AN
OXFORD
SECRET

An utterly gripping page-turner

FAITH MARTIN

writing as

MAXINE BARRY

Originally published as *The Jewelled Web*

JOFFE
BOOKS

Revised edition published 2020
Joffe Books, London
www.joffebooks.com

First published in Great Britain 1996
as *The Jewelled Web*

**Please join our mailing list for free Kindle books and
new releases.**

We love to hear from our readers! Please email any
feedback you have to: feedback@joffebooks.com

ISBN 978-1-78931-518-9

PROLOGUE

Oxfordshire, England, 1977

The old woman lay dying in her eighteenth-century four-poster bed. Around her, on walls of faded flock velvet, hung portraits by Gainsborough, Turner and Lely. Jessica, Lady Syramore-Forbes, didn't mind the dying so much, but the waiting was becoming tedious.

Outside she could hear the blackbirds singing in the ancient orchards and wished she too could be in the warm sun. Vancouver Hall overlooked the Aylesbury Vale, surrounded by gardens and two hundred acres of rich wood and farmland. Lady Syramore-Forbes smiled and, for an instant, a mere hint of her former beauty showed on her lined, ash-pale face. Then a fleeting shaft of pain made her slender body shudder in the midst of the magnificent carved bed. She wished yet again that the grim reaper would get on with it — though not just yet. Not until she'd seen Godfrey and signed the new will.

As if he'd been reading her mind, Godfrey James himself swept into the room. At sixty-two he was as thin as a whippet and nearly seven feet tall. As he loomed over her bed, Jessica laughed gently. 'Hello, Godfrey. You look perished, as always.'

1

Godfrey laughed. 'It's still cold up here, Jess, that's why.' It was a long-standing joke between them. Jessica knew that Godfrey didn't approve of people dying, and she, one of his oldest friends, had been in the doghouse ever since contracting cancer at the ridiculous age of ninety-one.

Without bothering to ask permission, Godfrey plonked his skinny behind on the bed, opened his pigskin briefcase and brought out a great wad of papers. Dear Godfrey, he'd always been able to get down to business straight away, a trait she had always shared with him, even in those faraway days when women were supposed to be barely capable of choosing a pair of gloves for themselves.

'It's all as you specified.' Godfrey's crisp voice quickly focused her still sharp mind on the matters at hand. She took the newly amended will and read every single word. Then she sighed and reached up to pull the bell rope above her bed. A moment later two women appeared at the bedside. Godfrey recognized them vaguely as a maid and the cook. 'Striker, Harringay, I want you to witness my signature on these documents,' she told them in a no-nonsense tone. Briskly Jessica signed her name in three places. Godfrey had the witnesses sign the corresponding affidavits, then signed himself. With a single nod of her head, Jessica dismissed the servants, then lay back wearily against the pillows.

'Now you're ready to kick the bucket, I suppose,' Godfrey said glumly, putting the new will back into his briefcase.

'I suppose,' Jessica said, but without much enthusiasm. 'Damn that grandson of mine for making me do this. Why is it I've had to spend one part of my life making the family fortune, and the other part cursing the family I've made it for?'

Godfrey grinned. 'Because you'd have been bored otherwise. It was all that marching with Mrs Pankhurst that did it.'

Jessica laughed happily, a sound that had been heard in many of the finest homes in England for over half a century. 'We got the vote, though, didn't we?'

'Worst thing that could have happened,' Godfrey shot back with a grin, then glanced down, his face clouding over.

Jessica looked at him fondly for a moment, then said softly, 'You can ask me, you know. Now that I'm dying, you can ask me anything. It's one of the few perks.'

Slowly Godfrey nodded. 'All right. Jess, why did you marry Lord Humphrey Arbuthnot Cliverton Syramore-Forbes? Lord, what a name! He was weak and not even particularly attractive. He spent money like it was going out of fashion and he didn't have a brain in his head.'

Jessica, flattered by the disgruntled disgust in his voice, smiled widely. 'Precisely because he was all of that and more.' She licked lips that had once been described as 'the most kissable in all the empire', but which now were thin and blue and painfully dry. 'He was weak, which meant that I could be strong. It wasn't easy for a woman to be strong in those days, you know. And he wasn't handsome, which meant he was easy to court and hustle up the aisle. What other woman would want to put up a fight for him? And because he liked to spend money, he didn't try to stop me from making it, no matter how much his contemporaries crowed and scoffed. And they did, you know. The Syramore-Forbeses, for generations mere landowners and farmers, turning into merchants! And merchants of the finest jewels in all of England? How they all laughed. But only in the beginning. Later . . .' Jessica chuckled with sheer delight. 'You know how we were lauded later. But most of all I married Humphrey because he had a title, which lent my business respectability and gave it an introduction into the upper echelons the whole country over. What other husband could have suited my requirements better?'

Godfrey found himself nodding even before she'd finished speaking, and then surprised himself by blurting out, 'But what about love, Jessie? What about that?'

Jessica smiled, a secretive smile that instantly aroused all Godfrey's barrister-like curiosity. 'Oh, I had that too.'

'From Humphrey?' Godfrey's voice was raised an octave in total disbelief.

'Of course not,' Jessica admonished with an almost coy chuckle. 'Oh, don't look so shocked, Godfrey. I did my duty.

James was Humphrey's son, just as Malcolm is his grandson. And much good may it do me.'

Godfrey nodded. 'You really think Malcolm intends to sell Halcyone's, don't you?'

'I'm sure of it. That's James's fault, of course. That boy was always obsessed with Ravenscroft and the family title. Anyone would think the earls of Ravenscroft were in line for the throne.' The final word wavered alarmingly, and Jessica took a deep breath, only then realising how short of it she was. Nevertheless she carried on grimly, wanting Godfrey to understand the reason for her recent actions. 'Malcolm wants the money from selling the business to refurbish and restore Ravenscroft. You know yourself, I've always channelled the profits back exclusively into Halcyone's. Let the old baronial pile disintegrate. I never liked that mausoleum of a house anyway. Besides, the two world wars have changed everything. Women don't buy grand pieces of jewellery anymore. They can't afford it. Halcyone's has needed to work harder and harder to retain its standards. Malcolm has never understood that.'

'But you trained him well, Jessie,' Godfrey reminded her gently. 'If you prevent him from selling, he'll only change the company beyond all recognition, and make a handsome profit from it into the bargain.'

From the moment the first Halcyone Jewellery Emporium had opened in Woodstock, it had stood for quality above all else. It hadn't taken long for its reputation to equal that of the oldest and most prestigious jewellers in England. Malcolm's recent desire to employ more modern sales and promotional methods had been the cause of more arguments between grandmother and grandson than almost anything else. That, and the way Malcolm was reportedly treating Francesca, his bride of only a year. Not even Francesca recently having given birth to twins, one boy and one girl, thus ensuring the Syramore-Forbes line, had succeeded in earning her her husband's respect, if local gossip was to be believed. Malcolm was abusing her, and Jessica didn't like it. Yet another black mark against him.

'True,' Jessica acknowledged Godfrey's assessment curtly. 'Which is precisely why I'm leaving it jointly to Halcyone and Justin in my new will. Since they're still babies, Malcolm will have twenty years to run the firm. I'm not betraying him totally, Godfrey,' she pointed out wearily.

'You know he won't like it. You leaving half to the girl child, I mean.'

'Tough,' Jessica said, her voice as hard as the diamonds that she regularly purchased from South Africa. 'A woman is, and always has been, the equal of any man, Godfrey,' she said firmly. 'And little Halcyone will be no exception, you mark my words.' She paused for breath, aware that she had spoken with more confidence than she truly felt. She had her spies at Ravenscroft, and they told her that little Halcyone was very much like her, Jessica, in looks and colouring. But would she grow up to be like her in other ways too? Would she have the spirit necessary to fight her father and brother for her rightful half of Halcyone's, after which she was named? Jessica firmly believed that a jewellery empire needed a woman at its helm — who else but women truly understood the allure of sparkling gems, the beauty of cold stone, the eternal lure, the fantasy, the pure *magic* that were precious stones? But it had to be the right woman. And if Halcyone was not woman enough to fight and win her own place in the family business then she was not the right woman for the job. It was as simple as that; hard too, but necessary, and Jessica had never been one to cringe in the face of brutal reality.

Jessica sighed. Oh, well, what was done was done. She'd rolled the dice, and could now only hope for the best.

She thought of the gift that she had entrusted for safe-keeping to Walt Matthews, the man she'd selected to keep watch over Halcyone's until her inheritors came of age. She'd given him strict instructions that the gift was to be given to Halcyone only on the day that she got married. It seemed such an inadequate gift, especially since, by her last Will and Testament, she had heaped upon such tiny, innocent shoulders a burden that might eventually crush her. But what else could she do? She had to give the infant her chance of a place in the sun. After all, little Lady Halcyone Syramore-Forbes was Jessica's only investment in the future.

And as the old lady lay there, the sunshine dying into evening, and herself dying right along with it, Jessica wondered how it would all turn out . . .

CHAPTER 1

Radcliffe College, USA, Present Day

The naked boy was beautiful. Sitting on a bar stool with a University of Toronto scarf draped loosely across his loins, he was motionless, his eyes fixed vaguely on the high window to his right. Fine shafts of sunlight haloed his hair, turning it blond. His features were too handsome for an artist's model, but Mrs Whittingham considered him a subject that her students might appreciate. Now the art teacher prowled slowly around her class of ten, sure that the chin was going to give several of them trouble.

The boy, a Harvard law student, couldn't have cared less if his chin was giving any of the Radcliffe women trouble. He was too busy trying to keep his mind from wandering to one particular student who had caught his eye the moment he'd stepped into the room. She was tall, with a cascading length of hair the colour of fire. He had felt the breath leave him the moment he set eyes on her.

'You all right, Jack?' Janet Whittingham asked.

He grinned ruefully at the tall, grey-haired woman. 'I could do with a stretch.' When she nodded, he draped a towel decorously around his waist and gingerly stepped off the stool. He stretched, wincing. Then, as casually as he could, he wandered over to stand behind the most beautiful girl he'd ever seen, and glanced at the drawing of himself. At that moment, the girl nearest to him, just to his right, whispered loudly, 'Her name's Lady Flame, believe it or not.'

Jack saw a dark, short-haired, plain girl looking at him with knowing eyes. 'You her friend?' he whispered back.

'And room-mate,' Wendy Gibbs acknowledged. 'We're in Fay House,' she added wryly as she watched him sidle up to her friend, and grimaced. She wasn't sure whether to curse the fates that had roomed her with Lady Halcyone Syramore-Forbes, or bless them. Flame, as she was called, for obvious reasons once you caught sight of those glorious locks of hers, was as friendly, open, honest and funny as she was beautiful.

Having successfully manoeuvred himself to where he'd wanted to be for the last hour, Jack could not seem to take his eyes off the hypnotizing sight of her hair. It was exactly the colour of fire; not red, orange or yellow, but a shade of all three, and it fell to her waist in rich, rippling waves. Her skin, unlike that of most redheads, was not pale or freckled at all, he noticed, but a rich cream. Her mouth was neither too big nor too small, her chin pointed but not unduly so. Her nose was long and thin but exquisitely shaped and . . . Jack caught his breath as, sensing his presence over her shoulder, she turned her head and looked at him. Expecting green eyes to go with the red hair, he found himself staring down into eyes as black as midnight — deep, dark, fathomless eyes that seemed to see right through him. He swallowed hard. 'Huh. Er . . . hi. I hope you don't mind. If I'm putting you off your sketching, I'll . . .'

'OK, Jack?' Janet Whittingham raised an eyebrow at him, and he quite happily scuttled back to his stool, more than ever aware that the rich ebony eyes were laughing gently at him. Settling back on the stool, he prayed that the memory of those wonderful eyes would not play a cruel trick on his libido. In a room of eagle-eyed fine art students, no telltale bulge would go unnoticed!

Janet Whittingham slowly circumnavigated the room, coming to a halt behind Flame. Looking at the drawing in front of her, she frowned slightly. There was something . . . odd about it. Flame had won a scholarship to Radcliffe through sheer hard work and talent, and Janet Whittingham had no quarrels with her presence in the fine art programme. Her drawing was technically brilliant, the best in the class. She had captured the play of light to perfection . . . perhaps too much perfection? Yes, Janet thought. Strange as it seemed, that was exactly what was wrong with it. She knew that there *was* emotion in Flame Syramore-Forbes's work. But not . . . not . . . Janet shook her head and sighed. It was no good. She couldn't quite place the problem. But she knew that Flame had made and designed several pieces of avant-garde jewellery for her friends, which were very much 'in' at the moment around campus. It made her wonder whether jewellery design, and not pure art, was really Flame's forte. With her background, it certainly wouldn't be unusual . . .

* * *

After class, the two girls went back to their room, a typical twin-bedded affair, bedecked in posters ranging from Dali to French Impressionist scenery. Flame neatly arranged her sketchpad, books and pencil case on her desk, while Wendy flopped with her stuff on to her unmade bed. 'Even your bed's been made,' Wendy grumbled. 'It's sick, I'm telling you, Forbes. Sick, sick, sick.'

Flame laughed, and obligingly flopped down on to her own bed. She was dressed in Levi's and a white shirt, but she still looked like a fashion model bumming it. Wendy scowled at her. 'Have I got paint on my nose, Gibbsie?' Flame asked, her voice drawling and light and strictly upmarket New England. Nobody would have guessed she was the daughter of an English earl.

'Sorry. I make a lousy room-mate. But you must have had loads of offers to swap rooms.' She looked up quickly. 'Right?'

Flame had. It hadn't taken long for the new freshman year to sort itself out, and the hierarchy had quickly placed Halcyone Syramore-Forbes very much towards the top of the pinnacle. For there was much more to Lady Flame, as she was widely known, than her looks. Intelligence, of course, but a warmth that went with it, and a generous nature that had the boys rubbing their hands, then, later, shaking their heads. For, against all expectations, Flame did not sleep around. But, above all, Flame rapidly became *the* person to see for costume jewellery. She'd made earrings out of Coke can ring pulls that had been all the rage, bangles out of wonderfully twisted ropes of copper, great chunks of carved rock pendants and, this semester's current favourite, painted iron and aluminium chokers and bracelets. She'd even had a write-up in the local press about her entrepreneurial spirit. High praise indeed for a first-year student.

'I'm happy rooming with you,' Flame said simply.

'You *are* sick,' Wendy said, but grinned happily. 'By the way, what did you think of our male model today? Nice, huh?'

Flame sighed, stretched out on her stomach on the bed and rested her chin on her hand. 'Why don't you go for it?' she asked softly.

Wendy rolled on to her side and stared across the short space that separated them, wondering if two women could be more different than themselves. 'Look, Flame, I'm ugly, OK? No, stop demurring like a prissy Victorian heroine. I am. Men and me just don't mix. Unless I can psych them out,' she added, giving an evil leer.

'You make dating sound like war,' Flame said, then looked at her friend candidly. 'You know I . . . I haven't . . . well, slept with a man before?' She made the confession haltingly, but with a certain amount of confidence. Wendy would not betray her trust, of that she was sure. 'I'm nineteen, and sometimes I feel as if I'm the only virgin on the face of the planet.'

Wendy nodded. The confession touched her, although she'd guessed within hours of meeting her that, incredible as it might seem, Flame was still a virgin. 'With a family like yours it's not uncommon,' Wendy mused. 'Big Italian families are always protective of their pretty daughters.'

Flame's family on her mother's side, Wendy knew, came from an old and very respected lineage that had been producing jewellery for the European aristocracy since before the time of the Borgias. The Corraldos. She wondered what it must be like, to come from a background like that. Wendy watched her friend, who was now curled up into an elegant feline position, looking for all the world like some ancient Greek's idea of a perfect virginal tragic heroine, and began to laugh.

'What's funny?' Flame began to laugh too, and her sensitive, finely defined face changed with startling ease into that of a carefree, healthy and uncomplicated young woman.

'Oh, nothing. Just us,' Wendy said. 'What a pair we make.'

Flame tossed her magnificent head. 'My mother told me, on my sixteenth birthday, that she'd actually gone out of her way to raise me with more freedom than was usual in our family.' She smiled, knowing she sounded pompous, and then thought about her mother. She knew that Francesca had suffered badly during her marriage to the English earl, Malcolm. Flame's father. A man she'd never even met. She knew, too, that Malcolm was responsible for separating her from her twin brother, Justin. Yet another member of her family she had never known. And being deprived of her son all these years had hurt her mother badly. Perhaps her bitter experience of marriage had soured Francesca towards men for the rest of her life. Why else would her mother, her beautiful, wealthy, eligible mother, have remained single for so long? The Count, the head of the Corraldo family, had petitioned the Pope for a divorce for his niece nearly fifteen years ago. It was a long time to live without the love and company of a man.

Wendy reached under her bed and brought out a reefer. Lighting it up, she watched without comment as Flame gave her a sad, admonishing glance and then leaped lightly to her feet to open the window. 'I can't wait,' Wendy said drolly, 'to hear about all these freedoms you were given.'

Flame laughed. 'Cynic! But it wasn't anything earth-shattering. Just the usual things. Like, after I was fourteen, I didn't have to go to church if I didn't want to. Mother had to go every Sunday, and still does. In spite of everything that's happened to her, she's still a devout Catholic. But I haven't been to church in years.'

'Lapsed Catholic? Oh dear. I fear for your immortal soul. Your grandparents would have fifteen fits if they only knew.'

Flame laughed. 'They probably would. Even this place is an example of what I mean. Mother went to Mount Holyoke. All the Corraldo women who wanted an education went to Mount Holyoke.'

'You rebel, you,' Wendy said drolly.

Flame winced, but, as she was still gazing out of the window, her friend didn't notice. 'Sometimes,' she said grimly, 'I feel utterly useless. Pointless, even.'

'Well, *Lady* Halcyone Syramore-Forbes, if your life is pointless, how does that reflect on the rest of us?' Wendy challenged, stubbing out the reefer with a savage crunch.

'I can't help it if my father was an English earl,' Flame said, stung.

'Was? Is he dead?'

'No. I don't think so.'

Wendy gave a sudden bark of laughter, and Flame moved back from the window to her bed, sitting with hunched shoulders and feeling ridiculously self-conscious. 'You don't think so?' Wendy repeated. 'What a family life you have. It's like a daytime soap.'

'I know,' Flame said sadly. 'But it doesn't feel like one. Do you realise I've grown up all my life with brown envelopes? Big, brown envelopes?'

'Huh?' Wendy looked up from her duffel bag, where she'd been searching for a bag of potato chips, and blinked. 'Envelopes?'

Flame grunted a half-laugh. 'Envelopes. At first, when Grandpa was busy with the custody fight for Justin, it was a matter of legal papers. Writs, affidavits, private investigators' reports, medical reports, you name it. For eighteen years my mother fought to get custody of Justin, my twin, and didn't even succeed in getting visiting rights. The English courts believe the heirs to English earldoms belong in England, not with their mothers. Then there were the other envelopes. The ones that come every week, even now.'

'And what's in those?' Wendy asked quietly, fascinated, and very much aware that Flame was pouring out her heart.

'Pictures of Justin,' Flame said, her voice so low Wendy almost couldn't hear it. 'Mother must have hundreds of thousands of them. Justin at his fourth birthday party — one of Grandpa's private-eyes shinned up a tree outside the grounds to take it. Pictures of my brother at Eton, collecting a cricketing prize. Pictures of him walking down a street, eating a meal in a restaurant, walking arm in arm with some girl or other. Do you realise my mother has never even spoken to him? Never even heard his voice?'

Wendy, for once, was lost for words.

'We talk about him all the time. I *think* about him all the time. I wonder what he's like. What makes him laugh. How he gets on with Father. I even find myself feeling sorry for him, for not knowing our mother and seeing for himself how great she is. Sometimes . . .' Flame's eyes began to shine in mute evidence of the tears that were perilously near the surface now '. . . sometimes, Mother and I will get the pictures out, and make up stories for them. In one, Justin would be happy, because of some incident we'd invent. In others he'd be sad, or angry. But we don't *know him*. On his eighteenth birthday party, for instance, he got drunk and peed into a policeman's helmet. Now what does that tell us? Is he a cretin, or just a normal eighteen-year-old? Is he weak-willed, letting his friends get him into trouble, or is he just more adventurous than they are? Don't you see? He's my twin, and although I could describe to you every detail of his face and the clothes he likes to wear, I couldn't tell you a single thing about who he is or what he thinks. And neither can his own mother.'

She stopped, aware that her voice had risen and begun to wobble. She took a deep breath and leaned back wearily against the wall. Wendy looked at her thoughtfully.

'So. What about your dad? The earl. The one you *think* is still alive?' she probed carefully.

Flame laughed self-consciously. 'Oh, nobody ever talks about *him*. If I even accidentally let slip his name around my family, it's as if I'm suddenly transported from sunny Italy and all that pasta to the depths of the Antarctic.'

'Oh, to come from an Italian family,' Wendy drawled. 'Who's your godfather?'

Flame laughed. 'Conte Giulio Pierluigi Corraldo.'

'Another aristocrat! Don't tell me. A Roman senator, right?'

'Hardly,' Flame laughed. 'The family business in Italy is based in Venice. I've never been to Venice,' she added as an afterthought, her voice subdued.

Wendy blinked. 'Neither have I. I've never been to Paris either. Or the moon.'

'No, I mean . . . My grandparents are from Venice. My mother too. Yet I've never gone there. I think it's because Grandpa, my mother's father, is really pissed about being the younger Corraldo son. His older brother wanted him out of Italy and well away from the heart of the family business. And because of that, I think Grandpa Michael wants us to be more American than Davy Crockett. That way, the Boston branch of Corraldo's is more his domain than ever. He never lets his older brother so much as set foot through the door when he visits the States. Even though the Conte, legally, owns half of it. Does that make sense?'

'Nothing about your family makes sense, Forbesie. Surely you've realised that by now?'

'Oh, I have, I have,' Flame laughed. 'Do you know, when I was fifteen, Uncle Enrico asked me what I wanted

14

for my birthday, and I said I wanted to learn how to make jewellery. You'd have thought I'd asked for the world to stop. And you know what he said? He said the Corraldo women never worried themselves about that sort of thing. And it's true. Mother says she's hardly ever set foot inside any of the Corraldo jewellery stores. Isn't that amazing? In this day and age they still run things like an exclusive male club.'

Wendy nodded sagely. 'That's why you refuse to show them your designs?'

'What? These little trinkets I keep knocking off?' Flame nudged a half-finished rock pendant lying on her shelf. 'My Uncle Enrico would laugh in my face.'

'I wasn't talking about them,' Wendy said. 'I'm talking about those wonderful designs in that portfolio you keep under your bed. Necklaces designed for emeralds and diamonds.'

Flame stared at her, then began to smile. 'There's no hiding things from you, is there, Gibbsie?'

Wendy grinned. 'Nope. Especially when you burn the midnight oil sweating over them for months on end.'

'Hmm, much good may it do me.' Flame grimaced good-naturedly. 'I doubt they'll ever come to anything. I haven't even had any formal training, for heaven's sake! I was just curious, that's all. You know, to see if I could do something that a real jeweller might be interested in.'

'Well, I thought they were great. So great, in fact . . .' Wendy turned and looked at Flame, wearing the expression she always wore when about to drop a bombshell '. . . that I photocopied them and sent a set off to Redex.'

'What!' Flame leaped to her feet, appalled. 'You did *what?*'

'I sent a copy to Redex. You know, that big new jewellery firm that launched itself with such a splash a few years ago.'

Flame knew all about Redex. Although her Uncle Enrico and grandfather never discussed business with their women-folk, Flame often overheard them talking. And Redex were beginning to worry them. Not only were they beginning to cut into Corraldo's market, they were thinking of opening a store on the East Coast. Worst of all, Corraldo's had lost several of their key staff to the rival company over the last two years, and the loss of the cream of their artisans had begun to tell on the quality of their merchandise. 'Oh, Wendy, how could you?' Flame asked, half aghast, half amused.

Wendy shrugged. 'You didn't have enough confidence to do anything about it yourself. So I gave you a push.' Seeing Flame's continued unease, she tried to cheer her up. 'Look . . . what's the worst that could happen? They send them back saying, "Thanks but no thanks," right? So what?'

Flame laughed, shaking her head. 'If Grandpa ever hears I sent some of my designs off to the competition, I'll be skinned alive. We Italians are a passionate bunch, you know!'

'*Mamma mia*,' Wendy drawled.

'Oh, well. I suppose the chances of anything coming of this Redex thing are practically nil. I wonder who's behind them?'

'I can't imagine,' Wendy said, bored with the topic.

'I did go into one of my uncle's workshops once,' Flame mused. 'I was only fifteen, but I caught on quick. They started me off on cuttlefish moulds, then investment casting. I suppose they thought the messy, boring stuff would put me off, but it didn't. By the time we'd gone on to stamping they began to mellow. And when I finally got my hands on some tools . . . Wendy, it was great. Gravers, scribers, dividers . . . That's how come I know how to make all this stuff now. It's not too bad, is it?' she added, uncertainly.

Wendy grunted. 'You need compliments so badly? You know your trouble, don't you? You're totally self-ignorant. Your jewellery is great. *You're* great. You know why people like you? Because you never judge. Let's face it, Flame, you've got what it takes to be a winner in this life — and I don't mean your family's millions, or your looks. I mean you. You've got strength. You've got the determination to do whatever it is you want, how you want; once you've built up your confidence a little more, that is,' she added pointedly.

Before Flame could reply, there was a sharp knock on the door. 'Come in,' she called automatically, then hastily got off the bed, surprised to see the Dean enter, her face grave and concerned.

'Halcyone. It is Halcyone, isn't it?'

Flame nodded. 'Yes. Is . . . is something wrong, Dean?'

'I'm afraid I have bad news for you, Halcyone. I've just received a telephone call from your mother. Your grandfather has had a heart attack, at his office.'

Flame felt the blood drain from her face as a picture of Michael Corraldo — tall, proud, silver-haired — flooded into her mind's eye. Her mother's father had always been the lynchpin of her world. The head of the household. The business genius who ran Corraldo's interests in the United States. A laughing man, full of love. She had always been his favourite. Despite his surprise, it had been he who had — eventually — allowed her to visit the workshop the summer of her fifteenth birthday, which suddenly seemed so long ago.

'Is he all right?' she asked tentatively, her voice sounding raw and tremulous. She swallowed hard, but met the Dean's steady, sympathetic gaze with unflinching eyes.

'I'm afraid not, Halcyone,' the Dean said softly.

'He's dead?' Her own voice sounded small, and faraway.

'Yes. I'm sorry. He is.'

CHAPTER 2

Oxford

Still dressed in her pink-and-white checked cake-shop uniform, the girl looked oddly out of place in the small, ancient college room. Justin watched her from his lounging position by the arched window, his blue eyes narrowed slightly against the glare of the pale December sun.

'This place is *old*, isn't it?' the girl asked, guilelessly.

'Most colleges in Oxford are.' Justin barely managed to keep the sarcasm out of his voice. She was just a girl who sold cream cakes in the covered market, after all. 'Have you been in Oxford long?' He smiled as he spoke, his charm easily stroking back into place any ruffled fur she might have, but his thoughts were anything but charming. He already knew the answer to his question, and wondered, briefly, if she would come clean. She didn't.

'Nah. Not long,' Gail lied without much finesse, and hunched her thin shoulders guiltily. Justin nodded, not at all surprised by the deceit, and slowly unfolded himself from the stone windowsill. With pure sybaritic pleasure, he stretched, displaying his fine body with a confidence that should have been arrogant but, strangely, wasn't. Gail watched the show appreciatively, most of her nervousness disappearing now that she was reminded of why she had agreed to come up to his college room in the first place.

She was small and dark, pretty but not overly intelligent, and in love with Oxford — and its men. During exam weeks she nearly overdosed on the atmosphere, for everywhere she went there were men dressed in sub fuse, the short black gowns they needed to wear in examination hall. She was twenty-five, but thankfully still looked much younger. Gail liked young men. Especially this one. He was tall, easily over six feet, with blond hair that lovely shade that reminded her of brass when it had just been cleaned. But it had been his eyes that had first attracted her — sky blue, wide, lovely and just a touch . . . cruel?

'What are you reading?' she asked, genuinely interested.

'PPE. Philosophy, politics and economics.' Justin felt his lips twitch but controlled the urge to sneer. To most of his fellow students, the cake shop was famous not only for its chocolate eclairs but also for Gail Trenchard. 'You know a lot about the way things are run around here. Ever think of entering as a mature student?'

Gail flushed. 'Don't be so bloody rotten!' Angrily she turned and headed for the door, but Justin got there before her. Catching her around the waist, he quickly dropped his head and kissed the tender skin under her ear.

'I'm sorry. I'm a bastard,' he said simply. He let her go and returned to the window, looking down into one of Wadham College's famous quads. 'I have to go home for the Christmas holidays soon. It's making me mean.'

Gail hesitated, her antennae twitching. 'What's wrong with home?' She moved quietly back into the centre of the small room with its simple bed, her anger quickly evaporating.

'Everything.' Justin gave a bitter laugh that was utterly genuine. 'It's got my father in it, for one thing. The Earl of Ravenscroft.' He said the title as if naming a poison.

'Your dad's an earl?' Gail squeaked.

He waited for her reaction, then smiled as he felt small, knowing hands slip up his back, then gently circle around his ribs. 'I hate him,' Justin said. 'I've plenty of reason to. Like Eton.'

'Eton?' Gail pressed her lips against his back, and felt the reaction go through his long, lean body in a sensuous ripple.

'Yeah. The torture chamber.' Justin shivered again, this time in a very different way, and Gail felt it immediately. Ducking under his arm, she stood in front of him, liking immensely what she saw. He was like a work of art from the Ashmolean Museum. And right now it was full of pain.

Slowly, carefully, Gail ran her fingers across his chest, careful not to let her fingers touch his nipples, instead pressing the centre of her palms over each of them and rubbing in a circular motion through the fabric. 'Tell me about it,' she said, then slipped off her shoes. Balancing with delicate expertise, she ran one foot up the back of his calf.

Justin gasped, closed his eyes briefly, then frowned. 'Eton was hell. Pressure from the masters to get a scholarship. Pressure from my old man to win the bloody cricket matches, and pressure from the gay lads to meet them behind the chapel.'

'And did you?' Gail asked gently, judging the delicious muscles in biceps and forearm before undoing the cuff buttons and caressing the inside of his wrists with velvet fingertips.

'No.' Justin swallowed hard, fascinated by his role as fly, when he was used to being the spider. 'Sometimes they'd form a gang to beat me up.' He gave a small laughing grunt of ironic hatred. 'I don't know why they couldn't leave me be.'

'Look in the mirror, my lord.' Gail used the title in a breathless whisper, then ducked her head and planted her mouth squarely over his right nipple. Justin gasped, and felt himself harden and throb.

'Gail,' he rasped. Wordlessly she began to undo his belt. Only when she was finished did she speak.

'You fought back, didn't you?'

'Sure I did. They made a first-class bully out of me,' he acknowledged miserably.

'Forget it. Forget them,' Gail hushed him. Straining on tiptoe, she kissed the length of his shoulders. His eyes snapped open, then slowly closed again.

'OK, Gail. I'm all yours. I won't struggle, I promise.'

Gail laughed into his smiling eyes, then sobered, for there was something else in his gaze. There was much more to him than was at first apparent. But it was pain. And anger. And hate. And Gail didn't want her fantasy world interrupted. So she gave a small, almost imperceptible shrug, and said teasingly, 'That's big of you.' Then, with a single, expert yank, she had the shirt off him.

Justin felt a moment of disappointment, and couldn't understand where it came from. Then her lips began to trail down his sternum, kissing with ever-increasing hardness until her tongue burrowed into his navel like a mole trying to dig through concrete. He threw his head back and his hands slapped against the wall, vainly seeking support. A small moan escaped him and he quickly clamped his lips shut, brutally cutting off the small sound of pleasure. Oh, he liked his women to moan and scream, of course, especially if he was at Ravenscroft and he knew his father could hear them. But in all his sexual experiences to date, Justin had never permitted himself to make a sound.

'What's the matter, my lord,' Gail breathed, holding his eye as she slowly sank to her knees. 'Don't you like it?'

'Oh, I like it,' he admitted, his voice breathless now. 'You love being in control of us, don't you, Gail? Making the clever men squirm? Do you . . . ?'

He broke off, gritting his teeth as Gail, with her knuckles, began to rub the growing, hardening bulge in his trousers. 'Does it make you feel equal, Gail? To dominate us like this?'

The tough, sometimes contrary zips that plagued jeans held no worries for Gail, and within a moment Justin felt the cool air on his naked member, and cursed the inadequate heating system in the old college. Then the coldness was gone, replaced by a hot tongue, licking him as if he were a lollipop, and he jerked helplessly against the wall, feeling the cold plaster press against his back. He fought desperately to keep the noises of desire from escaping him.

Gail looked up, saw the clenched jaw, the sweating, handsome face, and smiled. She was going to enjoy this. Slowly, taking her time, she ran her tongue to the tip of his shaft, then gently engulfed its head, sucking hard, nibbling with just enough verve to make him wonder if she would actually inflict some damage. Justin did wonder, and to his shamed delight heard his moan echo around the room. He dragged in a harsh breath and felt a single tear hover beneath his tightly clenched lashes. 'Have pity, Gail.' It was meant to sound like something Noël Coward might say, a sophisticated, amusingly indifferent request, but he himself could hear the entreaty in his voice. With a growing sense of helpless horror, he felt one of the bricks in the wall he had so carefully built up around himself crack and fall.

When he dared looked down, it was to see her hands curl around his thighs and slowly travel up to cup his balls and squeeze them, just hard enough to bring him up on tiptoe. Yet again his voice betrayed him, bursting out in a long, low moan that was both pleasure and pain, excitement and defeat.

So there was to be no pity for him. Not today, or tomorrow either, when he went home. He was not surprised. No dirty trick life had yet to play would have the power to surprise him anymore. Now, finally, he'd become immune. Whatever hope had persisted in holding on, as a last tenacious weed in the desert that was his soul, finally withered and died. And it was probably just as well. Hope meant pain. Now, perhaps, he could be truly free. The tear he'd been trying to imprison in his eye suddenly broke loose and trickled down his cheek, cold and comfortless against his skin.

* * *

The first thing Justin saw on entering his father's favourite salon was not the Earl himself, but the bottle of champagne sitting in a wine cooler on the Pembroke table. He'd arrived only minutes ago, driving up the twisting, familiar lane with that peculiar mixture of pride and hatred that had come to represent Ravenscroft and all it stood for. Justin liked many things about the house, perhaps most of all the title that went with it. He liked too the promise of money that Ravenscroft represented, even though money was hardly overflowing in the family vaults. In many ways, Justin loved Ravenscroft as fanatically as his father. But, unlike his father, Justin hated it too. Hated it because it was his father's. Hated it because it trapped him and dictated to him. It was like a huge, sucking leech. Even his poor, pitiful uncle was part of it, living up in the attics like some forgotten ghost, leaving drawings of flowers in the oddest of places, wandering about at night and lighting fires in the grates. Francesca, his detested mother, had befriended him and painted his portrait during her brief marriage to Malcolm, and now he went about at night, moving it from wall to wall. It had probably been hung in every room in the house by now.

'I expected you days ago. Term finished on the twelfth. Where have you been? London?' Malcolm snapped, eyeing his son with displeasure. Justin slowly walked into the centre of the room to face his father.

'I had work to finish,' he lied, his eyes unflinching.

'Was she worth it?' Malcolm looked up from his glass of champagne and eyed his son with a mocking smile. His hair was more grey now than blond, but it looked well on him. Attractive crow's feet crinkled at the corners of eyes the colour of summer sky. He was a man who had aged well and he knew it. Still, Justin reassured himself with grim satisfaction, get a few years over with and Malcolm would be old, not just middle-aged, and he, Justin, would be in the prime of his life. What fun and games he could have then.

'She wasn't, actually,' he said offhandedly, and poured himself a glass of the champagne.

Malcolm's lips twitched. He took a sip of his own champagne, then held it up to the light. 'Like it?'

Justin gave a small, bitter half-smile. 'Mouton-Rothschild, 1962. A very good vintage. Vineyard . . . the Chambrose vineyard, Bordeaux. Right?'

'No. It's the Froiux vineyard. But don't let it worry you; it's not your fault you're half Eyetie peasant.'

Justin's stomach muscles cramped, then slowly loosened as he successfully fought the urge to smash his still half-full glass into his father's mocking face. Slowly he smiled. 'You should know. You married the bitch in the first place. What's the occasion, anyway?'

'A celebration of the highest order.' Malcolm laughed in genuine glee. 'Michael Corraldo is dead. I thought about flying out and dancing on his grave. Want to come?'

Justin heard a small sound in the hall and glanced at the ajar door. 'Can we afford the air fare?' he said in a low voice.

This time it was Malcolm's turn to fight his anger. 'We'll soon be positively rich, dear boy! Michael Corraldo was the one who insisted on keeping the lawyers busy. Now that he's gone, your grandmother's estate can at last be settled.'

Justin laughed, remembering the state of legal limbo Michael Corraldo's lawsuits had forced his father to endure. 'Oh, of course,' he purred. 'What was it you always used to say? Halcyone's will be all mine one day. You'd deal with my sister's half. That's how the refrain used to go, wasn't it?'

At first Justin had often wondered about his twin. Francesca had taken her daughter when Malcolm had thrown her out, but she'd left her son behind. Did Halcyone care, or even know, that her father was trying to rob her of her birthright? As a child, feeling lonely and unhappy in his nursery full of toys, Justin had often wished that his sister were with him, and prayed at night for her to come and rescue him from his father. But she never did, of course, and as he grew older and became more hardened, his twin had receded in importance in his life.

Malcolm flushed. 'Don't worry, Justin. I always keep my promises. A little late in this instance, perhaps, but better late than never.'

Justin's eyes narrowed at the smug expression on his father's face. 'What do you mean? I thought you'd exhausted all the attempts at having the will invalidated?'

'I have. But, as I said, your peasant bitch of a mother must be as sick and tired of court actions and legal wranglings as I am. And now, with some Corraldo stock and Halcyone stock both going to you . . . she'll come over here. You forget, I *know* the way the bitch thinks. She'll do anything to ensure her precious *bambini* get their rightful inheritances.'

Justin finished his glass of champagne, his stomach churning. Was it possible his mother really was coming here? As a child he'd taken for granted his father's view of their ill-fated marriage. And it hadn't been hard to hate a woman who'd abandoned her son to sail off to America and the good life with her precious daughter.

Now, older and wiser, Justin was glad he hadn't been taken to America. To have been denied Ravenscroft! But to meet his mother face to face . . . He wasn't sure he was ready for that. Out the corner of his eye, he saw something move out in the hall; it was a mere shadow only, but for some reason he felt suddenly chilled. Then he shrugged. So what if the servants overheard? Unlike his father, Justin didn't give a damn what people said about him. 'So, what if she does come back?' He turned to once more face his father. 'What good can that do me? My dear little sister still has half the shares.'

'Your sister,' Malcolm gritted, 'doesn't count. Your mother,' he said the word as if it were something filthy, 'is executor until you are both twenty-one. And no doubt Michael Corraldo left whatever shares you and Halcyone are to inherit in Corraldo's under the eye of one of his many nephews.'

'I still don't see—'

'No, of course you don't, boy. That's why I've always been master in my own house, from attic to cellar.' Malcolm's eyes glittered.

Justin blanched, reeling and remembering once more the cellar. The cold, dark, cellar . . .

'I, on the other hand, see every reason why Michael Corraldo's death gives us the opening we've been looking for,' Malcolm carried on, reassured by the sight of his son's sudden pallor. 'As I said, Francesca has to come to England, if only to settle and protect her precious daughter's half-inheritance in Halcyone's. And once she's here it will be easy enough to get her to come to Ravenscroft.'

Justin laughed grimly. 'Like hell. She wouldn't set foot in this place, even if dragged by wild horses.'

'She would,' Malcolm said softly, his eyes cold and yet almost dreamy. 'To see you.' He contemplated his son thoughtfully. Things had not turned out as he'd hoped with Justin. The boy hated him and defied him at every turn. On the other hand, he was intelligent, handsome, and another slave for Ravenscroft.

Justin turned away, unable to hold his father's gaze. He strolled to the fireplace, leaning against it with a tired sigh. 'So what if she does come here?'

'My darling boy,' Malcolm said softly, and began to laugh gently. 'The moment the bitch sets foot in here, those shares are ours. I guarantee it. She'll sell us her daughter's half of Halcyone's and be glad to do it.'

Justin's head whipped around, his every muscle and sinew alert to the fact that there was something in his father's voice he'd never heard before. Certain that he knew his father's rotten soul inside and out, Justin found himself, for the first time since childhood, unsure about his father's thoughts. 'What are you planning?' he said, his voice both alarmed and cautious.

Malcolm dragged himself from his pleasant anticipatory thoughts to look at his handsome young son's distrusting face.

'Don't worry, Justin. Despite what you may think, I've always had your welfare at heart. I always intended that you should have it all, and so you shall. Ravenscroft, the title, and Halcyone's.'

Fascinated in spite of himself by his father's suddenly terrifying confidence, Justin felt his heart began to hammer in a mixture of excitement and fear. 'And you really think Mother will let you?' he said, his voice raised in a sneering drawl. 'She chose her daughter over me all those years ago. You think she'll have a change of heart now, and let you fiddle her precious "Flame" out of her inheritance?' His sister's nickname had been in use from the moment of her birth.

'That bitch,' Malcolm said with soft, lethal hatred, 'won't be able to do a damned thing about it. That I promise you.'

Justin stared at his father for a long, long moment. 'You disgust me,' he said at last. 'You're twisted. Warped.'

'And you're my son,' Malcolm said quietly. 'I made you. I can break you.' And with those ominous words Justin was once again ten years old, and in the cellar, where it was cold and dark. So dark . . .

For a second, father and son stared at each other, then Justin turned and strode from the room. Staring blindly ahead, he made for the stairs. He was scared and looked it. And, more than that, he was desperate, and not sure why. He only knew he had to do something. Fast. His life was rapidly falling apart, and as usual only two people were to blame. Malcolm. And, by extension, Francesca Corraldo, for leaving him to face Malcolm alone. He hated them both. And it was time he did something about it.

* * *

That night, Malcolm, a keen stargazer, was watching Venus. It was clear on the roof, but already a hard, sharp frost was forming, and the tiles beneath him were slippery.

He was glad the railings that circumnavigated the roof were sturdy and in good repair. From his telescope, Malcolm could see the play of light across the planet's surface, and he lifted his head briefly to adjust the magnification. Below, a barn owl shrieked and swooped on some unsuspecting prey in the little churchyard beyond the trees.

Behind him, a shadow moved silently in the pale moonlight.

A few seconds later, Malcolm screamed as he hurtled through the air, his arms and legs flailing like windmills as he plummeted past all four of Ravenscroft's storeys.

In the few seconds left to him, he realised that death was at last upon him, and he screamed in surprise. He screamed too in a short, wordless, agonized question, for in that final second before he was pushed he'd seen the face of his killer, but had been given no time to wonder why.

He only stopped screaming when his body broke on the expensively paved patio beneath the towering roofs, and his blood began to seep between the cracks to mingle with the rich Oxfordshire earth. Earth that had belonged to the earls of Ravenscroft for over five centuries.

CHAPTER 3

Francesca glanced up from the breakfast table as her daughter came yawning through the door, hair unbrushed and face free of make-up. Dressed in a baggy aquamarine sweater she had knitted herself and fawn trousers, she looked like a beautiful, ruffled cat. Flame flopped down on to the nearest chair and accepted the cup of tea her mother poured her. 'Mamma, I've got a confession to make,' she announced.

'Oh?' Francesca was instantly alert.

'Don't look so alarmed. It's nothing drastic. It's just . . .' Flame paused and decided to step softly. 'You know how popular my pieces of jewellery have been with all my friends? Well, recently I've begun to enjoy my jewellery work much more than the painting. And I began a portfolio of jewellery that was more . . . well, commercially serious, I suppose you'd call it. And Gibbsie, bless her interfering heart, sent them off without my knowing . . . to Redex.'

Francesca blinked. 'Oh. I see . . .' She crumbled a croissant anxiously on to her plate, then, curious, asked quietly, 'And what did they say?'

'That's just it. Gibbsie phoned this morning. They want to see me, and have made an appointment. Do you think Uncle Enrico will find out?' Flame asked nervously.

'I know Corraldo's aren't interested in seeing my work. Can you imagine what Grandpa would have said—' Flame broke off as she remembered that now she would never know what Michael Corraldo might or might not have thought of her designs.

Francesca looked down quickly at her plate, hoping she didn't look as uneasy as she felt. But her daughter was right — Corraldo's would never have taken her designs seriously, and Francesca knew that Flame would never push herself forward at Halcyone's — at least not yet. And who could blame her? She could well understand her daughter's need to prove herself with an independent company first. But Redex?

'So you want a career in jewellery design, but not at Halcyone's or Corraldo's?' Francesca asked.

Flame shrugged helplessly. 'I don't know, Mamma. I only know that I really felt alive when working on those designs. And if I'm good enough . . . then yes. I want to design jewellery.'

Francesca nodded. She had long begun to trust that her daughter could handle her own life very well indeed. As a child she'd always been very careful of her responsibilities. Her pet cat was fed regularly and never left to the house-keeper to feed, as had been expected by all the adults when she'd asked for a kitten as a birthday present. If she was ever going to be late, she always phoned. She had worked hard at school and kept her 'A' average, without needing any goad-ing, bribery or bullying. But, thankfully, Flame had never transferred this expectation of perfection on to others.

'Oh, I hate this,' Flame suddenly burst out. 'I thought I had my life all planned out. College, a painting career, and marriage. In that order.' Only the dancing lights in her eyes gave away the fact that she was mocking herself.

'Life has a way of throwing boulders in your way,' her mother warned, and Flame instantly forgot her own troubles.

'You're thinking about your own boulders, aren't you?' she said quietly.

Francesca sighed, and nodded. 'Yes, I suppose I am,' she murmured. And into her mind flashed a picture of Malcolm when she'd first met him. How handsome he'd been. And, she'd thought, kind too. What a mistake! He had married her only because she was a Corraldo, and therefore a fitting match for the heir to Halcyone's. He'd never loved her.

Flame reached out her hand and covered her mother's. 'Tell me how you feel. About Daddy's death, I mean.'

Francesca sighed painfully but answered as honestly as she could. 'Relieved, I suppose. I always . . . well, I never quite felt safe. As if he would reach out at any moment and take you away as well. As if he could destroy me all over again.'

'Mamma, you're the strongest person I know! Look at the way you went back to school and got your degree. And your job, translating manuscripts and interpreting for the Professor. Sorry, I didn't mean to interrupt. Was relief all you felt?'

'No. I also feel sorry for him now, because he never knew you, Flame. But now I can see Justin at last — I'll have the chance to see my son again, and you can meet your brother,' she half-sobbed.

'Has Justin written to you yet?' Flame asked eagerly.

Francesca shook her head. 'No, not yet. I dare say he's busy, what with the police investigation and the coroner.'

'But it was an accident, wasn't it?' Flame said. 'He fell while stargazing.'

'Yes. And now I imagine Lady Syramore-Forbes's will can finally be probated. Poor Justin must be feeling totally lost and bewildered. Perhaps I should go to him now. Oh, Flame, I long to do that! Just get on a plane and go. The moment I see him, I know everything will be all right.'

* * *

Two days later, Francesca picked up the post and walked into the lounge where Flame was waiting for the taxi to take her to the airport. She was obviously nervous about the meeting at Redex that afternoon, but trying not to show it. 'Relax.' Francesca smiled encouragingly. 'You'll do fine.'

31

'That's easy for you to say,' Flame grinned. 'You know I'm just a great big coward at heart.'

Francesca laughed. 'That, my girl, is something you most definitely are not.'

'Have you heard from Grandma yet?' Flame asked, trying to distract herself from the upcoming interview. What if Redex actually wanted the designs? She could never work for them. Not while she was half-owner of Halcyone's, that real-life fairy-tale castle of her childhood. She'd read all about it, had even seen a photograph of it once in an English magazine. Yet it had always been out of reach, a nebulous inheritance she could neither touch nor see. Now it was suddenly *hers*.

'No,' Francesca answered thoughtfully, reading a letter from her solicitor before putting it back in its envelope and reaching for the next one. 'But I know Venice will be good for her. It's funny how we all run home to Mamma when things go wrong. I did, she has, and you probably will in the future.'

'Now there's something to look forward to,' Flame said drolly. 'I envy her. Being in Venice, I mean. I'd love to see the city. And I remember Great-grandma Giulietta. I only ever saw her once, when I was what . . . six?'

'Well, why don't you write and ask if you can visit them? You'll have an Easter vacation, won't you? You should travel at your age. It'll be good for you.'

Flame watched her mother open an airmail letter, the idea both surprising and appealing. 'I'd like that. I'll do it. Mamma, you'll come too, won't you? Bring Justin. We can settle this ridiculous feud at last. The Syramore-Forbeses and the Corraldos shall not go the way of the Capulets and . . . Mamma, what's wrong!' Flame's last words came out sharply, for Francesca had sunk on to the sofa, her face white as snow. Flame ran to her, sinking on to her knees by her mother's feet, looking up into her wide, shocked eyes. 'Not more bad news?' she whispered. 'Oh, Mamma, I couldn't bear it.'

Francesca blinked, then slowly shook her head. 'I . . . I . . .' She looked down at the letter in her hand, then at her daughter. 'It's Justin.'

'Justin?' Flame whispered. 'He's all right, isn't he?'

'Yes,' Francesca said, her voice defeated.

'Then what is it? Mamma, what's wrong with Justin?'

'He doesn't want to see us, that's all.' Francesca looked numbly down at the paper in her hands, at the few short, terse sentences it contained.

Flame gently took it from her and read it, every word sinking into her heart like sharp pebbles, making it heavier and heavier.

Dear Signora Corraldo,

As you will have been informed by my solicitors, your ex-husband Malcolm Syramore-Forbes, Twelfth Earl of Ravenscroft, died as a result of an accident on the night of 20th December last year. There are, as you know, several outstanding legal family matters to be finalised, and if you have decided to come to England to discuss these with your legal representatives, I enclose the name and London address of my solicitors. I am now, technically, the thirteenth Earl of Ravenscroft, and the house and grounds, estates and titles, as expressed in my father's last Will and Testament, and according to British law, are now mine.

I write to inform you that ALL previous instructions of my father's, regarding yourself and your daughter, still stand.

Yours,

Justin Syramore-Forbes

Flame gasped, her eyes on the very first line. 'He didn't even call you . . .'

'Mother,' Francesca said, her voice breaking. 'No, he didn't. But I am his mother, Flame. I am!' With a heart-wrenching sob, Francesca buried her face in her hands and began to weep bitter, agonized tears.

* * *

'F.S. Forbes, Mr Dexter.'

The voice of his secretary interrupted Reece Dexter's perusal of the latest sales figures for Redex in San Francisco, and he impatiently fumbled for the button and pressed it with one long, calloused finger. 'Send him in.' A few moments later he heard the door open but continued to run his practised eye down the column of figures, unaware in his intense concentration that the minutes were ticking by. The report was far better than he had hoped. He turned the page, frowning over a discrepancy that had obviously been made by the accountancy department. He scribbled a note in the margin and was about to initial the document when a voice, cool as a frosty morning, halted his silver pen in mid-air.

'I thought our appointment was for ten-thirty. Not ten-forty.'

Reece Dexter's head shot up, his eyes widening at the sight in front of him. Vaguely he was aware that his breath left him in a whoosh, as if someone had just thumped him in the stomach. The girl was a goddess! Dressed in an impeccable Balenciaga emerald-green suit that consisted of pencil-slim skirt and double-breasted jacket, she was at once both slender and full-breasted, with long silk-clad legs and a tiny waist. But it was not her figure, stunning as it undoubtedly was, that held his attention, but her mass of hair, rippling over her shoulders like a curtain of fire.

Flame was just as thunderstruck. She'd spent the time waiting in the outer office psyching herself up. And, since she couldn't possibly work for Redex, she had managed to talk herself out of being intimidated by the vast size and wealth of the Dexter Corporation, which had interests far more diverse than just the Redex jewellery division. So, when she'd finally been shown into Reece Dexter's office, her courage had already been bordering on defensive belligerence.

Not wanting to disturb him, she'd all but tiptoed to his desk, only to be kept waiting minute after minute. No doubt this man was used to keeping his minions waiting. But Flame was in an unusual position — she was no out-of-work designer, ready to beg for her first big break. And if he thought he could be so rude and get away with it, he was in for one hell of a shock! Hence her opening statement. But the moment his head had snapped up, and she had been speared on those steely grey eyes, her bravado had fled. For several seconds they stared at each other, both stunned by the force of their first impressions, and then Reece Dexter began to laugh.

Flame gaped at him. She had been aware only of his eyes before — a steely blue-grey that had seemed to lance right through her. Now she became aware of everything all at once — the wide mouth that wore his laughter so well, the tiny crow's feet that appeared at the sides of his eyes, the long, straight, patrician sweep of his nose, the tanned, almost leathery skin that marked him at once as an outdoors man.

'Sorry. I didn't intend to keep you waiting.' Reece Dexter's voice matched the rest of him; it was strong, deep-timbred, and cut into the silence of the room like a surgeon's scalpel. 'And if I'd known what I was missing . . .' his voice softened unnervingly as his eyes ran slowly from the tip of her flame-coloured head to the high green heels she wore, then back up to her deep, chocolate-coloured eyes '. . . I'd never have wasted so much time on a list of boring numbers.'

Flame flushed, tingling from head to toe, and shifted her weight nervously from foot to foot. Angrily aware that she was acting like a schoolgirl, letting herself be overawed by mere good looks, her backbone stiffened. 'I wouldn't want to keep you from counting up your money,' she said, as sweetly as she could manage, but her eyes told him in no uncertain terms that she didn't appreciate flattery. And certainly not *his* kind.

Reece felt the laughter drain away, and in its wake sanity returned. He enjoyed beautiful distractions as much as the next man, but business had always come first with him, and always would. The sons of rich men had to grow fast and hard if they wanted to get out of the great man's shadow and blossom in the sun of their own making. Impatient now, he glanced behind her, but the room was empty. 'I was expecting a Mr Forbes. Has he been delayed?'

'I'm F.S. Forbes,' Flame said, having figured out from the receptionist that Wendy had written to them under that name. It was typical of her mischievous room-mate. And as Reece Dexter's heavy, dark brow shot up in questioning surprise, Flame did something she rarely did, and emphasised her title. '*Lady* Syramore-Forbes, in fact.' She didn't mention her first name. Halcyone was so unusual that this man couldn't fail to make the connection between herself and the prestigious English jewellery chain.

Reece took one look at her stormy face and fought back a grin. With her svelte figure, and sophisticated make-up, clothes and jewellery, she looked like a prize Persian cat who had been mistaken for some common-or-garden alley cat. With an effort he managed to keep his hands from reaching for her and stroking her ruffled fur back into place. Now that was a thought guaranteed to brighten up any morning. With even more effort, Reece dragged his errant thoughts back into line. 'I do beg your pardon,' he drawled, eyes twinkling irrepressibly as he turned on his swivel chair and slowly stood up. With easy, economical movements he moved to the front of the desk.

Flame took a step backwards. She couldn't help it. She had never expected him to be so tall, or so wide. Seated behind the desk, dressed in a dark grey business suit, he had looked less intimidating. Now she could see that he was easily over six feet tall, and had the wide shoulders and slim waist of a lumberjack. He seemed so incongruously out of place in the high-tech, ultra-modern office that Flame was half-convinced she was dreaming all this. And she was certainly acting strangely. Never had a man so unnerved her on their first meeting. In the space of a few minutes she had been furiously angry with him. Then she had found herself holding her breath as his eyes made a slow, thorough inspection of her that should have made her indignant but had only made her so very aware of her own femininity. He had laughed at her, and now he was intimidating her, simply by standing up. When he held out his hand, she saw at once that it was large and strong and . . . yes, those were callouses on his palms. Could this really be the head of a huge organisation? She could certainly never imagine *anyone* telling this man what to do.

'We seem to have gotten off on the wrong foot. Let's start again — I'm Reece Dexter, and I'm very impressed with the designs you sent me.'

Flame forced herself to accept his hand, and winced in anticipation of having her fingers crushed. Instead she felt her hand being engulfed in warm, incredibly gentle strength, and a low flush started deep inside her stomach and spread upwards, forcing her to take a sharp, surprised breath. 'Yes . . . er . . . well, I'm glad you like them. But I think there's something we should get straight right from the start.'

'Oh?' Reece looked down at her from his superior height, and a gentle waft of perfume played with his nose. Helplessly, his eyes dropped to the creamy lace blouse frothing between her jacket lapels and traced the outline of her thrusting breasts with a hot gaze. Quickly he jerked his eyes away and moved back to his desk, picking up her portfolio. Redex was too important for him to let himself be distracted by a potential employee. Redex was all his, the only part of the Dexter Corporation he could call his own. He was determined to make it the success story of the decade. Even so, he had to resist the urge to clear his throat like some lovesick schoolboy before getting this meeting firmly back on track.

'I, too, like to get things straight,' he began crisply. 'These designs show promise, but they are far from perfect. I take it you've had little or no formal training?'

Flame gasped, at once angry and wary. She felt that she had been wrong-footed ever since stepping into this office, and it was not a feeling she appreciated. 'No, I've had no formal training,' she admitted, 'but—'

'That's no problem. We have people here at Redex who can give you on-the-spot lessons. It's raw talent that counts, and that you have. But this design, for instance . . .' he held up a ruby and silver brooch '. . . isn't feasible simply because the welding needed would be impossible to do. But Grant

Longthorne — he's our chief metalsmith — will be able to teach you what is and isn't possible.'

'Look,' Flame cut in, 'there's been a mistake. I . . .' She was about to tell him about Wendy Gibbs sending in her designs without her permission, when her brain cut in with a different message altogether. 'Grant Longthorne? Wasn't he at Corraldo's?' She wasn't sure, but she thought she'd heard her grandfather mention that their metalsmith of over fifteen years had handed in his resignation last summer.

'That's right,' Reece said, his eyes narrowing warily. 'You obviously do your homework.'

Flame opened her mouth, then shut it again. So this was the man responsible for luring away all Corraldo's best people! She felt a slow, burning anger take the place of her previous helpless frustration, and took a deep breath. 'Mr Dexter,' she began, and almost growled in rage as, yet again, he interrupted her.

'Call me Reece. Since we'll be working together, I prefer—'

'We will *not* be working together!' Flame finally exploded, her small hands clenching into fists. 'You must be the rudest man I've ever met. First of all you keep me waiting, without so much as a "hello, please sit down", and then you keep interrupting everything I say!' She took a ragged breath, unaware that the action made her breasts rise and fall with eye-catching splendour.

Reece found himself having to choose between amusement, anger and desire, and found it impossible. He felt all three, and in spite of himself was glad. The morning that had started out so depressingly like all other mornings was turning out to be a rollercoaster ride, and at twenty-nine he was still young enough to appreciate the trip.

'If you'd just let me get in a word edgeways, *Mr Dexter*,' she all but sneered his name, 'I might be able to tell you that there's been a mistake. I don't want to work for Redex — in fact, now that I've met its boss, I wouldn't work for Redex if it were the last jewellery outlet on earth. Which it isn't.

As much as it might come as a shock to you, Mr Dexter, there are several companies far superior to this one out there.' She waved vaguely at the big panoramic windows where Los Angeles sprawled as far as the eye could see. 'Corraldo's of Italy, and Halcyone's of England, to name but two. And—'

'That's enough!' The voice cracked like thunder and Flame jumped, her angry words drying up instantly. She felt the power of the man a moment too late, and took a hasty step back as Reece Dexter stepped closer to her, his chin thrust menacingly forward, his eyes only inches from hers. She could see now that his eyes were flecked with orange, making them a strange combination of fire and ice. She swallowed hard, her heart pounding in a mixture of fear and something else. Something dangerous and exciting . . . 'If you don't want to work for Redex,' Reece began through clenched teeth, impatience making a small tic pulse ominously in his taut jaw just beneath his full, sensuous lips, 'just why did you send your designs to me in the first place?'

'I didn't,' Flame shot back, inordinately pleased to see the look of surprise wipe the superior expression from his face. 'A friend of mine did, without my knowledge or consent. I only came to explain to you in person what had happened. I thought it only *polite.'* She stressed the word mockingly. 'But having met you, I can see for myself what a wasted effort *that* was. Now, if I may have my portfolio back . . . ?'

Reece stared at her, aware that his body was stirring dangerously. He would have had to be made of stone not to be affected by her potent mixture of breathtaking beauty, blazing defiance and unintentional sexual challenge, but this went much deeper. He'd had women before, of course — many of them. But none, not even from his teenage years, had affected him so strongly, so completely, and on such short acquaintance as this aggravating little virago. Aware that she was still staring at him questioningly, with angst in every taut line of her lovely body, Reece grabbed the portfolio off the desk and all but slapped it into her outstretched hands. 'By all means, my lady. And I wish you luck with them. Although I can't see Corraldo's, or Halcyone's, falling over themselves to accept them. I only offered to help you because Redex is still relatively new, and I have a policy of encouraging new talent.'

'Oh, really?' Flame shot back heatedly. 'And here was I, thinking you had a policy of stealing it.' And with that excellent exit line, Flame turned on her heel and stomped to the door.

Reece watched her go, breathing hard. He winced, then in spite of himself grinned as she slammed the door behind her, leaving the room feeling strangely empty. She had come and gone like a cyclone, leaving chaos in her wake, and already, absurdly, he was beginning to miss her. He sat slowly down in his chair, very much aware that his body was still tingling and that the air still carried the caress of her perfume.

Ruefully he shook his head. She was too young. Too damned cocky. And he didn't need any added complications in his life. The son of a billionaire had enough problems without that. Still, it seemed a pity to let all that fire and beauty just walk out of his life . . .

CHAPTER 4

Justin walked casually into the Junior Common Room and looked around with a bittersweet pang of regret. He'd become fond of the JCR, with its smoky atmosphere and horrible coffee machines, and knew he was going to miss it. For a moment he felt angry at being forced to leave Oxford, then he shrugged it away, idly leafing through the pigeonhole in search of correspondence. What he found was a blue air-mail envelope, addressed to himself, and he felt a long cold snake coil up his spine as he stared down at the unfamiliar handwriting. Reluctantly, his eyes lifted to scan the post-mark, which was Boston, USA. Although he'd never seen her handwriting, he knew instinctively that it belonged to his mother. But why had she waited so long to reply to his letter? Malcolm had been dead for nearly three months now. Could it . . . ? Justin's throat went dry. Could it be a second chance? He'd written her that spiteful note while his emotions were still see-sawing between fear and elation, anxiety and a giddying sense of relief. He'd wanted nothing more than to clear out the cluttered closet of his life, and that meant ensuring that his mother stayed safely on the other side of the Atlantic, where he didn't need to worry about her. But what if she'd realised he'd not been clear-headed when he'd penned that letter? What if she'd decided to wait, give him time to adjust and then write again, asking . . . asking what?

'I should watch out for old McDuff, Juzzer. He's on the warpath.'

Justin jumped, the jaunty sound of his nickname smashing into his thoughts.

George Campbell-Bean, a fellow PPE student, stuck a great meaty paw into the 'C' pigeonhole and began to sift rapidly through the mail. At six foot two, George was an inch taller than Justin. He had thick chestnut hair and deep dark eyes, and was widely considered to be one of the most handsome men in Oxford. He was thickly muscled too, and had worked hard to get into the Oxford Eight. He was looking forward to his first Oxford/Cambridge boat race, and only two things spoiled what would otherwise be a very comfy life indeed. First, he was poor; his father was suffering in the recession, and the small retail outlets he ran in Scotland were feeling the pinch. And the second, perhaps even more irksome fly in the ointment was Justin Syramore-Forbes. Justin, who with his pale blond hair and blue eyes should have looked washed out and effeminate next to George, but never did. Justin who, with his slender and graceful build, should never have made the Oxford Eight, but who had, and who was, unbelievably, an even a better oarsman than George. Justin, who had a title and reeked of money. But the thing that really irked George the most was that he quite liked the Earl of Ravenscroft. There was something about Justin that struck him as . . . pitiful.

George read the letter from his father and groaned out loud. 'The old man's threatening to cut off the dosh.'

'Marry a rich old trout, Georgie, my boy,' a laughing voice belonging to Scott Tate advised.

'Don't I wish,' George grumbled half-seriously.

Scott, dressed in his usual black, was a third-year jurisprudence student. There was something both innately playful and yet cruel in his nature. He watched Justin with his usual close intensity. 'You've decided to leave Oxford?' he finally asked, and Justin shrugged. Alarm bells were sounding far off in the back of his head. Scott saw too much. And that could be dangerous. 'Why do you think that?'

'Oh, come on,' Scott chided. 'You know I'm always right.'

'So modest! Since you seem to know it all, tell me what I should do about the mess I'm in now.'

'You mean about Halcyone's? Or the death duties? Or about Walt Matthews? He is the one guarding your dear sister's piece of the pie, isn't he?'

Justin was aware he'd gone cold, and only hoped he hadn't gone white. 'You've been busy.'

'I'm always busy,' Scott said. 'Don't worry. I'm on your side. And I'm not studying law for nothing, you know.'

'Three years at Oxford qualifies you as a legal eagle, does it?' Justin asked, half amused, half angry. He knew that Scott Tate was cultivating him, of course. He knew, too, that having a pet lawyer was no bad thing. He wasn't his father's son for nothing. 'Let's go to my room.'

'Said the spider to the fly,' Scott added drolly, following Justin up the XI staircase and into his cramped room. Justin put on his small electric kettle and reached for the Earl Grey.

'Death duties are crippling, aren't they?' Scott asked, accepting his mug and lounging elegantly on the sofa. He knew Justin as well as research would let him, coupled with his own observations of the last seven months. Justin was, as Scott's down-to-earth mother would have put it, 'right screwed up'. And with a family history like his, it was hardly surprising.

'True. It's rather funny, actually.' Justin took a sip of his tea. 'I thought that all my troubles would be over when Dad died. But I only swapped one set of problems for another. There's no way I can stop my sister from claiming half of Halcyone's now that the will's been probated. And I'm going to have to sell two of the farms and the acreage that goes with them just to cover the death duties and tax on Ravenscroft and leave me with some working capital.'

'So what's your plan?' Scott said, taking it for granted that he was on board.

Justin eyed him over the rim of his mug, his face expressionless. 'What makes you think I have a plan?'

Scott laughed. 'Justin! Come on, give.'

Justin shrugged. He didn't trust Scott Tate, of course. He didn't trust anybody. But Tate was the greatest brain in the Oxford student body. And he was, next to himself, the biggest bastard. Together, he knew they could make a formidable team. 'As I see it,' he began slowly, feeling his way cautiously, 'I have no choice. Apart from the remaining farms, Halcyone's is the only money-making machine I have. So, I have to leave Oxford and run it, before my twin begins to turn her greedy little eyes this way.'

'Good. Possession is nine-tenths of the law. See, I did pay attention during all those lectures,' Scott drawled.

'Which means I have to make myself so indispensable to Halcyone's that without me, the whole edifice falls. And that shouldn't be too difficult. Walt Matthews is no genius, and under his so-called leadership the company has just been ticking along all these years.' Conditioned by his father to look on the company as nothing more than money, and money that would eventually be used on Ravenscroft, Justin had discovered, with ever-growing delight, that the small Woodstock shop had a magic and atmosphere that in its own way was every bit as unique and compelling as that of Ravenscroft itself. This revelation had fuelled even more his ever-growing hatred of his dead father. 'I want Halcyone's,' Justin said quietly, almost to himself. 'It's the one thing Malcolm never touched, the one thing that Jessica left to me.'

'Quite,' Scott said succinctly, fascinated by the convoluted way that Justin's mind worked. 'But do you know how you're going to go about getting it?' Justin shrugged. 'Well, most of all you need capital. How much money, in real terms, have you got?'

Justin laughed out loud. 'Apart from the cash left over from the sale of the farms? None. Oh, I've got property worth millions coming out of my ears, plus art treasures hung on Ravenscroft walls worth more millions, but they're held in perpetuity and can't be sold. Banks look upon businessmen favourably, but what experience do I have?'

Scott nodded. 'So, the same applies to you as to Georgie-boy,' he said. 'You'll have to marry money, my lord. Some peasant whose father is rolling in ready cash. There are plenty of them about. You want me to make up a list, get you invited to the right parties?'

Justin stared at him. 'You're serious, aren't you?'

'The question is,' Scott said slowly, 'are you? Will you marry money to get Halcyone's, or is the sacrifice too great?'

'No sacrifice is too great,' Justin said immediately, then realised it was true. He would do anything not to fail.

'So,' Scott said briskly, 'you marry money. Then you have to ensure that Halcyone's makes even more money.'

'I've been thinking about that. Apart from branching out into costume jewellery, which I can just about set up with the cash I do have, the company's biggest asset is its reputation. And reputation sells — especially to royalty.'

'Come again?' Scott said, blinking.

'Ever heard of the Principessa Sofia Elena di Maggiore? She's one of those many Italian princesses who choose to ignore the revolution.'

'There are hundreds of those,' Scott said dismissively.

'True. But in her case she has the money to live up to the title. Her grandfather founded a wine dynasty. He produced good cheap plonk, and the result was, his fellow vintners refused to speak to him, and grew old and poor with great dignity, while the Maggiore clan got stinking rich. The Principessa's father, and then her husband, have carried on the good work.'

'Fascinating,' Scott said drolly. 'But is it relevant?'

'Oh, it's relevant,' Justin assured him. Since coming to the painful decision to leave Oxford and make a go of Halcyone's, Justin had thrown himself into researching his task wholeheartedly. 'And the plan is simple. The family's jewels, while fabulous, are old and cumbersome. The Principessa is rich and jewel-obsessed. In three years' time she'll be forty, and, to cheer herself up, she has decided to treat herself to a suite of jewellery. Her choice of words, not mine. Rumour has it that the amount of money she's set aside to pay for it is vast. *Vast,*' Justin reiterated softly. 'So, the good lady is "shopping around" for a jeweller.'

'And you're going to throw Halcyone's hat into the ring?'

'It's a good hat. It's new enough to appeal to the Principessa's spirit — after all, her money was made by her grandfather, as Halcyone's was made by my great-grand-mother. But the company's also just old enough to have that certain . . . patina? . . . that comes with age. Our craftsmen are the best. And Halcyone's is English.'

Scott frowned. 'I'd have thought being British was a disadvantage. Don't Italians stick togeth . . . Wait a minute,' Scott's voice rose. 'This princess is Italian? And it's widely known, in the top jewellery circles, that she's ready to commission a company for the new jewels?'

'Yes.'

'Then surely Corraldo's would have put in a bid?'

'Yes,' Justin said, thinking of Enrico Corraldo and his uncle, the Conte.

'*Yes,*' Scott echoed, not sure whether to laugh or shake his implacable friend by the scruff of his neck. 'Don't you think Princess Sofia whatsername will jump at the Corraldo's offer? It's older than Halcyone's, Italian, and just as famous.'

'I'm sure she's got Corraldo's at the top of her list. But then, Halcyone's hasn't entered the arena yet.'

Scott grinned. 'You've got something else up your sleeve?'

Justin shook his head. 'I don't need anything else. The Italians *do* stick together, but they also hold a grudge. The Principessa won't have forgotten, let alone forgiven, the fact that her grandfather was made to feel like an outcast in his own country by his neighbours and peers. And one of those neighbours and peers just happens to be a direct ancestor of the present head of the Corraldo family.'

'Right,' Scott said doubtfully.

Justin smiled. 'You forget, jewels are not like any other business in the world.' His voice softened lovingly. 'Halcyone's manufactures dreams. Glamour. The ultimate in fantasy, in status and power. You think it all sounds a bit nebulous, counting on the whims of some Italian princess? In a way it is — in another way, it epitomizes exactly what Halcyone's is all about. And that's where we have an advantage over outfits like Redex. They're a new American firm. They're giving even the mighty Tiffany a run for its money. Even so, they're too new to appeal to the Principessa.'

'OK. So let's say you do get the commission. What then?'

Justin laughed. 'Your working-class morality is showing, Scott. Do you know what happens when a firm gets the royal seal of approval? Matrons flock. The *nouveau riche* go bananas. The reputation spirals. We get the Maggiore commission and soon everyone will want a Halcyone original — even if it's only a measly £5,000 pair of earrings.'

Scott caught the sound of excitement, for the first time ever, in Justin Syramore-Forbes's voice and couldn't help but feel it too. 'You're really keen on this, aren't you?'

'Yes. Strangely enough, I am.' Justin looked out over the lawns. He would regret not graduating from Oxford. But at last he had control of his life, and he was going to win.

'So your father's gone, and you're learning what it is to be free,' Scott mused. 'Was it worth it, Justin?' he asked softly.

Justin swung round as if Scott had just lashed a red-hot poker across his back. Then he relaxed and turned back to the window. 'Do you think I murdered my father, Scott?' he asked, his tone so casual he might have been asking if he thought it was going to rain tomorrow.

Scott smiled. 'I think,' he said calmly, 'that I don't really give a damn whether you did or whether you didn't.'

* * *

Several thousand miles away, Reece Dexter's long black limousine pulled to a halt at the private airstrip five miles from LA. Waiting was one of the Dexter Corporation jets, a gleaming black and silver craft of streamlined elegance and ostentatious power. Once inside, he helped himself to a small measure of bourbon and liberally laced it with water. He glanced at his watch, swiftly calculating the time he'd be in the air. He'd seldom had reason to visit Italy before, and he was looking forward to it.

As the jet taxied and took off into the darkening sky, Reece pulled forward a dossier on the Principessa Sofia di Maggiore and began to study it. She sounded like an interesting woman. And that thought led him on to contemplate the most interesting woman of all — Lady Forbes. Oh, he'd quickly had her checked out. No wonder the little madam had all but told him to take his job and shove it!

How easy it was to conjure up her fiery presence. He just closed his eyes and there she was, spitting venom and insults and making him want her all over again. Reece shook his head angrily and snapped on an overhead light. He'd already made his mind up to forget her. But, as the jet climbed higher and levelled out, Reece couldn't help but feel that it was a mistake to give up on his beautiful cyclone so soon.

And Reece Dexter was not a man used to making mistakes.

CHAPTER 5

Venice

After landing at Marco Polo airport at Tessera, Flame made her way to the train station, and by the time her train had pulled into Santa Lucia she could hardly wait to explore the city. She selected the Giudecca Canal as a starting point, and decided to take the most popular and scenic vaporetto. The ride was one she would never forget.

Venice was sinking. And yet, for all the peeling woodwork, crumbling stone and faintly smelling water, the city had a grandeur that rose above it all. It was so unashamedly Gothic and unrepentantly flamboyant. Whenever the boat turned a corner, another domed building gleamed white in the sun, the fourteenth-century Venetian metalwork by Gian Paolo Boninsegna competing with the beautiful Baroque church façades by Alessandro Tremignon.

She was just approaching her stop when she saw a magnificent gondola pass by, and for a second her heart stopped as she spotted a dark head, half-hidden by the gondola's white curtain. No — it couldn't be . . . Flame shook her head, angry at herself for imagining, even for one moment, that the obnoxious Reece Dexter could possibly be in Venice.

Really, the man was a menace, plaguing her dreams every night. Telling herself to stop imagining things, Flame made her way to her great-grandmother's house, the magnificently named Palazzo d'Oro, situated in a labyrinthine set of *calli* off the Salizzada San Moise.

The main door was opened instantly by a middle-aged man, who half-bowed and addressed her in Italian. 'Signorina Syramore-Forbes? I am Marco, the Contessa's manservant. May I take your cases?'

A moment later, Flame found herself in a small open-air courtyard. Greenery climbed up every wall, and hanging baskets trailed blue, red, yellow and orange flowers over the sides of their moss-filled domes. But the real eye-catching feature of the courtyard was the fountain in the centre, a naked marble woman pouring from a ewer into the water below, where water-lilies and golden koi carp competed in the splendour stakes.

'This way, please, *signorina*. The Contessa is most anxious to meet you again.'

In the long gallery, one eccentric portrait by Lorenzo Lotto made her stop in mid-step. By the time Marco showed her into her great-grandmother's room, her mind was crammed with images of paintings by Sebastiano Ricci, Giambattista Tiepolo and Alvise Vivarini. It was only Marco, ponderously announcing her, that snapped her attention back to the immediate present.

'Flame, *cara,* you look magnificent. Doesn't she, Mamma?' Maria Corraldo rose from her position on a gilt sofa and walked swiftly across the oriental carpet to take Flame by the hands and squeeze them lovingly.

'Indeed she does.' A warm, thoughtful voice had Flame's eyes swinging from those of her grandmother to those of her great-grandmother, and her breath caught. Contessa Giulietta Maria Granti was a vision, even at eighty-one years old. Dressed in blue Venetian raw silk, she rose to her feet without the aid of a stick. Her hair was silver and was arranged in a shapely chignon. Diamonds and sapphires sparkled above her breast in a spectacular fan-tailed peacock brooch. 'Flame. How well they named you, *cara*,' she said, and kissed her great-granddaughter on both cheeks.

Giulietta liked what she saw. Tall and lissom with a figure like Venus. A perfect complexion was the key to any woman's beauty, and Flame not only had that but the deep, dark mysterious eyes to complement it perfectly. She nodded and straightened her old shoulders. So much for looks. It was what lay beneath that counted.

'Have I grown a second nose, Great-grandmother?' Flame asked, and Giulietta began to laugh. The girl had spirit!

'Not that I can see. And call me Grandy.' As they talked, Giulietta led her to a comfortable sofa and poured tea.

'Venice is wonderful,' Flame enthused, taking a cup of weak-looking brew. 'I want to see it all, you know, before I go back to Radcliffe.'

'Of course you must,' Giulietta agreed. 'And what's the first thing you want to see?'

Flame felt herself hesitating. There were so many things she could say — the Bridge of Sighs, the Doge's Palace, the San Marco bronze horses or the clock tower. Instead, there *was* one place she wanted to see more than anything else. 'Corraldo's,' she said softly, then glanced sharply at Giulietta as she and Maria exchanged knowing glances.

'See, I told you,' Maria said softly. 'Flame is determined to go where angels fear to tread. I told you she won that prize only last month, for her jewellery designs?'

Giulietta nodded and looked at Flame thoughtfully.

Flame shrugged. 'It was only a small prize, Grandy, but I do already have some designs that might be of interest to Corraldo's. I've worked on refining them all semester.' Flame did not add that since Reece Dexter's crushing indictment she had researched her designs more thoroughly and made sure there were no longer any glaring technical errors. Such as impossible welding! 'Do you approve, Grandy?' she asked softly.

'What's to approve? You surely know what you are doing. And now that you've had some tea,' Giulietta smoothly changed the conversation, 'do you want to see your room? I put you in the Pope Clement XIII suite. It overlooks the canal.'

The suite turned out to be breathtakingly magnificent. Flame had never seen furniture so . . . gold. Palazzo d'Oro meant 'golden palace', and it certainly lived up to its name. Flame made her way to a small balcony. Opposite her was a large limestone *palazzo*, and below a long, green, winding canal. It was bliss!

* * *

Three days later, Flame and her great-grandmother were seated in the Granti gondola, a long black affair that bore the Granti coat of arms in gold on the side, silently traversing the Grand Canal. It was nearly ten o'clock at night, lights twinkled all around them, and Flame was on her way to her first *festa*. 'I wish Mamma were here to see this,' Flame mused. 'She's spending more and more time in San Francisco nowadays.'

Their gondolier chose that moment to burst into a passable baritone and Flame laughed aloud. It was all too much: the transport, her dress, the jewellery. She felt like a fairy-tale princess thrust from the pages of folklore and forced into the twentieth century. Maria had insisted that neither of her two evening dresses were suitable for the occasion, and had looked out a dress from Giulietta's vast selection. Off the shoulder, tight-waisted and full-skirted, it was of a colour that could not easily be named; silver, grey, pewter-blue, it was all these and more. Because it was made of the finest Thai silk, it was luminous, shifting, ever-changing. Giulietta's private hairdresser had thrown up her hands and nearly danced a jig on first sighting Flame's hair, and had spent hours arranging her mass of waves into a style that sat high on her head but at the same time allowed long, thick tendrils to cascade over her shoulders on to the silk of her gown. The combination of cool grey silk and flaming hair had taken everyone's breath away, including her own. Women just didn't dress up like this anymore, she had demurred, laughing.

'Except in Venice, *cara*,' Giulietta had said, reaching for three red velvet boxes which opened to reveal diamonds and emeralds that turned Flame's knees to water. Now they lay heavy against the skin of her throat and hung from her ears. But it was the tiara on her head that occupied Flame's thoughts the most. She could feel the tight bands digging into her head, heralding the ominous beginnings of a headache. A simple arch of emeralds and diamonds, it looked spectacular against her hair, but the style was old and very heavy.

At that moment, their gondola docked next to one that looked remarkably like the gondola Flame had thought she'd seen Reece Dexter using. But she gave it little thought. Ahead of her was a *palazzo* filled with the cream of Venice's elite. What if she made some awful gaffe?

Giulietta glanced across at Flame's suddenly nervous face and took her hand. 'Courage, *cara*. They will not bite. And remember — you will easily be the most beautiful woman there. They should all fear *you*.'

Inside, Reece Dexter smiled at the Principessa Sofia di Maggiore and reached for another glass of champagne. He knew that the commission was lost, but was not too concerned. It had been a shot in the dark anyway. His company was too new to be trusted with a royal commission, but Reece didn't count the journey as a wasted one. He'd made deals with more modern thinkers, totalling more than a million dollars.

He turned as yet more guests arrived, and his eyes widened in shock at the vision walking through the door. It was her! His lovely cyclone. Reece felt his breath catch in his chest as she began to walk down the steps, and his body once more caught fire, leaving him both angry and amused. And he thought he'd forgotten her. Like hell! He found himself walking towards her, determination in his step and in the look on his face. Fate was obviously trying to tell him something. So why fight the inevitable?

Flame saw him a moment later and stopped so abruptly that Giulietta cannoned into the back of her. '*Cara,* what . . . ?'

'Lady Forbes,' Reece said loudly, stepping directly in front of her and giving her no chance to try and dodge him. With eyes filled with devilment, he executed a perfect but mocking bow. 'Now what do you suppose the chances were that we would ever meet again?'

Flame bit her lip, dismayed at the familiar heat suffusing her body. He was wearing a black dinner jacket that did little to disguise the almost primitive power of his body and masculinity, and again Flame felt that cowardly desire to take a step back from his overwhelming charisma. Behind her, Giulietta's eyes began to sparkle.

'I'd have thought they were slim enough for me to feel safe,' Flame snapped, then could have kicked herself as his eyes locked with hers in a long, knowing, purely sexual understanding.

'You're too young . . . and beautiful . . . to want to be *safe,* Lady Forbes,' Reece chided gently, but he was inordinately pleased that at least he'd made as great an impression on her as she had on him.

At that moment, Giulietta flicked open the Spanish lace fan she was holding, the movement catching Reece's eye. 'You must introduce me,' he chided her yet again, making Flame feel guilty over her slip in etiquette and angry enough to want to spit tin tacks. The thought of sharp steel objects piercing his flesh was a most satisfactory one.

'Contessa Giulietta Granti, Mr Reece Dexter,' she gritted.

'Dexter?' Giulietta queried at once, her interest in this fascinating stranger doubling. 'The Dexter of Dexter Mining?'

Reece smiled modestly. 'I wouldn't have thought a lady as lovely as yourself would have any interest in mining, Contessa.'

Flame's jaw dropped. He was being charming! He was actually flattering her Grandy! She glanced at the older woman and saw her smile. Flame drew in her breath sharply. How ridiculous! How could Grandy be so taken in by this great big . . . oaf!

'As a relation by marriage to the Corraldos, I have a great deal of interest in people who mine gemstones. I assume Redex is your creation?' Giulietta raised a delicate brow, at the same time watching Flame's ominously darkening face with a great deal of amusement.

Reece shot a quick look at Flame. 'It is,' he answered Giulietta's question first. 'And you, Lady Forbes. Are you also related to the Corraldos?' he goaded.

Flame smiled sweetly. 'My mother is Francesca Corraldo, yes. Daughter of Michael Corraldo. You may have heard of him?'

Reece had. Oh, how he had! 'Please excuse us, Contessa. You won't object if I steal your lovely companion for a dance?'

'Not at all,' Giulietta said, and weathered the furious glance her great-granddaughter sent her with a nonchalant smile. Flame opened her mouth to state categorically that she didn't *want* to dance, but the words were left unsaid as Reece slipped a hand around her waist and all but lifted her feet off the floor. Before she knew where she was, she was crushed against the solid wall of his chest and swept away into the waltzing throng.

'Now just wait a minute!' she finally found the breath to protest. 'It's polite to ask . . . oh, I was forgetting. You don't know the meaning of the word, do you?'

Reece smiled down at her. 'Perhaps not,' he agreed through gritted teeth. 'But I do know other words. Like industrial espionage, for instance.'

Flame blinked. 'What?'

'You heard me. So a friend sent your designs in to Redex without your knowledge? Like hell! Tell me, did your *Uncle* Enrico find what you had to tell him about our set-up at Redex interesting?' He wondered what this treacherous little minx would try to pull on him next. And wondered even more why he was so looking forward to it . . .

'What *are* you going on about?' Flame snapped, then gasped as his hand tightened on her waist like a vice, pulling her against him so tightly she could feel every outline of his body — from the muscles lined in ridges against his flat stomach to the long, lean, powerful sweep of his thighs and even . . . She blushed. She could even feel the hardening presence of his manhood pushing against her silk-clad hip.

'Don't play innocent with me, Lady Forbes,' he growled. 'And I can't keep calling you that. It's not even correct. What's your name?'

'Everyone calls me Flame,' she said. If he really thought she was spying for Corraldo's, who knew what he would have made of her first name being Halcyone! 'But you're being ridiculous! I have no interest in—'

'Flame?' Reece looked down at her, his storm-cloud-grey eyes softening like melting silver as he stared at her hair. 'How apt.'

Flame felt her heartbeat pick up again and thud crazily against her ribs. Suddenly air was hard to come by, and she was no longer sure that she even cared. The music from the orchestra swelled into a crescendo, and she found herself being whirled around in arms that had grown to feel like extensions of her own body. He was impossible, his moods swinging like mercury from angry to seductive, from charming to near brutal. She could feel the electricity sparking from him and an answering sizzle ignited in her own blood. She could feel her nipples tighten and thrust against his chest, and she was glad of the barriers of material separating them, even as a more primitive, wanton desire wished they would melt away. Their eyes met, clashed, duelled. Suddenly the music stopped, and the two of them with it. Flame waited, not sure what to expect next. Then Reece smiled, a strange, half-frightening, half-seductive smile. 'So, it's not a coincidence that we meet again, after all,' he murmured thoughtfully, and shrugged his broad shoulders. 'No matter.' And with that totally cryptic but thrillingly ominous observation, he abruptly kissed her hand, turned on one well-shod heel and disappeared into the crowd.

Flame stared after him with wide eyes. Her hand still tingled from the brief imprint of his lips, and her mind tumbled around in giddying circles. Her tingling breasts rose and fell with every panting breath she took.

What on earth had she gotten herself into!

CHAPTER 6

Hundreds of miles away, Justin walked into a room and stood on its threshold, taking in the scene with a jaundiced eye. It was a typical Mayfair party, and he smiled and accepted a glass of tepid champagne. He wasn't in a party mood. Oh, he'd had his fair share of leading the 'Sloane Ranger' existence. He'd pissed into several fountains and thought it hilariously funny, courtesy of four glasses of the finest Napoleon brandy. He'd indulged in the usual experiments with women and booze, but never drugs.

The hostess, a woman of fifty, homed in on him, dressed in a mini-skirt that showed off admittedly still very good legs, her ample breasts jiggling behind a silver lamé halter top. 'Justin! How wonderful to see you.'

'As if I could bear to stay away from you for long, Julia,' Justin felt himself smile, heard himself flatter, and watched the reaction with all the detachment of a scientist watching a bug struggle under a microscope. He'd learned charm at a very early age — on a variety of nannies, schoolmistresses and, later, lovers. It was now already such a spontaneous response that he was barely aware he was doing it — like breathing. Justin's smile, appealingly boyish, cleverly frank and fresh, was a purely physical response to well-tried stimuli.

'You must let me introduce you to this year's debs. You know you've caused quite a scandal, leaving Oxford that way. That's no way for an earl to behave.'

'On the contrary,' Justin smiled, hiding his annoyance at the silly woman with ominous ease, 'I thought that's exactly how an earl should behave. After all, who ever heard of an educated earl? That's almost indecent.' With his hostess eating out of his hand, Justin quickly got what he wanted, which was an introduction to the girl who was top on Scott's list of single heiresses. At least three stone overweight, she had short black hair that curled in natural waves around a moon-shaped face. Bright brown eyes tended to resemble buttons in what would otherwise have been a passable face.

'Felicity Mainwaring, meet Justin Syramore-Forbes, Earl of Ravenscroft.'

Justin smiled first at the men clustered around her, surprised to see George Campbell-Bean among them, then pivoted with lithe grace to look down into the face of the woman whose sole attribute was her money. 'Miss Mainwaring,' he said formally, but reached down and kissed her hand.

'Flick,' Felicity Mainwaring corrected in a broad Yorkshire accent. 'What am I supposed to call you?'

Justin, straightening from his continental gesture of gallantry, met her eyes and found himself smiling. 'People call me a lot of things. Some of them totally unmentionable.'

Flick grinned, showing strong, even white teeth. For a moment something about it puzzled Justin. 'I bet! But suppose I wanted to be polite?'

'We all call him Juzzer,' George chipped in, his Scottish accent blurred with good whisky.

'George, you're pissed,' Justin said with quiet good humour, and everybody laughed.

'I hope so, ye miserable Sassenach,' George slurred, then promptly shut up, aware that Flick Mainwaring was giving him a sharp look. It was so obvious what was going on, Justin wondered why everybody was pretending. Every one of the five men clustered around her was after her for her money — himself included. They were all willing to overlook her looks, her awful accent and her unfortunate dress sense, which tonight was a lime-green confection of tiered lace that made her look like a fondant gateau from a gourmet's nightmare. And Felicity herself? Justin turned from George and encountered bright eyes alive with mocking humour and obvious intelligence, and felt an almost physical jolt. She knew! All these men around her, of impeccable pedigree and noble stock, were all cash-poor and willing to court a plump Yorkshire lass for her father's money. And she knew it! He let go of her hand, surprised to find he was still holding it.

'You live in London, Juzzer?' Flick asked, beckoning a waiter and selecting, of all things, a pint of Guinness from the well-stocked tray. Justin blinked as he watched her take a sip, and shook his head.

'No. I have an estate in Oxfordshire. Farmland, mostly. I love it,' he said simply, and only then noted her silent approval. Scott had briefed him well — her father had made his real fortune in coal, before the slump in prices, but had instilled in his only child from an early age a love and respect for the land.

'I expect you're used to dos like this,' Flick said, gesturing to the smoky room filled with *Harpers & Queen* ex-debs of the year, politicians, 'city' gentlemen and women who wore bored, hard veneers the way furniture wore chintz.

''Fraid so. I expect you managed to avoid them, though?'

Flick grinned, and again Justin stared, wondering what was so different about it. Then, as she caught his eye and nodded happily, he realised what it was that was nagging him. The grin was genuine. Wide, unselfconscious and wonderfully free of ennui or artifice. It was so unlike the smiles he was used to seeing on the faces of his women. 'I like a woman who can grin as if she means it,' Justin said, meaning to flatter, and it was only when she fixed those frank, placid brown eyes on him that he felt vaguely ashamed.

'Glad to hear it. I do a lot of grinning, I'm afraid. Like when I saw this dress. My father bought it for me. It's his idea of elegance. Isn't it magnificently ugly?'

'Magnificent, old gal,' George slurred. The others had slunk off, and Justin glanced at George briefly. 'You ought to go outside and get some air, George,' he said pleasantly enough, and their hostess, who had been taking it all in like a desert plant drinking in the rain, took the hint.

'Yes, come along, George. Let me show you my prize fuchsias. I was thinking of entering them at the Chelsea Flower Show this year. Tell me what you think.' She all but marched him away. If Justin and Flick Mainwaring actually married, it would be the matchmaking scoop of the century for her. And later. . . She looked back over her shoulder, her eyes hot and eager on Justin, whose tall stature and silver-blond hair made him stand out like a beacon. Love in the afternoon with the Earl of Ravenscroft. Lovely!

Justin, oblivious to the erotic thoughts of his hostess, led Flick Mainwaring out into the ballroom. He had no idea whether she could dance or not, and was glad to hear a simple waltz. He took her hand and felt her fingers close around his in a strong grip that was unexpectedly pleasant. Then, with an easy, effortless glide, he began to waltz, surprised and then not at all surprised when Flick matched him movement for movement with a grace that was not quite, but very nearly, his equal. The waltz swept on into another, and then another. Flick never said a word, and, unwilling to break the contentment of the moment, Justin remained silent also. It was the first time that he could remember when he'd been with someone, anyone, who didn't expect or want anything from him. Nobody gave. But here, dancing with Flick, he felt strangely at peace. Once he felt a timid tap on his shoulder, but when he looked around and saw Michael Bell, one of Flick's poverty-stricken suitors, he simply ignored him, and the third son of a minor baron melted obediently, if sulkily, away. Flick watched it all and still said nothing.

It was nearing midnight when they finally stopped dancing and drifted back once more to the main salon. There they made their way to the buffet tables, and Justin watched as Flick piled up her plate. Instead of feeling embarrassed or contemptuous of her, he found himself admiring her. It took guts to stand up and be counted in the roomful of lean jackals circling all around them, who screamed in terror if their scales told them they'd put on just one ounce.

'Shall we take it into the garden?' Flick suggested, and Justin willingly agreed. He was reluctant to begin the seduction — he was not sure how to go about it without insulting her. Damn it, why had she made him like her?

'So, what do *you* want my money for, Juzzer?' Flick looked up in alarm as Justin made a choking sound. His wine had gone down the wrong way. She obligingly thumped him on the back, hard, and Justin nodded his thanks. His eyes still watering, he looked at her ruefully.

'You don't know how to play the game,' he reproved softly.

Flick shook her head. 'Oh no. I just choose to play by my own rules, that's all. As you do.'

Justin took a slow — this time careful — sip of his wine and gave himself a mental shake. She was clever, this girl. And possibly dangerous? He felt his blood begin to race. 'You think you've read me so well, do you?' he asked, his smile both questioning and a little uneasy.

'From what I've heard, and what I've seen, I think so.'

Justin stared at her for a long moment, then said softly, 'You could be wrong.'

Flick cocked her head to one side. 'I've been wrong before,' she owned. 'But I'm not wrong very often.'

Slowly, Justin leaned back in his chair, aware that his nerves were tightening. 'Are you going to be kind, Flick?'

In the act of lifting her pint of Guinness to her lips, Flick stopped dead and looked at him, her eyes sharply assessing. 'People have given you a hard time, haven't they?'

Justin shrugged and looked away, unable to hold her steady, honest gaze. 'Don't they do the same to everybody?'

Flick said nothing, patiently waiting until, forced by the growing silence, he looked at her once again. 'Some people can take it better than others,' she said quietly.

Justin stiffened. 'You think I'm a coward? Or just weak?'

'Neither,' Flick said, then, to Justin's total bewilderment, added thoughtfully, 'I think it would have been better for you if you were.'

* * *

Flame, at that moment, was watching Reece Dexter's broad back disappear into the *festa* crowd, unaware of Giulietta beside her.

'He wants the Maggiore contract, of course,' Giulietta confided, and, when Flame blinked in incomprehension, quickly explained about the Principessa's commission.

'So that's why he's here,' Flame murmured to herself, fighting back an insane surge of jealousy. He was here to flatter some Italian princess out of her money! She might have known. For one gigantically insane and ridiculously romantic moment, she had thought he'd followed her. Lord, how stupid, how naive could you get?

Giulietta would have had to be blind not to see the sparks flying between Reece Dexter and her young charge, and the old lady was a firm believer in fireworks. She'd have to invite that young man over for tea one day.

'Where is she — the Principessa?' Flame asked.

Giulietta shrugged. 'She's just left, *cara.*'

Flame tensed. Had she left with Reece? Were they even now making love? She wouldn't put it past him to try and seduce the commission out of her. Assuming that Reece had now gone, the evening felt oddly flat. Angrily, Flame dismissed him from her mind. He was a hateful man.

At two-thirty a.m. the *festa* drew to a gradual close. The ride back was quiet and lovely, and the two women got home just as the dawn was breaking. Inside, Flame eagerly took off her tiara, and gave such a loud sigh of relief that not even Giulietta could ignore it.

'Is the headache very bad, *cara?*' she murmured sympathetically. 'There's aspirin in the bathroom.'

'How did you know?' Flame asked, rubbing her temples.

'I'm not a mind-reader.' Giulietta laughed. 'It's just that it always gave me a headache, and my mamma before me.'

Flame grimaced. 'It has such pretty stones, too. It's a pity it's so heavy.'

Giulietta glanced at her quickly, aware of something in her voice. She watched Flame staring at the tiara for a moment, intently observing the look in her beautiful eyes, then nodded abruptly. 'Why don't you draw a design for a lighter, more modern tiara?'

'What?' Flame dragged her eyes away from the luminescent stones. There was something magical, almost hypnotic about them. Now, in the early morning dawn, elated after a truly magical night, the gems seemed even more mesmerizing than ever.

'You've been practising designs for months now,' Giulietta encouraged. 'Draw me a sketch, *cara*. If I approve, I'll have the tiara dismantled and remodelled to your design. It'll be yours. I'll give it to you as a twenty-first birthday present.' Venice at dawn was a time for grand gestures, after all.

* * *

That night — or that morning, by the time she climbed under the covers — Flame dreamt of Reece Dexter. Strange, disturbing dreams, where they floated in circles to music, his lips swooping on hers in ever more demanding kisses until they were clinging together so tightly that she could feel herself melting into his body. Six hours later she woke up, and the first thing she saw was the tiara on her bedside table. The sun shone through the windows straight on to it, ricocheting emerald and silver light on to the wall and ceiling. The phantom shadows seemed to Flame to be otherworldly, like the reflected rays from an ancient power. Slowly she sat up and reached for her sketchpad. Tentatively at first, she began to draw. Time flew as she lost herself in the concept, colour and beauty of the stones. By the time the afternoon sun had gained colour and heat, Flame had produced three designs, all totally different from the other, all hauntingly beautiful.

Giulietta stared at them, speechless. She had never dreamt that Flame might possess a talent as great as this. On the spur of the moment she decided to send the tiara and her preferred design of the three to her favourite jeweller at Corraldo's and pay him double to have the tiara remade within the week. She would trumpet her great-granddaughter's talent from the rooftops! That should give the old Conte something to choke on, she thought with a grim smile. The Conte was a dangerous man to cross, but if Flame was ever to be taken seriously as a designer, Giulietta knew that cross him they must.

* * *

Reece Dexter stood thoughtfully at the window of his hotel, looking out across the breathtaking panorama that was the Grand Canal. But his thoughts were not on the city, fabulous and beautiful as it was, but on something even more intoxicating. Flame Syramore-Forbes.

He smiled as he thought of her name, even as a tide of want and anger washed over him. Just who was she? The outraged innocent she seemed, or a scheming, business-minded piranha? His smile turned into a rueful grin as he admitted that, at this stage, he didn't much care. She had entered his life with all the shattering force of a bomb blast, and he was glad. A peaceful life had never much appealed to him.

Nevertheless, he'd have someone check her out. He wanted no more nasty surprises. If she wanted to play games, he was more than willing to let her. Oh yes, more than willing. Since he would win . . .

As he looked out of his hotel room across the city of canals, his mind filled with images of her. She had taken him by surprise once. Now it was his turn. His lovely little cyclone was going to learn that nobody got the better of Reece Dexter. And he would make sure that they both enjoyed the lesson.

CHAPTER 7

Justin heard the bell over the shop door give its discreet musical chime and looked up, his face breaking into a smile at the sight of Flick. Since the party in Mayfair they had seen a lot of each other. Flick could talk about anything and everything, and prised out of Justin thoughts, ideas and philosophies he himself had never been aware existed. And the more he saw her, the more he wanted her. Having her solid and comforting presence by his side would be a much-needed boost during the inevitable confrontation with his mother and sister. With Walt Matthews on their side, he needed somebody in his corner. And Flick's business sense was second only to his own. What a team they would make. Together Halcyone's would soar.

'Flick.' He came to meet her, taking both her hands in his. 'Let me show you around.' He led her to the back room, which was small, crammed with equipment and eerily silent. Only the occasional whine of a drill or blast of a blowtorch ever penetrated the quiet, almost monk-like atmosphere. As if aware of the aura created by the craftsmen who were bent over pieces of work in various stages, Flick walked on tiptoe.

'I dare say all you know about jewellery is that you like wearing it, right?' Justin grinned, glad of a chance to show off Halcyone's flagship store. Woodstock was his domain.

'I don't actually,' Flick said softly, and Justin's eyes sharpened on her, noticing that she wore only a simple watch.

'Philistine,' he teased, but felt suddenly uneasy. Quickly he led her to the nearest workbench, where Gunther Voss was crouched over a stone. 'How's it going, Gunther?'

'Huh?' The old man looked up, and Flick was surprised to see just how old he was. He looked eighty if he was a day.

'Gunther Voss here escaped from Germany just before the war. He's a Jew,' Justin added matter-of-factly, and although Flick winced, Gunther himself merely smiled sadly. 'Jessica nabbed him the moment he set foot on English soil. My great-grandmother knew a good deal when she saw one.'

'She saved me from the authorities over here,' Gunther explained. 'We all loved Lady SF,' he added enigmatically. He turned back to his work, Justin forgotten.

Flick leaned closer, meeting Gunther's sparkling eyes. 'And what exactly are you doing, Mr Voss?' she asked politely.

'I'm joining two pieces of stone together, the bulk of the material being the inferior variety, miss. Observe . . .'

With liver-spotted hands that were as steady as rocks, he plucked a tiny piece of diamond from a tray with a pair of tweezers and held it under a microscope. 'The top half, or, as we say, "crown", is a real diamond — see the way the light catches it?'

Flick nodded, fascinated by the stone, by the man, by the lure of something new. She could sense that this wonderful old man lived for his craft, and his obsession was both exciting and a little sad. 'I simply cement this crown to the lower part, or "pavilion". And the finished result is a diamond that is not quite a diamond. It looks almost as good, but is not as expensive. It is one of the ways in which both jeweller and customer achieve a compromise that pleases us both, yes?'

'And I thought you were cheating, you wicked man!'

'Oh, I am wicked. Totally,' he assured her. 'I know all sorts of ways to cheat. Why, in my younger days in Germany, I used white zircon for diamonds, red spinel for rubies, and blue spinel for sapphires. I've even known craftsmen paint the back of pale emeralds to enhance the colour.'

'Naturally he doesn't do any of that here,' Justin put in, his tone just a touch sharp.

'Naturally not. Lady Syramore-Forbes's shops are the finest in the world, for quality of stones and quality of work. Nobody has ever suggested we cheat,' Gunther said, then glanced at the composite stone in his hand, obviously new ground for Halcyone's, his distaste obvious. Justin felt himself flushing.

'This new range is keeping up with the fashion, Voss,' he said coldly. 'Women today want cheaper jewellery that still has that touch of quality. Composites are a logical step. All the continentals are doing it.'

'Of that, I have no doubt,' Gunther said quietly. 'Excuse me, miss, I have to get back to work.'

'Of course.' Flick straightened from the workbench and shot Justin a furious look.

Justin had told none of his staff yet, but costume jewellery would be the next step. Multiple chains, foreign expansion. He had it all mapped out.

'Come and look over here. You can see how an earring is made, from conception to the finished thing . . .' Flick followed him from bench to bench, seeing his eyes deepen as they watched the senior stonecutter turn a dark green shapeless lump of emerald into a perfect oblong called a 'baguette'. Flick had never seen him so animated, so satisfied before, and it came as something of a surprise.

During the past weeks he'd taken her to the ballet, to parties and even punting on the Cherwell at Oxford, always the epitome of an English earl. But she had never been fooled. He used his outward appearance only for protection. It hadn't taken her long to get a sketchy but fairly accurate picture of the man who was the true Justin Syramore-Forbes. His lonely childhood had scarred him deeply, as had his father. His lack of friends, brought about by his father's determination that he should act the 'little earl' at all times, had left him perpetually lonely. And in spite of being a stud, he'd had little success with women, where it mattered. She could tell, by the way she was constantly able to surprise him, that he had no real idea of how women thought, or what they wanted. What an enormous help his mother would have been, if only she'd been granted custody of him. Unstinting love, given without expectation of reward, was what all children needed and what Justin had never had. It had left him emotionally crippled, unable to express his feelings, unable even to understand them. And she knew, without false modesty, that she had been able to help him a little. He was now genuinely fond of her, and of all her suitors she'd narrowed the choice down to two — Justin and George Campbell-Bean. Last night she'd made up her mind and called her father, telling him to brace himself for a wedding. Hers.

'And something like this . . .' Flick quickly snapped her attention back to the present as Justin selected a simple but exquisite sapphire teardrop earring and held it up to the light. '. . . is what comes out at the end of days of hard work. Like it?' He held it up to her ear, then shook his head. 'No, it's too dark for you. You need diamonds with your dark hair. Black and white. I have just the thing for you; come on.'

Flick let him take her hand and lead her out into the showroom. Selecting a key from a chain of them that he wore on his belt, Justin opened a glass display case and withdrew from the bottom locked drawer a red velvet box. Placing it on the glass counter top, he turned it to face her, then opened the lid. On a nest of black velvet lay a diamond necklace that made even Flick gasp. It was so packed with glittering stones that at first she was too dazzled to take in its overall design. When she finally began to look in more detail, she gasped again. Twisted strands of diamonds were roped into a tortuous plait from which hung a single, huge diamond.

'The main diamond is a "brilliant" cut. It has that star shape at the bottom, see?'

'Just,' she laughed, blinking and shaking her head. 'It's magnificent. How much is something like that worth?'

Justin shrugged and put the necklace back on to the black velvet. 'I'd rather not say,' he said softly, then straightened, his face suddenly tight and nervous. 'I was rather hoping you'd accept it as a gift.'

'What?' Flick gasped. 'You know I couldn't accept this . . . *fantastic* thing. It's so . . .' Flick shook her head, staring at the necklace speechlessly. 'Justin, I just couldn't.'

'Not even as a wedding present, Flick?'

She looked up quickly, the diamonds forgotten. His shoulders were tense, his hands gripping the edge of the counter like a man holding on to a life-raft. Others saw only his arrogance, his confidence, his jaunty, cocky exterior. Now, looking at his tense, handsome face, she saw his pain, his uncertainty, all his fear and pent-up rage. For the second time that day, Flick wished she hadn't come. But it was not her nature to be cowardly. For others, a letter might do. For Flick Mainwaring, a job like this demanded an eyeball-to-eyeball conversation. 'Oh, Juzzer. Do you always make things so difficult?' she sighed at last, biting her lip as his shoulders slumped forward.

Justin shook his head but his eyes remained fixed on the necklace. 'I take it that means no?'

'That's what I came up here to tell you.'

Justin nodded. His mouth was so dry that for a moment he couldn't seem to prise his lips apart. When he did, he found his voice was quite normal. 'Was it something I did? Or something I didn't do?'

Flick sighed. She could never remember feeling this bad before. She felt as if she were kicking an injured animal, and although her big heart bled in her chest, her common-sense brain told her now, more than ever, that she was doing the right thing. Justin Syramore-Forbes was like the flawed diamond one of the workmen had shown her just a few minutes ago. It looked brilliant, it was as hard as any stable diamond, but just one tap in the wrong place and it would shatter. He needed an expert craftsman to mend him, and that she was not. She wasn't convinced he *could* be mended . . .

The lost look of agony in his eyes was more than she could bear, and, leaning over the counter, she gently reached for his hand, alarmed to feel that it was so cold. 'Justin,' she said softly, 'you didn't do anything wrong. I think . . . I think you've hidden so much of yourself from others that you've hidden it from yourself too. I think . . .' Flick, for the first time, found herself unable to say, simply and honestly, what she meant. 'Oh, Juzzer, let's face it: we both knew, right from the start, that this was . . . well, a business contract. You wanted money, and I wanted a man I could live with.'

Justin nodded miserably. 'You're quite right, of course,' he drawled, but the mocking, accepting words bore no resemblance to the painful feeling of betrayal and despair clogging his chest. 'So . . . if not me, then who?' He straightened and deftly shut the box. He could barely feel his fingers, but continued to act automatically, glad that she could not see that she was killing him. She was also killing his hopes of an easy takeover of his rightful inheritance stone-dead. Halcyone's. Now, more than ever, Halcyone's was paramount. It would never let him down. Never break his heart. Never raise his hopes and then dash them.

Flick, relieved that he had taken it so well, relaxed slightly. 'Your old friend, as it turns out,' she said gently. 'George Campbell-Bean.'

Justin was sure he smiled, because he could feel the cramped muscles in his face moving. 'Good old George. But why him?'

Flick shrugged. 'George is just right, when you think about it. He's a Scot, and he understands the true value of money. But most of all I can persuade him it should be me who takes over Daddy's company. And when he realises I can keep him in the style to which he wants to become accustomed without him even having to work, he'll be ecstatic.' Flick reached out and touched his cold cheek. 'You know I'd have made an awfully nagging wife, don't you, Juzzer?' she added gently. 'You'd have been miserable within a month.'

'I accept you've saved me from a fate worse than death,' Justin agreed. He wanted to kill George so much it made him ache.

'You bet,' she laughed. 'And you couldn't really see us together, could you?' she asked, hopefully.

Justin shook his head. No, not much. He'd thought of them at Ravenscroft, where Flick could have turned the house into a home for the first time ever in its miserable history. He'd thought of coming home and finding a fire, and a meal, and Flick, big with his child. He'd thought of nights spent in his huge four-poster bed, no longer cold and alone, but wrapped in her warm thighs, his head cushioned against her ample breasts. He'd thought of her laughter, her rock-like, steadfast common sense, her comforting presence. 'No,' he said quietly. 'I never thought of us together. Not really.'

'Just my money for Halcyone's, hmm?' she teased. 'But it *is* a wonderful place. You will be able to keep it, won't you? You belong here — I could see that today.'

'Oh, I'll manage somehow,' Justin said hollowly. 'This is all I have now. And Ravenscroft, of course . . .'

Flick reached up impulsively and hugged him. His hands splayed over her back, drinking in her warmth and affection. He took a deep shuddering breath. 'Flick,' he said, his voice cracking, and in horror he heard the raw emotion in his tone. He pulled away quickly. 'Good luck with George. He'll go through all your money, give you sixteen kids, then run off with the barmaid at the local.'

'Don't worry. I'll keep him on a tight leash. Treat 'em like a dog, and they'll purr like a cat.'

'Sounds good to me,' he agreed shakily. 'Well, see you around.' He moved quickly to the door, feeling light-headed.

'Trying to get rid of me already, eh?' Flick teased, stepping out on to the pavement and walking to her car, parked at the kerb. 'I bet you already have the next heiress lined up, hmm?' She got into the front seat. 'I'll send you an invite to the wedding,' she called as she pulled away.

He watched her move out of sight, then walked to the tiny car park at the rear of the shop. He drove to Ravenscroft and went straight to his bedroom. There he lay face down on his bed and began to cry. Softly at first, he was soon sobbing, long drawn-out sounds of misery that brought his Uncle Roger down from the attic.

Standing silently in the doorway, Roger, a loving, simple-minded soul, watched his nephew crying. He rather liked Justin. He didn't try and make him stay in the attic as Malcolm had, and he never told him off about hanging up his paintings. He wasn't Francesca, of course; she was an angel. He would wait forever for Francesca to come back into his life. But he didn't like to see Justin crying. He knew crying meant he felt bad.

On the bed, Justin reached for a pillow and brought it to his stomach, curling around it into a foetal position, his slender shoulders shaking uncontrollably. But even in his misery he knew that he was not beaten. Malcolm hadn't beaten him, and neither would Flick. Nor would his whore of a mother nor his bitch of a sister. He would get even with them all. Oh, yes, he'd get them all.

Roger was glad when Justin finally stopped crying.

* * *

Flame checked the board one more time, relieved to see that the flight from New York had arrived at last. She couldn't wait to see Wendy again.

Reece Dexter too was glad the New York flight had arrived. He was looking forward to spending a few days with his father. It seemed they hardly ever saw each other anymore, and he was intrigued about the 'surprise' Owen Dexter had hinted at over the phone. He was just moving towards the barriers, his height and power cutting an easy path through the throng, when he saw her. She wasn't difficult to spot. Nobody else had hair that colour! Immediately his mood sky-rocketed, and he took a deep, calming breath.

As wonderful, as appealing as it was, it was also frightening. He couldn't resist her, and why should he want to? After all, she posed no *real* threat. She was just a distraction in his life, and one he badly needed. His life had become little more than a mundane routine of late, but there could be no danger of falling into a rut when she was around. A bed full of thistles, perhaps. Or roses . . . soft, sweetly perfumed, velvety roses. Reece took a fortifying lungful of air and moved into battle.

Flame was craning her neck, waiting for the first stream of passengers to arrive, when a familiar voice had her spinning around in a heady mixture of hot pleasure and cold anger.

'You really must stop following me around, Lady Flame. It's becoming embarrassing.'

Flame's eyes widened as his bulk filled her vision. He was wearing a faded pair of old Levi's that clung to his muscular thighs like a second skin, and an open-necked shirt of dark blue that revealed a small sprinkling of dark hairs on an impressively wide and muscled chest. He was standing so close, hemmed in against her by the crowd, that she could feel the heat from his skin. So intent was she on controlling her breathing and trying to regain her equilibrium that it took a moment for her to react to his words. When she did, she rose to the bait beautifully. 'Me? Following you around? Of all the big-headed, self-centred . . .'

'Ah, ah, ah,' he chided gently, waving a calloused finger right under her nose. 'Not in front of the natives.'

Flame took a quick glance around, but nobody was taking any notice. 'Look, why don't you just go away?' Flame asked coldly. 'I'm expecting a friend and—'

'A friend?' Reece cut in, yet again interrupting her in mid-speech. His eyes narrowed slightly. 'A male friend?'

'No. My room-mate from college, if you must know. Not that it's any of your business.'

'Oh? I got the distinct impression that you were trying to make yourself my business. First you lie and cheat your way into my office. Then you turn up at the *festa*. Now here. Really, I'm flattered by all your attention.'

Flame floundered, gasping against a sudden hot sweep of rage. Just who did he think he was? And to make matters worse she knew that deep down she was interested in him. She just couldn't seem to help it. Reece watched the conflicting emotions flash across her face, enjoying the spectacle enormously.

'You . . . you . . .' Flame couldn't think of a word ugly enough to call him, and searched instead for another line of attack. 'You can talk about lying and cheating. Or do you seriously expect anyone to believe that you aren't prepared to do anything — *anything*,' she hissed, 'to get the Principessa di Maggiore to give Redex her commission? Everyone knows you've been cosying up to her shamelessly. You're making a complete fool of yourself.'

Reece grinned slowly. 'Jealous, Lady Flame? You really don't have to be, you know. You've already won. I'm intrigued by you. You've caught my eye, as my grandmother would have said. Now, when shall I pick you up tonight?'

'What? Do you seriously think I'll go anywhere with—?'

'I thought the Antico Martini might be nice.' He named one of Venice's premier restaurants with a casual shrug. 'Or would you prefer the Alla Colomba?'

Flame stared at him, at the mocking fiery eyes, the relaxed, arrogant smile that made his lips look even fuller than . . . Angrily she shook her head. Lord, she was going mad! 'I wouldn't go to McDonald's with you,' she spat, and then whirled as an amused voice said, 'But I would. I'd go anywhere with you.'

'Wendy!' Flame whirled around and saw her friend, and almost kissed her in relief. She had been so intent on trying to cut Reece Dexter down to size, she hadn't noticed that the plane had disgorged its passengers.

Reece grinned. So she was meeting a girlfriend after all. He felt so relieved he almost laughed out loud. 'Thank you,' he acknowledged Wendy's obvious flattery, and, to Flame's fury and Wendy's amusement, reached across the barrier and kissed her hand. 'I'm glad somebody appreciates me.'

'Don't count on it,' Flame said acidly. 'She doesn't know you yet.'

Wendy looked at Flame, then at Reece, and smiled. So it was like that, was it? 'Come on, let's get out of here,' Flame said, tugging on her friend's arm.

'I'll be seeing you,' Reece called out as the two girls made their way towards the exit. Flame, her colour high, stared straight ahead.

'Not if I see you first,' she muttered under her breath.

Beside her Wendy began to laugh. 'Who *was* that?'

'Just a man,' Flame said crossly.

'That has got to be the understatement of the year,' Wendy drawled. 'Let me collect my cases and we'll have a good chinwag, OK?'

Flame nodded ruefully. 'Sorry, Wendy. But that man gets under my skin.'

'I could tell!'

Flame grinned, but, as she drove her friend to the *palazzo* her smile faltered. Reece was dangerous. Exciting. And worse: confusing. Something told her she was headed for trouble.

Suddenly she wasn't in a vacation mood.

CHAPTER 8

Conte Giulio Pierluigi Corraldo looked like a matinee idol from the fifties. Dressed in a dark blue smoking jacket with long silk lapels, casual grey trousers and, of course, Gucci loafers, he was likely, Flame was sure, to set every feminine heart over the age of fifty fluttering like butterflies. But since this was her first meeting with her famous great-uncle, and since he had chosen to make it so formal by inviting her into the impressive library, she pushed this somewhat irreverent thought aside and smiled warmly.

'Hello, uncle. I've been looking forward to meeting you for a long time.'

Conte Giulio took a few steps forward and kissed her on both cheeks. 'It was not my wish that we remain strangers for so long, great-niece.' His voice was smooth, reminding Flame instantly of olive oil. It also reminded her of a condescending art teacher she'd known back in high school. His two-tier class system that placed boys firmly on the top tier had annoyed her then, and she found a similar emotion beginning to creep into her bones now. Suddenly it was not hard to understand why Grandy disliked the Conte so much and had insisted on accompanying her.

'Well, I'm here now. And enjoying Venice enormously.'

'Ah, Venice. Who doesn't fall under her spell, hm?' Conte Giulio glanced at Giulietta's mocking smile and returned one of his own. 'Contessa Granti. As lovely as ever.'

He moved to a globe of the world that opened out to reveal a drinks cabinet and poured them glasses of chilled white wine. Giulietta took her proffered glass of wine with an almost imperceptible little toast. 'So, now that I can see for myself why everyone is talking about the new "Flame" in Venice, I cannot find it in my heart to blame them,' Conte Giulio smiled. His great-niece's triumph over Venetian society had not gone unnoticed.

Flame didn't like her grandfather's elder brother, and she had the strong feeling that it was mutual; she was glad of Giulietta's silent presence. That the old Contessa was making the Conte uncomfortable was beyond doubt.

'Please, take a seat.' The Conte waved magnanimously at the sixteenth-century wooden chairs scattered about the imposing library, but Flame chose a cosy little settee set some yards away. Giulietta opted to sit, ramrod-straight, on one of the chairs. Flame fought the intense desire to giggle nervously. The ticking of a ponderous wall clock, the heavy silence aided by thick velvet drapes at windows and doors, all added to a stilted ambience that was fast settling over them. It was not at all how she had expected her first meeting with her great-uncle to be. How formal he was. How unlike all her other relations, who were so open and natural. No wonder her grandfather, Michael, had been only too happy to get out of Italy and run his own show in Boston.

'Giulietta informed me the other day that you have designed some interesting pieces. Mainly necklaces and tiaras, she tells me?' The Conte, frowning a little over their disobedient choice of seats, settled himself behind an impressive desk.

'More than interesting, Giulio,' Giulietta interrupted, her voice like honey. 'Flame has already had an offer from Redex.' She then had the immense satisfaction of watching the head of the Corraldo dynasty go white.

'Has she indeed?' he managed, and gave a sickly smile that showed even, slightly yellowing teeth. 'But Redex is very new, isn't it?' he added, and their eyes locked, their mutual antipathy so obvious that Flame fidgeted nervously in her seat. The Conte's eyes narrowed. He knew all about Reece Dexter's 'accidental' meetings with his niece. The Conte's spies were everywhere. He'd thought the man was simply out to acquire a pretty mistress. But what if Dexter really was after his lovely great-niece for her designs? What if she really was good?

Flame nodded. 'Yes, Redex were interested,' she admitted, leaning forward eagerly on the settee, her long flame-coloured hair falling over her shoulders and cascading over her breasts. 'I enjoy designing enormously.'

'And she does it so well,' Giulietta purred. 'In fact, I'm going to pick up one of Flame's pieces tomorrow. She has redesigned the Granti emerald tiara. My jeweller says it'll be ready tomorrow.'

The Conte stared at her, his body going rigid. 'You have already commissioned her?'

Giulietta nodded, her eyes narrowing. '*Sì.* I intend to wear the tiara throughout the summer season. Naturally I'll tell all my friends about it . . . *all* my friends,' she stressed gently, and smiled as she saw the fury escalate behind the Conte's dark eyes.

'Well, there's not much call for tiaras these days,' he said softly, then turned to Flame, unable, as usual, to hold Giulietta's mocking, fearless stare. A man used to dominating his family, and especially his womenfolk, the Conte hated the Contessa with a passion that was unusual, even among Italians. Expecting Flame to be a softer target, he shrugged in what he hoped was the epitome of regret. 'Earrings, believe it or not, are the greatest sellers. Along with rings, of course. Have you turned your hand to those yet?'

Flame, ever sensitive to feelings, sensed immediately the contemptuous condescension lying just behind her uncle's unctuously smooth voice and felt her backbone stiffen. 'No,

Uncle Giulio,' she said steadily, holding his eye with her own. 'I haven't yet. But I shall now.'

Giulietta smiled, applauding her great-granddaughter's spunk. But Giulio Corraldo was surprised. Not by the merest flicker of an eyelash did he show it, of course, but he was aware of an unpleasant feeling of . . . not foreboding, exactly. That was ridiculous — no mere slip of an American girl could discomfit him. But his niece was not obliging him the way he'd imagined. And was there the merest hint of disrespect in her voice?

'Yes. Well. Your success with Redex is not important. Dexter was after the Maggiore commission, of course,' he continued smoothly, 'but I happen to know that he has not been successful. Corraldo's are still the hot favourite,' he finished, still smiling like a shark. It was obvious that Giulio was determined to win the commission.

But his mind was whirling. What had Michael been thinking of, letting her work at Corraldo's during her vacations? 'Well, you are young yet,' he said dismissively. 'You haven't even finished college. Tell me, what formal training have you had at design?'

Flame met the hard brown eyes head-on, not fooled for one moment by the polite curiosity in his voice. 'I've had no formal training in design, Uncle, as I'm sure you know,' she said coolly. 'But I've been producing jewellery since high school. I've even won the odd prize here and there. But, as you once said, to my grandfather I believe, good designers are born, not taught.'

Giulietta smothered a chuckle with her hand, disguising it as a delicate cough. Giulio felt a flush of anger rise in his face, and he quickly turned aside to select a cheroot from a silver-embossed humidor. He lit it from a gold-leaf table lighter with almost ridiculous panache, and when he turned back to smile at his niece, his face was once again matinee-idol smooth. 'Designers of any real talent are rare,' he proffered, blowing two perfect smoke rings.

'True,' Flame nodded, her fiery hair rippling with the movement. 'That's why Grandy has arranged for me to see Ramon DeVira and show him my work.'

Giulietta stiffened as the Conte shot her a knowing look. The Contessa's lips firmed angrily. She was in no doubt that the Conte was determined his niece should fail.

'You admire Ramon's work, Uncle Giulio?' Flame asked sweetly.

Giulio smiled, but his face was beginning to feel stiff.

Not for an instant had it occurred to him that the beautiful creature sitting before him, dressed in grey trousers and an eye-catching tiger's-head sweater, would have the gumption or temerity to challenge his authority. Conte Giulio permitted no member of his family to do that. He would have to put this upstart American beauty in her place. She was too much like Giulietta for comfort. 'Who does not admire the great DeVira's work? Of course, he is a great friend of Giulietta's,' he added delicately, and smiled at Giulietta's tight, angry face. Complacently he blew another smoke ring.

'Are you implying he might say my work is good when it isn't, just to please Grandy?' Flame asked, letting amusement creep into her tone.

'Of course not!' Giulio snapped, knowing instantly that he'd blundered.

Flame nodded and smiled gently. 'Well, Uncle, it's been wonderful to meet you at last,' she lied diplomatically. 'I hope you don't mind if we rush away? There's an exhibition of Art Deco jewellery at the Accademia. Have you seen it yet?'

Giulio opened his mouth, then closed it again. Not only had she goaded him into losing his temper but now she was actually dismissing *him*. '*Si*, I have seen it. It is well worth a visit,' he continued, rising graciously to his feet. 'Please, don't let me detain you any longer,' he added smoothly, hiding his fury and discomfiture well. 'Run along, children, and enjoy the exhibition.'

Flame, quite prepared to let her uncle keep his dignity and have the last word, smiled warmly. Giulio accepted their goodbyes, and it wasn't until Flame looked questioningly at her Grandy that he realised Giulietta had not even risen from her chair. 'I'll be out shortly,' the old lady said quietly. 'I just want to have a quiet word with your uncle.'

Flame nodded, her eyes twinkling, and Giulietta's lips twitched. How well they understood each other!

The Conte watched the door close behind her, his eyes narrowed to mere slits. Fuming, he took a seat facing the old Contessa and waited. He didn't have to wait long. Giulietta rose to her feet with an ease that belied her years, and walked to the desk, looking down at the Conte with eyes totally devoid of respect. 'I know you, Giulio,' she said softly. 'You'll do everything you can to hold that girl back, just because she has the talent you've always wanted and never had. You'll deny her the help Corraldo's could give her, just because she's a woman, and because she doesn't give a damn about you and what you think. But remember — I have influence in this town too. I have friends . . . friends like Sofia di Maggiore . . .' She paused to watch the Conte's face tighten ominously. 'And let's not forget, Corraldo's is not the only jewellery house in the world. She owns half of Halcyone's.'

At the mention of the rival company, the Conte's mouth twisted into a sneer, and all pretence of sophistication fled as he lunged to his feet, breathing deeply. His face ugly, he leaned on the desk and snarled into her face. 'Let her go to Halcyone's, then. Because no one in Italy will take her seriously. I promise you that!'

Giulietta, far from looking intimidated, or even surprised, merely nodded her head. 'You are a poor excuse for a man, Giulio,' she said softly, and, turning on her heel, walked swiftly from the room, her back straight, her head high, oozing a dignity that made the Conte snap the pencil he'd been holding clean in half. Once the door was shut he threw the ruined pencil away and reached for a single sheet of thick, cream-coloured paper that bore the Corraldo crest at the top in navy-blue ink. Quickly, he wrote the date and the name and address of Ramon DeVira, who was, as Giulio knew, currently in Paris. As he wrote, he began to smile. If Giulietta thought Ramon would drop in on her once he was back in Venice and look at her niece's little drawings, she was in for a rude awakening. And so was Flame Syramore-Forbes, if she thought she would be allowed to break into the exclusive and elite jewellery clique in Italy.

* * *

Giulietta insisted on taking her out to dinner that evening and stared at her so thoughtfully that Flame began to fidget. 'Have I got a spot on my nose or something, Grandy?' she asked curiously.

'*Cara,* you could have sauce dribbling down your chin and still every man in this room would want you.'

'I agree.' The words, spoken with a drawling American twang, made Flame drop her fork and look up at the man towering over them. They were at the Al Graspo de Ua, a beautiful restaurant near the church of San Bartolomeo. Feeling pleasantly full after her starter of *salame con funghi e carciofini sott'olio* and a main meal of delicious *costolette milanese,* she was feeling in a mellow and generous mood. Now though, looking up into mocking grey eyes with their depths of orange fire, Flame might have known something would spoil it. And who could succeed in doing that better than this man?

'Grandy, you remember Reece Dexter?' she said with a long-suffering sigh.

Giulietta inclined her head gracefully, and Reece nodded back. When he returned his gaze to Flame, one eyebrow rose in a telling arch. Flame looked away, but her tongue tip flicked out to lick her pink lips nervously. Every muscle and sinew in her body was taut, and already her adrenalin was running high. Damn him, why did he always stir in her this alarming reaction?

'I know you won't mind if I join you for coffee,' Reece lied, grabbing a spare chair from the next table and sitting down before either of them could object. Giulietta hid her smile of approval behind her napkin.

'Mr Dexter, Grandy and I were just about to leave,' Flame tried vainly to reassert herself, but her voice sounded more petulant than superior.

'Oh?'

Flame could see he was not going to budge. Not an inch. She leaned back into her chair as their waiter filled their wine glasses with an excellent Chablis. She felt as if she was sitting on a keg of dynamite, and she couldn't stop her eyes from straying to the lighted fuse. He was wearing navy blue, the expensive suit doing nothing to make him look more respect-able. Reece Dexter oozed a primordial power and masculine sensuality that not even Savile Row could tame.

'Relax, *cara,*' Giulietta murmured. 'Venice at night is the domain of lovers. Haven't you realised that yet?'

'We're not lovers, Grandy,' Flame hissed angrily, know-ing what her great-grandmother was doing, and wondering why she felt the overwhelming need to keep Reece Dexter at arm's length. Out of the corner of her eye she saw Reece smile, and her anger escalated dangerously. 'Nor will we ever be lovers,' she said firmly.

'We won't?' Reece's drawling voice cut through the elec-tric atmosphere like a knife. She turned and saw him looking at her with such a phony look of avid interest that before she could stop herself she aimed her foot under the table and gave him a hefty kick on the shin. He winced, but in the next instant he leaned his elbow on the table, cupped his chin in his hand, and said in a fair imitation of a breathless little voice, 'Come on, *do* tell. Are we going to be lovers?'

Flame stared at him, wondering what on earth to say. He was wearing such a silly expression and . . . yes . . . he was actually fluttering his eyelashes at her! Suddenly she found laughter gurgling in her throat. This man was . . . insane. Absolutely insane!

'Why don't you step outside?' Giulietta purred. 'It's such a lovely evening for a midnight stroll.'

'In this country we do not push ourselves on to strangers and ask such personal questions,' Flame snapped at him, trying to regain her much-needed equilibrium. 'But of course, I'm becoming used to your rudeness,' she added sweetly, looking daggers at him.

Reece let his eyes roam over her lovingly, the orange flecks in his eyes expanding as they caressed her, warming her skin wherever his gaze touched her. She too was wearing navy blue, and the evening gown glittered in the candlelight. With her hair piled atop her head she reminded him of some exquisite candle. Flame by name, flame by nature, of that Reece was convinced.

'I think it's time we left,' Flame said, catching Giulietta's eye and trying to breathe deeply. Loath as she was to admit it, Reece Dexter's look had the ability to rob her of breath. Already she could feel her nipples tightening and tingling, and she only hoped they didn't show against her dress.

'Good idea. Where are we going?' Reece asked, but he'd evidently made enough mischief for one night, for he made no move to rise.

Flame leant ever so slightly closer to him, and through the corner of her mouth whispered tautly, 'Do you want a kick on the other shin?'

Reece, ostentatiously leaning closer still, whispered out of the corner of *his* mouth, 'Don't tell me you're only in this for kicks, *sweetheart?*'

Flame helplessly felt her eyes meet his, and fell into their depths. It was like floating in a grey, choppy sea. The swells were high, and dangerous, but exciting, oh, how exciting! She felt her heart thunder in her chest, and deep inside her something sprang to life. Quickly she pushed her chair away and stood up. She felt totally disorientated, and, looking down into his laughing face, she shook her head. She was out of her depth here, and she knew it. He knew it too, damn him! 'Goodbye, Mr Dexter,' she said pointedly, and, not looking back, she walked away from the table, her hand on Grandy's arm, her mind reeling. He was impossible. And so rude. But, as angry as she was, her nipples were still tingling, and her legs felt weak and watery.

Reece watched them go, his laughter slowly dying. He had made her really angry with him tonight — but he had also made her want to laugh out loud. It might take time to bring her around, but he was patient. He knew he only had to wait and to keep chipping away at her resistance, as Michelangelo had chipped away at his marble blocks, and soon he would have her where he wanted her. Naked, and in his bed. Reece smiled at the thought, but it was a tender smile, and not at all the wolfish masculine grin he imagined it to be.

* * *

Justin heard the bells long before he reached the church. It was the second Saturday in May, and the Yorkshire air was full of the sound of bees, birds and bells. But the natural beauty all around him had done nothing to ease the ache that persisted in throbbing in his chest. It was ridiculous, he knew, to feel the way he did. It was not as if he was in love with Flick, after all. As he made his way through the narrow roads of the village, he wondered, not for the first time, why he was putting himself through this.

Black limousines bedecked with white ribbons had already disgorged several little bridesmaids, cute as buttons in pink lace, when he pulled up in front of the church. Nervously, he checked the buttonhole in his grey suit as he walked between the gravestones, and nodded at a male usher in the doorway, who asked him cheerfully, 'Which side, sir? Bride or groom?'

Justin, very much aware of the irony of the situation, said flatly, 'I'm a friend of both.' He took his seat towards the back of the church, shivering slightly as he did so. No matter how hot the weather outside, the stone interior of an

English church was always cold. Next to him, a woman in genteel lavender extracted a lace hankie from her handbag, in preparation for a good cry. Children ran in the aisle, chased by disapproving parents. On pedestals at the altar stood cascades of flowers — roses, carnations, orchids, ferns. A wasp was causing an annoyed sensation in the front pews, and the vicar, resplendent in white cassock, was waiting in front of the altar. Justin felt odd. Strangely numb and faintly amused, he felt as if he'd wandered into some strange dream or a particularly bad art-house film. He could see George standing by his best man. His hair had been newly cut, and he was dressed in a smart navy-blue suit. He wondered how much Flick had had to pay for it, and then he jumped as the organ began to play the bridal march.

Suddenly everything was quiet. And then he saw Flick.

She was dressed head to toe in white. Her hair was glossy under her veil, and as she walked by him in that curious, halting walk all brides used on approaching the altar, Justin felt himself reel. It should be him standing at the front, watching her walk towards *him*. And then George stepped out to meet her, and he didn't care how ridiculous he was, or how cliched the situation. He just wanted to be somewhere else — anywhere else. But he was trapped. Trapped by his own masochistic nature and the strangers hemming him in. Bitterly, he fought back the urge to get up and run, and acted instead like the well-brought-up little boy that he was. He sat when everyone else sat. He sang when everyone else sang, and bowed his head when everyone else did. And, like everyone else, he listened in silence as the vicar asked if anyone had just cause as to why the marriage should not take place. He had not heard Flick's voice for over a month, and when he heard her saying her wedding vows a cold clammy wave made him shiver anew. When he heard George's voice, the rolling, loud Scottish burr made him flinch. He was glad when it was over. He looked away as the new Mr and Mrs Campbell-Bean walked down the aisle, and hoped neither of them saw him. Outside he managed to manoeuvre himself away from the couple, who were indulging in the usual wedding photographs, and all but ran to his car. There he got behind the wheel and took a deep breath, hunched over the steering wheel, feeling as if he'd just run a particularly gruelling marathon.

Looking up, he could see them, framed in the church's arched door. Flick was leaning against her husband and George was looking down at her, his big stupid face grinning like a cat that had the cream.

Justin gunned the engine and roared away.

* * *

At the exact moment that Flick and George took off from Manchester airport to fly to Greece for their honeymoon, Justin arrived back at Ravenscroft. He showered and changed, ate a sandwich, and watched the sun set over his impressive grounds and farmland. He looked perfectly composed. Then he sat at his writing bureau and took out his desk calendar. The first Saturday in June was ringed, reminding him of a charity rowing event at Henley. The warden at Wadham had rung him up a few weeks ago to ask if, as an 'old' Oxonian, he cared to sit in as one of the eight, since an Oriental Studies student who was on the original team would be in Japan for the summer, and thus unable to row. Justin had accepted gladly, just to get in some practice and have a good time with his old friends. And George, of course. George, who would be back from his stingy two-week honeymoon. George, who was determined to be on the winning team come the next Oxford/Cambridge boat race.

Good old George, who was, at best, a very poor swimmer . . .

CHAPTER 9

At the Palazzo d'Oro, Flame had taken over Giulietta's study, which now housed sketch after sketch of Flame Syramore-Forbes originals. Giulietta had worn her tiara on several occasions, and the word was out that there was a new designer in town. But, stung by the Conte's sarcastic comments about there not being much call for tiaras, Flame had spent the last week working on nothing but rings and earrings, finding, to her chagrin, that they were the hardest to design. Rings were so simple, it seemed that everything that could be done with or to a ring had been done. How could she possibly think up anything original?

When Francesca walked into the study just before lunchtime, Flame looked up from the bureau and gasped in pleasure. 'Mamma! You never said you were coming over!'

Francesca hugged her briefly, then stepped back and looked at her daughter critically. 'You've been up to something.'

Flame grinned. 'Of course!'

Francesca's mock scowl vanished as both women erupted into gales of laughter, which brought the others. With four generations of Corraldo women in the same room, an hour swiftly passed in gossip, tea, and much praise for the little gifts

Francesca had brought with her from San Francisco. Flame showed her mother her designs, and she was awestruck at the talent and potential they so clearly depicted. Francesca then told them about San Francisco, her recent work for the Professor, the latest fashions to hit New York, and everything else except what she had flown several thousand miles to actually tell them.

'Flame was telling us that she's thinking of giving up Radcliffe and concentrating instead on her designing. Her friend Wendy flew back to the US some time ago,' Maria said, during the first lull in conversation for over an hour.

'Oh?' Francesca's first reaction was one of dismay. Then, when she began to consider it more fully, she began to wonder. It had taken only a few minutes, looking at Flame's designs, to see that they were good — more than good.

'I won't do it if you're really against it, Mamma,' Flame said quietly, tacitly earning the approval of both the older women. 'I know I've missed the beginning of the semester but I can catch up.'

Nevertheless, when Francesca shook her head and said softly, 'I think you're old enough, and wise enough, to make your own choices now, Flame,' everyone was secretly relieved.

Flame, for her part, felt a lump rise to her throat, and she swallowed hard. 'Thank you, Mamma. And I haven't made up my mind yet. I'll wait until Mr DeVira has seen my work. I don't want to do anything rash.'

'Very sensible, *cara,*' Giulietta murmured approvingly, then, her eyes twinkling, added mischievously, 'but I hope you don't apply those same sensible rules to that charming American.' Turning to Francesca, she said, *sotto voce,* 'He's fallen head over heels for your lovely daughter, Francesca.'

'Oh?' Francesca mused, as Flame, at the same instant, snapped crossly, 'Nonsense!' Watching her daughter flush at the gentle teasing, Francesca told herself she was being silly to worry. After all, Flame was nineteen. But she knew only too well how passion could carry a woman away, misleading her into thinking things that were false were true and into seeing love where none truly existed.

90

'Don't worry, *cara*,' Maria whispered, sensing her daughter's unease. 'Giulietta really does like him.' And that said it all.

Francesca caught Flame's exasperated eye, and smiled brightly. 'Well, you have had an eventful time lately . . . And . . .' sensing that she would never have a better opening, she took a deep breath and added softly, 'so have I. As it turns out.'

'Oh?' Three pairs of eyes turned towards her, and this time Francesca felt herself blushing.

'I've met a man,' she blurted, then groaned softly. 'That's not what I meant to say at all. At least, it is, but it's not how I meant to put it . . .'

'It's not a crime, *cara mia*.' Giulietta smiled across the table. 'Tell us about this man. How old is he?'

'He's fifty-six,' Francesca said, almost defiantly, but, since none of her companions made any sounds of shock, she carried on quickly. 'He's an American, Owen Dexter. The Second.' She took a quick, fortifying sip of spritzer, and looked straight at her daughter. 'He's asked me to marry him, and I've accepted.'

'*Cara!*' It was Maria who first broke the surprised silence, and, getting out of her chair, she quickly came around the table to hug her daughter, tears already beginning to trickle down her cheeks. 'You can't know how long I've waited for you to say those words,' Maria choked. 'I thought that awful *bastardo* had wrecked your life for good . . . Oh, Flame, *cara*, I'm sorry. Forget I said that,' Maria turned her appalled face towards her granddaughter and crossed herself. 'One mustn't speak ill of the dead.'

Flame, far less concerned about her dead father and much more concerned about her soon-to-be father, waved her hands vaguely, her eyes still locked with those of her mother. 'You say his name is Dexter?' she queried, fighting off her panic. Francesca nodded, happily unaware of her daughter's unease. 'Do you love him, Mamma?' Flame asked softly, standing slowly.

'Yes, Flame, I do,' Francesca said softly. 'Very much.'

'Then I'm glad. So glad,' she added, and watched her vision waver as her own tears of happiness began to flow. It didn't take two seconds for mother and daughter to be in each other's arms, both weeping freely. It was ten emotional minutes later when Flame and the others learned more about Owen Dexter II.

'He's a widower, with one grown son. I met him in San Francisco, of course, when the Professor and I attended that conference. I didn't want to say anything to you all until it was really serious between us, and . . . well . . . things just happened so fast.' Francesca, more than happy to answer any and all questions, was not aware of how her face lit up when talking of her future husband. But everyone else noted it, and without exception were sincerely glad. If anyone deserved a second chance at love, it was Francesca. But Flame had to know.

'This son. His name's not. . .' Please God, she prayed, don't let her say yes. 'He's not called Reece, by any chance?'

Francesca looked surprised. 'Yes, he is. How did you know?'

Flame swallowed a gigantic lump in her throat. Her heart sank into her boots, but somehow she managed a smile. 'Well, it's a small world after all,' she said brightly, wincing at the falseness she could hear in her tone. 'You remember I told you about Redex, and it not working out? Well, it's owned by the Dexters. I met Reece when I went for my interview there.'

'He's also right here. In Venice,' Giulietta chimed in, her eyes thoughtful as she ruminated on this latest twist.

'Owen said his son had started his own company, but I had no idea it was Redex,' Francesca said, shaking her head.

Flame flushed in fury. Just wait until she saw him! Oh, just *wait*! Giulietta quickly stepped into the awkward silence. 'I wondered why you were spending so much time in San Francisco,' she said craftily.

'Yes, tell us all about Owen, Mamma,' Flame said eagerly, praying that he wasn't, couldn't possibly be, anything like his arrogant son. Surely the world only had room for one man like Reece Dexter!

Francesca was defensive. 'I can assure you he's a most respectable man. And independently wealthy. You approve?'

'Approve?' Flame looked into her mother's anxious eyes and cursed herself for being so selfish. So what if she and Reece didn't get on? She would *not* let it spoil her mother's happiness. 'If you're happy, I'm happy.'

'Thank you, *cara*,' Francesca said softly. 'I know Owen will love you too.' And with those gentle words Flame felt, for the first time, a little trickle of cold unease slip down her spine.

'I never thought of that,' she said quietly. 'I hope he likes me. He does know about me, doesn't he?' she added, chewing nervously on her lower lip.

'Of course he does, *cara*,' Francesca said gently. 'He knows every last detail of my life. And I his. Don't worry, Flame. Owen and I are both old enough to accept life as it is, and not as we'd like it to be. He loved his first wife very much. They were married for twenty-two years before she was killed, and he was devastated. Since she died, he never looked at another woman. We both know what it's like when life treats us cruelly. Which is why, when we finally found each other, our love is that much sweeter. Can you understand, Flame?'

Flame nodded. 'Oh, Mamma, I'm glad. So glad that you've found a man to love at last.'

'Thank you. And you don't have to worry. I know he'll adore you. Owen is a man with a lot of love in his soul. And you'll like him too. I know you will. You all will,' Francesca added, looking at the silent women around her, for once in her life feeling confident, assured and very much in love. 'He's here with me in Venice. I've invited him over for tea so you'll be able to see for yourselves how wonderful he is.'

Maria looked at her and prayed silently that Owen Dexter was a man who would not break her daughter's heart. Giulietta sipped her tea in silence, and ran through a mental list of all her friends, gauging which one could tell her the most about these Dexters who were making so many claims on Corraldo women. Flame watched her mother, and hoped that she would remain happy forever, and that, please God, Owen Dexter really would grow to like her.

* * *

Scott Tate turned his Jaguar XJS into Ravenscroft's drive and roared up it, startling some deer that roamed in the woods on the north-facing side of the estate. As he was shown into the library by the butler, his eyes were drawn to the now infamous portrait of Roger Syramore-Forbes by Francesca. So Justin's potty uncle must still be wandering about. 'Help yourself to a drink,' Justin offered, and shut the door firmly behind the exiting servant. He didn't trust the butler. He might be spying for his mother.

'So, what's up?' Scott settled into a large wing-backed chair and took a healthy swig of his drink.

Justin tossed a file on to his lap. 'We've heard from the Principessa,' he said casually, walking to the big bay windows and looking out. Rhododendron bushes gave way to sweeping lawns, while at the bottom of a small hill a vast pond, alive with water-lilies, was spanned by an old, elegant wooden bridge. On the other side of the hill, an impressive white gazebo nestled in front of a copse of maple and copper beech trees.

Scott read quickly. Basically, it was a 'nibbling' letter.

The Principessa had been delighted to hear that Halcyone's had made a bid for her commission, for the Principessa had the greatest admiration for the respectable English company. She would visit them as soon as she was in England, this coming weekend, and would like if possible to tour their famous Woodstock emporium. There were no guarantees and no hints as to who was the favourite in what was fast hotting up to be one of the greatest prizes in the jewellery calendar of that year. Already Bulgari were stepping up their campaign, as were Cartier and several French independents.

'You know the way these people work,' Scott mused. 'Does it look good for us?'

'Yes,' Justin said calmly, taking a sip of Scotch. 'So far she's let everyone come to her to make their pitch.'

'So the fact that she wants to come to Woodstock is encouraging?'

'Very,' Justin agreed, a small frown settling between his eyes. 'What we have to decide now is how to play it. Bulgari would have given her glamour, glamour and more glamour. A little spy I have in Italy tells me that they actually gave her a show, complete with a catwalk, champagne and live music. Apparently the models were dressed in the plainest of white or black gowns, to show their jewellery off to its best advantage.'

'I can't see that going down well in Woodstock somehow,' Scott drawled, and Justin, for the first time since Flick's wedding, actually smiled.

'No. But I don't think that will be to our disadvantage. Bulgari guard their makers and designers jealously. I doubt our Principessa even had a sniff inside their workroom. So I was thinking of going the exact opposite way, and as well as showing her the "quaintness" of our little emporium, I thought of giving her the guided tour of the back room.'

'Flatter her with technicalities, you mean?' Scott caught on quickly. 'Let her see how the little men work. Flatter her intelligence by putting on the "old craftsmen" scene and talking to her as if she actually has some idea of what goes into creating a work of quality?'

'Why not?' Justin shrugged casually. 'I doubt she's actually been near jeweller's oil in her life. Or held a soldering iron. Why not let one of our men, Seth perhaps, help her make a simple little thing? A pendant, perhaps? With a single stone that she can help set herself. Let her keep it as a gift?'

Scott leaned forward, nodding eagerly, his eyes alight now with the avaricious gleam of a vulture scenting meat.

'Yeah. The French will try to seduce the pants off her with a presentation piece of fancy jewellery — probably a tiara or something . . .'

'Right,' Justin agreed. 'And the Americans will probably try to do the same thing we do, but they're so commercially orientated they can't hope to do it with the same panache as we can. They'll probably show her around some huge forty-storey office building full of computers, and explain how they earned forty million dollars in the last fiscal year. I'm also having all our best pieces held over from selling until the Principessa has seen them. I've got a man checking out if any of our earlier works have landed up in a museum somewhere. They sometimes do, you know. If they have, then a quick tour of them with her royal ladyship will impress on her just how well thought of Halcyone's designs truly are.'

Scott nodded. 'You do realise that once all this reaches the ears of the Corraldo clan you'll have your mother and sister to contend with, don't you?'

Justin's face tightened ominously. 'I know. It won't matter to Flame, or my darling mother, that it was my idea, my work and effort that's making all this possible. When my dearest mother and her precious daughter arrive in England they're going to have the devil's own job getting anywhere near me or Halcyone's. I've heard my darling sister fancies herself as a designer. She's caused quite a stir over some revamped tiara her great-grandmother gave her to play with.' Justin's lips twisted into a cold smile. 'But if she thinks Halcyone's is going to be her stepping stone to fame and fortune she can think again.'

But even before Justin had finished speaking, Scott was shaking his head. 'I don't think that's the right approach. For a start, there's no way, now that Jessica's will has finally been probated, that you can *stop* them gaining access to Halcyone's. And you know the old saying — have your friends close, but your enemies even closer.'

'You mean let them stay here? At Ravenscroft?' Justin asked, the thought making him feel physically sick.

'It'll be easier to keep an eye on them,' Scott pointed out.

Gloomily Justin conceded the point. 'OK. I'll make vague reconciliation noises.' He left his chair to pour himself another Scotch and walked once more to the window. Suddenly the pastoral scene wasn't so beautiful anymore.

'When do we do the royal tour?' Scott asked. 'Saturday?'

'No!' Justin said sharply. Then, more quietly, 'I'm going to Henley Saturday.'

'Can't you skip it, Juzzer? This is far more important.'

Justin swallowed his whisky in one gulp, a strange smile flickering briefly across his face. 'Sorry.'

'It can't be that important,' Scott said irritably.

'No,' Justin agreed, taking a sip of his drink. 'But it will be infinitely satisfying.'

* * *

'You're going to do *what*?' Reece said, a slow grin spreading across his shocked face. Opposite him, Owen Dexter gave a sheepish, utterly happy smile.

'I'm going to get married.'

Reece slowly sat down, shaking his head. They were in his suite at the Cipriani, one of Venice's most prestigious hotels. 'I don't believe it. So that's the surprise you've been hinting at all this time.' Reece quickly recovered from the shock and walked to the bar, pouring both of them a celebratory Napoleon brandy. This called for a drink! His father moved with a spring in his step Reece hadn't seen since his mother was alive. And he looked younger, happier. He should have guessed that only a woman could do that to a man.

'I want you to meet her right away,' Owen said, never having doubted that his son would react favourably to his news. They were so close, and so sure of their relationship, that they feared nothing, not even the upheaval such a major step would cause in their lives. Reece, for his part, had loved his mother deeply but, after the initial period of mourning and grief had passed, he'd often wished his father could find happiness with another woman. Now he'd gone and done it, Reece felt like shouting for joy.

'This is such a surprise. I never guessed . . . I don't know anything about this lady! Tell me all about her. What does she do?'

Owen laughed. 'She's an interpreter for a famous professor. But that hardly begins to cover it. She's so beautiful, Reece, and so gentle. She has a heart as big and warm as the Sahara! She's Italian, and — this will really kill you — her family are the Corraldos!' Owen Dexter grinned and clinked his glass against that of his son's, unaware that Reece had frozen to the spot and was staring at him blankly. 'Looks as if I'm marrying the competition, son. Do you think Redex will survive?' Owen had no doubt that it would. His son had taken control of the Dexter Mining Corporation some ten years ago, and had never given his father a reason to be sorry. And he had no doubts now that his first totally independent company, Redex, would continue to be a great success. And, speaking of the Dexter Mining Corporation, he had a message for him from their office in Colombia. But that could wait.

Reece smiled automatically at his father's enthusiasm, but his face felt stiff and cold. 'Oh, I expect it'll limp along. I've met some of the Corraldos, in fact. Venice is a small city. Which branch of the family does she belong to?'

Owen shrugged. 'I'm not sure. It's so big! But she talks about an uncle who's a count. And about her grandmother, a Contessa Granti. Ring any bells?'

They did. Oh yes, they certainly did. 'How old is she, Dad?'

Owen laughed. 'Don't worry, son, I'm not marrying a teenager. She's a mature woman, ten years younger than me. She's been married before, but has been divorced for years. She has two children — a boy and a girl.'

'The girl . . .' Reece said, his voice perfectly calm. 'Is she here in Venice? I think I might have met her.'

'Yes, she is, as a matter of fact,' Owen said, not letting on for a moment how nervous he was about meeting her. Francesca's children meant so much to her. He knew the heartbreaking circumstances surrounding her son, and it was only natural that she should be so close to her daughter. Owen was scared stiff that Flame would not take to him. And it was so important that she did. Determinedly pushing aside his fears, he wrapped his arm around his son's broad shoulders and took a long swallow of his brandy. 'Francesca tells me she's quite something, and if she's anything like her mother I know it has to be true. And from the pictures I've seen, I can tell you, she's quite a stunner. She has this mass of long red hair . . .'

* * *

'Oh, Grandy, what am I going to do?' Flame asked, when she and Giulietta found themselves alone, just before dinner.

'I don't see your problem, *cara*. Reece is going to make a fine stepbrother.' She watched Flame's appalled face go white and bit her tongue to hold back her laughter.

'I hadn't thought of that!' Flame moaned.

'So I see,' Giulietta said drily. 'But your mamma has found someone she wants to marry. So what if he's Reece's father?'

'So *what*? What if he turns out to be just like his son?' Flame huffed.

'What if he is, *cara*?' Giulietta challenged. 'It's only you who seems to object to Mr Reece Dexter. Everyone else loves him. Especially the Principessa di Maggiore, so I hear. Hasn't she just invited him to a little dinner party?' Giulietta couldn't resist mischief-making.

'Oh, stuff the Principessa di Maggiore,' Flame said crossly. 'This is serious. I bet he knew all along what was happening. I bet he was laughing himself sick all this time. No wonder he wanted me at Redex!' she suddenly burst out, sitting bolt upright on the sofa as the thought struck her like a body-blow. 'He knew all along who I was! All he wanted was a spy at Corraldo's and he thought I would be perfect. Of all the underhand, rotten, cheating, *insulting* things to do! Did he really think that just because my mother and his father were getting married I'd agree to work for him and spy on my own relatives?'

Giulietta sighed. 'Has it not occurred to you that he might be as surprised as you are about this wedding announcement?'

'In a pig's eye!' Flame snorted inelegantly.

'At least talk to him. You're going to have to sort out your differences, you know, unless you want your mamma to feel as if she's stepped into the middle of a war zone.'

'You're right, I suppose,' Flame said with a sigh. 'I'll call him and ask to meet him somewhere.' She felt her heart thump at the thought of being alone with him, and hoped that the hot flush she felt deep in her stomach had not spread to her face. She walked over to the telephone and called the Cipriani. Where else would someone like Reece stay? 'Reece Dexter's suite, please,' she said primly to the hotel switchboard operator, and a moment later heard his voice.

'Reece Dexter.'

It leaked into her ear like hot syrup and funnelled down, spreading into her breasts and bringing her nipples to instant attention before seeping lower, seeming to flood right into her loins, making them convulse wonderfully. Flame took a sharp, shaking breath.

'I want to talk to you,' she snapped, angry at her own reaction. There was a moment's startled silence, then his voice again, this time hard and ominous.

'Good. I want to talk to you. Meet me at the San Marco landing stage tomorrow night. Nine o'clock.'

'I'll be there,' Flame snapped back, and slammed the phone down. Lord, she was beginning to seriously dislike that man.

Except she wasn't. God help her, she didn't seem able to.

CHAPTER 10

Owen Dexter II looked at the four women facing him and smiled. He couldn't help it — they looked so serious and so beautiful. Beside him, Reece had no difficulty picking out his father's bride-to-be. She was lovely and obviously very nervous, and he found himself relaxing slightly.

Francesca stepped forward and then hesitated, not at all sure what to do next. Owen's son was so much . . . more . . . than she'd expected. Taller. Broader. Overpowering.

'Hello, Francesca,' Reece said, sensing that she was lost for words and willing to take the initiative. Until he could judge for himself what kind of woman she was, there was no point making waves. And, in truth, he didn't want to. He had enough to contend with with her damned daughter.

'Reece,' Francesca murmured. 'I've been looking forward to meeting you for so long.'

Reece saw Flame lift a hand to her head and sweep back a lock of long flaming hair. Inexorably his eyes moved above Francesca's head and met those of her daughter. Flame stared back at him defiantly. She hadn't expected to see him before their assignation tonight, and his appearance with his father for tea had unnerved her. She let a small, defiant smile settle

101

across her lips and saw his eyes narrow ominously. If he wanted to play games then so could she.

He dragged his thoughts back to Francesca. 'Dad's been like a lovestruck teenager ever since he arrived. Now I see why.'

Owen grimaced humorously. 'Children. Who needs them?' He faced Francesca's family and smiled. 'Well, I can't say I haven't been warned,' he murmured. 'In your daughter, darling, I can see the lovely young woman that you must have been, and now it doesn't hurt so much that I never knew you back then. In your mother, I can see the lovely lady that you will become, and in your grandmother I can see that our golden years together will be filled with beauty and grace.'

Maria blushed as Owen took her hand, and then instantly relaxed as she found herself looking up into the gentlest pair of blue-grey eyes she'd ever seen. At five foot ten, Owen Dexter was by far the most handsome man she'd met in a long time. His hair was silver, and sprang crisply back from well-defined temples and forehead. His face was square, strong and honest, with a solid jaw and slightly large nose. His mouth was wide, and looked as if it smiled a lot. 'I'm glad you could come,' she said. 'I know you must be a busy man.'

'Never too busy to meet my new family,' Owen said. 'Or to get married,' he added softly.

'Francesca, you never told us you wanted to marry here,' Maria scolded, but she was ecstatic. A Venice wedding was something never to be forgotten, never to be repeated.

'I thought I'd surprise you all. I hope you're happy?'

'Happy? Mother, we're all overjoyed!' Flame cried.

'Owen, this enthusiastic young thing is what you'll have to put up with, I'm afraid. Think you can manage it?' Francesca hugged Owen's arm as he moved to stand in front of Flame, who immediately became nervous again.

'Oh, I think I shall manage,' he said drolly.

'Mamma, you're marrying a tease!' Flame admonished happily, as relief washed over her. It was still early days, but she already felt she would have no difficulty growing to love and accept her new father. And Owen, smiling down into deep chocolate eyes that were almost an exact replica of Francesca's, knew that he now had a daughter in his life.

Francesca smiled. 'I know. He's a dreadful tease. Think *you'll* be able to put up with *him?*'

Flame looked at her soon-to-be stepfather and tilted her head in consideration. 'Well . . .' She drawled the word out thoughtfully. 'I suppose one can put up with anything, if one has to,' she said magnanimously, eyes twinkling.

Reece watched her winning over his father and snorted, quickly covering the disgusted sound with a cough.

'You're so kind.' Owen bowed formally, and grinned.

They moved into the orangery, where the scent of flowering orange trees filled the air. Tea was served, and conversation, led by Giulietta, flowed easily. Flame retreated to one corner and Reece to the other, and, apart from throwing daggers at each other with their eyes, they managed to refrain from throwing actual objects — although Flame for one had to clench her fists several times to prevent herself from lobbing a Dresden shepherdess at his supercilious head.

Everyone was aware of the simmering tension between them, and Owen wondered if Francesca had realised its source. It was obvious that his son and his daughter-to-be were wildly attracted to each other. Obvious, too, that they were both, for some odd reason, determined to fight it, tooth and nail.

* * *

Justin felt the sweat rolling between his shoulder blades as the cox called out the stroke. Glancing at his oar, he saw it slide into the water in perfect symmetry with those of his rowing mates seated in front of and behind him. In, out. In, out. The banks of the Oxfordshire countryside flashed by in a green blur as the two teams shot past the lines of spectators. But Justin was oblivious to being watched, oblivious to the gliding speed of a boat in perfect motion. Instead he stared at the back of George Campbell-Bean's head, two seats in front of him. In, out. In, out. He knew that the rival team was behind him, but for once he had no thought for the outcome of the race. Only what would come later. In, out. In, out.

Soon they were in sight of the finishing post. The cox's voice rose in growing excitement as the other boat began to edge closer to them. Ahead, he could hear George grunting as the speed picked up. Muscles were stretched and aching, sweat was pouring, and Justin felt himself reacting to the challenge. They passed the finishing line first, but the others were only a few strokes behind. It was then, when the excitement was at its height, that Justin made his move.

A branch in the water, a rivet going in the boat, a bad break with a large rock in the river could all conspire to sink a boat. But now they were past the finishing line, danger was the farthest thing from anybody's mind. Groaning men let their calloused hands relax on the oars and bent their heads as they panted for breath. And in one, violent rocking movement that nobody would later be able to pinpoint, the boat lurched and overbalanced. Around him Justin heard the startled cries of his team-mates, and then the cold grey Thames closed over him. But whereas his rowing mates began to thrash and kick for the surface, Justin, the only one prepared for it, was already diving under the floating boat, his eyes never having left that of the man two oars in front of him. George was thrashing about, dangerously close to panic, and when Justin grabbed his legs and yanked, he let out a startled groan and grunted as his head, in a whiplash movement, banged against the side of the boat.

Justin could feel his lungs beginning to strain, but he ignored it, pulling George down further, surprised he wasn't struggling more. Then he saw the red gash on the side of his temple, and his heart turned over. George was hurt. And suddenly it wasn't right anymore. Two men in a life-and-death fight had an honour of sorts — a primitive fairness that Justin could understand. But this . . . this was not a duel between two equals. This was . . . murder!

He saw the telltale bubbles forming around George's mouth at the same instant that he became aware of a dark object closing in on him. Looking up he saw Eric Haithwaite, the lead oarsman, swimming down, his eyes squinting against the cold. Justin, whose eyes had already adjusted, saw at once that he was heading straight for them. Seeing that Eric's vision was fast becoming adjusted to the water, Justin knew he had no choice, and felt a great surge of relief. Quickly, he moved his hands from George's legs and began to swim upwards, catching George under his arms and tugging up. He kicked strongly and headed for the surface, all the time a silent scream of rage and frustration resounding in his head. Why couldn't things work out the way he wanted, just once in his life? He hit the surface and took a huge gulp of air. Beside him he saw Dale Dix, another member of the team, treading water. 'Help me get him out, for God's sake,' Justin screamed. 'I saw him hit his head before going under.'

The crowd, who had been laughing at what they had thought was a comic show, began to quieten as they watched the men race for the shore, and a slow, low murmur began to ripple through them as they watched the struggle.

'How long was he under?' Eric shouted, already tipping George's head back and forcing open his mouth.

'I don't know,' Justin lied as Eric began desperately blowing into George's mouth. He felt blissfully numb. It was no longer in his hands whether George lived or died, and he was no longer sure which he wanted. He wanted Flick to suffer and perhaps . . . perhaps come to him for comfort. How long would a wife of only three weeks mourn her husband? Aware that his fellow team-mates were crowded around watching them, his instinct for self-preservation rose to the fore. 'I saw him go under and went straight after him, but he sank like a stone.' Die, George, die! 'What the hell happened anyway? Did something hit us?' he asked innocently.

But nobody, it seemed, knew what had happened.

'I should have got to him quicker,' Justin mumbled, and Dale slapped his shoulder and squeezed briefly.

'Don't knock yourself out. Out of all of us, you were the quickest to react.' Justin nodded grimly, staring at George's pale, suddenly childlike face. Please don't die, George, he prayed desperately. And then he saw Flick, pushing her way through the crowd, slipping and sliding down the bank, the paramedics not far behind. Justin had to look away.

'I've got a pulse!' Eric suddenly cried, and Justin slowly stood up, his limbs feeling like lead. He took several steps back as the paramedics took over, competently administering oxygen. Justin stared at Flick's white face as she held her husband's hand, then turned away. He felt like crying, but of course he didn't. Earls of Ravenscroft never cried in public.

'We've got a strong pulse, and he's breathing.' The older of the paramedics beckoned for a stretcher. Justin watched in silence as the stretcher was carried through the parting crowd to the waiting ambulance.

Eric turned and looked at Justin. 'He owes you his life, Juzzer. Hell, that was quick thinking on your part. And I thought I was quick off the mark.' For a while all three men stood, shivering in the cooling air, reaction over the near tragedy beginning to take its toll. Then, aware of the staring crowd, Eric took a step closer to Justin and, before Justin had any idea of what was happening, raised his arm in the air. 'Well done, Juzzer,' he yelled, and the crowd, always anxious to cheer its heroes, began to clap and applaud. Justin blinked as a flashlight captured the moment and he realised, with a sinking heart, that the local newspapers originally hired to cover the event had got a much better story than they had bargained for. Everyone loved a hero, and what a hero Justin made — handsome even when drenched. Justin smiled ruefully, accepting the accolade of the crowd wearily, looking tired and haggard. The eyes that followed the ambulance as it screamed away were blank.

* * *

Flame was glad of the full moon as she walked quickly to the deserted San Marco landing stage. As she drew to a halt at the canal's edge, she noticed the gondola. Long and black, beautifully sleek, it gleamed silver in the moonlight. She sighed softly, breathing in the damp, intoxicating, unique atmosphere that was Venice at night.

'At least you're on time.' A voice that turned her bones to jelly suddenly filled the night, and Flame gave a small startled cry. She looked down at the gently rocking gondola and there he was, standing at the back, his hand resting on the steering pole, for all the world looking like a man who made his living riding the Venetian canals. He was dressed in tight-fitting black jeans and a white shirt, and his feet, incredibly, were bare. As Flame stared down at him she swallowed hard. Suddenly the night was his accessory, the city a laughing ally, and she felt hopelessly outgunned. She took a step back.

'I thought we were here to talk?'

'Oh, we are,' Reece agreed grimly. 'I nearly got my ear chewed off this afternoon by Dad. By the way, that was quite some act you put on.'

Flame stiffened. 'I was not acting. Strange as it may seem, I actually like your father. He's so unlike you.'

'How long have you known about them? Oh, stop looking down on me and get in!' She was wearing a simple white summer dress that had the annoying habit of swishing gently around her bare legs with the slightest breeze and he was uncomfortably aware of the silken sheen of her bare skin, and the gentle but ample swelling of her lovely young breasts. With her standing above him like that, Reece felt like some humble human supplicant floundering in the presence of Aphrodite.

Flame took a deep, fortifying breath and did as she was bid, stepping into the curtained interior. It was a relief to be safe from his piercing eyes for a few moments and she looked around her in surprise. The gondola was carpeted from end to end in a midnight-blue carpet, but there were no benches.

Only large, soft cushions lined the floor. She felt the gondola move beneath her, and quickly pushed aside the curtains. Reece was steering them away from the landing stage and out into the Grand Canal. 'What do you think you're doing?' she demanded, her voice sharp with anxiety and something else. Something excited. Something breathless.

'Relax. I won't capsize us.' And, indeed, he was handling the gondola like a professional, but not for anything would she ask him how, or where, he had learned the skill. Inexorably, he took her further and further away from the safety of land, out into the privacy of the lagoon. Nervously, she watched the city fade into the night. She could see the lights of the Lido in the distance, but Reece was not heading for the island. Instead he steered them far away from the commercial hot spots and out into waters where boats seldom ventured. She should have been afraid, but she wasn't. Her heart began to race as he secured the boat and came towards her. He moved like a cat, every movement economical and full of silent strength. He stood looking down at her for a long moment, and then moved slowly towards her. Quickly, Flame scrambled back under the cover of the long, dark green velvet curtains. Reece turned up the lamps, their golden glow bathing the interior of the gondola with gentle light. Flame had backed up as far as she could go and was half sitting, half lying against a wad of cushions. Her hair spilled across her breasts like silken fire, her eyes and skin glowing in the lamplight.

'This is an unusual place to meet, isn't it?' she asked nervously. Reece saw her swallow and lick her lips, the unconsciously enticing gesture making him groan low in his throat. She heard it, of course, and he saw her eyes widen. But not just in alarm. Deep in their dark depths he saw a fire that matched and answered the one that had been growing inside him ever since he first saw her. He had always known this moment was inevitable . . . 'Reece,' she whispered frantically. 'We have to be adult about all this.'

Reece smiled wolfishly. 'Oh, I feel *very* adult,' he assured her, eyes darkening as they ran over her waiting body.

The gondola was so small she could hear every tiny sound, their harsh breaths, the sound of her silk dress against the satin cushions every time she moved, the slap of the water against the hull. Slowly, he moved towards her and knelt at her feet, his hand reaching out to take one ankle. His fingers curling around her flesh sent tiny shocks of molten heat up her leg and deep into the core of her. She felt her womanhood contract fiercely, the sensation making her gasp aloud. Holding her eyes with his own, Reece slowly slipped off first one sandal and then the other. His anger was forgotten. So what if she had been leading him on? He was more than willing to be led. Nights like this were as rare as the precious gems he mined, and he would not let this moment pass him by because of anger or suspicion. Those could be dealt with later.

'We shouldn't,' Flame whispered, her words choked with desire.

'No,' he agreed, and gently curled his fingers around the backs of her calves and stroked upwards, leaning forward as he moved until his face was just inches away from hers. Flame could feel his clean, warm breath feather her cheeks, and in the glow of the lamps the flecks in his eyes gleamed like gold dust in the grey rock of his eyes. Except they were not hard at all; his eyes caressed like velvet wherever they touched her. Of their own accord, her arms lifted and encircled him, her hands running across the wide expanse of his shoulders, feeling the heat of his skin on her fingertips through the tough cotton of his shirt. Of their own accord her fingers ran lovingly through the silky, nut-brown hair at the nape of his neck and then down, over his spine and the deep strength of his back. He drew his breath in sharply. He could feel her weaving her silken web around him like some golden spider from myth, but he didn't care.

He leaned forward as she rose up, their lips met and clung as if they'd been fashioned just for this moment, and the sweetness of it made him moan. Flame gasped as he gently forced her back against the cushions, his head moving lower to kiss her nipple through the white silk of her dress. She gasped again, feeling her flesh tighten into a pulsing tiny bud that radiated sparks of desire as his mouth and lips sucked incessantly. She arched under his pleasant weight, feeling a tightening, spreading throb begin to drum between her legs. Leisurely, his fingers went to the large buttons that ran from the hem of her dress to the top, undoing them one by one and spreading the dress aside, exposing her lovely breasts and white panties. Flame moaned as his bare hands slid warmly over her ribs, his thumbs moving in caressing circles over her flat belly and moving up. His tongue flicked over her now bare nipples, laving them lovingly, before he slid down her, allowing his tongue to blaze a burning path between her breasts, down her stomach and into her navel. She moaned again, her legs thrashing in helpless reaction, and her eyes flew open as his lips travelled over her panties and rubbed between her legs. The ceiling above her was dark and wooden and she stared at it hard as Reece began to kiss her thighs, his hands holding them firmly apart. She was unable to resist, unable even to think or protest. Her body was screaming at her that this was right, right, right, even though some dim and fast diminishing part of her insisted that it was wrong, wrong, wrong.

Then she was completely naked, and she closed her eyes helplessly, surrendering to his mastery, giving herself up to the passion that lay claim to her. This moment had an inevitability about it that she, as a mere mortal, could not hope to alter. Even the man himself was like a force of nature — wild and insistent, a power that could not be tamed and one that she didn't want to tame. She had never felt so cherished, so aroused, so . . . *feminine* in all her life, and she never wanted the moment to stop. She cried out as his lips found the heart of her womanhood, and her hands grasped the wooden railing above her, her body arching on the cushions in wild abandon. She cried out again, her voice sharp and hoarse, then bit her lip in sudden shame, shocked by her own cries of pleasure.

'No, Flame, no,' Reece murmured hoarsely, and quickly moved back up her body, his lips stopping only to trace the delicate contours of her collarbone. 'I want you to cry out, my little cyclone.' He watched her slowly open her eyes, which were deep and almost black with passion. 'I want to hear you.' Reece shucked off his shirt, exposing a wide, muscled expanse of chest, lightly sprinkled with dark hairs. Flame's fingertips itched to touch them and she gave in to the temptation, thrilled at the way his breathing laboured at her slightest touch. 'I want to hear you being pleasured,' Reece continued hoarsely, his eyes almost silver now with desire. 'I want to touch you, hear you, smell and taste you . . . oh, sweetheart, how I want to taste you.'

He slid off his trousers, his movements awkward but quick, and Flame, still reeling from the heady eroticism of his words, barely had time to admire his tanned skin, the strong, masculine sweep of thighs and large, thrusting manhood before he was once more upon her, his passion hot but restrained, his desire strong but gentle. This time, when his mouth found the heart of her womanhood, she no longer tried to hold back her cries, and, when she could no longer fight the tightening waves of her first orgasm, she moaned without inhibition, aware of the shuddering pleasure in her body, aware of her voice, thick and dark and passionate as she rode the crest of a wave that travelled over every pore of her body. A girl no longer, the woman who had taken her place embraced her new self joyously. Wonderful moments later, she opened her eyes slowly and found his face right above her, so dear and familiar it made tears smart in her eyes. His face was tight with tension and desire, and he looked more male than ever. Gently she reached up and cupped his face. 'Thank you, Reece.'

'Sweetheart,' Reece swallowed with difficulty, knowing he could ruin this moment forever if he didn't handle the next few minutes very carefully. 'You are . . . a virgin, aren't you?' he said gently. Her responses had been so new to her, her inexperience so obvious, that — incredible, wonderful, mystifying as it might seem — Reece knew that he was the first man to touch her. The revelation was still cannoning through him, making him want to shout with joy and thank her rapturously for the precious gift she was giving him. But he was also very much aware of the responsibility that was now his, and he was determined not to hurt or disappoint her, as well as to protect her from any possible consequences of what they were about to do.

Flame nodded, a little shy at the admission. 'Does it matter?'

Reece shook his head. 'It might hurt. Just a little. Will you mind?'

Flame half rose and leaned on her elbows behind her. Looking down at their entwined bodies, hers looked whiter, leaner, while his was dark and powerful. She gasped as she saw his thrusting member resting against her trembling thighs. It looked huge and so blatantly male that her loins turned liquid in anticipation of cradling its long, hard length. The thought was both terrifying and wonderful. When she looked back at Reece, she saw clearly the tense look in his eyes, the gentle, questioning gaze cutting right through her defences and into her heart. 'It's all right,' she whispered, feeling strangely tender, aware for the first time that, in his own way, Reece was as vulnerable as she was.

'I'm glad.' He expelled his breath in relief, not aware that he'd been holding it. 'It's nothing to be afraid of, sweetheart, I promise,' he said gruffly. Sensing she still needed a little time to adjust, he leaned slightly away from her and, holding her eyes with his own, took her hand and guided it down to him. He moaned as her fingers closed around him, and her eyes widened in surprise. He felt so hot, so hard, and her body clamoured for him so responsively that for a moment she was stunned. How could she have spent all this time knowing so little about her own body?

'Reece,' she whispered in wonderment, and his eyes shot open at the want in her voice. Briefly, he smiled.

'That's right, sweetheart,' he murmured encouragingly, a feeling of tenderness for her making his voice thick and breathless. 'This is what you do to me.'

Flame gently leaned back, and as he nudged her legs apart with his own, she felt no fear, only want, only a sense of rightness, as he began to fill her. There was a little pain, but it was an exquisite pain, unlike any she'd ever experienced before, and when he began to move inside her, and she began to feel a climax building that made her first one seem like nothing more than a mere foretaste, she forgot everything save the man who was filling her with such new sensations, with such wonderful ecstasy. 'Reece!' she cried his name and instinctively hooked her legs around him, her ankles locking behind his bent knees, her body undulating beneath his. Reece moaned, his body tensing and quivering like that of a nervous horse. Flame closed her eyes, uncaring that now he had become rougher, his body thrusting with ever-growing urgency into hers as she was swept up in a wave of pleasure that catapulted them both from the real world for long, fabulous moments, and showed them instead a world of mind-blowing sensation and fulfilment.

It was a long time before Flame drifted, reluctantly, back down to earth. Lying in arms that gently cradled her, she closed her eyes in an effort to keep the world at bay. They had made love with all the passion and tenderness of true lovers. But they were still so far apart. She could sense it. 'Reece, did you know that your father and my mother were seeing each other?' she blurted the question out, realising too late that it sounded more like an accusation than a question. She felt him stiffen and move away, and a moment later he began to get dressed. Only then did he answer her.

'No. Did you?'

She shook her head, watching him dress with an aching heart. With every article of clothing he donned, he seemed to be moving farther away. 'No. But it doesn't really matter, does it?' she asked, her voice almost desperately hopeful.

'No,' Reece agreed, wanting to say more. But what, exactly? For a mature man, he found himself feeling strangely tongue-tied. It was annoying. He ought to be able to handle after-sex conversation much better than this. He always had before; a witty word, a laughing comment, and he and his partner parted friends. Why was it so different now, with this girl? Deep down he knew the answer, and it was unnerving. Unnerving enough for him to want to get away from her and her intoxicating presence, to find somewhere quiet where he could think everything over carefully. If he was right, and he was dealing with . . . love . . . the word whispered softly in his brain, making him shiver . . . then he needed to be careful. For both their sakes. Hell, this should never have happened so soon. Especially when he'd known she was so innocent. His anger was obvious, but Flame, seeing it, thought it was directed at herself. Suddenly she was ashamed of her nakedness and quickly pulled on her own clothes, wanting to say something, but not knowing what to say, wanting something else to happen, but not knowing what. Just something that would make everything all right again. Something that would make sense. But nothing did.

In silence, the gondola moved placidly but swiftly across the lagoon towards the shore, its two passengers tense and silent with the confusion of their thoughts.

* * *

That same night, hundreds of miles away, Flame's twin also lay in bed, weeping softly. But his were tears of frustration, of pain, of fear. And the only person to hear and offer silent, unrealised comfort was Roger, who stood undetected in the shadows, his round eyes fixed anxiously on his nephew. Eventually Justin stopped crying, and Roger was glad. He didn't want Francesca to come home and see her baby son crying. She might think that Roger had not looked after him properly for her, while she'd been forced to live in exile.

But Roger knew how to look out for Francesca.

He'd always known.

CHAPTER 11

Owen grinned at his face in the mirror as he scraped the last of the shaving cream from his chin. It didn't look like the face of a man who was about to be married in six hours' time. Even here, in Venice, amid her family and friends, he still couldn't quite believe his luck. Couldn't actually believe the last five months had been real, and not some wonderful, blissful dream.

Owen had been raised in Texas, only moving to the West Coast after he had married Clare. He had been twenty-four then, and already the owner of a nifty little manufacturing company specializing in auto parts. But it was in California that his fortunes had really taken off — both financially and socially. Within a decade he was a multi-millionaire, and, much more importantly, the father of a young boy. Despite the gruelling hours and hard slog, all the travelling and entertaining, Owen had never let his family suffer. Clare and Reece had always travelled with him — not just to the glamorous places like Hawaii, where he owned a hotel, or exciting places like Rio, Las Vegas, London and Paris, but also the out-of-the-way spots. The middle of the Australian outback, where he owned opal mines; Burma, where he had a share in ruby mines; and several places in Colombia where the finest of emeralds could be found.

Perhaps because of the uniqueness of gem mining, or because, as a boy, Reece had been most impressed with these out-of-the-way places, he had grown to value his father's mining interests above all others. And Owen had not discouraged his enthusiasm. Right from the start, his son had shown intelligence, strength and many of Owen's own stubborn characteristics. But he'd seen his friends become alienated from their offspring, and had been wary. He'd seen too many of Reece's schoolfriends turn to drugs or alcohol in an attempt to shuck the heavy responsibilities loaded on them by their parents to ever make Reece suffer the same fate. From the time Reece could understand the value of money, he'd had to work for what he wanted. Not for him the biggest stereos, the best racing bikes, the fastest cars. And Owen always took the time to be with his son: at basketball games, which they both loved; on simple picnics with Clare; or just lounging around the house talking.

Yes, everything in Owen's life had been perfect. He and Clare had enjoyed a reputation for fidelity, love and loyalty that was fascinating to the rest of the inhabitants of their wealthy and privileged world where divorce, affairs and scandal were rife. Reece was a son to be proud of, his company was ever-expanding, and Owen never thought it would end. But end it did. One day Clare left to pick up some flowers for a dinner party they were giving and never came back. A drunk in a Buick had seen to that. Owen had lived in a state of shock for a year. A year in which Reece, aged only nineteen, had all but taken over making decisions about the company, coping with his own grief alone, a fact that Owen only began to realise many years later. Years when the numbness began to erode, when the horror began to recede, and the loneliness began to grow and life became a dull, grey ordeal.

Until the day Professor Vallery had brought his translator/interpreter and assistant to one of their conferences. Owen was a financial backer of the Vallery Museum, which often exhibited archaeological findings. Owen had entered the museum's quaint and antiquated boardroom, and the first thing he had seen was Francesca. Dressed in a simple navy-blue business suit, she was discreetly interpreting Professor Vallery's conversation to the museum chairwoman. And he felt *something*, for the first time in years. At first it was only admiration — Francesca had a lovely figure, a lovely profile, a lovely voice. Then, as he was introduced, he noticed she had lovely skin, a lovely small hand, and a lovely smile. Then, as the meeting progressed, and Francesca began not only to interpret the Professor's findings and wishes but to add valuable input of her own, he realised she had a lovely mind. And her loveliness continued.

The meeting disturbed him. Long after Francesca and the Professor left for their hotel, Owen felt restless. The next day he had lunch at the hotel where he knew she was staying. Naturally the Professor invited him to join them. Naturally he did. Naturally, he fell in love with Francesca. It was that simple. That easy. That right. He was not a fool. He didn't expect a lovely woman like Francesca to love him back. He had been quite literally speechless when he'd realised that she did.

The moment was forever etched in his mind. They'd been driving over the Golden Gate Bridge on their way back from the opera, when he had glanced across at her and seen, in the reflection of car headlights, her eyes on him, soft and unmistakably those of a woman in love. He had almost driven them over the edge and into the bay below.

Now, putting on his tie and jacket and heading downstairs to the breakfast table, he was glad he hadn't. So very glad. Life was wonderful again.

'Good morning, Owen.' Giulietta, who'd insisted Owen stay at the *palazzo*, was the only one up. Reece had been on the phone all night to Colombia and was due to fly out right after the wedding. Owen knew that the trouble at one of their mines wasn't what was bothering him. His son had changed recently, and Owen couldn't quite distinguish where the change lay.

Of his wife's three ladies, as he always thought of Flame, Maria and Giulietta, Giulietta was by far the sharpest. 'Hi, Giulie, old gal. What's cooking?' he drawled loudly.

'American oaf,' Giulietta shot back, then reached for the coffee pot. 'I take it you're prepared for the ordeal to come?'

'You mean the dreaded Conte?' The Conte was to give Francesca away and it would be the first meeting between the two men. 'I suppose I'll manage. But from what I can prise out of Flame, I gather he's the original three-headed troll.'

'He is . . . overpowering. If you let yourself be overpowered,' Giulietta admitted.

'And Flame didn't,' Owen guessed, biting into his toast.

'No. She didn't. And I'm glad to see the condemned man can eat a hearty breakfast,' Francesca said from behind them, having arrived just in time to catch the tail-end of their conversation. Owen rose quickly and kissed her as she joined him at the table, his face brightening visibly. Maria was not far behind her daughter, and, after tut-tutting about the bride and groom seeing each other before the wedding, nibbled nervously on a croissant. They'd performed a minor miracle in getting everything organised in only a fortnight and Maria was worried they'd missed something. Flame was nowhere to be seen. Giulietta and Maria discreetly retired, and together Owen and Francesca sat at the table, elbows resting on the top, coffee cups in hands, gazing at each other like teenagers again. This time, the second time for both of them, things would be perfect.

Owen had had to probe gently, day after day, week after week, to get the true story of Francesca's first marriage out of her. She was not the sort of woman to cry on his shoulder and make a fuss. She had borne her problems, huge though they were, with tremendous fortitude. When he had finally learned the whole truth — the cruel facts behind her marriage — he had been horrified for her. He was so angry on her behalf that for the first time ever he had found himself hating a man. He simply couldn't imagine how he would have felt if he'd been forced to live without ever having known his son. And, thinking of children . . .

'Have you noticed,' Owen began cautiously, 'how our two children seem less than . . . well . . .'

'I have,' Francesca admitted nervously, then reached across and took his hand. 'But it won't affect us, will it?'

'Not on your life!' Owen shot back, and, raising her hand to his lips, kissed her knuckles, his eyes full of adoration as she blushed delightfully.

'Owen. I'm so lucky to have you, and I don't want to spoil this wonderful day. But I *am* worried. I can't put my finger on it, but I feel as if something . . . I don't know how to explain it. I feel that something really . . . awful is going to happen.'

'Don't say that!' Owen said sharply, then could have bitten off his tongue. 'I'm sorry. It's just that since Clare died so suddenly . . . I hate anyone to say things like that.'

Francesca was instantly contrite, and, reaching out her hand, bare of all rings, she lay it across his. 'Sorry, *cara*. And on this day too. I haven't told you, really told you, how happy you've made me, have I? After Malcolm, I thought I would never even want to look at another man again. And until you walked into that silly little museum boardroom, I never have.'

Owen swallowed, hoping she hadn't noticed the lump her words had brought to his throat. He was, after all, a Texan! Francesca, of course, did notice, and smiled both in happiness and in love. Nothing could spoil this day for her now. Nothing.

* * *

Conte Giulio Pierluigi Corraldo stood before his mirror and checked his naked body. A few moles, a hint of flabbiness around his middle, a few grey hairs on his chest. For a man his age he was in superb shape, and he knew it. Quickly, he dressed and left for the office. Just because he was attending his niece's wedding this afternoon, it didn't mean he wouldn't put in a full morning's work.

When he arrived, a servant of the Contessa was waiting for him in the foyer. He looked nervous as the Conte led the way to his private office. 'You have them?' the Conte asked peremptorily, holding out his hand. Shaking slightly, the old man handed over a large portfolio. Wordlessly, his face a mask of distaste, the Conte withdrew some money from his wallet and handed it over. The servant hurried away. The Conte knew the old man had a wife dying of cancer, but he suspected that Giulietta's manservant wanted money only to buy more alcohol for himself. The Contessa would quickly realise what had happened, of course, and fire him, but that was none of the Conte's concern. The man was weak and could be exploited, that was all. He settled himself in his large chair and opened the portfolio. For a long time, he gazed speechlessly at the beautiful Flame Syramore-Forbes originals. The only copies . . .

* * *

Reece slipped a deep red carnation into his buttonhole and checked he had the ring, laughing at his own nervousness.

But you didn't get to be your father's best man every day. A bellboy knocked on the door and handed over a brown envelope. Reece tipped him generously, and ripped it open quickly, recognizing the postmark and handwriting. Inside was his report on Flame. Much of it he already knew, but it was her English family history that stopped him dead in his tracks. Halcyone's! She owned half of Halcyone's too? Good grief, was there any jewellery company she didn't have her claws hooked into? Was she planning to marry the head of Tiffany's? Was she after the chairman of Cartier? He wouldn't put it past her. Angry, but also a little amused, Reece slammed down the envelope and wearily rubbed his hands across his eyes. And he'd been feeling so guilty about the other night. That wonderful night in the gondola when he'd thought he'd found the answer to his dreams, and then felt like a tongue-tied boy. He'd felt so nervous he had hardly said a word to her afterwards. And all along, she must have been coolly making her own plans. What better target could she possibly have for herself than her new stepbrother, who was also owner of Redex and one of the premier gem-mining corporations in the world? The same mining corporation, incidentally, that supplied both Corraldo's and Halcyone's of England with the bulk of their gems? Reece swore violently. Being bested, outmanoeuvred and outsmarted was one hell of a new experience, and the feeling of creeping humiliation was not one he particularly relished.

Looking out over the tranquil canals, Reece shook his head. Lord, he felt tired. She was exhausting him with her constant, nasty little surprises. He'd known a lot of men who'd been had, of course; in his world, gold-diggers were a common hazard. But he'd never thought he'd fall victim. He'd always been too smart for them before. Until, that was, a red-haired siren had tricked her way into his office, his life, his thoughts, his . . . heart.

Reece swore again and shook his head. No, she hadn't got that far. Oh, she'd nearly succeeded. She played the out-raged innocent so well. Innocent? He glanced again at the letter lying on the table. Innocent as Jezebel! But a little voice kept insisting that his anger wasn't real, but an excuse he needed to dodge the real issue. One that, at twenty-nine, he'd begun to think he'd never have to deal with at all. He was in love, and the timing couldn't be worse. Soon he'd have to go to Colombia where his only problems were poisonous snakes and spiders and an unprofitable mine. But he'd be back. And Lady Flame Syramore-Forbes had better watch out then!

* * *

Francesca and Owen were drinking the last of the coffee when the mail arrived. Among the messages of congratula-tions there was the usual large brown envelope. 'It's a report from . . . a man in England. He's looking out for Justin and Roger for me,' Francesca said quietly.

Owen nodded, understanding at once. 'Well, open it, sweetheart.' He squeezed her hand lovingly, watching

Francesca's face as she did just that. Briefly she read the report and glanced through a set of photographs at the familiar face of her son and a few long-lensed shots of Roger, usually taken as he stared out of an attic window. Only when she had stared at Justin's face for several minutes did she realise the envelope still contained something bulky. Opening it out, she pulled out the front page of a newspaper. Puzzled at first, she quickly unfolded it and gasped. Owen moved quickly from his chair to walk behind hers and glance down over her shoulder. What he saw was a picture of Justin. It was grainy, but not even rough newsprint could disguise the quality of the fine, strong face. Justin was wet, his blond hair plastered to his skull. His face, though, was unusually tense, and the caption above the extraordinary picture said it all. 'HERO OXFORD BOY SAVES CHUM FROM DROWNING'.

'Oh, Owen,' Francesca breathed, and quickly read the story. In glowing terms it told how, after winning a charity match against their old rivals at Henley, the Oxford boat had overturned. One member of the team, George Campbell-Bean, had hit his head on the side of the boat and sunk. Only the quick thinking and heroic actions of his rowing mate, Lord Justin Syramore-Forbes, Earl of Ravenscroft, had saved him. Thinking little for his own safety, the Earl had dived under the boat and brought the stricken Campbell-Bean to the surface. The lead oarsman had given mouth-to-mouth, and Mr Campbell-Bean had later recovered in hospital. The Earl's old college, which he had left in his first year in order to take over the reins of the Halcyone jewellery chain, later held a dinner in the Earl's honour.

Over the page there was another picture of Justin, this time looking even more handsome and distinguished in evening dress, sitting at high table, surrounded by dons and a few close friends. 'Oh, Owen, isn't he wonderful?'

Owen smiled and nodded. 'We'll be able to see for ourselves soon. I know we were going to have our honeymoon in Rome, but perhaps after a few days we could continue it in England? What do you think?'

Francesca gasped and stood up, the paper falling to the floor, briefly forgotten. 'Oh, could we? I'd love that! But . . . let's not go to Ravenscroft straight away.'

Owen nodded. After so many years, Francesca was terrified of meeting her son, and who could blame her? As he kissed her gently, and then more firmly, he knew it was not going to be easy. From what he'd learned of Malcolm, and judging by the way Justin had reacted after his death, who knew what garbage Malcolm had drummed into the boy? He knew, too, that the letter Justin had written to his mother after Malcolm's death had not been a kind one. Still, the boy obviously couldn't be all bad. Mixed up, undoubtedly. But, Owen thought, his arms tightening around Francesca in loving possession, once he met Francesca, he would love her. How could he fail to? It would take time, but he was determined to incorporate Justin into their family, just as surely and as lovingly as Reece would be incorporated. They would all learn to love one another. Owen wouldn't have it any other way. Anything less would only hurt Francesca, and he was determined nothing would ever do that again. Not Justin, and not their wayward son and daughter. Reece and Flame had better get their act sorted out, or else!

'*Cara*,' Francesca murmured against his lips, her eyes closed, her heart pounding with happiness. Nothing could ruin this day for her. Nothing.

At her feet, the photograph of Justin stared up at them.

CHAPTER 12

The church of San Sebastiano had seen many weddings. The bride today was beautiful but mature, her wedding dress the colour of antique ivory. It had been Giulietta's own wedding gown, and Francesca had been close to tears earlier, when her grandmother had helped her don the classical dress. The groom was handsome, in his silver-grey suit that contrasted flatteringly with his tanned, leathery skin. The church was packed. Jewels glinted, and corsages of the finest roses, orchids and gardenias abounded. Orange blossom filled the ancient church with scent, aided by carnations, violets, freesias, orchids and roses. The huge, impressive organ began playing the bridal march, and Francesca glided up the aisle for the second time. As she joined Owen at the altar, where the Conte, as official head of the family, gave her away, all eyes were on the bride, who looked radiant.

Giulietta remembered her own wedding and smiled. Maria remembered Michael Corraldo and reached for her lace handkerchief. Flame, in her capacity as chief bridesmaid, could do nothing other than face Reece, and her eyes were dark, fathomless pools every time they alighted on him. What was he thinking? How did he *really* feel about her? Did he love her, just a bit? But she could hardly bear to meet his eyes as the bishop began to talk about the sanctity of marriage. Owen had told them Reece would have to leave for Colombia the day after the wedding to deal with some trouble at one of their emerald mines, and that had been the first time she'd realised that the Dexter Mining Corporation mined precious stones, not coal or tin. It had been yet another oddly discomfiting revelation in a week where she was already feeling off-balance.

The church was reverently silent, and again and again Flame felt her eyes being pulled in Reece's direction. The sun shone through the stained-glass windows, angling small diadems of red, green and blue on to his dark head and impressive shoulders. With a lurch in her abdomen she recalled what it felt like to cling to those shoulders as his body drove into hers and her eyes closed briefly. She must forget about that — it was obvious Reece had. Determinedly she looked away, watching her mother kneel beside Owen, her head bowed to receive the blessing. Vainly she tried to force all thoughts of Reece Dexter from her mind. She fiddled nervously with her bridesmaid's bouquet of orange blossom and pale peach carnations. She was dressed in an apricot-coloured floor-length gown of light velvet, cut very simply. With her flaming hair and cascades of amber and beaten-silver jewellery dangling from her ears and around her neck, she looked stunning.

Francesca had eyes only for Owen. How different this wedding was from . . . no. Francesca refused to compare this to that other occasion. Malcolm had seduced a young girl, with lies that promised love and fidelity, while all the time coveting her Corraldo connections. This was Owen, who loved her. There was simply no comparison. She let the priest's words wash over them, feeling warm from her heart to her head. When Owen slipped the ring, a single diamond set in platinum, on her finger, Francesca closed her eyes briefly. This time, it would be all right. This time, with this man, she would be happy. When she opened them again, Owen was looking at her, his eyes soft and gentle, and she smiled, her smile like a ray of sunshine in the dark interior of the Venice church.

* * *

Justin bowed, just slightly, and raised Principessa Sofia Elena di Maggiore's hand to his lips, where he lightly brushed her knuckles. His eyes never left hers. Sofia di Maggiore was beautiful, in a unique way. She was just under six feet, with raven hair and a figure that could only be described as statuesque.

'Principessa, welcome to Ravenscroft. I hope you had a pleasant journey?'

Sofia inclined her head, her dark, almost black eyes sparkling with polite flirtatiousness. 'I did, *grazie*. And I thank you for your offer of overnight accommodation at this lovely house, but I promised Guido I would meet him tonight in Monaco.'

'Lucky Guido,' Justin murmured, and glanced behind him to where Scott Tate and a little grey-haired woman who'd arrived with the Principessa were standing. Her chauffeur remained in the car. 'Well, would you like to come into the blue room? You and your companion must be thirsty.'

'Oh, forgive me my rudeness. This is Signora Corlino. She is my . . . how do you English put it . . . my right hand? Wherever I go, the *signora* goes with me. To fix my hair, answer my telephone; she is indispensable to me.'

'I understand,' Justin acknowledged politely, and led the small party into the salon that he'd carefully prepared for the occasion. The Principessa surreptitiously took in every treasure to be seen — the genuine Constable that rested over the Adam fireplace, the Wedgwood figurines, a matching pair of Ming vases that were stood on Sheraton pedestals either side of the big lead-paned windows.

'What would you like to drink, Principessa, *signora*?' Justin deliberately included the *signora*, guessing rightly that Sofia regarded her maid almost as fondly as most English children regarded their nannies. The *signora* was promptly served the tea she requested, and Sofia could not mistake the quality or pedigree of the bone-china teacup and saucer that was used. Justin asked the butler to go down to the cellars and named one of the finest wines he had for the Principessa. She could not fail to be impressed by being offered a £5,000 glass of wine, and Justin considered every penny of expense well worth it.

It was approaching noon, and Sofia was persuaded to stay for lunch before going on to tour the Woodstock emporium. The dining room, like the salon, had been especially prepared, and every inch of wood gleamed. The finest silver, china and crystal were on display and the simple meal of salmon mousse, crab salad and gooseberry fool was well received.

After having got off to a flying start, he was not about to falter now. He refused to give a thought to what was happening in Venice right at this moment. He had received an invitation to his mother's wedding, and promptly declined by return of post. Then he'd set about learning all about Owen Dexter. Learning that he owned mines that supplied Halcyone's with the bulk of its finest stones made him furious. Even worse, Reece Dexter owned Redex. Who knew what tricks his little sister must be playing to take advantage of all that? She must have thought it was Christmas!

Justin was determined to give Sofia his wholehearted attention as she accompanied him to Woodstock in the Syramore-Forbes Silver Ghost Rolls-Royce. Naturally, the shop was spotlessly clean. The carpet, a traditional deep-pile purple Aubusson, had been cleaned, its colour subconsciously wafting the essence of royalty to the people that entered. The glass display cabinets had been polished until it was hard to believe the impressive pieces of jewellery on display were actually protected by glass at all.

And yet Justin had not altered one thing. The floorboards underneath still undulated beneath the feet. The paintings on the wall were still higgledy-piggledy and quaint. The shop was still small, almost dark, and unutterably

English. The Principessa was charmed, and above all, surprised. This room was as unlike the elegant, light airiness of Bulgari and the other jewellery establishments she'd been in as the town of Woodstock itself was unlike Rome, Paris or Amsterdam. But Sofia, as well as being woman enough to be impressed by Halcyone's, the country mansion and Justin's own very potent handsomeness, was also a businesswoman, and, after being suitably charmed and impressed by the shop, she quickly began to inspect the jewellery it displayed. Since deciding to commission the jewellery, Sofia had learned a lot about the art, allowing her to inspect with a shrewd eye the pieces of jewellery that were on display. Which were, she saw at once, perfect. She would have expected little else from a company of Halcyone's repute.

Justin expertly guided her through the collection, displaying his own knowledge and pandering to her own minimal expertise. 'This is Belle Époque,' he murmured, after ten minutes spent poring over the display cabinet. 'It came into fashion round about the turn of the century, and its era was over by 1914. My great-grandmother said Belle Époque was gay but not wanton, exuberant but disciplined.'

Sofia nodded, and, not to be outdone, added gently, 'The shapes are very fluent — and they have softer colours. I expect that's because of the influence of Art Nouveau?' Justin smiled into her dark eyes, more than willing to let her win their tiny battle of wills. 'Indeed it is. I particularly like this piece. It's in the style of René Lalique. He's famous for his glass, of course, but he also made jewellery, especially in the basse-taille style.'

The Principessa nodded. 'I like those peridots.'

Justin nodded, and made a mental note of the hint. 'I agree. I like their soft greens too. Actually that piece was made in honour of Edward, the Prince of Wales. It was his favourite stone.' Sofia accepted the point, and they moved on. Justin had been very eclectic in his choice, and as well as Belle Époque there were stunning examples of Art Deco pieces, mainly brooches, with their mathematically precise geometric designs, as well as post-war pieces, the domain of the surrealists, and even some contemporary pieces. Sophia was more than satisfied. The workmanship was exquisite, the designs satisfying, and of course, Halcyone's had an ambience that was seductive. When the day came to make her final list, Halcyone's was going to be close to the top.

'If you have time, Principessa, I'd like to show you into the workrooms. But of course, if you don't particularly want to see how the pieces are created . . .' Justin let his voice trail off, very well aware that Sofia was already hooked.

'Really? Your craftsmen work here? In this shop?' Sofia jumped at the chance, as Justin had always believed she would.

The workroom had been deliberately left exactly as it was. Except the craftsmen had come to work in their best suits and had visited their favourite barber before coming in, in honour of their royal guest. From the moment she set foot in the room, heard the high-pitched whining of drills, smelt the solder in the air, the oil, almost the sweat and toil of the working man's efforts, Sofia was impressed. Never before had any of the others let her even near one of their workrooms. Justin began with glamour, and steered her to Gunther Voss, cutting a rough ruby into a perfect lozenge, a process Sofia found fascinating. Then they moved on to the apprentices working hard with saw and file on copper and aluminium, which needed special handling. Although the latter points were far less glamorous than the cutting of stones, Sophia found it no less fascinating. And Justin's pièce de résistance, having Seth help Sofia make a simple pendant, went better than Justin could have hoped. Sofia had no idea that Seth's offer had been anything other than a genuine, spur-of-the-moment decision. Justin had chosen his subject well. Enamelling was something Sofia had given very little thought to. It was something that could be made quickly, it was colourful and it produced startling results in next to no time. It was also something that Sofia could do successfully, providing she was carefully led by Seth, which she was.

If Signora Corlino was surprised by the sight of her mistress sitting at a dirty workshop with an old man behind her, guiding her hand, she didn't show it. And Sofia, for her part, was fascinated by the process. Tiny pieces of coloured enamel, already shaped and cut, were actually being assembled, by herself, right in front of her eyes to produce a pendant depicting a simple but beautiful and stylized cream lily. 'There it is, Principessa, ma'am,' Seth's rolling Dorset burr was both respectful and gruffly English. 'I always said you could do it, now, didn't I?'

Sofia nodded, barely able to take her eyes from the pendant in front of her. Never before had she enjoyed an hour more. When she had started it had been a simple, plain oval of gold. Now it was a work of art. And she had done it. 'It's lovely. How clever you are, Seth.'

'You set it, Principessa, ma'am. I merely helped.'

'Of course, it needs to be finished,' Justin explained. 'Enamel is a high-quality flint glass, coloured by the introduction of various oxides and salts. It's been immersed in a weak nitric acid for a few minutes to get rid of any impurities; that's why it was still moist when you applied it. Now it must be put in a muffle that works at temperatures of between 700 and 900 degrees Celsius to dry and harden it again.'

'I never realised it could be so . . . satisfying. Before I've always passed over enamels as . . .' Sofia shrugged helplessly.

'Second-class?' Justin helped her out and nodded. 'Yes, most people think that, but it's simply not true. There are also more styles of enamelling than you might think. What you've just done is called cloisonne, but there are others; champlevé, basse-taille, Limoges — which require thin plates of copper and plique-à-jour, which is similar to what you've just done, except it has no background.' Sofia listened attentively, still buzzing from the high of actually making her own piece of jewellery, something she'd never expected to do. Justin watched her avid eyes follow the pendant as Seth prepared it for the muffler. 'Once the pendant has been dried, I would be honoured, on behalf of Halcyone's, if you'd accept it as a gift in gratitude for your time and patience. Perhaps you can leave an address with our manager?'

Sofia nodded happily. 'I'd be delighted to, Lord Justin.'

Justin nodded. Of course, Sofia would not get the pendant she had just made. It was too clumsy, so ill-fitted. But Seth would take it all apart and reassemble it, and in a week's time Sofia would accept a fine piece of enamelled jewellery and could happily, if inaccurately, boast that she had made it. The Principessa left soon after. She was glowing.

We've got her, Justin thought exultantly. Then smiled grimly. Provided nothing went wrong.

* * *

Flame, who got slightly tipsy at the wedding reception, caught the bouquet that Francesca tossed over her shoulder and, amid much laughter and teasing, happily waved off the newlyweds, along with the rest of her family and guests. Slowly, almost reverently, she lifted the bouquet to her nose and smelled the beautiful fragrances. Traditionally, whoever caught the bouquet was the next to be married. Quickly, she looked around for Reece.

But Reece was already gone.

That night she miserably slept off her slight hangover, and rose the following morning feeling just a bit ropy. At the breakfast table, the early morning post had brought a letter from Radcliffe. Flame had been expecting it, since she'd made up her mind to leave, and had written to the Dean explaining her reasons. But the Dean, apart from accepting her withdrawal with regret, had written with far more devastating news. Wendy Gibbs had been found dead in her room. Knowing that they had been friends, the Dean had thought she should know. The coroner's report, the Dean informed her sadly and as gently as she was able, had found the cause of death to be massive trauma caused by the accidental taking of a crack overdose. Flame began to weep, bringing Maria and Giulietta anxiously to her side. But Flame was inconsolable. She'd been Wendy's best friend and had not even guessed that Wendy had had such a terrible problem. And now it was too late to help her . . .

CHAPTER 13

Francesca and Owen came back from their weekend in Rome looking every inch the happy honeymooners. But the moment Francesca walked into the salon she knew that something had happened. Maria rose and kissed her warmly, but her eyes were troubled. 'Mamma,' Francesca said, and watched as Maria reached for Owen, and to his delight planted an equally warm kiss on his cheek. 'Mamma, something's happened. Where's Flame?' she asked sharply.

Giulietta rose painfully to her feet. 'She's upstairs, *cara*. She's had some bad news, I'm afraid.'

Owen and Francesca listened grimly as Giulietta related the facts of Wendy's death. Francesca sighed deeply. 'I have to go and talk to her.' She turned, caught Owen's eye, and held out her hand. Owen felt a wave of relief hit him. Their first crisis, and Francesca had turned to him as naturally as a sunflower turned its face to the sun. Upstairs, Flame was standing by the window, looking out over the city she had come to love.

'Flame, *cara*. Giulietta told me about Wendy. I'm so sorry.' Francesca came swiftly to her side, pulling Flame against her, holding her tight to her breast.

'Mamma, I'm sorry. I wanted to wait before telling you. This is your honeymoon, after all!'

'Rubbish!' It was Owen who spoke, his voice gruff with emotion. 'We never want you to feel that you can't come to us, at any time, with any of your troubles.' It sounded so inadequate, but he felt his position as stepfather was too new for him to go to her and do what Francesca was doing. But her pain was so obvious that Owen longed to do so. He remembered holding Clare the same way when they'd received the news of her mother's death in a San Antonia nursing home. Francesca looked at her husband, her eyes full of pain and love. She smiled, a heartbreaking smile of gratitude. Flame sniffed and took a shaky breath, pulling herself together and slowly drawing away from her mother. Well, at least the worst was over.

Except it wasn't. Not by a long shot.

Later, when she had forced herself to eat a desultory dinner with her family, she made her way back to her room, determined to work on another jewellery piece. But when she reached into the dresser drawer, only a blank space looked back at her. For a moment she simply stared, then frantically pulled out the other drawers. But she already knew that the portfolio was gone. She had not misplaced it, and although she would ask, she already knew that neither Giulietta nor her grandmother had 'borrowed' it. Slowly, numbly, she fell back on her bed.

Someone had stolen it. But who? And why? Nobody had access to it, here at the Palazzo d'Oro. There was only herself, her family and . . . Reece. Reece, who owned Redex. Reece, who had admired her earlier efforts and been impressed enough to want to employ her. Reece, who needed new designs to ensure the success of his jewellery company. Reece . . .

* * *

Justin moved his hand down the back of his dancing partner, very much aware of the warm, rhythmic movement of her flesh. Desiree Deville was Scott's latest idea: the French heiress to her father's vast farmlands, she was single, reasonably attractive, and very sought after. At the moment she was sighing loudly in his ear and he felt the unmistakable pert pressure of her nipples sliding against his chest with a mixture of amusement and anxiety. He had discarded his jacket earlier on, when the party had begun to heat up in more ways than just the temperature in the room.

A live band pounded music into the room from one corner, the amplifiers so loud that all the partygoers could really make out was the steady 'thump, thump, thump-thump' of the lead guitar. Justin didn't mind. He hadn't minded when the lights had been gradually dimmed until he and his partner were swaying in complete darkness. He didn't mind the drunken chuckles all around him as men and women got groped. He didn't even mind the raucous or mellow suggestions being given by acid-heads. He was now in a state of blissful, if not terminal, numbness.

'So this is how you English really party?' Desiree had to shout into his ear, and Justin nodded, disinclined to try and talk above the din all around him. 'And I thought those polite little soirées Daddy took me to at the Connaught were all there was to you English!'

Justin smiled again, his strong white teeth flashing eerily in the gloom. He knew that Desiree was nearly drunk, but then, so was he. He needed to be, even to attempt Scott's scheme. The damned man was becoming obsessed by the idea that Justin should marry money — and quickly. And it was only because Justin knew that he was right that he was here, holding this giddy French tart in his arms, letting her rub against him like a cat on heat. Now that Francesca had married her billionaire, and the Principessa had made it clear in her gushing letter how close Halcyone's was to getting the commission, he needed to solidify his position quickly. And the letter he had received from his mother yesterday had clinched it. She and her darling hubby were coming to visit him next weekend. And he couldn't put them off. Not this time. He was dreading it. Just thinking about it threatened to cut through his armour of uncaring like a laser.

Sighing, he filled his palms with Desiree's rear end. He knew she would not consider him as a husband until after she'd checked out his performance in bed. In a way, he couldn't blame her, but in another way he felt totally humiliated. Sex was fine when it was fun. He supposed it would be beautiful when love was involved. But sex to secure a fortune . . . Quickly, he grabbed a passing glass of champagne off a tray and took a big swig. Hell, he felt awful. Everything seemed to be collapsing on top of him.

'Hmm. That's nice,' Desiree slurred, burrowing her nose even further into his neck. Justin winced at the scent of her hairspray in his nose. She was a small girl with a chic cap of dark hair, cut in a Vidal Sassoon geometric style. A slender girl in a silk sheath that was almost see-through.

Desiree sighed again and her hand slipped from his waist to run across his flanks, pressing him ever closer to her. She could not fail to feel the hardening state of his arousal, and she gave a half-lewd, half-intoxicated giggle, a sound that made Justin wince. Flick would never giggle. Flick! Desiree felt a shudder ripple through her dancing partner and smiled. She had a wide, greedy mouth that was used to getting what it wanted. Spoiled all her life, Desiree made no bones about going after what she desired. And she'd wanted the Earl of Ravenscroft from the moment his friend, Scott-whatever-his-name-was, had introduced them.

'It's all right, darling,' she purred into his ear, bringing Justin back from the brink of despair just in time. 'Let's find a quiet spot, hmm?' she suggested, all but dragging him from the crowd, giggling as she made her way to the back of the house, towards a dark and deserted conservatory. He felt her fingers fasten on his trouser belt, and stood rock-still, breathing deeply as she expertly pulled down the zip and tugged on his briefs. He gasped as the sensation of her moist, hot little tongue lapping his balls almost made him cry out. Almost.

Justin gritted his teeth, even as Desiree's hands came out to clutch his calves, stopping him from retreating. She'd been looking forward to this treat for too many hours now to let the Earl's typical English reticence rob her of her pleasure.

Although he knew no one would be able to hear him even if he started to scream blue murder at the top of his considerable voice, Justin kept his mouth grimly closed as Desiree began to lick his turgid member, from stem to top. The sweat began to trickle from his forehead as she took him fully into her wide mouth, her lips foraging ever downwards. He was big, Desiree discovered rapturously, her mouth stretching wider, her tongue massaging harder and harder. Justin began to shake, aware that climax was not far away, and quickly pulled her off, a tremendous surge of disgust lancing through him. Surprised but undeterred, Desiree moved up his body like a sensuous snake and kissed him hard on his panting lips. 'You like, *cherie*,' she mouthed into his ear, her voice raised and breathless.

Justin's eyes snapped open, still wild with lust. 'Yes, I liked,' he admitted, half-truthfully. And, unable to help himself, he added, 'Perhaps you'll like this,' and lifted her off her feet in an instant, bumping her back against the cold plates of glass that comprised the walls as she eagerly hooked her legs around his waist. She was wearing no underwear, and the action opened her wide to Justin's fully turgid manhood. Without hesitating he thrust into her, a savage smile etched on to his face. Trust an Earl of Ravenscroft to come through. Ravenscroft needed a male heir to secure its future. No damn problem. He closed his eyes, needing to shut out the sight of her avid, aroused face. He felt sick.

Desiree grunted, her nails digging into his shoulders, thrilled. He was so out of control, this cool-looking, blond-haired English aristocrat. Who would have thought . . . Desiree moaned as he pulled away and then thrust into her again, filling her ruthlessly. She squirmed at the familiar tightening in her belly. 'Oh, *oui, oui*,' she murmured, her voice a high squeak. She began to mutter in French, a strange combination of swear words, encouraging expletives and threats. Justin, who couldn't speak a word, found the alien sounds strangely threatening. This was supposed to be his future wife? He didn't think he could bear it. But with controlled strokes he brought her to one crashing orgasm after another, his own body held in tight control, the pounding of his loins echoing the growing pounding in his head until at last, when Desiree thought she might actually faint, Justin erupted into her, his body at last slackening in post-coital weakness.

As he released her, Desiree slowly slumped down the wall on to her bottom, wondering what her sophisticated Parisian friends would say if they could see her now. Loved to near death by an Englishman, of all things! And the French thought the English were so . . . wishy-washy. Aware of how ridiculous she must look, with her dress up around her waist, her hair a mess, her breasts rising and falling as she fought for breath, she began to laugh. She couldn't help it. She must look so funny!

Justin opened his eyes and stared at her, for a few seconds unable to believe it. She was laughing at him! He felt a wave of utter despair, frustration and desperation wash over him, making him yearn to scream and scream. Then, as quickly as it came, the overwhelming rage was gone, leaving in its place a frightening emptiness and a sense of total futility. Wearily he pulled up his briefs and zipped his trousers back into position.

'I'm sorry . . .' for a moment he couldn't think of her name '. . . Desiree. There's been a mistake.' Then, without a word, without even trying to help her to her feet, he turned and walked away. Scott and Ravenscroft could go to hell. He was already there.

Desiree watched him go, still laughing.

* * *

Flame was enjoying London. She had thought that staying with her Aunt Aria and her husband Geoffrey would make her feel as if she were taking a step back into childhood again, but nothing could be further from the truth. She was treated like a fully fledged adult right from the start, and it felt good.

Francesca's eldest sister, Aria, against all expectations, had married an Englishman soon after Francesca had married Malcolm. Now both in their late sixties, Aria and her placid husband had been happily married for twenty years. They still lived in the same leafy suburb that Geoffrey had lived in all his life, in the same house that he had shared with his mother until she had died at the ripe old age of ninety-three.

Flame had arrived in England barely a week after her mother's wedding. She hadn't wanted to stay in Venice after the discovery of her missing portfolio — people were bound to ask her about her work, and she'd told nobody about the theft. They could only come to the same inescapable conclusion as her, and she simply couldn't bear to jeopardise her mother's happiness. Owen would be forced to tackle Reece, and she didn't want to be responsible for coming between father and son. She'd much rather deal with Reece herself . . .

Francesca had asked Flame to accompany Owen and herself to England on their honeymoon, but Flame had refused to play gooseberry! Because she knew they couldn't stand the thought of her living alone in some soulless hotel room, she had agreed to stay with her Aunt Aria. Within an afternoon it was all arranged, and Flame flew out of Venice two days later. But not before posting a letter to Reece. She knew he was in Colombia, and she was glad that she'd never have to see him again. She would contrive always to be somewhere else when he visited his father. But that didn't mean he was going to get away with what he had done. So she had poured out all her scorn and contempt in a letter addressed to the Dexter Mining Corporation office in Colombia and posted it immediately, just in case her nerve failed her. After that catharsis had drained her, she had left Venice without a backward glance.

She had liked her aunt and uncle at first meeting at Heathrow airport. Geoffrey, now retired, was the epitome of a gentle, placid man who adored his round, loquacious wife. Their house was modest, but lovingly decorated and cared for. The garden, Geoffrey's one claim to passion, was a mass of colour, scent, topiary and neat flowerbeds. Over the last week, Aria had foisted huge meals on Flame that she could never eat, while Geoffrey had constantly regaled her with lightly amusing tales of his years in the civil service. Under their mixed, well-meaning attempts to make her feel better, Flame slowly began to emerge from the burdens of her grief. Grief for her lost friend, and a little grief for her own lost innocence. But the grief over Reece's betrayal would not budge. It stayed with her, making her soul leaden, and reducing her heart into a painful ache in her chest. Why had he done it? Why had he made love to her so wonderfully, so beautifully, so tenderly, and then turned so cold and scheming afterwards? What kind of man was he?

For a while she had foolishly and childishly thought that she would never like or trust another man again. But with Geoffrey around as a constant reminder of how different men could be, Flame was able to slowly and unflinchingly examine her own part in her misfortunes. It made her realise that she was almost as much to blame. She could even smile ruefully now, when she thought back to how naively she had behaved. At night she could only thank God that she hadn't been truly in love, only in love with the idea of love. But somewhere, deep down, a little voice mocked her, accusing her of self-deception. For the first time she began to understand just how great her own mother's suffering must have been. Reece had only stolen her work from her. Malcolm had stolen Francesca's son.

Thoughts of Justin reminded Flame anew that the weekend was fast approaching. Owen and Francesca were in York — she'd received a postcard of York cathedral only that morning. Now, seated on a Thames riverboat, taking a slow leisurely cruise past the famous and beautiful Houses of Parliament, Flame sighed deeply. Her parents, after finishing their tour of Britain with a few days in Edinburgh, were going to travel down to London on Friday night and meet up with Flame at Aria's home. Then, the next day, they were to travel to Ravenscroft. Ravenscroft. The word made Flame shiver in foreboding, and she quickly turned her thoughts to other things.

Giulietta had called that morning, and Flame had assured her Grandy that she had already completed three of the five commissions Giulietta had arranged for her to do for her English friends. She had completed a sapphire and diamond necklace design for the Countess of Vane, a set of black-pearl drop earrings for a Mrs Frances de Witt (who, despite her name, was as English as rhubarb), and a brooch for Lady Elspeth Astram. The two others were already in draft stage, and could be posted to her clients before the weekend. Flame had heard from the three who had already received their sketches, and they all assured her they were delighted with them, and promised to have their jewellers make up the items *exactly* as her drawings specified. Flame supposed they were all being genuine, but she was very much aware that her confidence was at a low ebb. They might, after all, just be saying that because she was Giulietta's pet.

Shrugging off her negative thoughts, Flame tried to concentrate on the scenery around her. But they were now passing the Tower of London, or the 'Bloody Tower' as her pre-recorded tour guide told them, and Flame once again felt herself shivering. How many kings and queens had been beheaded behind those ancient walls? And that thought took her straight back to Ravenscroft again. Ravenscroft, which her mother so hated. Ravenscroft, which housed Roger, the kind, gentle, simple man Francesca spoke of constantly, whom she so obviously had loved, and still did love, in spite of the fact that he was the brother of her hated first husband. The private detective firm who watched Justin informed Francesca regularly of Roger's wellbeing also. As far as they could tell, he was happy in her son's house. It pleased Francesca, Flame knew, that Justin had not had his uncle put into an institution. Francesca knew also that her portrait of Roger was still at the house. The story of it appearing in a different room every morning had become something of a legend in its own time in the village and surrounding valley. So Justin hadn't destroyed it. That, surely, could only bode well for the future? Flame hoped so.

Flame also knew that Justin was doing very well at Halcyone's. Giulietta, who seemed to have spies everywhere, had told her not long ago that Halcyone's might even get the Principessa di Maggiore's commission. She hadn't even realised that Justin was going after it. How wonderful it would be if Halcyone's got it. Flame herself might be able to design some of the pieces for the collection.

The boat docked and Flame stayed in her seat, letting the last of the summer tourists file past her before getting out and slowly walking to a bus stop. She was aware of becoming more and more nervous about the upcoming weekend. Meeting your own twin brother for the first time when you were both coming up to your twentieth birthday was odd, but it shouldn't be frightening, surely? And from what she knew of her twin, what was there to be frightened of anyway? He treated his uncle kindly. He was a good businessman. He was a hero, a man capable of risking his life to save a friend from drowning. But he was also Malcolm's son. More Malcolm's son than she could ever be Malcolm's daughter. What poison had Malcolm fed into his veins? That was what worried her mother the most. Just how much influence did the spectre of her father still wield in the house he so obsessively loved? Just how deep did his venomous influence go? Flame shook her head, telling herself she was being ridiculous. Was it really possible that Justin could hate them? Or was he, too, just frightened, as she was? Frightened of meeting his real family at last? Frightened that they wouldn't like him, as she was frightened she would fail to impress him?

Flame sighed and wearily fought off an attempted pickup by a boy waiting in the queue behind her. Whatever their mutual fears, she and her mother were going to meet Justin in a few days' time. It was a meeting that was inevitable. It was a meeting that meant so much. But, try as she might over the coming days, Flame simply couldn't shake off the painful, distressing feeling that it was all too late.

* * *

Thousands of miles away a man walked wearily up a mud-clogged dirt track to a bungalow almost swamped by trees and climbing vines. The rain poured down with a steady drumming relentlessness while all around him he could hear the shrieking, angry chattering of monkeys. He wore the heavy-duty boots, thick slacks and oilproof jacket with an ease that spoke of years of practice. Anyone who'd known him in the city would not have believed it was the same man. A battered hat pushed down on his head protected him from the worst of the rain, but rivulets of water trickled down his face and dropped on to his chest, soaking him wherever it could. He moved with a panther's loping ease and economy of effort. Despite having been up and working for over thirty-six hours, he nevertheless sprinted lightly up the bowed wooden steps to the veranda surrounding the bungalow and pulled off his hat.

'Jake? The damned Ute has broken down again,' Reece yelled as he shucked off his dripping, mud-caked boots and eased the heavy oilskin off impressively wide and muscular shoulders.

The screen door opened and an old man stepped into the cool, moist air, the grin he gave in welcome a mile wide. In rapid-fire Spanish, he promised to send one of the men with a pickup truck. Slapping Jake gently but firmly on the back, Reece went thankfully inside, the lino beneath his bare feet feeling cold and clammy. The room was sparsely furnished. Mosquito netting hung at the windows, giving the interior a dim, slightly sinister appearance. Sitting down on a sagging sofa that had definitely seen better days, Reece gave a heartfelt sigh and ran a strong sinewed hand across his face. Lord, he was tired. There had been nothing but problem after problem this week. And a bad case of secondary flooding on the lower fifth levels hadn't helped either.

The old man took one look at his friend's haggard face and quickly retreated into the kitchen, coming back within minutes with a braised chicken and rice meal, a glass of neat whisky and two items of mail. Reece opened the brown envelope first, knowing it was some papers he'd been expecting from his chief engineer who'd had to fly to San Francisco on a mission of diplomacy and bribery. He grunted as he looked through them, relieved that his latest bout with red tape had been successfully won. At least for the time being. Redex would have no shortage of sapphires this year.

He had forked a healthy amount of chicken and rice into his mouth, and drunk one gulp of his whisky before noticing the postmark on the second letter. He knew the handwriting wasn't his father's, though the postmark was Venice. His innards tightened as his nostrils caught the vague but beautifully familiar scent wafting from the notepaper. Flame! She'd written to him. He couldn't help but feel a warm glow start in the pit of his stomach. She had seemed so far away, so out of reach, and now, suddenly, she was right beside him. He could almost imagine he could reach out and touch her. He missed her so much, he literally ached!

Eagerly, Reece opened the letter and began to read.

CHAPTER 14

Roger heard a car driving up the tree-lined avenue and craned his neck to peer through the top half of the attic window. The car was long and dark blue, and a pretty shape. Since Francesca had taught him how to draw, he always noticed shapes. The car door opened and a man stepped out. Roger had never seen him before. He had silver hair and was smiling. Next came a young girl from the back. She was pretty. And he'd seen her hair before . . . His still handsome, still oddly youthful face creased into a ferocious frown of concentration. Suddenly, he laughed. 'Jessica,' he said. The girl wasn't his grandmother, of course. He knew she had gone to God. But the girl outside had her hair. Had Jessica lent it to her? But then all of Roger's puzzled thoughts were swept away in a giant moment of utter joy, for getting out of the passenger side of the car was Francesca. Francesca! He'd looked after everything for her, and now she was back! But she looked all stiff and scared. Suddenly Roger felt the distance between them, and it hurt him. He had to get to her. Quick! Quick! He began to run. He had to hear her voice again. Quick, quick! See her smile . . .

Flame had thought she was prepared for Ravenscroft, until now. There were flowers everywhere — in the garden, growing up the walls of the house, peeping through hedges and climbing up arches and the stumps of trees. The house was so outstandingly Elizabethan, and the diamond-shaped leaded panes in the windows glinted in all their facets, reminding her of insect eyes. She shivered and looked across at her mother. What must she be feeling now?

Francesca was feeling very odd indeed. It was exactly the same as she remembered and yet different. Malcolm was gone, and without her tormentor the house became just a house again. A huge, old, graceful *object*. Francesca laughed and turned to Owen, walking towards him, her arms outstretched. 'Owen, I'm free. I'm free at last.'

Just at that moment the door literally flew open. Owen, seeing a grey-haired man come charging down the steps like an out-of-control bull, instinctively took a protective step in front of the women. Roger, seeing Francesca disappear behind the silver-haired man's back, skidded to a surprised halt, his feet leaving marks in the gravel. 'Francesca,' Roger wailed, stricken, and Francesca felt her heart leap.

Roger! Dear, sweet Roger, her one and only friend during the nightmare years of her first, short marriage. Quickly, Francesca stepped around Owen, her eyes shining, her arms held out in welcome. 'Francesca,' he said again, and began to shake. His shoulders, still stooped, began to shiver visibly and his hands moved restlessly at the end of his arms, as if he wasn't sure what to do with them.

Flame and Owen realised simultaneously who this childlike man was, as Francesca ran towards him. 'Roger!' She was as quick as a deer. Within seconds she was holding Roger's trembling body in her arms, aware of his warm breath burrowing in her neck and of the small, quiet whimpers that rumbled through his chest. 'Oh, Roger, I've missed you so,' she said at last, taking a step back to look at him, careful to keep her hands firmly on his shoulders, remembering how it upset him to be released too suddenly. 'How handsome you still are. And young! You don't look a day older than when I left.'

'Silver,' Roger said.

'Yes, your hair is silver now, instead of gold. But I like silver better,' Francesca assured him.

Roger's mouth gaped open. He thought he hadn't forgotten a single thing about his best friend in the whole wide world, but he had. He'd forgotten how she could be so right about everything. She pointed out things he'd never even think of if he lived to be a hundred. 'Love you, Francesca. Knew you'd al-always come back.'

Flame, watching them together, seeing for herself the intent devotion in Roger's eyes for her mother, felt tears of her own slip down her cheeks and she hastily rubbed them away. Owen, relaxing now after the initial tenseness of the meeting, licked his suddenly dry lips. He'd never had to deal with mental disability before. He only hoped he didn't blow it. He wanted Roger to be friends with him, too.

'I never wanted to go away and leave you. You do know that, don't you?' Francesca said anxiously.

Roger nodded emphatically. 'Know. Was there. Heard him make you go away. Hate him.'

Francesca shook her head, her face becoming serious. 'No, Roger. You mustn't hate Malcolm. Hate is a bad thing.'

Roger's trembling increased with shocking speed and a very real fear sprang into his eyes. 'Francesca? I done something bad?'

Francesca shook her head and took his large, trembling hands in hers. 'No, Roger, you haven't done anything bad. I'll always love you,' Francesca said, her voice breaking.

Roger grinned again, the simple, uninhibited expression of joy changing his face utterly. 'Love Francesca.'

Francesca nodded, her heart full. 'I know. Roger, I want you to meet . . .' She tugged gently on Roger's hand, leading him to her family, and he came as docilely as a cow being led to the milking shed. 'Do you remember my other baby?'

'Not Justin?'

'That's right. The little baby I took with me. Remember?'

'Remember,' Roger said, his chin tucking down into his chest in shyness as the girl with Jessica's hair smiled at him.

'Well, this is that baby, all grown up. This is my daughter, Flame.'

Roger's chin touched his sternum, but he lifted his eyes. Vulnerable, slightly scared eyes. Flame reacted without thinking. 'Hello, Uncle Roger. I love you too.'

'You do?'

'Yes. Mamma's told me all about you. You're one of the main reasons I've come to Ravenscroft today. To meet you.'

Roger's mouth fell open for the second time. No one had ever come to see *him* before.

Francesca squeezed her daughter's hand in mute thanks, then turned to Owen. 'And this man is my husband, Roger. His name is Owen.'

Roger frowned. 'Husband means Malcolm.'

'Not this time, Roger,' Francesca said gently. 'You see, when a husband dies, his wife is free to take another husband. Do you see?'

Roger stared at Owen. 'Husband bad,' he insisted.

'No, Roger. Malcolm was bad . . . as my husband, I mean,' Francesca added hastily. 'Owen as my husband is good, Roger.'

Owen, realising Roger was still staring at him in a mixture of wariness and bravado, knew it was going to be up to him. He smiled. 'Roger, I don't want to hurt Francesca. I want her to be happy. To protect her. Understand?'

Roger frowned. 'Protect?' he said thoughtfully, then nodded. 'Yes. Protect her. All right.' He smiled, and Owen felt a warm glow spread into his heart. 'I protect Justin,' Roger said, unaware that the mention of his name put the tension right back into the small group again. 'Knew you wanted me to watch over him. So I did.'

'You've been looking after Justin for me?' Francesca repeated. 'Oh, Roger, you're more . . . more wonderful than I remembered. Thank you. Thank you.' She kissed him on his eyes, just as Roger remembered, and when he opened them again she was rubbing the back of his hand across her cheek, a thing she only ever did when something special happened.

Suddenly, Roger remembered. 'Painting,' he said, tugging on her arm, forgetting his own strength so that Francesca was nearly pulled off her feet.

'Roger, wait. Not so quick,' Francesca smiled, not at all alarmed by his sudden show of strength, remembering of old that it was born only of an eagerness to please. They were in the hall now. The same grandfather clock ticked ponderously in the same corner. The same suits of armour gleamed dully in the dim light. Owen and Flame kept close behind them as Roger mounted the stairs, his hand still firmly clasping that of his Francesca. Halfway up the stairs Francesca stopped dead, making Roger turn in surprise and follow the line of her eyes. On the wall was her painting of him. Roger nodded.

'Put it there this morning. Forgot.'

In the portrait, Roger was seated on a rocking horse and rays of sun came through a window. The sweet, innocent, almost shockingly naive handsomeness of its subject was breathtaking. 'It's your masterpiece, Mamma,' Flame gasped.

Roger was impatient. 'Painting,' he said, and tugged again, jerking Francesca ever upwards. She knew where they were headed of course. The attics. Roger led them straight to a corner room and threw open the door. Scattered around were the oddest of items: a twenty-year-old perfume bottle, yellowed and cracked. A pair of shoes, an old comb that still bore some strands of her dark hair. A crystal-bead necklace she'd long since forgotten.

'Roger. They . . . they were all mine,' she whispered.

Flame was instantly reminded of a shrine. It was touching, yet disturbing. For a second Flame felt cold, as if a ghostly hand passed through her, tickling her heart as it went. Then Flame let out a small, involuntary gasp. Everyone turned to look at her and then at the painting she was staring at. It was Francesca, of course. She was sitting on the floor, looking slightly to her left. A disembodied hand, obviously not her own, was rubbing against her cheek. The painting was crude, obviously the work of an amateur but just as obviously that artist's own private masterpiece. For, shining above the lack of balance, the disproportionate length of leg and the size of the head, love shone in the painting. Warmth, tenderness, togetherness, *devotion* became epitomized by the smoothness of the girl's cheek and the chunky hand it was touching. Francesca's cheek. Roger's hand.

Francesca moved towards it on legs she could hardly feel. 'Roger!' she breathed. 'I never . . . we never got around to paints.'

'I used your paints,' Roger admitted. 'Remembered how you used paints. Wanted you to stay here.'

'And in this painting, she did stay, didn't she?' Flame whispered, swallowing a hard lump in her throat.

Downstairs, Justin poured his second brandy and stared out of the open salon windows. He'd seen their arrival and heard them come into the hall. Everything in him had been poised, quivering, ready. And for what? They hadn't even called out his name. He threw himself into a high-backed leather chair with enormous deep wings, where he felt safe. He stretched his legs in front of him, seeing where his heels had worn a thin spot in the carpet. The carpet was his too. Every stone, every piece of wood, every bit of plaster in the house was his. Not Roger's. Not his darling mother's. Not the billionaire she had married.

Justin took another swallow of Cognac. He'd decided the best way to handle his mother would be to become her long-lost son. Play up to her and exacerbate whatever guilty feelings she might still harbour about leaving him. And he'd been ready to do just that. Ready with the fatted calf. Ready with the red-carpet welcome. Ready to hug and kiss and even cry, if he thought it was called for. And what had happened? They'd fawned over Roger and disappeared into the damned attics! It was almost funny. Justin could feel laughter, a tight, burning laughter begin to bubble in his chest, and he closed his eyes, his fingers tightening on the glass, making it shake. Why hadn't they come to him, if only to deride him, to demand things of him? To tell him he was a bastard, or a victim, or something. Anything. But their absence was more than he could stand. Not even his mother could be bothered to put him before anything else, just for once in his life.

The glass, unable to withstand the brutal pressure of his tightening fingers, suddenly broke. Justin yelped, staring at his hand in numbed surprise. The glass had cut him in several places, the stinging alcohol quickly finding the cuts and adding to his pain. He shook his hand angrily, like a dog shaking itself after being stung by a wasp, and pieces of glass fell from his lap on to the carpet. They were quickly followed by his drops of blood. Justin stared at them, mesmerized. At that moment the door opened and Justin looked up, panic in his eyes. But it was only the butler. 'Get some plasters and antiseptic. And a bowl of warm water,' he snapped grimly.

On the stairs, Francesca watched the butler hurry away. She so wanted to meet her son that she felt physically ill. 'Oh God, why did I let myself be distracted? Roger . . .'

'Roger's need was immediate,' Owen interrupted quietly. 'He needed you utterly and totally. You responded in the only way you could. Justin's a lucky man to have you as his mother.'

Flame nodded. 'Owen's right, Mamma. I know you've been thinking of Justin all the time. So have I.' Francesca nodded, but this was not the way she'd wanted things to be. All she'd ever wanted was to find Justin, hold him safe in her arms and tell him how much she loved him. Why hadn't it happened that way?

The butler came back, carrying a bowl of water and a small first-aid kit, and all but ran into them, loitering in the hall. 'Oh. Er . . . my lady . . . I mean Mrs Dexter. Er . . . your son is in the blue salon. If you'd like to follow me.'

Francesca moved stiffly, very much aware that now the time was upon her, she was completely unprepared for this moment. Flame followed, not sure what she felt. Or wanted. She'd never had a brother, and yet she was about to meet her twin. What if he hated her on sight? What if . . . ?

The door was open and the butler hurried in, setting the bowl down on a piece of Sheraton furniture. Francesca, Owen and Flame stared silently at the man standing in front of the fireplace. He was dressed casually in a white shirt, faded jeans, and comfortable, obviously old riding boots. He was lean, tall, blond-haired and incredibly good-looking. He looked just like his photographs and yet the reality of his flesh and blood — most of all his blood — made him seem somehow *more* than real.

'Your water and antiseptic, my lord,' the butler said, beginning to turn a queasy shade of green, a colour that deepened as Justin took a deep breath and pulled a particularly large piece of glass from the soft pad of his thumb. Justin, tight-lipped, looked up in time to see his manservant sway alarmingly. 'That'll be all, Chamberlain,' he dismissed with a wry smile. 'Take a bottle of something from the drinks cabinet. You look terrible.'

'Yes, my lord. Thank you,' the butler said, quickly backing out and around Francesca, who was stood rock-still halfway through the door. Justin poured a good dollop of antiseptic into the bowl of water and dunked in his hand, breathing sharply at the stinging pain. He looked up from the reddening water and his eyes went straight to those of his mother. They were brown and stricken.

'Are you all right?' Francesca whispered, white to the lips.

Justin looked puzzled for a moment, then pulled his hand from the water. Immediately blood began to trickle from the cuts. 'Oh, this? Yes, it's worse than it looks.' He nodded at the carpet, still littered with the remains of his glass. 'I was having a celebratory drink, and the glass shattered. After being around for five hundred years or so, you can't blame it for going brittle.'

Francesca feasted on his voice, even as a roaring began to sound distantly in her ears. This was her son. Her son!

Justin dunked his hand once more into the water and reached for a towel and quickly wrapped it around his hand.

Slowly, he turned from the table. 'So, you're Francesca,' he said, his voice emotionless. He seemed so cool. So . . . unapproachable.

Francesca nodded. The last time she'd seen him, seen the colour of his skin, seen the movement of his limbs, felt the impact of his eyes, he'd been only weeks old. She'd been able to hold him in the crook of her arm as easily as a bouquet of flowers. Now he was a man, taller than she was. She felt the sadness hit her like a tidal wave. All the years she'd missed. His first steps. His first tooth. His first naughty prank. His first girlfriend. The terrible numbness swirled around her. She'd had to give him up. Malcolm had physically ejected her from the house, yelling at her, telling her she could have the brat, that daughters were useless, but that his son would stay in Ravenscroft. She could still feel the awful sensation of helplessness as she'd watched the door slam, cutting her off from her baby. She felt suddenly as cold as she had then, and her legs buckled. Blackness rushed up, rapidly enveloping her. 'Justin,' she said, and fainted.

Justin blinked and watched her collapse into a heap on the floor, for a moment too surprised even to think. Owen was the first to move. Rushing to his wife, he knelt beside her and lifted her head from the floor and checked the pulse in her neck. Flame, for the first time in her life, felt a moment of paralyzing indecision. Then she turned and looked at her brother. Justin, echoing her, turned at the same precise moment. Blue eyes locked with dark brown. 'You're Halcyone?' he said, once more angry at the name his sister had been given. It was as if the jewellery empire was already hers, since they shared the name.

'Flame,' she corrected automatically, feeling distinctly unreal.

Justin's eyes narrowed for a moment on the colour of her hair. For the first time he noticed how lovely she was. She was wearing a light silver and green summer dress, a simple, pleated affair that she wore with all the panache of a fashion model. Her face, he was shocked to realise, looked a lot like a feminine version of his own, despite her dark eyes. He turned away from her, pained by the revelation, and glanced once more at Francesca, still pale and inert in Owen's arms. 'Is she all right?' he said, his voice quiet and controlled.

Owen looked up. 'I think so. She's just . . . overwhelmed by everything.'

'There's some brandy in the cabinet. I'll get her some,' Justin offered.

Francesca, slowly opening her eyes and only dimly aware of what was going on, watched his retreating back with longing, stricken eyes. Mutely she held out her arms to him, wanting him, needing him, loving him so much she felt she could hardly breathe.

But Justin didn't see.

Justin never did.

CHAPTER 15

Justin knew she was watching him because he could feel her eyes on him like a physical caress. It unnerved him, but at the same time strangely calmed him. At least she was now giving him her full attention. He poured a measure of brandy with quiet, methodical efficiency and turned, bringing the offering back to the woman now being helped to the sofa by her husband. Justin stood in front of her, the brandy glass outstretched. Her face was returning to a more healthy honey tan. Her wide eyes were no longer so stricken, and when she accepted the glass from him he forced himself to withstand the jolt of her eager, hungry look. How could this woman be his mother?

'Are you feeling better now?' he asked politely, backing off just a step but still unable to break free of her orbit. She had the pulling power of a pulsar, a star determined to drag every bit of debris into its field and destroy it. Like a natural catastrophe, she had come into his life and wrecked it. He hated her, and yet, in spite of himself, Justin was fascinated. For his mother was beautiful, and he hadn't expected that. She was also much younger-looking than he'd expected, and well dressed in a cream dress with an orange trim.

'I am feeling better now. Thank you,' Francesca murmured, her hand shaking a little on the glass as she brought it to her still pale lips and took a tentative sip.

'If I'd known you fainted at the sight of blood I'd have stood with my hands behind my back,' Justin heard his voice gently tease, and felt his lips curl into a whimsical smile.

'It wasn't that,' Francesca said, twiddling the glass nervously in her fingers. 'It was seeing you again, after all this time. I've wanted it so much, yearned for it for so long, that now it has finally happened . . .' She shrugged helplessly, all the time her eyes fixed on him, drinking him in. This beautiful young man in front of her was her son! Half of her had gone into making him; her labour and sweat had been the power that had impelled him into this world he now inhabited with such ease and assurance. But how could she now possibly fit into his world, a world that had been built without her? How could she find a place in his life, when he had no need of her?

Justin, aware only of the strangely burning, oddly unfamiliar emotion in her eyes, could feel the draining power of her attention, sapping him of his anger, his pain, his will. He turned abruptly away and found himself facing Flame. All at once he felt surrounded; outnumbered, outmanoeuvred. He needed to change it — quickly. Get back once more in the driving position. Raising one eyebrow, he smiled at her. 'I don't suppose you're a nurse?'

'Nurse? No,' Flame shook her head, feeling just a little tongue-tied in front of this cool Adonis-like male who was her brother. She hadn't the faintest idea how his mind worked. Didn't have even the smallest clue as to what made him tick. But she was no longer the eager little college girl she'd been just a few short months ago, ignorant of life and love. Intellectually, she wasn't at all intimidated by her brother, his fancy house and his very English nature. In other ways, though, she knew she was vulnerable. After all, she and this man, this stranger, owned half of Halcyone's each, and she needed it in her life, now more than ever. She craved a salve to paste over the heart that Reece Dexter had so blithely broken, and what better salve was there than work? She would throw herself into Halcyone's and slowly but surely push Reece out of her thoughts. But what must Justin think of her, just walking in, out of the blue, to claim her share?

Suddenly, Flame became aware of pressures she had not even considered before. She was his sister, the one who had received, by any measure, the thick end of the wedge. In Francesca, America and the Corraldo family, Flame had had all the love, attention, luck and privileges that anyone could possibly hope for. He, by stark contrast, had been left behind with a man whose very nature was cold and cruel. Flame couldn't help but feel that she owed this stranger a great debt. It was an added burden that she was only now beginning to understand.

'Why do you want to know if I'm a nurse?' she asked curiously, knowing she could never just blurt out her thoughts, but would have to employ patience and persistence if she was ever going to know this reticent young man better.

'I thought you might lend me a hand,' Justin lifted his injured hand with a wry smile, 'if you'll pardon the pun.'

Flame smiled. 'Of course. Come here, let's see if the bleeding's stopped.' Together they walked to the bowl and Flame carefully peeled away the towel. Most of the bleeding had stopped, revealing several deep but small cuts. 'It's not as bad as it first looked,' she said to her mother around Justin's broad shoulder, and gave her a reassuring smile.

Francesca nodded, feeling more and more human by the moment, and took another reviving sip of her brandy, watching her children avidly as Flame competently rubbed antiseptic on to her brother's cuts and then covered them with surgical plasters. How right they looked together! How wrong it had been to raise them apart. Twins, Francesca thought fiercely, were special. They had shared a womb, shared nourishment and protection together. Right from the very start of life they were joined, irrevocably.

Justin was fascinated by his sister's closeness to him after all this time. How often he had heard Malcolm denigrate her, shrugging off her presence in the world as sheer irrelevance. Now she seemed to him to be anything but irrelevant. When she was finished, Justin looked down at his throbbing hand and found it trembling slightly. Quickly he let it hang by his side and with his free hand pulled the bell rope above the mantel. Within minutes Chamberlain came reluctantly into the room, a dustpan and brush in his hand. 'You can take the things away now, Chamberlain,' Justin said blandly, his voice neither condescending nor familiar, his eyes barely flickering over the servant as he came into the room.

Flame, Francesca and Owen watched in silence as Chamberlain deftly cleared away the broken glass and retrieved the bowl and its accoutrements. Each were thinking much the same thing. How very much the Lord of the Manor Justin was. Francesca and Flame had always lived in a house where servants cooked and cleaned for them, of course, and Owen and Reece had lived with a housekeeper ever since his wife had died, but both the Corraldos and the Dexters had very different relationships with their employees from the one being played out in front of them now, enjoying a mutual first-name relationship that bore no mark of servility. But Justin, in all probability, didn't even know Chamberlain's first name. He didn't ask, he ordered. And Chamberlain oozed respect and servility in every pore. Owen felt sorry for him. Francesca felt a shiver of unease, remembering how the servants had all talked about Malcolm behind his back. Did this man Chamberlain complain about her son too, in the privacy of the kitchens?

Flame wasn't sure what to think. She hadn't expected Justin to fall into their arms in welcome; that was patently not the English way. On the other hand, he was not being openly antagonistic. He was not angry with them, or at least not openly so. Both Flame and Francesca had discussed this meeting at some length, and had been prepared for almost anything, including downright rejection. But this was still somewhat unnerving.

Justin took a seat in his favourite leather chair and stretched his impressive legs out in front of him. His gaze, direct and unflinching, took turns settling on each of them. Francesca, feeling the worst of the meeting was behind them now, began to relax. All she had prayed for was a chance. And it seemed Justin was prepared to give her that.

'Justin I . . . feel I have to talk to you. Get it all out in the open. Do you mind?' Francesca began, her voice quiet and yet possessing a power Justin was only just beginning to understand. He felt a swift wave of panic rise and then quickly fall in his gut. He smiled.

'Of course not. That's why you came, isn't it? To talk.'

'To explain, perhaps, more than anything. That's what has hurt me the most all these years,' Francesca continued simply. 'Not being able to explain things to you.'

Justin wished he had a glass of brandy himself as he felt those eyes sucking him dry. He'd had no practice with mothers. He'd didn't know how to protect himself from their brand of talons.

'What exactly did your father tell you?' Francesca, after a moment's hesitation, decided that only honesty, stark, simple, and in its purest form, would suffice now.

'Tell me?' Justin stalled desperately. He'd already had to contend with every destructive emotion going — hate, envy, jealousy, despair. Did she have to add confusion as well?

'Malcolm must have told you something about why I wasn't here during your childhood. What was it, Justin? I have to know. Before we can even begin to . . . to . . . understand one another, we must understand the past.' Francesca was on the very edge of the sofa now, leaning towards him urgently.

Justin shrugged, unwilling to be dragged down into the depths of melodrama. 'He didn't talk about you much,' he lied, hoping the words made her feel unimportant. 'I gathered that your marriage was one of passion, a spur-of-the-moment thing he quickly regretted. And knowing Father, I expect he made you begin to regret it too.' Justin, angry at himself for giving her even that much credit, plunged on. 'You got fed up with him, he with you. The only problem, as I see it, was us. Halcyone and me.'

'Flame,' Flame put in quietly.

'Sorry. Flame and me,' Justin corrected with a faintly mocking smile, then turned to his mother again. 'In the circumstances, I suppose the decision you made seemed logical. You wanted to split, you had two kids. So you gave the boy to the father and then took the daughter for yourself. It seems simple enough.'

Francesca closed her eyes briefly, a tight ache in her throat making her pause before being able to continue. 'I thought it had to be something like that.'

'So you grew up,' Owen said slowly, 'thinking that your mother left you of her own accord?'

Justin tensed. Suddenly he was on thin ice and he didn't like it. 'That's how I saw it.'

'It's not true,' Francesca said simply. She didn't raise her voice, she didn't protest, she didn't rant or rave, just stated it as a fact. A fact that Justin believed for one giddying, wonderful moment. Then he shrugged.

'Does it really matter?'

'Of course it matters!' Flame cried, her voice echoing the shock in her eyes. 'How can you say that? Mamma never left you! She never abandoned you. Malcolm forced her to go.'

Justin glanced at her, surprised by her sudden passion. What did it matter to her? She'd grown up in a cosy little home, all Italian sweetness and light. '*Dad* made her leave?' Justin deliberately used the word 'dad' and watched Flame flush guiltily.

'That's exactly what happened,' Francesca said. 'I found out he was having an affair. It . . . I won't deny, it gave me an excuse to ask for a divorce. But he was terrified I'd be given custody of you. So . . . he threw me out of the house, saying I could have Flame but not you.'

Justin was silent for a long time. He knew how his father's mind had worked. And yet . . . 'Why didn't you fight for me?'

Francesca almost flinched. With a mother's keen ear she could hear the little boy under the whiplash tone, easily decipher the cry from the heart and accurately read the agony behind the anger.

'I did!'

'She did!'

'She did. Like a mad thing!'

All three spoke at once, but it was Flame who spoke last and most vehemently. 'I grew up with you, Justin, although you might not know it. Every day Mamma and Grandpa and their lawyers would talk about their strategy. I grew up hearing about court cases and custody cases, ward-of-court cases, everything the law could think of in order to get you back. And always Mal— our father, won. I listened to Mamma crying every night when she lost the latest round. She fought for you constantly for every year you grew up! She fought with everything in her — I know. I was there!' Flame heard her voice breaking with frustration and unshed tears and took a deep, shaking breath. She had to make him see. It was so vitally important. But before she could continue, Owen took up the challenge.

'You've grown up at the top of this country's hierarchy, Justin. You must know more than anyone how impossible it would have been for your mother to get custody of you. You were living in England, heir to an earldom and millions of pounds' worth of estates. Your father was alive and well and so very, very well connected in the legal world. How would it have gone? Malcolm would have called up an old Etonian friend of his who was sitting on the bench? Judge X. Invited him down to the old club? Had a good meal and a good glass of port? And then got around to this bothersome custody case. Some Italian tart trying to take your son, eh? Can't have that, old boy. That's how it would have gone, isn't it, Justin?'

Justin sighed and ran a weary hand over his forehead. Grimly, he nodded. 'Yes, that's how it could have happened.'

'That's how it did happen, Justin,' Francesca said quietly. 'I never gave up fighting for you. Not until your eighteenth birthday, when I knew you could come and see me of your own free will. And I wrote a letter, asking you to come.'

Justin started. 'Letter?'

Francesca sighed deeply. 'You didn't get it, did you?'

Justin's lips twisted grimly. 'You should have had more sense than to send it here. Dad—' He stopped abruptly, aware he was revealing much more than he had intended. 'No, I didn't receive it,' he said simply.

'I didn't write to you here,' Francesca said quietly. 'I wrote to you at your school. I thought you would definitely receive it there . . .' She trailed off as their eyes met, both thinking the same thing. It was left to Justin to voice it.

'So. Dad had his spies even there.'

'What did he tell you about Mamma?' Flame asked curiously, and Justin shrugged impatiently.

'He put her down, of course. What can you expect?' Then, looking challengingly at his twin, asked bluntly, 'And did the Corraldos sing his praises to the rafters?'

'No,' Flame admitted quietly. 'Nor did they lie.'

'How do you know?' Justin shot back, angered by her certainty. It wasn't fair that she could be so sure and secure while he was awash with confusion. He'd been comfortable with his illusions. Now they were being shattered one by one and he felt helplessly adrift, badly in need of a place to anchor himself. But where?

'I know my mother would never lie to me,' Flame answered him directly, and that was when Justin knew how wonderful Francesca must have been as a mother. Suddenly he was consumed by jealousy. Why hadn't he been the one to grow up able to speak with that quiet, simple, sure voice? The bitch! Why should she have all the good luck? 'And she'd never lie to you, either,' Flame added, thankfully unaware of his suddenly violent and vindictive thoughts.

Justin took a deep, calming breath. He was overwhelmed by what he was hearing, these revelations from the past — if they were even true, of course. And the confusion of it all just made him angrier. He would stick to the plan: play them along, keep them off guard. He could take on the role of strayed lamb returning gratefully to the loving fold, couldn't he? By the time they'd learned he'd grown from lamb to wolf, it would be too late. Halcyone's would be his. It was the one thing that mattered in all of this. The past was the past. His father was dead. Only Halcyone's mattered now. Oh, they were clever, these people. They hadn't even mentioned it. Did they really think he was so stupid? They were here for him only to estimate how easily they could take Halcyone's from him. He'd heard rumours that Corraldo's had kicked Flame out. The famous Conte, it seemed, was hardly impressed with her. He also knew the fuss her so-called designs were making. His oh-so-sweet sister was determined that Halcyone's should be hers. And Francesca, the perfect mother, was determined she should have it. Over his dead body!

He managed a wan smile as he turned to his mother. 'So,' he said softly. 'You're never going to lie to me?'

Francesca felt a cold shiver snake down her spine and determinedly ignored it. Justin was due his anger and disbelief. It would take time, but she would make him see. Make him understand that she loved him. 'No. I won't ever lie to you. I love you too much ever to do that.'

Justin smiled. 'You already have lied. How could you love me? You don't even know me.'

Francesca paled, but after a moment reached into her bag and brought out a long set of pictures in a plastic billfold. Justin all but reared back as she offered it to him. 'It's you,' Francesca said. 'I carry you around with me, always.'

He saw a picture taken at his sixth birthday party. One taken at Eton. The latest was of him in a rowing boat. 'How did you come by these?'

'I had to keep in contact with you somehow,' Francesca said simply. She was no fool — she knew that underneath his air of charm and politeness he must be seething, and she could sense in him a sinister, almost unnatural self-control that alarmed her. 'I had to watch you grow up in the only way I could . . .' Francesca swallowed hard. 'Justin?' Justin looked up from the photographs of himself, unaware that his eyes had darkened to a stormy grey. 'I cheered when I received reports about your wins at cricket. I cried when I heard about your dog — Toby, wasn't it? — having to be put down.'

'Reports?' Justin latched on to the single word and Flame stiffened. There was something dangerous in the air suddenly. Something . . . alien. Something unhealthy.

'You have to understand,' Francesca cried. 'I loved you. I missed you. I needed to be with you in any way I could. So I learned about your life, sharing in it as best I could.'

'By spying on me?' Justin said softly. 'These pictures . . .' he waved the billfold vaguely in the air, his eyes fixed on those of his mother. 'They were taken with a telephoto lens, weren't they?'

'Yes. Your father wouldn't let me, or anyone representing me, anywhere near you. I was forced to resort to drastic measures.'

Justin nodded, his eyes now almost pewter in colour. 'Like hiring a private detective to sp— watch me for you?'

'Yes. I had to make sure you were safe.'

'Safe?' Justin half barked, half laughed. 'With my father? Do you know how twisted . . . oh, forget it.' Abruptly he folded the photos away, snapped shut the billfold and handed it back. 'I'm flattered that you cared enough to go to all the trouble,' he lied with such throwaway ease that even he was surprised.

The bitch had been spying on him all these years. Had her seedy little PI been anywhere about when he'd taken his first girl to bed? Had he taken a little snap of him on a loo somewhere? Was nothing sacred to this woman with the magnetic orbit? Well he, for one, was not going to get sucked in. His sister was obviously under her spell, as was her latest husband. Now he understood that his feelings of being watched, of having spies all around him, were justified. His paranoia doubled, his head whirling with the possibilities of betrayal and treachery. Who reported back to her from Halcyone's? Had her spies been around at Henley? Did they know about his humiliating loss of Flick? Did they know about George? Justin forced himself to take a deep breath. He couldn't panic. Not now. But she was pitiless, this woman. Worse than his father. His father had never . . .

'Justin, you're quite pale. Are you feeling all right?' It was Flame who spoke, forcing him back from the precipice. Yes, Flame. His beautiful little sister. His mother's pet. His enemy. Well, they wouldn't have Halcyone's. Never!

'You must want to see your rooms and unpack,' he said with a courteous smile. 'I know Uncle Roger will be glad to have your company . . . again.' He got up, aching all over. Hell, he was tired. These Corraldo women were formidable adversaries. And to think he'd almost succumbed, almost let them fool him into thinking they actually cared about him. Holding out like a carrot the tempting promise of love, while all the time ferreting out his weak spots. But he had their measure now. Oh yes, he understood them now all right . . .

'You will be all right, won't you?' Francesca asked anxiously, standing up and quickly walking towards him, her hands reaching out to clutch his shoulders. 'Your hand . . . ?'

Justin managed to stand his ground and manfully gritted his teeth as her hands touched him. How gentle they were. How full of love and concern her eyes looked. How deadly she was.

But he was deadlier. He would win.

Justin nodded. 'Oh yes,' he said softly, his own eyes looking warm, his own voice sounding gentle and trusting. 'I'll be all right. I can promise you that.'

CHAPTER 16

Flame knew she could not go forward until she had said goodbye to Wendy Gibbs properly. She still harboured too much guilt over her friend, still wondered constantly if she could have prevented the wastefulness of her death. And until she made peace with her dead friend, she'd have no peace at all. The day was hot, one of September's last hurrahs to summer, and she and Roger were sitting on the banks of the river that crossed the boundaries of Ravenscroft's grounds near a charmingly disused watermill, set amid weeping willows. How Wendy would have loved to paint it. She knew, too, that Wendy would have enjoyed Flame's own success. The women Flame had designed pieces for were ecstatically happy with the finished jewels. One, a countess, had worn her piece to a Royal Gala Performance, and a leading fashion magazine had featured it in one of their articles.

The countess's unique and lovely jewellery, she happily told us, was the design of a young lady I'm sure we're all going to hear more about in the coming weeks. The co-owner of one of our most prestigious firms, Halcyone's, she is set for a glittering career.

It had reaffirmed her decision to dedicate her talents to jewellery, and her mother had been delighted. It had been much harder to gauge her brother's reaction, however. When she had shown him the clip he'd read it with every outward appearance of being pleased, but his eyes had worn that now all-too-familiar look of calm caution. It was as if he was waiting for something to happen . . . waiting for her or Francesca to hurt him in some way.

But the time was coming for Flame to visit Halcyone's and familiarize herself with her inheritance. Justin's reluctance to let her see it worried her. And it worried Owen more, Flame could tell. Their weekend at Ravenscroft had been extended. It was now Thursday, and still Justin had made no hints about their leaving. And while he didn't, Flame knew, Francesca wanted to stay. Her delight in simply being in Justin's company was impossible to deny. It was obvious from the look in her eyes whenever Justin came into the room. It was obvious in her voice whenever she talked to him. But, Flame thought, a frown replacing her earlier smile, was it obvious to Justin? Flame didn't think so. Had his obviously nightmarish existence with Malcolm made him incapable of believing in anything good, anything loving? Although Justin himself never talked about his father, there were hints about how barren his childhood must have been. Hints from the older people in the village who remembered things. Hints from some of Justin's friends they'd met over the days. Hints in the things Justin said, or didn't say. And the more they learned, the more Owen and Flame worried.

'Got one!' the voice all but shouted in her ear, and Flame nearly leaped out of her skin. She turned just in time to see Roger straighten up from his stomach, where he'd been leaning over the river, dangling a jam jar in his left hand. In the jam jar were two minnows, tiny fish that teemed in the clear, unpolluted waters at Ravenscroft. 'Pretty. Blue, red,' Roger said excitedly, and Flame leaned easily against her uncle's solid form as she looked closer at the jam jar. The minnows did, indeed, have a red and blue stripe down their small sides.

'They're like rainbow trout, only much smaller,' she said, and looked on, warmly amused, as Roger laughed long and loud.

'Eat trout. These are small.'

Flame laughed. 'You like trout, don't you?'

'Yes. Like eating.'

Flame, beginning to develop her mother's uncanny rapport with this lovely man, knew there was something more behind the words. She thought about it, and then nodded. 'You like eating with us, don't you? At night, all together. Francesca and me, and Justin and Owen?'

'Yes.' Roger, with fierce concentration, tipped the minnows out into a bucket where five more of their fellows swam in glum consternation, and squelched a piece of white bread into the bottom of the jam jar. Then, on its piece of old kitchen string, he slowly, delicately lowered the jar into the water.

Flame lay on her stomach beside him, uncaring if her face got muddy or if her dress got grass stains on it. She rested her chin on her hands and sighed contentedly. They'd have made a good portrait for Wendy. A good artist would be able to capture Roger's uncanny patience. He had the stillness of a hunting leopard and yet the gentleness of a lamb. When he'd had enough, the fish would be tipped back into the river, suffering nothing more than inconvenience for his sport. A good artist would make full use of the dying summer countryside around them, the touches of ochre and orange beginning to appear in the bushes and grasses around them. A good artist. Like Wendy. She must say goodbye to her. Until she did, she knew, she'd never really be able to accept it. She had to go and say goodbye. Fly to Kansas, where she had been returned to her shocked family to be buried. Flame sat up abruptly. Until she saw the stone for herself, with Wendy's name on it, until she saw the wilting flowers on her grave, she couldn't let her go.

'I'm going back now, Roger.' Flame gently laid a hand on Roger's tense shoulder and saw him turn his head.

'Go home?'

'Yes. I have to tell Mamma something. Are you going to carry on fishing?' Roger nodded. Flame slowly got to her feet and hunted in the grass for her flip-flops. A tiny, cooling breeze played across the top of the river and lifted the hem of her summer dress. With another smile at her uncle she turned and began the long walk back to the house. She wasn't afraid of leaving Roger alone. She knew he could swim.

Wendy Gibbs had never been able to swim.

* * *

In the library, Justin picked up the phone. In front of him was a magazine, a famous and prestigious women's magazine that did the rounds in the finest homes of England. In the centre spread was a piece about a party a certain socialite had given. Nothing unusual or noteworthy in that, of course. Except that she was wearing what the women's editor called 'a Halcyone original, as stunning a piece of jewellery as I've ever seen.' Except the piece had not come from Halcyone's design workshop. It had come from his sister. His dear little sister whose fame as a designer, both in Italy due to Giulietta's handiwork and now in Britain, was fast growing. And her talent, Justin had begun to realise over the last few days, was becoming the most dangerous thing about her. There were others, of course. She was bright, but thankfully still trusting, and he'd managed so far to keep her away from Woodstock. She was also stunningly beautiful, but at least, being his sister, she could never use that weapon against him.

He'd used his time well. He'd watched all three of his visitors, listening, learning, making mental notes. And the most interesting titbit of all was the fact that his twin was nursing a broken heart. But who had broken it? Someone in Venice? And could he use it to his advantage?

He dialled the number and waited. Scott answered on the eighth ring, sounding angry and breathless. It wasn't hard to guess what he'd interrupted. 'Scott, it's me. Have you seen the latest *Deb's Debut?*'

'What? Oh, that rag. No, why?' In the background a querulous female voice asked him to come back to bed.

'Well, buy a copy. Read it and weep. Then get your arse over here. Pack a bag; you can stay this weekend. It's time you met my loving family.' He hung up before Scott could protest, then stared at the photo. In it some ageing matron had shot a precocious smile at the camera taking the picture. She was dressed in fussy sapphire silk, her hair piled up in a ridiculous pompadour. But her own stupid sense of dress and obvious delight in publicity only succeeded in making the one piece of excellence on her body stand out all the more. It fairly leaped out at the reader, who, in most cases, would be women of rank and money. It was the necklace. Sapphires, diamonds and, of all things, amber, leaped out at the eye. The odd combination should have clashed, should have looked stupid and amateurish, but instead it looked determinedly original, defiantly fresh, bright and professionally brilliant. Damn her! With a snarl Justin picked up the magazine and threw it into the fireplace. It was not lit, of course, but the symbolic burning was completed in his mind. He'd have to burn her, too, of course. Flame. Flame by name. And Flame by fate. He'd burn her all right. And soon.

Outside, Roger watched him from the shadows of the hall. He'd forgotten the minnows now. But he remembered something else. He remembered another time when Justin had been upset. The night when Malcolm had gone to the roof to look at his stars. The *last* night that Malcolm had gone to look at the stars . . .

* * *

During the same hour that Flame flew from Heathrow Airport to New York, where she intended to take another flight to Wichita, Reece Dexter left his makeshift bungalow deep in the heart of Colombia in a battered jeep. Flame was sad, and anxious about the ordeal ahead of her. Reece was livid. The letter burned a hole in his pocket. He careered over the rutted road, bouncing around inside the less than luxuriously sprung jeep, getting bruises he barely noticed. He'd had women, of course, but no one special. That was why she'd been able to take him by surprise. He'd fallen in love without even realising it at first, but he was not a man to be afraid. He'd needed time to think and make sure he didn't blow it — for both their sakes. And then, out of the blue, *she* had the gall to write to him, accusing him of stealing her designs. As if they were so *damned* precious. As if he cared a jot about them. And it hurt, dammit, it *hurt* that she thought so little of him. Well, he'd see if she still had the gall to make him out to be a villain when they were face to face. Then they'd see if she cared to take up where she'd left off, in person rather than on paper. And if she didn't have the sense to apologize and back down . . .

Reece's handsome face curved into a smile of almost blissful anticipation as the jeep hurtled towards the small airport where he'd had his private jet flown in. His blood was boiling as the jeep skidded to a halt outside the ramshackle buildings. He could see his Learjet, sparkling and looking incongruously out of place at the end of the grass runway, but he had a telephone call to make first.

The line was atrocious, and it took some time to get the operator to track down Ravenscroft's number, but eventually he managed to get through to his father. Holding one finger in his free ear in an effort to better hear over the crackles and whines, he shouted, 'Dad? Dad? It's Reece. Can you hear me?'

'Reece. I . . . the mine was . . . everything OK?'

Reece cursed the state of the Colombian telephone system and raised his voice another notch, ignoring the radar operators, who looked at him with fascination. It was not often they got Learjets landing at their airstrip, and whenever they did it was due to a drug-running operation. 'Dad, where is Flame now? Is she there?'

'No. Going . . . airport.'

'Which airport?'

'Kennedy. Leaving for Kansas . . . at . . .'

'When?' Reece roared, all but shattering the windows in the tiny control room, his eyes squinting as he tried to make out his father's words. 'Noon flight to . . . the 25th. OK? But, Reece, she's . . . bad news . . .'

It was impossible to hear, but he'd learned what he needed to know. He yelled goodbye and hung up, then glanced at his watch. Why the hell was she going to Kansas of all places? But time was too short to ponder that one, so he nodded to the gaping airport officials and left the building at a run. It was a long jog to the plane but he wasn't even out of breath as the co-pilot lowered the steps for him. He gave him their destination and leaned back in his seat, absently fastening the belt. He'd be in New York long before her flight was due. Slowly, he began to smile. They needed a private place to start their own version of World War Three, and what could be more discreet than a private jet, flying thousands of feet above the earth? Cocooned from the world, far away from protective relatives, far away from help. Reece's smile turned to a grin. They'd see how brave she would be then.

The days in Colombia had been long, miserable and lonely, and the thought of seeing her again was intoxicating. He cursed himself for being a fool, for falling for a woman who was so dangerous, but he comforted himself with the realisation that soon they'd have the whole sorry mess sorted out. He was a man who always handled his problems rationally. When he wasn't being goaded beyond endurance by a certain red-haired cyclone . . . And if she really thought she could write poison letters to him and not have them rammed back down her audacious, lovely little throat, she was in for one hell of a rude awakening.

And he felt like just the man to give it to her!

CHAPTER 17

Flame's plane arrived at New York from Heathrow dead on time. She disembarked wearing the black outfit she had chosen, having decided against changing on the plane or booking into a hotel. The dress was satin, with a modest V-neckline, long, tight-fitting sleeves and a pleated, elegant skirt that came three inches below her knees. She wore medium-heeled shoes of black velvet that showed off her ankles and slender calves to perfect effect. She was just about to take a seat when a middle-aged man dressed in a pilot's uniform stopped her. 'Lady Flame Syramore-Forbes?' He held out an ID card. 'I'm Colin Doyle, one of the pilots for the Dexter Corporation. Our private jet is waiting for you at the end of the runway. Mr Dexter thought you might prefer to travel privately.'

Flame smiled. How like Owen to be so thoughtful.

'There's a limousine waiting, your ladyship. May I take your case?' Flame had packed only an overnight case and smiled as she handed it over.

The jet was a picture of sleek power. Stencilled on its side in gold lettering were the words 'Dexter' and the aircraft's individual numbering. But as she left the car and followed the attentive pilot up the portable stairs into the plane she suddenly felt uneasy. Her spine was icy, as if trying to warn her of something. She almost laughed at herself, when, once aboard, she looked around the luxurious interior. Opposite her was a black swivel chair, positioned with its back towards her. It was facing a large coffee table in the middle of the single cabin, which was stacked with up-to-date magazines and light reading. Another comfortable chair sat opposite, and in one corner was a coffee machine. Nothing sinister to be seen! She moved forward, the carpet beneath her feet making her feel as if she were walking on cotton wool. Behind her the door closed. The pilot secured the hatch and nodded to her with a polite smile before disappearing quickly into the cockpit and shutting the door behind him. A moment later she heard and felt the powerful engines roar into life. Quickly she headed for the chair facing her and it wasn't until she sat down, buckled her belt and then faced front that she saw that the chair that had had its back to her was occupied.

Reece had the immense satisfaction of seeing the colour drain from her face. He'd been aware of her the moment she stepped into the plane, of course — he could hear her quiet breathing, even though his own heart thundered in his chest. He could smell her light, flowery fragrance and his skin had erupted into gooseflesh as she had unknowingly passed him. Now, looking into her eyes, wide and dark with dismay, he fought back the giddying rush of pleasure just the sight of her gave him, and smiled mockingly.

'Hello, Flame.'

She blinked. At first she thought she was imagining him; that her yearning for him had at last made her crack, causing her to conjure his image out of thin air. But the coolness of his voice quickly put her right on that score. 'I didn't expect to see you again,' she said, her voice even colder than his.

'I can imagine,' Reece said, his voice grim but his eyes strangely bleak. 'Now that you've had your say, me having mine would only be a nuisance. Isn't that so?'

Flame frowned. She didn't have the faintest idea what he was talking about, and she wasn't going to stay to find out. Angrily she began to unfasten her belt.

'Don't be a fool,' Reece snapped. 'We're already taking off. Do it back up!' He barked the final order at a near shout, and he watched in irresistible admiration as her chin shot up and her eyes flashed defiance. But Flame could feel the powerful plane racing along the runway and she rebuckled her belt, her mouth mutinous. 'Now, where exactly is it you want to go?'

'I know where I'd like *for you* to go,' she hissed, her eyes glittering like onyx.

Reece, in spite of himself, laughed. 'Temper, Lady Forbes, temper. Now be a good little girl and let me know where you want to go. Pilots get nervous if they don't know where they're supposed to steer the plane.' For a moment, Flame stared at him, tempted to tell him she wanted to have the plane turned around, but that would sound childish. And, from the glint in his eye, it was exactly what he was expecting.

'Wichita,' she said, forcing the words out like crushed ice. Reece's eyebrow shot up and disappeared into his silky dark hair and her fingers itched to smooth an errant lock back against his head.

'What's in Wichita?' he asked, his voice rich with amusement.

Suddenly her face lost its defiance and a pinched, tight look he couldn't remember seeing before flickered across her eyes. She swallowed hard and looked out of the window as the skyscrapers of New York receded below. 'Wendy is,' she said simply. 'You remember her? You met her at the airport when she flew to Venice for the summer vacation.'

Reece's eyes narrowed. There was more to this than met the eye. 'I remember Wendy,' he said, his voice fond. 'She was the one with the good taste.' Flame looked at him curiously. 'She liked me,' Reece reminded her, his eyes twinkling.

'Just goes to show she never did have any sense!' she shot back, then felt awful — not for Reece but for Wendy. 'Oh, God, I never meant that,' she said and slumped back in her chair. Leaning her head against the cushioned rest, she closed her eyes. 'She's dead,' she said dully, the words sounding so final she felt herself shudder.

Reece's eyes turned bleak for a long, long moment. Then he unbuckled his belt, although the seatbelt sign was still on, and knelt down beside her. Slowly, he reached out and ran a finger gently down her cheek, wincing as she shied away from him. 'I'm sorry,' he said, all anger and amusement gone from his voice now.

Flame opened her eyes and looked down at him. His face was so close that her breath suddenly became a rare commodity. His eyes were fixed on hers, those fascinating orange flecks in the grey irises almost shimmering. She could see that he'd forgotten to shave that morning, and, without a thought for the consequences, the backs of her fingers rubbed experimentally against his strong, square chin. His bristles rubbed pleasantly. Hastily she snatched her hand away. 'I . . . I missed the funeral but . . . I heard about it the same day I discovered you'd stolen my designs.' Suddenly her voice was rock-hard again, and the look she turned on him was one of contempt.

Reece abruptly remembered the letter and stood up, moving away from her as if she were contaminated. Looking down at her, he cursed himself for being a fool a second time.

'I'm sorry about Wendy,' he said, and meant it. She'd been a funny, quirky little thing. It seemed such a waste. 'How did it happen?' he asked, walking to a panel in the plane's side and opening it out. A small but fully stocked bar awaited inside. He poured himself a measure of Scotch and added ice and water. For her, he poured a small glass of brandy. When he turned, she was still watching him, her body tense with unspoken anger, her eyes fixed on his with wary caution. Wordlessly he handed her the drink then moved back to his seat.

'Why did you come here, Reece?' Flame asked, ignoring his question. She was looking down into her glass as she spoke, but when she heard a rustle she looked up to find Reece holding out paper. She made no move to take it. She already knew what it was. Her letter. Again her chin came up an extra inch. 'If you're waiting for me to apologize for that—'

'I wouldn't be so stupid,' he interrupted her ruthlessly, a habit of his that she was beginning to get used to. 'The day you actually take responsibility for anything you do will be a day worth noting in my diary. What I would like, however, is an explanation.'

Flame, stung by his accusation, caught her breath quickly. 'I would have thought that was self-evident,' she shot back, leaning forward in her seat and only then realising she still had on her belt. Angrily she grappled with it, but couldn't get the dratted thing undone.

With a long-suffering sigh, Reece left his chair again and knelt down beside her, ignoring her as she reared back. His fingers undid the belt, yanking on it angrily. As he did so, his fingers skidded across her thigh, and Flame gasped. Ignoring her, Reece went back to his seat, but his hand was shaking as he retrieved the glass.

Just then a buzzer sounded, and Flame watched Reece depress a small button on the armrest of his chair. 'Yes?'

'We're on course for Kansas City, Mr Dexter, but you weren't sure that was our final destination?' Flame recognized the pilot's voice and felt like kissing him. His intervention had at least given her a few minutes' breathing space. And did she need it! She was breathing as heavily as if she'd just run a hundred-yard sprint.

'Is there an airport at Wichita that can take us? If so, land there and have a car waiting, please.'

'Yes, Mr Dexter.'

'Please,' Flame repeated, her voice mocking. 'I never thought I'd ever hear you say that.'

'My father taught me manners,' Reece gritted, annoyed at her criticism. 'Which is more than I can say about your mother. Just where do you get off, writing something like this?' He waved the letter angrily in the air between them. 'Or did you think you were safe, since I was thousands of miles away?'

Flame felt anything but safe, but she was not going to be intimidated. 'I stand by everything I say in that letter,' she shot back, her voice rising to the level of his.

'Like hell!' Reece snarled back, leaning his hands flatly against the coffee table, his face thrust aggressively towards hers. 'This says I snuck about Giulietta's home and commandeered those designs of yours.'

'Yes. It does, doesn't it?' Flame said sweetly.

Reece's expression didn't change. His eyes still glittered dangerously, like a thunderstorm, complete with its own lightning. 'Come on, Flame. You have a brain as well as . . .' he gulped noisily 'everything else. Are you trying to tell me you never use it? Or don't you have to?' he implied insultingly.

'Why you . . . you . . . of course I have a brain! And use it!' She heard herself screeching like a harridan and took a shaky breath. 'Right from the start you wanted those designs. You even called me in to Redex to talk about them. What's the matter, Reece?' she asked, her voice becoming sarcastic now. 'Aren't you used to being turned down? Did I hurt your fragile male ego that much?'

'You're making no sense, girl — zero,' Reece argued, making her feel annoyingly unsure of herself. 'Tell me something, sweetheart, what's to stop you suing me for theft?'

'Nothing!' she shot back, stung.

'Precisely. But if those designs of yours suddenly turn up for sale at Corraldo's, what do you do then, Flame?' he asked softly, and saw the blood drain out of her face. 'Do you sue your own family? No doubt the Conte will have passed them on to someone unsuspecting. Your mother's younger brother, perhaps? Think about it,' he added, his voice softening at the stricken look in her eyes. 'The Conte hates your guts. It would be no problem for him to bribe one of Giulietta's staff to steal the portfolio. He knew damn well you wouldn't be able to do a thing about it.'

Flame opened her mouth, then closed it again. She didn't know what to say. it made such perfect, appalling sense.

'I hate to have to break it to you, *sweetheart,*' he mocked, his eyes almost playful now, 'but those designs of yours aren't *that* important to me. I went to Venice to bid for the di Maggiore commission.'

Flame smiled, as nasty a smile as Reece had ever seen. It looked so painfully out of place on her beautiful face that he itched to kiss it off her smirking lips. 'OK, *honey bunch,*' she said softly, leaning her own hands on the table now, their faces only inches apart. 'I admit I wasn't thinking straight about the designs. But I sure had you figured out in other departments. You went after the Principessa di Maggiore with everything you've got,' she drawled suggestively, and her eyes strayed downwards, past his eyes, down the deep, strong course of his chest, to the waist of his jeans and down below, where she could see the bulge of his manhood. Beneath her very eyes it swelled against his jeans, and she felt an answering contraction deep inside her. Startled, she looked up into his eyes, which were so close to hers now that she could see the irises dilate.

'You evil-minded little vixen,' he said, but he was grinning as he said it, and for Flame that was the final straw. 'Don't tell me you're jeal—'

Flame hit him. And it was no delicate slap either. She put everything she had into it, swivelling her whole weight in the chair and whiplashing it back. Her hand tingled painfully as it connected with his cheek, and she shook her fingers automatically, just managing to stop herself from yelling in the process. Reece's eyes were wide with shock. Flame stared at him, appalled. His eyes were way past thunderstorms now; they were in the territory of hurricanes.

'I hope you enjoyed that,' Reece said, his voice so calm and neutral that Flame felt momentarily lost. Until his next words made it clear exactly where she was — right up the creek! 'Because I'm going to enjoy immensely what happens next,' he all but whispered, and moved.

Flame had never in her life seen anybody move that quickly. One moment he was facing her, a solid coffee table between them, the next he was on top of her, hauling her out of the chair and on to her feet. She didn't even have time to gasp before his mouth was on hers, his tongue thrusting into the unprepared sweetness within. She moaned, but not in fright, as she felt his hands find hers and fold them against her back, pushing her body up against the entire length of his. She could feel the muscles of his chest pressing against her breasts, and her nipples sprang to immediate, sensational attention. Her belly quivered against the belt of his jeans, and her knees buckled as she felt the thrusting power of his manhood swell against her inner thighs. Her breath began to ache in her lungs and small pinpoints of light were just beginning to dot her vision when Reece finally lifted his lips, allowing him to watch her draw in a deep, ragged breath.

Her eyes were like hot chocolate now, rich and sweet and irresistible. Without a word, he hooked his feet around her ankles and overbalanced her, only his strong arms and lithe grace preventing her from toppling to the floor like a sack of potatoes. He lay over her, his hands still on hers, only now holding them prisoner on either side of her head. He gazed down at her, breathing harshly, one side of his cheek redder than the other where she had hit him. His lips swooped once more on to hers, and she opened up beneath him, their tongues doing an exotic duel. Flame gasped as she felt him transfer both her hands into one of his, her body tingling in anticipation of his touch.

She moaned, undulating beneath him as he caressed one breast through the cool satin of her dress. His hands moved down, stroking over her belly, tracing the material to the hem and then slipping beneath to stroke her legs. Flame gasped, her panties becoming damp with desire as he stroked up past her stockings and on to her bare, sensitive skin. Her eyes feathered closed as his finger cunningly rubbed against her cleft and, through the material, found her small bud of pleasure and began to rub. Her legs lost all power, and her back arched helplessly, thrusting her ever harder against him. In response, he increased the speed and pressure and Flame found herself bursting into waves of rippling pleasure. She gasped, drawing breath straight from him, robbing him of his own precious oxygen. Their lips drew apart at last, both gasping for air. She opened her eyes then but he was already moving down her body.

Although he took his remaining hand away from hers, she still lay motionless on the aircraft floor, her hands above her head. Quickly he reached beneath her and pulled down the zipper of her dress, pulling it up and away from her, baring her shoulders and strapless bra. He unbuttoned the front-fastening undergarment and threw it away, where it landed against the beige carpeting, a small, defiant scrap of black silk. He stared down at her for a long moment, and then his palms were against her nipples, rubbing in circular caresses that once more had her eyes closing in ecstasy. When his tongue replaced his hands Flame cried out, uncaring if they could be heard by the pilot and co-pilot in the cockpit. She only knew she had been waiting for this for so long, even though she hadn't realised it. She felt the dress being pulled down and along her legs, the cool satin making her shiver. Then his hands were tugging down her damp panties, and her heels dug fiercely into the carpet as his hands separated her thighs and his lips found the very heart of her femininity.

Reece inhaled her musky, intoxicating scent as his teeth nibbled delicately on the small, throbbing rosebud against his tongue. He brought her swiftly to climax, and as she lay, shaking in the aftermath, he rose unsteadily to his feet. Just what was it about her that ensnared him so? He didn't know, or care. He only knew he wanted her, totally, completely, and with an urgency that was intolerable. So they weren't going to have a cultured, civilized relationship but a hectic rollercoaster ride. Did it really matter? All his life he'd been sensible, responsible, level-headed. This was one problem that couldn't be tackled logically, and he'd been a fool to try. As if a few weeks apart to sort out where they stood had done one damned whit of good!

He could feel her eyes on him as he tugged his shirt off over his head, too impatient to undo the buttons. Their eyes melded together as he dropped his hands to unbuckle his belt. Her eyes left his only long enough to feast on his proud, erect manhood as he slid off his jeans and knelt once more beside her. She reached for him, her fingers running up his ribcage and to his nipples, where they tweaked and playfully pinched. Her heart thundered in triumph at the look on his face, which was tight with desire. She could still see the imprint of her four fingers and thumb on his cheek, but they stood out as white now against his tanned, healthy flesh. His hair was rumpled and mussed, and she felt her body clamour for him. There was no mistaking the mute appeal in her eyes, and Reece quickly reacted to the urging tug of her hands. Smoothly, he slid between her thighs and felt her calves hook around his in a strong, erotic clamp. Her hands dug into his buttocks, her body rising in a silent demand to hurry. Reece pushed into her with one sure, smooth motion, her tight body cradling him so completely that he had to grit his teeth and use every ounce of willpower not to explode into her there and then.

Flame cried out his name at their union, and her nails raked his back. She'd forgotten everything, save their passion. Her hair spilled back against the carpet, like a pool of fire, and Reece pushed his fingers into it, his lips once more finding hers. He moved above her, rising and then thrusting into her, using his great strength to make sure he didn't crush her, while at the same time making sure that their coupling was as complete as it was possible for a man and woman to make it.

Flame felt first one, then two, then three rippling orgasms tear through her body, and she clung to him as if they were two pieces of wreckage floating on a storm-tossed sea. She heard him curse and then groan, and watched as his eyes became glazed, losing all sense of self, all sense of control. She felt his warm semen flood into her, and her hands clutched possessively at his shoulders. She felt his collapsing weight pin her to the floor with a warm smile of wonderment, and tenderly stroked his dampened hair as his head fell on to her cushioning breasts. He drew in great, ragged gasps that, she dimly realised, her own body was also making, and a sense of gentle relief swept through her.

It was going to be all right after all. How could it not be, when they could make each other feel like this?

* * *

She awoke to the sound of buzzing. For a second she was totally disorientated. There was a droning sound that seemed vaguely sinister and she was staring at the leg of a chair. She shot up as someone moved behind her and all at once realised where she was. The jet! Behind her Reece pulled himself up into the chair and, naked as the day he was born, pressed the button on the arm rest. His eyes, however, were on her. 'Yes?'

'Ten minutes until Wichita, Mr Dexter.'

Flame scrambled for her clothes, hopping from foot to foot as she tried with more haste than grace to slip into her panties. 'Thanks, Colin.' He watched, a gentle smile curving his lips as she put on her bra, fumbling with the catch. He licked his lower lip, remembering when she had bitten it. It had been the last time . . .

'Aren't you getting dressed?' Her voice, small and unsure, broke into his pleasant thoughts, and he smiled.

'Sure. Scared I'll disembark buck-naked?'

'It wouldn't surprise me,' she said saucily, and then, as she looked down at the black dress in her hands, her face changed. Wendy!

Understanding at once, Reece wordlessly climbed into his clothes and finger-combed his hair. He watched as Flame reached into her handbag and repaired her make-up. The silence was a gentle one. Often their eyes met, lingered and then moved back to overseeing other movements. Reece the fastening of his seatbelt, Flame the reapplication of her lipstick. It didn't matter. They could feast their eyes on the sight of each other whenever they wanted. They'd both forgotten past suspicions and past angers. They had no place in the present, sad but tender silence.

The car that waited for them was a long black sedan, and as Flame consulted the map that was in the glove compartment, Reece drove towards Wendy's home town. On the outskirts, they stopped and asked for directions to the cemetery. They found it easily. The church was wooden, with peeling white paint, and the graves were lined up in neat rows. Wendy's was easy to find — it was the last one in the last row. Great mounds of dead flowers crackled drily in the wind. Flame stumbled on the uneven ground as they made their way towards it, and Reece's hand shot up to her elbow, holding her steady. She glanced at him gratefully. 'I'm so glad you're here,' she whispered, her words so quiet they were almost lost on the breeze. But he heard, and his hand squeezed her arm, giving her strength. 'Oh, Wendy,' she whispered, her vision of the block of granite wavering as tears sprang to her eyes. 'You deserved so much more.'

In the car, she had told Reece the way Wendy had died, and she could see by his expression that he was as angry and puzzled as she was. Why did things like this happen?

She bent down to her friend's grave, pushed some of the dead flowers aside and laid down her own. 'Goodbye, Wendy,' she whispered, but only a solitary crow flying overhead answered her.

CHAPTER 18

Flame collected her rental car at Heathrow and quickly headed for the motorway. Beside her, Reece watched her driving, surreptitiously admiring her skill. Her skirt slid smoothly around her legs whenever she used the pedals, and he found his eyes straying again and again to the point where her seatbelt rubbed against her breasts. When he caught her looking at him with a shy, gentle smile on her face, he grinned back.

'Face it, cyclone. You're like catnip.'

Flame laughed. 'Catnip? How romantic. And why do you call me cyclone?'

'It's a legacy from that day I first saw you. You stormed out of my office leaving the place looking as if it had been hit by a cyclone.'

'The place?' she queried softly, glad of the excuse of driving to keep her eyes on the road instead of on him.

'All right then. Me. You left me feeling as if I'd been hit by a cyclone. And not just the once, either,' he added slyly, and in an instant they were on the gondola again. Flame swallowed hard and almost missed her exit off the motorway.

Reece studied the beauty of the passing English scenery with interest. He planned to set up a Redex store in London, but he wasn't in any great hurry. England was such a beautiful, ancient, peaceful place that Reece found it hard to think of work at all, which was a new sensation for him.

Flame watched him, whenever traffic permitted, and smiled to herself at his nickname for her. Cyclone. Well, at least she'd made an impression!

By the time she turned into the Ravenscroft drive, Flame had convinced herself that she and Reece had put the rocky past behind them and were ready to start work on a brand-new future. They were so different in many ways, but she was confident it would happen. She would *make* it happen.

Beside her, Reece stared at the house, giving a low, telling whistle. She grinned at him. 'It's quite something, isn't it?'

It was. It screamed Elizabethan elegance at him as she drew to a halt outside the most impressive set of doors he'd ever seen. There was no doubt about it: his father had married into the English aristocracy. He climbed out of the car and opened the door for her, and as she took his hand, a shiver rippled over her, making her frown. For a moment her fingers clung to his and she was afraid to let go. Then he glanced at her quizzically, looking down at her from his superior height, and the moment passed. Determinedly she let go of his hand and together they turned to enter Ravenscroft.

Scott Tate stepped from the shadows of the vast porch, dressed in casual cream slacks and a light lemon-coloured shirt. With the top two buttons undone in acknowledgement of the heat, he knew he looked good.

The girl was stunning. Why hadn't Justin warned him? 'Hello, I'm Scott Tate. And you must be Lady Flame?'

Flame smiled politely and responded with a brisk handshake. She felt Reece move restively by her side and turned to him, her eyes silently apologizing for their unexpected visitor. 'This is Reece Dexter.'

Scott Tate looked at Reece Dexter and smiled. Reece didn't smile back, but put out his hand, leaving Scott no choice but to take it. 'Hello. You must be Owen's son.' Reece nodded briskly.

'Mamma?' Flame called, heading off in the direction of the blue salon, tugging eagerly on Reece's hand to make sure he followed her when she heard her mother's happy reply. Reminded anew of how young she was, Reece felt a moment's unease. For the first time he became aware that the age gap between them spanned a decade.

Scott watched them go, anger written all over his face. He was not used to failing in the 'first impression' stakes and he knew, instinctively, that he had just experienced a first. Beautiful as she was, young as she was, vulnerable as he had supposed she was, she had won the first round with ease. She was not going to be a pushover. Especially when she had Reece Dexter under her thumb. Scott cursed the big American's presence but knew he could do nothing about it.

At that moment he turned and saw Justin standing half-way down the stairs, watching him. Scott smiled mockingly, wondering how long he'd been there. 'So that's the famous Flame,' he drawled. Justin's eyes never flickered, but a smile played a crooked time on his lips, and Scott fought back the sudden desire to shift restlessly on the balls of his feet. He wasn't sure he could read Justin anymore. 'Were you expecting the visitor she brought with her?'

'No, I wasn't. And it's very interesting they should arrive together,' Justin mused. 'My sister is like . . . a mountain lion, Scott. She's sleek and golden, and quite, quite beautiful. And she's a predator, with claws and teeth. She'll have half of me, if she can. Rip Halcyone's in two and gobble half. But I won't let her. Do you understand?'

And in that instant Scott knew that Justin was not quite sane. Oh, he was rational and functional, and acting normally enough so that anyone who didn't know him would be fooled, but to someone who knew him as well as Scott did . . .

Scott nodded quickly, not wanting to antagonize him. He'd play along, for the moment. He needed time to think. 'She's certainly got our friend from Redex dangling on a string,' he agreed. 'Perhaps that's her weak point. She needs to keep men under her thumb.' He shamelessly played up to Justin's paranoia. There might be something in it for him.

'I doubt Walt would be comfortable under any woman's thumb, and he's Flame's top man in the company. I still think Grandma Jessica was a witch,' Justin mused, looking up the stairs to the portrait of the youthful beauty who had turned into his ancient, wily great-grandmother. 'It was as if she could see into the future, appointing him to look out for things. He's old now, of course, and married with grandchildren. But he's sharp and tough. We'll have to watch him.'

'Have they met yet?'

'No. I've managed to keep them apart. So far. But he's clamouring for a meeting, and since that article about Flame's designs came out . . .'

Scott nodded. Flame had done several more designs for the English nobility, and her reputation was growing amazingly fast. But, at the moment, Scott had more interesting things to think about. Wooing and marrying the half-owner of one of Britain's leading jewellery stores would be a fast way up the ladder for any man of guts, initiative and action. He didn't doubt that he could soon seduce Flame Syramore-Forbes. The Yank would be no problem. Reece Dexter might have a head start, but Scott Tate was a master at breaking couples apart. He'd done it many times in the past when he'd wanted the woman for himself. His only problem now was Justin.

'If I could get close to her, I might learn something useful. She's too vain ever to suspect that *I'd* be the one using *her*. What do you think?' He turned a questioning eye on Justin, outwardly just a man exploring a possibility and seeking an opinion, inwardly a man desperately trying to read what was in Justin's mind. It was impossible. Justin's ice-cool gaze never wavered.

'It wouldn't hurt if you could get close to her,' Justin finally said, but added dampeningly, 'if you think you can.' Scott laughed that off, and Justin watched him saunter away.

For the first time his face registered an expression. It was scorn.

At that moment, Owen came into the hall, no doubt to find out why Justin was not entertaining his precious son.

'Why don't you come and meet Reece?' Owen asked pleasantly. He was interested to see what Reece would make of Justin.

'I'll be in in a minute,' Justin promised tonelessly. Once more alone in the hall, Justin could hear the buzz of female voices, excited, laughing, close and loving. By his sides, his hands clenched into fists. Scott was turning against him, he knew that. Up above, the portrait of Lady Jessica gazed down on him. He could have sworn the eyes were laughing at him.

Slowly, Justin turned and walked in the direction of the salon. And there, Francesca looked up, the familiar expression of longing leaping into her eyes the moment she saw him. Justin was glad that she was so hungry to make him love her. So hungry to make him think she loved him . . .

'Justin,' Francesca said, getting to her feet. 'I want you to meet your stepbrother, Reece.'

Justin took his first good look at Reece Dexter. What he saw shook him. There was strength there. And intelligence. He was not at all like Owen, who had none of his son's obvious power. Instinct told him that this man whistled nobody's tune but his own. He hid his dismay and anxiety instantly, and moved smoothly across the room, holding out his hand, confident that he looked the epitome of a civilized English gentleman. This man would need a very clever kind of manipulation. It would be no good to try and make friends. He was too sharp to believe it. He must think of something more subtle. And he already had a good idea how to turn Reece Dexter's unexpected presence to his own advantage.

'Hello, Reece. Welcome to Ravenscroft.' The two men shook hands, and Reece nodded, his eyes curious. So this was Flame's twin. They looked nothing alike. He met bland blue eyes and saw something darker inside them flicker. What was it? Pain? Anger? Fear? Reece thought fear, but wasn't sure.

'I hope I'm not putting you out, showing up like this.'

Justin shook his head, and said, almost sincerely, 'Not at all. I'm glad you're here.' Reece's eyes narrowed briefly, but then, their mutual sizing-up completed, both men simultaneously moved apart, Reece to stand near the Adam fireplace mantel, and Justin to lounge languidly in a large armchair opposite his sister. 'So, how was . . . everything?' he asked quietly, giving the impression of tentative sympathy.

He looked so unsure of himself and his emotional ground that Francesca had to fight the urge to go to him and cup his tense, pale face in her hands and tell him it was all going to be all right. Only last night in bed, she and Owen had been talking about him, saying how self-controlled he was, how afraid to show any sort of emotion. She knew, deep in her heart, that her son was emotionally stunted. Growing up with Malcolm, how could he not be? For days she'd been trying to gently reintroduce him to his feelings, to show with her own unstinted displays of emotion and love that it was all right to open up, all right to show anger, love, fear, confusion, and everything else that made people human.

Flame, unaware of her mother's thoughts, shrugged tiredly. 'It was a bit grim. I never . . . I never really understood her, you see,' she admitted sadly. 'And now she's gone, I never will.'

Justin looked away, his eyes going to the window, and Francesca sighed. There it was again — that cold curtain. How long would it take her to free him of Malcolm's frigid legacy?

'Justin,' Francesca said softly, and then was lost when he turned to her, one eyebrow half-raised. She shook her head helplessly. 'Are you all right?'

Justin looked into her eyes, once again so anxious to suck him in, and smiled. 'Of course I am. Why?'

Again, Francesca could only shake her head helplessly. 'No reason. You just seemed . . . far away suddenly.'

Justin smiled. He *was* too far away. Too far for her to be able to stick her claws into him. 'Why don't we have tea out on the lawns? Near the rose garden. It's a great day, and Flame needs cheering up.'

'That's a great idea! We'll make it a picnic! I'll go tell Chamberlain.' Francesca left quickly.

Reece sensed that there was a great rift in this strange family, and felt once more like a stranger on the outside, looking in. There were bad vibrations in the air around here, and he glanced at his father curiously. Owen gave an almost imperceptible shrug.

'Well, I'd better go change,' Flame said, once more unable to think of a thing to say to her brother. It was only when she was in the hall, headed for the stairs, that she realised she was shivering. How . . . odd . . . Justin seemed to be. Or was she imagining things? But then a hand touched her shoulder, warm and strong, and she turned to find Reece right behind her.

'Don't tell me a cyclone is afraid of a little frost?' he whispered and winked.

Flame laughed and covered his hand with her own. She leaned closer and gently kissed him, loving the way his lips moved like cushioned velvet beneath hers. She shook her head. 'Justin is so cold, isn't he? But with you around, I'm never scared,' she whispered, and meant it. If she'd known how quickly he would soon leave her, she might not have been so confident.

* * *

As they sat for their picnic, there was a graciousness, a timelessness evident all around them that was perfectly complemented by the raw-throated call of wood pigeons in the trees and the heavy scent of roses on the still, hot air.

Chamberlain had arranged the picnic artfully. The garden table and bench seats were polished to a sheen, a check cloth laid over the table. On it was piled every kind of picnic delicacy Cook had managed to muster in the two and a half hours' notice she'd been given. Roasted chicken legs rested in baskets lined with lettuce, fresh crusty rolls, still warm from the oven, awaited pots of this year's strawberry, raspberry, gooseberry and blackcurrant preserves. A Dundee cake, a rich cherry cake and a farmhouse cake awaited the knife, while plates of ham, cold roast beef from yesterday's joint and sausage purchased from the village store awaited relishes and pickles that had been in Cook's family recipe book for centuries. In tall crystal jugs, ice cubes swam in real lemonade, fruit punch and freshly squeezed orange juice. Dark green Royal Worcester plates lined with real gold sat beside silver cutlery bearing the Ravenscroft crest. In a silver bowl, fruit of every description had been artfully arranged — peaches fresh from the greenhouse and still warm, cherries, plums, bananas, apples, apricots, grapes, oranges and kiwis. It was, Owen thought with affectionate humour as he took his place at one end of the table, a typical picnic, Justin-style. Odd, yet strangely touching. Owen had to admit that he had not been able to understand his stepson at all, except to conclude that he was dangerous. Something was in the air, something nasty, and it worried him.

At the other end of the table, Justin poured himself a glass of lemonade and reached for a bread roll. With calm ease, he inserted his knife into the juicy flesh of a peach with all the cold precision of a surgeon. Behind the ice-blue eyes, his thoughts were writhing. Francesca, aware of the dark undercurrents, sighed unhappily but reached for a roll and handed it to her husband, the gesture intimate and loving. Justin pretended not to notice. Reece watched and listened, and under the table pressed his leg against Flame's. She responded by splaying her fingers across his knee and squeezing. He drew his breath in on a hiss and looked across to see Scott Tate watching him, his hard eyes predatory and angry. Reece felt no anxiety about the other's man's fuming presence. He'd dealt with men like Scott before.

His father looked happy, Reece thought, as the lovely dark-haired woman who was his wife reached for a piece of chicken and offered it to him. Reece felt good about

Francesca. There was a gentleness in her that was both strong and loving. She was not his mother, of course, not Clare, but she was a woman in love.

Francesca caught him watching her, and tensed. Then Reece smiled at her, and in that instant she knew that he had accepted her. There was a blessing in his eyes that was unmistakable. She answered with a radiant smile.

Justin saw it and looked away, giving the impression to anyone watching that he was embarrassed by the open display of affection. But it was not embarrassment that rippled through him. It was pain. The memory of his last visit home from Oxford, when Malcolm was still alive, suddenly flared up in his head. He raised a hand briefly to his temple where a stab of pain pounded beneath his skin and bone and rubbed it gently. Francesca saw the telltale movement, noticed his averted eyes and saw instantly his anguish. Her heart lurched; her conscience shrieked.

'Justin,' she said automatically, then, when he turned to her, she took a deep, shaking breath. How often had she said his name and then, when he looked at her, been unable to say what she wanted, too afraid to reach for the ice wall he'd built around himself and try to melt it down? But she would do it. She had to do it. Although she couldn't have said why, Francesca instinctively knew that time was running out. That something dark and powerful, something hard and painful, was looming on the horizon, and meant to take her son away from her for a second time. Something that had the power to destroy them all.

CHAPTER 19

'I'm going to Halcyone's tomorrow,' Flame said determinedly, and glanced at her mother. 'Do you want to come?' They were all in the lounge, replete from the picnic and feeling mellow.

Francesca sighed. She knew this moment had been coming for a long time, but it didn't make it any easier to deal with. 'No, *cara*, I don't think so,' she said softly. 'Besides, you won't need me,' she added, accepting that her daughter was all grown up now and well able to take care of herself. Francesca couldn't have sided with her against Justin, and Flame wouldn't have expected or wanted her to.

Justin slowly folded the paper he was reading and put it down. 'It's not a good time, Flame,' he said, as he had said so often before, but before he could say more, Flame shook her head.

'I'm going tomorrow,' she repeated, not a trace of antagonism in her voice. Justin stared at her for a long time, but he knew she wouldn't back down.

'I thought that you didn't have much to do with Corraldo's? The business side, I mean.'

'I don't. That's why I need to start learning right away. But I know how well you've done on the administrative side of things, and I wouldn't dream of . . . well . . . pushing in.'

193

Justin smiled wryly. Like hell! His eyes met those of Reece, who was watching them all silently, and his smile twisted. 'It looks as if I'm outnumbered, doesn't it?' he said softly. 'But exactly what is it that you think you can do? Halcyone's already runs like a well-oiled machine.'

'I'm not going to go in like . . . a cyclone, Justin,' Flame said, casting Reece a loving look. 'I just want to look and watch and learn.'

'I see,' Justin said drolly. Flame drew in a deep breath.

'Justin, shall we go into the library?'

He shook his head. 'There's no need for that. You'll obviously get your own way, no matter what I say.' He didn't add the words 'you always do' but they leaped into everybody's mind, as he'd intended.

'You make me sound like a . . .' Flame began hotly, then saw her mother give her a quick, pleading look, and took another deep breath. 'Justin, Halcyone's *is* half mine. I only want to find my place there. I don't want to take it over!'

Justin looked at her and smiled sadly. 'If you say so.' He picked up the paper and began to read. Francesca was torn between the desire to shake him by the shoulders and cry her heart out. He saw them, her, as enemies. It was not fair! It was not *fair*.

Flame felt relieved, ashamed and angry all at once. She glanced at Reece, who was watching her speculatively. Had Justin set him to thinking that she was some sort of spoiled brat? That had obviously been his intention. Then Reece smiled at her, silently applauding her stand, and still so obviously on her side that she almost laughed in relief.

Justin disappeared behind his paper, desperately fighting to keep his fury under control.

The tension seemed slowly to dissipate, and, since it was still such a lovely day, a general migration to the swimming pool, tucked discreetly out of sight of the house in a grove of silver birch trees, took place. Scott Tate decided the opportunity to flirt with Flame was too good to miss, but Reece ignored him. In normal circumstances his presence would have put all of Reece's territorial male instincts on alert, but it was so obvious that Flame didn't feel one whit attracted to him that he could watch them with detached amusement. Although she was talking to Tate, her concentration was on Reece. He could clearly feel her attention, her curiosity and, in a little measure, her concern, even from several yards away.

If she had but known it, she could relax totally. He was through judging her without any proof. Through thinking the worst of her. He was prepared, now, to get to know her in depth, to let this feeling between them run its course and find its own level. Somehow he just knew that it would be on a plane little short of paradise. The thought made him smile, and when she caught him at it, he gave her a tiny salute and turned away. And there was Justin, watching them. Reece straightened and finished the last of his wine.

Justin, to his surprise, leaped agilely from the lounger, quickly taking the hint. 'Come on, I'll show you to a room. You have quite a choice, actually.' Everyone smiled at the understatement, but Flame looked strained. Once out of earshot, Justin absently plucked a moon-daisy from a herbaceous border they were passing and said, 'So you mine gemstones. Any particular kind?'

Reece looked at him, then back to the house. 'I imagine you know exactly what kind,' he answered bluntly, disinclined to play games. 'Dexter's provides at least sixty per cent of Halcyone's yearly quota. Or are you seriously trying to tell me that you haven't thoroughly checked out your new in-laws?'

Justin smiled, and again Reece was surprised that he didn't show petulance, or at least anger. It was what he would have expected of a spoiled aristocrat, and the fact that Justin was refusing to fit the pattern raised his caution to downright wariness. 'Of course I have,' Justin admitted softly. 'And, unless I miss my cue, isn't this where I'm supposed to warn you about my sister? She looks like an angel but fights as dirty as any demon.'

'Why don't you then?' Reece asked softly. 'Warn me.'

'I have a feeling I don't have to,' Justin shrugged. 'Somewhere along the way you had the right idea about her. Before long, she'll slip up again, and you'll get to see her horns once more.'

'And here I was thinking that twins were supposed to be so close,' Reece drawled.

'Close?' Justin looked at Reece and shook his head. 'I'm already too close.' At that, Reece abruptly stopped walking, and Justin did the same. Up until now they'd been sparring, but there was a quality in Justin's voice that changed everything. He sounded genuine.

'You sound afraid,' Reece said, no criticism intended, but Justin flushed.

'You'd be scared of her too, if you had the sense you were born with,' he snapped, then shook his head. 'Just forget I said that. Where's your car? I'll have Chamberlain bring the case in. Which wing would you like to sleep in? If you intend to bring some ladies home from the village, perhaps a room as far away from the rest of us as you can get?'

Reece looked at him steadily. 'I don't think you and I are going to get along,' Reece said, his voice still bland.

'No. It doesn't seem likely,' Justin admitted.

'I'll take a room in the same wing as everyone else,' Reece said abruptly, and wondered why the fire in the cold blue eyes shifted a little.

'Right. This way then.' Justin showed him to a room that was magnificent. Four-poster bed, original tapestries, furniture that screamed 'class' at him, and two paintings that, he felt sure, would have had Sotheby's licking their collective lips. He walked to the windows, which overlooked one of the loveliest valleys he'd ever seen.

'Very nice,' he said, and turned as Chamberlain walked in with his case. It looked very battered and cosmopolitan in the impressive room.

Justin dismissed the servant, then looked briefly at Reece. 'Will you be staying long?'

Reece shrugged. 'Not long. I have to get to Australia.'

'Opals?' Justin hazarded.

'Opals,' Reece acknowledged.

Justin nodded, turned and left. Reece watched the door shutting behind him, and had the very nasty sensation that he had just been had.

Justin descended the stairs thoughtfully. He was not unhappy with Reece Dexter. No. Not unhappy at all. He had such a great deal of potential.

* * *

That night, in the library, Justin and Scott sat alone. Justin poured them a Scotch. 'You've seen to the writs?'

'All but sewn up,' Scott assured him. 'Old Judge Warburton will be free the beginning of October, and we're ready to go. We won't win. Flame's claim on one half of the company is airtight. But that's not the point, is it? The publicity will be bad enough to worry her, but not bad enough, I hope, to do us any lasting damage.'

Justin nodded. So far his mother and sister knew nothing about his plan to take them to court to sue for the other half of Halcyone's. If he could use their need to be well thought of in society to shame them into letting him buy Flame out, so much the better. If not, he'd have to think of something more . . . drastic.

* * *

In the main salon, Flame moved restlessly before the shelf of books, trying to look as if she was choosing some night-time reading. But she was very much aware of the man stretched out on the sofa, making no attempt to hide the fact that he was staring at her. 'What's the matter, Reece?'

He shrugged. 'Nothing.' What could he say? So he didn't like her twin brother. He didn't have to shout it from the rooftops. He watched the way her back tensed at his curt answer, and had the strong urge to get up and kiss her spine, pressing his lips against the cool green cotton of her dress, feeling the heat from her skin beneath his lips. He could almost hear her small gasp of pleasure, almost feel her shiver of reaction. Getting to his feet, he moved towards her. 'What book are you looking for?' His eyes twinkling mischievously, and he added quietly, 'Little sister of mine.'

'I'm not your sister,' Flame spat quickly, giving him a furious look before seeing that he was teasing her. So intent was she on his smiling eyes, she didn't notice the figure that stepped onto the terrace outside the window. 'Oh, Reece. You're impossible,' she scolded.

'*I'm* impossible,' he grinned, looking scandalized. 'You know,' he said softly, reaching out for her and taking her bare arms in his hands, drawing her a step nearer to his solid body, 'when I got that letter I wanted to kill you for thinking so badly of me.' A simple pressure from his hands had her stumbling against him, and although her eyes flashed anger and outrage, her body began to melt as she felt the steady pounding of his heart against her breast and the heat of his skin seeping through her clothes. Flame felt a deep-rooted kick of sexual reaction bolt through her body, and she gasped.

In the doorway, Owen and Francesca came to an abrupt and fascinated halt. Reece was holding Flame close against him and her back was arched away, even as her hands were pressed against his impressive shoulders. Their faces were close and furious, and there was a tension in the room that made the air zing.

'Yeah,' Reece repeated softly. 'But then I thought . . .' his voice dropped to a whisper that only she could hear '. . . if you were dead, what would I do with the rest of my life?' She gasped as his hands, strong and determined, splayed across her back and pulled her even closer into him. Her nipples immediately thrust against his chest and her legs weakened, trembling against his muscular thighs.

'You could always do it and find out,' Flame said, her voice little more than a throaty purr.

'I just might,' Reece said, but his voice was no more than a whisper now and he bent forward and kissed her. The moment their lips met, Flame collapsed against him, only vaguely aware that it was his strength, and his alone, that kept her upright. The tension that had been building inside her all afternoon, making her flit around like a butterfly in a garden of steaming flowers, erupted in a way she had never known possible. In a second she felt, heard and saw everything. The blur of his head coming towards her; the flashing pewter of his eyes. The scrape of his shirt against her breasts; the cool tough denim of his jeans against her bare leg. The sound of his voice; the dull thud of his strong heart in his chest. The smell of him that was soap and aftershave and a certain, indefinable, tangy scent that was all male. And, above all else, the feel of his lips on hers, crushing her and yet not hurting her, the darting spear of his tongue in her mouth, possessing her and yet not diminishing her. She moaned against his lips, pressing closer into his hot, strong body. With one simple kiss, Flame was on fire.

Owen and Francesca drifted away from the door and walked quickly down the hall. Out of earshot they looked at each other, both confused. 'Oh, Owen,' Francesca said, and Owen, unable to do anything else, began to laugh softly. After a second, Francesca too began to laugh. What else could they do?

In the salon, Reece reluctantly, very reluctantly, began to lift his head, but their lips seemed fused. With a moan of defeat he pressed against her again, and Flame's clinging hands pulled him closer.

Outside on the terrace, Justin lounged against the stone balustrade, a cooling September breeze blowing over him. He hardly felt it. He watched the straining couple through the diamond-shaped panes of glass and could feel their passion. And, like Francesca and Owen, he too began to laugh — but for a very different reason.

Reece all but hauled her out of the room. At the foot of the stairs he quickly lifted her into his arms and ran up the flight of stairs to his room, arriving barely out of breath. He slammed the door shut behind him with his foot and carried her over to the bed. His hands pushed away their clothing and feasted on her flesh as he joined her on the mattress. Flame gasped as his lips found her nipples and laved them lovingly. 'No,' she murmured, surprising him into stillness. He tensed as he looked down at her, naked and aroused.

'No?' he queried softly, his eyes curiously vulnerable.

'It's my turn,' she said softly, and with strong hands she pushed on his shoulders, flipping him on to his back and then kneeling over him. The tension went out of his face in a moment, and the orange flecks in his eyes began to expand and flare into pulsating life as she bent and kissed his nipples, delighting in the small sigh he gave. Shyly at first, her hands explored his body, her fingers stroking his arms and shoulders, moving down over his ribcage and across his flat belly. Her lips followed her hands, and when her tongue delved into his navel Reece moaned. Above him, the painted cherubs that adorned the ceiling smiled impishly down at him and Reece grinned back at them. Then Flame's fingers found his manhood, and the smile quickly fled and was replaced by a grimace of pleasure. Her hands cupped his balls gently, marvelling at their silken texture. Curious, she bent her head and licked them delicately and was almost bucked off the bed as Reece thrashed helplessly. Firmly she pushed his thighs apart and tried again, loving the way his head moved from side to side on the pillow. She could feel his powerful thigh muscles contract and quiver and the sense of power she felt was both humbling and elating.

Moving up, she knelt above his up-thrusting penis and waited until he opened his eyes. Then, and only then, did she slowly impale herself on him, gasping as his strength filled her, her eyes locked with his. Her moan mixed with his as she contracted her inner muscles to stroke and tease him. Slowly, rising almost to the tip of his manhood and then back down again, she began to ride him, her head thrown back, her hair flaming down her shoulders. Reece's hands moved to caress her breasts as he watched her exploring and experiencing her womanly powers. She was magnificent. She was his.

In that second he knew they had been destined for each other. He might have fought it, denied it, cursed it. But it was unconquerable. He felt his heart swell with pride and passion, love and happiness as she gazed down at him, moistening her mouth with her pink tongue, her eyes round with wonder one moment, and the next half-closed with passion and satiation. Flame looked down at his face, contorting now as the strength of his orgasm began to cannon through him, and she cried out, her own body climaxing, her own belief and faith in their future strong and alive within her.

'Reece! Reece. I love you.'

'I love you too,' he gasped, his hands reaching out to grab her as she collapsed over him, her body heaving and shaking in pleasure. 'I'll always love you.'

But as the sun set on the beauty that was Ravenscroft, and as they held each other with the tenderness only lovers knew, neither of them could have guessed that in less than twenty-four hours, he'd be gone.

CHAPTER 20

The moment Flame awoke, she felt different. For a few seconds, blinking up at an unfamiliar, curlicued ceiling, she was confused. Then, in a flash, she remembered. Reece! Turning over on to her side, she lay watching him for long, silent, precious minutes. He looked so much younger in sleep, and so much more vulnerable, that she felt a lump rise in her throat. She leaned closer, her fingers gently curling around a lock of rich brown hair on his temple. How long his eyelashes were, and so thick! Her caressing fingers awoke him, and the eyelashes she found so fascinating parted to reveal his thunder-and-lightning eyes. He smiled, his firm, strong lips curling into a look of laughter that changed his whole face. 'Good morning,' he said softly.

'Good morning,' she replied, suddenly shy. She tucked the sheet a little higher over her breasts, the movement making a wayward lock of hair fall over her eyes. Impatiently she moved to brush it back but he was quicker. His hands were gentle as they moved over her scalp and when he lifted his head from the pillow to kiss her, she felt her heart almost stop. It was one of those wonderful moments, the kind you never, ever forgot. 'Reece,' she said gently, and ran her hand over his chest, her fingers itching where the fine mat of silky hairs tickled her skin. 'I meant what I said last night.' Her eyes were almost sombre as they looked into his, and his hands stilled on her silky mane of hair. 'I love you.'

Reece caught his breath and let it out slowly. He'd woken up beside women before, some of whom had even said 'I love you'. But he'd never said it back. Or wanted to. Until now. 'Thank you,' he said gently, his large, calloused hand cupping her cheek, his thumb rubbing gently just below her eye. 'I love you too.'

Flame looked at him anxiously. 'Don't say it if you don't mean it.'

'I never say what I don't mean,' he replied, and cocked his head to one side. 'What's wrong?'

'Nothing. It's just that . . . we had such a bad start. I wasn't even sure that I liked you at first and you made it more than clear that you didn't trust me,' she said, a huge but slightly questioning grin spreading across her face.

Reece laughed drily. 'I made myself that clear, huh?'

'As crystal!'

'Well, even I make mistakes sometimes,' he teased, his voice oozing such arrogant magnanimity that she thumped him playfully on the shoulder. 'Ouch. It's not smart to damage the goods when they already belong to you,' he reproached, ostentatiously rubbing his shoulder.

Flame looked him deeply in the eyes. 'And are you mine, Reece? I mean, *really* mine?'

'Always,' he promised softly, relieved to see the worried look in her eyes fade away. 'Now, don't you think you'd better go back to your own room and get dressed? Just in case your mother, or my father, come a-calling?'

Flame giggled as she tiptoed back to her own room, feeling deliciously wanton. Reece laughed softly and folded his arms behind his head. Above him the cherubs grinned down. So, he was committed at last. For the first time in his life, he was in love. It felt good. No, more than good. It felt wonderful!

Back in her room, Flame quickly showered and chose her outfit carefully. The dress she chose was predominantly white, made of gauzy chiffon, and cut on the most simple of lines. Sleeveless, it had a deeply cut 'V' at both neck and back, an elasticated waist and a billowing skirt. A pair of white strappy sandals emphasised her shapely calves and ankles, as she skipped to her dressing table. There she donned the lightest of make-up, just a dusting of tawny eyeshadow, a touch of mascara, and a coating of peach-coloured lipstick. She decided on an elegant French pleat for her hair. She was ready for Woodstock. Or at least, as ready as she'd ever be.

Sighing slightly, she made her way to the dining room, where Francesca looked up from her cup of coffee and the morning paper. Owen greeted her with a kiss on the cheek, and Flame took a plate and walked to the buffet table, selecting crispy bacon and scrambled egg from the vast array of choices. She had just taken a seat, and told herself she didn't care that Reece wasn't there, when he walked through the door.

'I thought I heard the sound of food being served,' he said cheerfully, his eyes hungrily going to the buffet table laden with eggs, bacon, sausages, kippers, fruit, cereals and toast. He was dressed in faded Levi's, a loose white shirt, and worn, comfortable-looking brown leather boots. His hair was still damp from the shower, his chin newly shaved, and he smelt of soap and aftershave. He still moved with a lithe grace that made Flame gasp. Never before had she met a man who exuded such raw power. Reece Dexter reminded her of a wolf. And he was *her* wolf.

He sat next to her, and immediately her every instinct leaped into awareness of him. She would swear she could feel the heat from his skin sliding across the few inches separating them, playing on the bare skin of her arms. She didn't need to look to know that gooseflesh had spread across her skin.

Across the table, Owen and Francesca watched, fascinated by the contrasting sight they made — Flame so beautiful, young and feisty, Reece so handsome, laid-back and powerful. Francesca couldn't help but feel excited for her daughter. And afraid. She knew what it meant to be overwhelmed by a man. Not that she was comparing Reece with Malcolm, of course, but still . . . A woman was so helpless when it came to fighting her own heart.

In the doorway, Roger hesitated. He hadn't come down yesterday because he'd seen the stranger arriving. Now he moved from foot to foot, his movement catching Reece's eye.

'Roger!' Francesca rose from the table to gently lead him by the hand. 'Roger, this is Reece. Owen's son. Reece, this is Roger.'

Flame had told Reece all about Roger on the plane back from Kansas, and now he stood slowly and held out his hand. Roger's eyes widened as he rose and continued to rise. He was taller than anyone Roger had ever met before. Then he spoke.

'Hello, Roger. I'm glad to meet you at last. Flame and Francesca talk about you all the time.' As Roger shrugged his sloping shoulders and lowered his eyes shyly, tucking his chin defensively into his chest, Reece waited, still holding out his hand. Eventually Roger looked up at his hand. Slowly, he put his own hand into that of the tall stranger's grip. He felt strange lumps and hard bumps on the hand, and when Reece pulled it away Roger stared at them, intrigued. He didn't know hands could be hard. Everyone else's were all soft. Reece glanced quizzically at Francesca, who smiled and gave a slight shrug. She knew Roger would speak in his own good time.

Once Roger had helped himself to breakfast, he sat down and hunched over his food, eating quickly and with intense concentration, seeming to forget that anyone else existed. Reece watched him, his eyes gentle, and the sight warmed Flame's heart.

It was just when she was looking at Reece so adoringly that Justin and Scott walked through the door. Justin hadn't been sleeping well. Although he looked as handsome as ever, and greeted everyone with his usual polite charm, Francesca wondered if he was feeling ill. It would be impossible to tell with Justin. That damned English reserve of his would demand that he keep up appearances no matter what. And, of course, today was the day Flame went to Halcyone's for the first time. He was obviously miserable about it.

'Has everybody made plans for the day?' Owen asked, determined to break the silent deadlock. There was something darker uncoiling behind the tense silences that worried him. He didn't want Francesca caught in the middle.

'Yes. Reece and I are going to Woodstock today,' Flame spoke first and quickly, determined to get it over with. 'I think it's long past time I took a look at Halcyone's for myself.'

'You haven't visited shop?' It was Roger who spoke, his voice so surprised that even Justin felt uncomfortable.

'No, not yet, Uncle Roger,' Flame admitted, wondering how she could possibly explain it to him. 'I . . .' Flame glanced quickly at Justin and found his expression had not changed. She found herself unexpectedly feeling sorry for him. 'I've been busy with my own work.'

'Pretty pictures?'

'Yes. Pretty pictures.'

'Flame designs jewellery, Roger,' Francesca said. 'Already she's had several reviews in the best magazines. And she's already designed several pieces for the English aristocracy.'

'Have you kept a record of them?' Reece asked softly, and Flame looked at him, suddenly anxious to show him her newest designs. His opinion meant so much to her, and he would be able to tell her honestly if she had really ironed out all her kinks since doing her first set of designs. She knew she'd learned a lot technically, and was impatient to know what he thought of her latest creations.

'I'll look them out for you,' she said, then added teasingly, 'but, Mr Chairman of Redex, they're not for sale.'

Francesca drew her breath in sharply. Why was Flame playing with fire like this? But, amazingly, Reece laughed, looking not at all angry at the near-insolent hint. 'I'll remember that.' He gave her a speaking look, which she weathered with a wide grin, and then, sensing his stepmother's discomfort, turned to Francesca and began to talk, keeping the conversation purposefully light, away from any subjects that could be misconstrued.

At ten o'clock the party had split up into distinct groups. Owen and Francesca left for Oxford, a city Owen had fallen in love with on sight, and Justin and Scott retired to the library to discuss business. Flame, walking into the hall and very much aware that Reece was behind her, turned and gave him a heart-stopping look over her shoulder. 'The designs are in my room,' she husked.

'I'd like to see your designs, Flame,' Reece said, his eyes twinkling with laughter.

'Oh, you! You're impossible,' Flame laughed, and ran lightly up the stairs. Right behind her, watching her back, watching the way the skirt of her dress swished against her shapely legs, watching the way her hips and delightfully rounded derriere swayed as she walked, Reece wondered if he'd ever be able to keep his hands off her.

Flame opened the door and let him walk in first, her heart beating like a drum gone crazy. As soon as she'd closed the door he pulled her into his arms and kissed her hungrily, his lips forcing hers open with thrilling strength and ease, his tongue darting inside. She clung to him, her hands running over his strong, smooth back. For long, silent, fulfilling minutes they kissed, their tongues and lips exploring each other ravenously. Eventually, though, breathless and looking satisfactorily flushed, Reece pulled away and took a deep breath. 'Are all breakfasts around here going to be like that?' he asked, his voice rich and amused and still husky from passion.

'I hope not,' Flame laughed, moving away from his heady orbit and self-consciously licking her lips. She could still taste him. 'Reece,' she said, her voice and eyes mischievous, and he grinned and shook his head.

'Uh-uh. If we start on that we'll never get out of this room.'

'Spoilsport,' she shot back, but walked to the locked drawer where she kept her work. 'Here they are.' She spread them out, watching in silence as he looked through them with slow concentration. He noted, with his engineer's brain, the precise and technically correct aspects of her drawings, only then taking in the actual beauty of the objects she'd created. There, on paper, the stones he was used to seeing as a miner — misshapen, dull-coloured, cold, hard, lifeless lumps of rock — were transported into things of beauty: a peacock's tail of aquamarine, emerald, sapphire and peridot. An eagle's-head brooch of amber, gold, onyx and agate. And so it went on, drawing after drawing; necklaces, brooches, earrings, tiaras, rings and bracelets.

Finally, a good hour later, Reece looked up, meeting her eyes without flinching. 'They're perfect,' he said simply. And meant it. 'You've redefined and strengthened your own sense of style. These . . .' he flicked the pieces of paper with his finger '. . . breathe Flame Syramore-Forbes. You *can* feel it, can't you?' he pressed softly, and Flame nodded, unable to speak. Wordlessly she packed the portfolio away. Reece felt a brief, businessman's regret that she'd never design for his company, and pushed it away. Who the hell wanted to mix business with pleasure anyway?

'You do want to come to Woodstock with me, don't you?' she asked, only now realising that downstairs she'd spoken for him without consulting him first. 'I mean, if you haven't got anything else planned?'

'Of course I'll come with you,' Reece said softly, almost chidingly, and reached for her hand.

* * *

Justin reached into the desk drawer of a writing bureau and withdrew a long white envelope, embossed with a royal coat of arms. Wordlessly he handed it over to Scott, who read it briefly and with growing jubilation. 'We've got it!' he crowed, quickly scanning the polite lines from the Principessa Sofia Elena di Maggiore, informing them that, after due consideration and much weighty contemplation, she had decided to award Halcyone's of Woodstock the commission for her celebratory birthday jewellery collection. There followed a list of items she wanted the commission to comprise. Quickly, greedily, Scott scanned them. It made even him blanch. The list contained no less than six tiaras, twelve necklaces with matching earrings and bracelets, thirty pairs of earrings, twenty-five individual rings, ten brooches, and a myriad number of items, including shoe buckles, belt buckles and handbag chains. 'Bloody 'ell,' Scott breathed, his cockney accent rising along with his excitement. 'This lot will be worth millions.'

'Nine point five, in fact. It says so at the end of the list,' Justin said nonchalantly.

'You don't sound very happy. When did you get this?'

'Yesterday.'

'So why aren't you climbing the rafters?'

'Read the letter again. Properly.'

Scott did so, and it didn't take long to find the problem. The Principessa had quoted her reasons for the choice of Halcyone's in depth, but as well as mentioning the firm's unblemished reputation, growing expansion, international prestige, years of experience, gifted craftsmen and impeccable management, she also quoted the growing reputation as a designer of Halcyone's half-owner, one Lady Flame Syramore-Forbes. Not only had the Principessa seen all the pieces Flame had designed for Giulietta's friends, Giulietta would have made sure that the Principessa was aware that the new Corraldo collection, already acclaimed an artistic success, was in fact the true work of her great-granddaughter.

Reading between the lines, the Principessa was making it perfectly clear that it was Flame who was to do the bulk of the designing, and the contract to Halcyone's was to be legally binding only after the Principessa had seen and approved of the designs. 'That . . . makes things difficult,' Scott said at last in magnificent understatement.

Justin stood ramrod-straight at the window. 'It makes the court case impossible. One whiff of it and the Italian bitch will pull out.' Already word would have leaked that Halcyone's had got the contract. If they should suddenly lose it . . .

'You think Flame knows?' Scott mused. 'That's why she's chosen today to go to the shop?'

'Why else?' Justin smiled coldly.

Scott slowly folded the letter and handed it back to Justin. 'So. What do we do now?'

Justin turned back to the window, the paper crumpled in his hand. 'We wait. I'll find a way to bring her down. Haven't I always been able to find a way?' he added silkily.

Scott thought of Malcolm Syramore-Forbes's providential 'accident' and just managed to stop the shiver of fear that shot up his spine. 'OK, Juzzer. Whatever you say.' He all but ran from the room. Things were getting out of hand.

* * *

Flame and Reece parked in the town and walked to the shop. The building was old, and full of that graciousness that only age can bestow on a building, and Flame's heart swelled with pride. It was so British. So respectable.

The window display, she saw at once, was both understated and classic. A black swathe of fine velvet covered the wide sill, and on a single black marble stand was a fabulous diamond necklace. This shop was her future. Corraldo's was closed to her, and she simply *couldn't* work for Reece at Redex; it would place too much stress on them both. No, this shop was her last and only hope. But would her designs be up to the standard of workmanship this company boasted? The men behind this elegant façade, working away in the back, had centuries of experience and expertise between them. They had seen fads come and go, styles change, the popularity of the stones themselves change. What would they make of her designs? A young, female, upstart American?

It was Reece's gentle hand on her arm that gave her the courage she needed. Looking once into his soft grey eyes, seeing the gentle smile, the encouraging to-hell-with-them-all twist of his lips, she flushed at her own dithering and, taking a deep breath, walked defiantly through the door and into her future.

Whatever that might be.

CHAPTER 21

Flame liked Walt Matthews on sight. He'd travelled down to Woodstock to congratulate the staff at the main emporium on the news of the Principessa's contract, and had been surprised to find they knew nothing about it. Walt had sent out for champagne. One of the things Walt had learned during his term as reluctant 'minder' for the absent Lady Halcyone Syramore-Forbes was that a company that didn't grow was a vulnerable company. Only the staying power of the 'Woodstock Elite', with their superb skill and craftsmanship, had kept Halcyone's afloat. That and Walt's modest contribution.

For nearly twenty years Walt had enjoyed his unique position in the company, but never abused it. Under his gentle guidance, no forced redundancies had been made, nor had the company made a loss in all the years since Jessica had died. Neither, he freely admitted, had it made any vast profits. Knowing and accepting his own limitations, Walt had been both glad and alarmed when Justin Syramore-Forbes had come to see him last spring and informed him he was leaving Oxford to take over as general manager.

Walt needn't have worried. During his months in control, Halcyone's had been transformed. The London store had sold more items of quality dress jewellery than any other outlet, including the big chains, and the quarterly profit was massive. Plans were afoot to increase exports by twenty per cent, and already the company had won one of the most prestigious and major commissions in recent history. It was all very impressive. And very fast. Walt wondered sometimes if it wasn't too fast. The boy was driven to succeed, that much was obvious. But what chances, what risks was he taking to achieve these marvellous results?

But for all that, Walt had no objections to Justin's leadership. Besides, there was nothing he could do to prevent Justin taking over. He could only wait until Halcyone Syramore-Forbes came over from America to claim her rightful inheritance.

So he had been both surprised and relieved when, midway through their toasting, the manager had entered nervously and told him that a lady claiming to be half-owner of the company was outside, inspecting their stock. Walt recognized her at once. She was Lady Jessica as a young girl — the hair alone was enough to convince Walt of that. He went to her immediately, one gigantic hand held out. 'Hello, Lady Halcyone. I'm Walt Matthews. You may have heard of me?'

Flame smiled in genuine pleasure. 'Please, call me Flame. And of course I've heard of you. My great-grandmother made you trustee of my shares. I'd like to thank you for doing such a good job for me all these years. I'm only sorry we haven't had a chance to meet before this.'

'Well . . . you've come at just the right time,' Walt said, indicating the door behind him. 'We're all drunk as skunks on champagne.' He glanced at Reece curiously.

Flame blinked. 'Oh?'

'Don't look so worried,' Walt laughed, already at ease with the young beauty in front of him. 'It's the Principessa contract of course. I insisted on getting in some champagne for them. You don't mind, do you? They're usually such decrepit old stick-in-the-muds, you'll never get the chance to see them let their hair down again.'

Flame grinned. 'Of course I don't mind. But what exactly did you say we're celebrating?'

Walt stared at her for a second, his sense of unease growing. 'So he didn't tell you either?'

'Who? What?' Flame felt her smile slip, at the same time glancing towards the door as a muted blast of cheering slipped through.

'Halcyone's has won the Principessa di Maggiore contract,' Walt said bluntly, and Flame gasped. 'It's worth nearly ten million,' he added casually, and grinned.

Reece moved forward to hug her briefly, and found Walt Matthews looking him over carefully. 'Congratulations,' Reece whispered in Flame's ear, then turned to Walt, held out his hand, and introduced himself. 'Reece Dexter.'

Walt made the connection at once, of course, and was suitably impressed, both with the man himself and the baggage that went with him. He looked at Flame, his eyes speculative. Flame blushed, Reece grinned, and Walt looked anxiously behind him as yet another rowdy burst of cheering filtered into the shop. What would the Earl say if a customer came in, only to be greeted by drunken cheering?

'We'd better get back there and calm them down,' Walt said, a little shame-faced by his part in their downfall. 'If I'd known the boss was coming, I'd never have suggested the champers. Please, don't think they're like this all the time. When you meet them you'll understand . . . well . . . come and see for yourself.'

It didn't take long for Flame and Reece to see what Walt meant. After silencing them with a simple wave of his hand, Walt introduced her with a simple, 'Gents, this is the other boss, Lady Halcyone Syramore-Forbes. Your ladyship — the Woodstock Elite.'

Red faces, white faces, sheepish faces stared back at her apprehensively. Flame spotted a half-full bottle of champagne. She picked it up and looked at it. The room fell totally silent. Looking around at the old faces, some openly anxious now, she grinned. 'Well, at least you left some for me!'

Walt laughed, and with it the tension broke. Glasses were found for her and Reece, and Flame toasted them, giving a short impromptu speech, which rambled a bit, ranging in topic from how glad she was at last to be at Halcyone's, how wonderful the company was, how good the craftsmen were, and congratulations on the Principessa contract.

The next three hours were taken up with drinking and getting to know the individual craftsmen. For Reece especially, it was a voyage of discovery on how superb jewellery was made. Perhaps not surprisingly, he was most impressed with the stonecutter, Gunther Voss. What he wouldn't do to have a man of Gunther's calibre at Redex!

Flame was both surprised and touched to discover that all of them were totally familiar with her work. Seth Weems even went into rapturous detail about one of her necklaces, designed for the English countess. Without exception, Flame discovered they liked and approved of her designs, and this led to her second surprise of the day. It was Walt who unexpectedly dropped the bombshell. After Seth's blush-inducing recital on the excellence of her work, Flame tried to slow them all down. 'Well, I don't know if it was all *that* good,' she laughed, holding up her hands. 'After all, I'm still very new at all this.'

'Talent comes from God,' Gunther Voss pontificated solemnly.

'Hear, hear,' Walt said. 'And whatever you do, you must be doing it right, otherwise Princess Sofia wouldn't have insisted on you being her official designer.'

'What?' Flame gasped, her hands stilling on the brooch she had been examining. 'She wants me to design the collection?'

'Halcyone's, until your brother took over, has been pretty much just coasting along,' Walt explained. 'Justin's ideas have bucked up the company no end. He was the one who went after the contract. He was the one who introduced the dress jewellery, the export plans . . . But the Princess chose us as much because of you as because of your brother.'

'I . . . I never knew,' Flame mumbled, both gratified and afraid of this new development. She could appoint herself chief designer now if she wanted to, and no one would question her right. But it meant that the entire success or failure of the commission could rest with her. What if the Principessa didn't like her designs? What if she couldn't complete them in time? She gave Reece an agonized glance. Without needing a word, he walked over to her and took her cold hands in his.

'Don't worry. You can do it.' He leaned closer and kissed her gently on the lips. 'You can do it all.'

* * *

Justin knew the moment they came back that things had changed. He was in the hunting room, polishing his shotgun. Made by Purdey, it had cost over thirteen thousand pounds, and was made of the finest wood. Highly finished in silver and polished till it glowed, the weapon was a work of art. Now, oiling and cleaning the gun was like second nature to him, and was a perfect exercise in relaxation. Flame found him wiping the barrel with a rag in long, loving strokes. He looked up at her entrance.

'Hi.' She took her gaze hastily from the weapon in his hands and found her brother's eyes no less disturbing. 'Sorry to interrupt . . . I met Walt Matthews today.'

'Oh?' Justin took his eyes off her long enough to crack the shotgun back into position, the noise making Flame jump in cold-skinned reaction. 'I didn't realise he was in town.'

'He came up to congratulate the Elite on the Principessa contract.'

Justin didn't comment on her new vocabulary, but his voice was slightly acidic as he asked, 'And just what did the . . . *Elite* . . . have to say about it?'

Flame flushed. She'd done enough massaging of Justin's fragile ego. It was about time she made it clear that not only was she in England to stay, but she was also in Halcyone's to make her mark. 'They were delighted, of course. But Walt was a little surprised you hadn't told us about it.'

Justin reached for a different polish and began to rub it over the engraved silver. 'I take it he stole my thunder?' he asked, his voice almost bored, and for the first time Flame realised how disappointed he must be.

'Oh, hell, I hadn't thought of that,' she admitted sympathetically. 'You worked so hard for the contract; you should have been the one to tell them. I'm sure Walt didn't mean to . . .'

'Undermine me?' Justin offered mildly. Standing the gun on its butt, he looked down the barrel. Flame made an instinctive movement towards him.

'Watch out!' she cried sharply. Justin looked up, surprised, and Flame bit her lip, feeling foolish. 'I thought it was dangerous to do that.'

'Only if it's loaded.'

'Oh. Well. . . I'll let you get on with it then,' she said, a little ashamed of herself for showing her ignorance of the gun so clearly. 'Are you going shooting later?'

'No. I'm just keeping it clean. It's worth over thirteen thousand.'

Flame blanched, then nodded. How little she knew of his life — of the English way of life. At the door she paused, determined to do what she had come to do. She turned around, waited for him to notice her, then said quietly, 'Why didn't you tell me about the commission, Justin?'

Justin looked surprised. 'I assumed you knew. Being a Corraldo, I mean. They know all the news before anyone else.'

Flame gazed back, no longer fooled by his air of bewilderment. In a few sentences he'd managed to make her the outsider again — the rival. She belonged to the Italian branch of the family. 'We're not at war, Justin,' she said softly. 'You and I could make the perfect combination. You've already proved what a great businessman you are — Walt is very impressed with the changes you've made in just the short time you've taken over. I'd be quite happy to head up the creative side — I could design, you could sell. Don't you think that's better than . . . squabbling?'

Justin bent back to his gun, dismissing her. Finally, dejected and sad, she moved away, closing the door softly on her twin. Outside, Scott touched her arm. 'I need to speak to you. It's important,' he added earnestly.

Flame sighed and nodded towards the library. Reece, through the open salon door, watched them disappear down the hall, his eyes thoughtful.

'OK. What is it?' Flame asked once they were alone. 'It's about Justin,' Scott began. 'You know he considers Halcyone's his by right, don't you?'

'I know,' she agreed. She didn't see the door open slightly. 'But now that we have the Maggiore contract, it's more important than ever that we stop this stupid feud.'

Even before she'd finished speaking, Scott shook his head. 'It's already too late. Justin was all set to take you to court. He even had a sympathetic judge lined up.'

'But why? What good did he think it would do?'

'He wanted the bad publicity to shame you into selling out to him. He'd have parted with millions to get you and your mother out of his life. That's how much he hates you.'

'Just why are you telling me this, Scott?' she asked suspiciously. 'What's in it for you?'

Scott tensed, wondering just how much he could tell her. Then a movement behind her caught his eye, and he guessed instantly who was listening in. Dexter! 'I've got you all wrong, haven't I?' he said, unable to resist the opportunity to cause trouble. 'All this time Justin's been telling me what a grasping, manipulative little bitch you are, and I didn't believe him. But now . . . I wonder.'

Reece listened, smiling. He was looking forward to Flame putting him right. He even began to grin in anticipation.

'Justin doesn't stand a chance against you, does he?' Scott continued, hoping Dexter was getting an earful. 'Admit it — you loved the little rickety shop, the stinking air of wealth. All this time you've been playing our little Redex friend along, just in case things went wrong and you needed a safety net to fall back on. I have to admit it, you really are some operator.'

Flame stared at him, appalled. 'Scott, you're mad,' she said angrily, her voice carrying clearly to the doorway, where Reece's grin widened. Behind him he heard the telephone ring and Chamberlain answer, but he was too busy waiting for Scott Tate to feel the full brunt of Flame's temper to take much notice. Then Chamberlain coughed discreetly behind him and Reece turned quickly, feeling guilty at being caught snooping by the butler. 'Telephone for you, Mr Dexter. Australia. It's a matter of some urgency.'

In the salon, Flame stamped her heeled foot on to Scott's and had the immense pleasure of hearing him yelp. Reece, lifting the telephone receiver, heard it too, and laughed. A moment later, all his amusement fled. There had been a cave-in at one of Dexter's opal mines. News was still patchy. Reece uttered a few terse comments and hung up. He sprinted for the stairs and hastily packed, but nevertheless found a piece of paper and scribbled a hasty note to Flame before racing away. If any miners were trapped . . .

In the salon, Flame heard a car start up and squeal out of the drive with a spattering of gravel. Scott, looking out of the window, recognized the car and the driver and turned back to Flame. 'I think that was Reece,' he said softly. 'I can't think why he's in such a hurry,' he purred. 'Perhaps it was something to do with his listening at the door?'

Flame turned, saw the open door and remembered Scott's accusations against her. That she was out to take away the company from Justin. That she had merely been using Reece. And she hadn't actually denied it! He must have thought . . . Her heart lunged, and an icy wave of despair hit her.

'Reece,' she breathed. 'Oh, no! *NO!*'

CHAPTER 22

Flame rushed out into the hall, but the house felt so empty, she already knew in her heart that Reece was gone. Nevertheless, she ran to his room, staring in dismay at the empty wardrobe. Numbly she went to the window, tears smarting in her eyes. Why couldn't he have hung around a little longer? Let her explain. If only he'd trusted her, just one more time . . .

She didn't see Justin leave his room and start to walk past the open doorway. The sight of Dexter's room, so obviously abandoned, made him stop in his tracks. Justin stared at his sister's shaking shoulders curiously for a long, long moment, then noticed a small white square of paper propped up on the dresser. Curiosity drove him forward, and he stealthily picked up the note and slipped it into his jacket pocket. Warily, he backed out of the room unobserved, and returned to his bedroom.

Quickly, he scanned the note.

Flame,

There's been a cave-in at one of our opal mines in Australia. I'll call you as soon as I arrive. Hope you gave Scott Tate hell! Go to it, cyclone! I'll come back as soon as I can.

Love you. Reece.

Justin smiled bitterly. How sweet. They were so sure of themselves, those two. Damn them! With a determined effort he fought back his anger and took a deep breath. He was still in control. He could still cause them pain. Carefully, he tore the note into tiny pieces and chucked them in his wastepaper bin. Only then did he go downstairs and inform Chamberlain that should Reece Dexter call for Lady Flame, he was to be told she was not available.

* * *

Venice

Returning to Venice was like coming home. Flame left Ravenscroft the same day as Reece, anxious to get away from Justin, who watched her with such burning venom. She was tired and despondent, but determined to do what she had come to do. Namely, research the Principessa di Maggiore as thoroughly as was humanly possible. She was determined that not one of her designs would be turned down as inadequate, and to accomplish that she needed to learn everything there was about her illustrious client in advance — her likes and dislikes, her favourite colours, favourite fashion designers, even the cars she drove. Anything that would give her an insight into the Principessa's personality. And who better to help her with that than Giulietta?

Her great-grandmother met her at Marco Polo airport in her 1950s classic Bentley. It didn't take Giulietta long to realise that there was more to this visit than mere business, and, when Flame very carefully skirted any mention of Reece Dexter, Giulietta smiled wisely. Nevertheless, she followed Flame's lead, and kept their discussions strictly on the matter at hand.

Flame listened attentively, noting down everything of use — even her choice of pet, a smoky grey Persian cat. Opulence, Flame concluded, was going to be the key to the Principessa's heart, and opulence she would get.

She thrust Reece to the back of her mind. If only, she thought sadly that night, crying into her pillow, she could put him to the back of her heart as well.

* * *

In the main salon, Justin turned to face his mother, his expression even more bland than usual. 'As I said, I have no idea why Reece left,' he repeated. 'I imagine he simply decided he'd been on holiday long enough and that it was time to get back to work.'

Owen, seated on the sofa, said nothing. He deliberately hadn't made any calls to his office since coming to Ravenscroft, deciding that Francesca needed him more. Besides, he was seriously thinking of retiring, and he had to learn to let go sooner or later. But it was not like Reece to leave so suddenly.

Justin watched his mother speculatively. He was more than ever convinced that Francesca's guilt could be played upon. 'I've decided to set up a second team to create a portfolio for the Principessa. I know . . .' he held up his hand as Francesca opened her mouth to defend Flame's abilities. 'I know that Flame is supposed to be doing it. But I have to think of the company. If she and Reece are going to argue at the drop of a hat, and Flame is going to fly off to Venice in a huff whenever things don't go her way, I need to ensure that Halcyone's has a back-up plan. Just in case.' He allowed his shoulders to droop wearily and ran a hand across his forehead. 'I know I'm not the artistic one, but I have workers relying on me. They need a pay cheque every week, and I need to keep the company afloat. I have to think of everything, anticipate any problems. I can't afford to rely on luck, or trust in blind faith.'

Francesca stared at his slumped shoulders and bit her lip. He sounded so tired. Perhaps Flame shouldn't have gone off to Venice so . . . abruptly. After all, it was because of Justin's efforts that Halcyone's had the contract at all. 'I'm sure Flame will come up with some good designs, *cara,*' Francesca said, not noticing how her son winced at the Italian endearment. 'You shouldn't work so hard, darling.'

Owen frowned. He didn't like the way this conversation was going. 'Of course Flame will come through. It was a good idea of hers to leave for Venice,' he stoutly defended her. 'Giulietta's a sharp old girl. She'll help Flame get a feel for the Principessa.'

Justin glanced at him bleakly and smiled. He let his eyes slide to his mother. *See*, his eyes said. *See how you're all against me? How you all leap to her defence?*

Francesca half-reached for him, but he was already turning away.

She wanted to cry.

* * *

Flame came downstairs the next day, dressed in a charcoal-grey trouser suit with a pearly-grey silk blouse that made her hair look even more striking than ever. Giulietta was glad she was being so businesslike, especially considering the first port of call on their itinerary.

In San Marco square, Giulietta headed straight for the Corraldo store and Flame felt her footsteps drag reluctantly as they drew level with the window display. Then, her eyes widened. There, spread out on the wide velvet-covered table, were her designs!

'The famous Corraldo autumn collection,' Giulietta said. 'Just in case you were beginning to doubt your abilities,' she added crisply. 'Now, let me point out the ones the Principessa liked best when we looked them over last week.'

Her eyes twinkled, and Flame laughed. 'Grandy, you manipulative old fraud, you!'

Giulietta pointed out a wren brooch. It looked pert and full of life, even though the stones were all in the brown colour range — mostly tiger's eyes, amber, onyx and smoky topaz. 'The Principessa noted that he looked ready to burst into song,' she said, and turned to look at her great-granddaughter. 'You did that, *cara*,' she said, her voice husky with emotion. 'You should be delighted that the design transferred so well from paper.'

Flame nodded, pride warring with outrage. Her name should be on those pieces. But then, Giulietta had made sure that everyone already knew they were hers anyway. Determinedly she shrugged off her anger at the Conte and instead concentrated on what mattered. So the Principessa liked the little brown songbird, did she? Why? Then, in an instinctive flash, she understood. 'You know,' she said quietly, 'there haven't been many jewellery pieces done on musical themes. Didn't you say the Principessa loves the opera?'

Giulietta smiled, looking well pleased. 'Indeed she does, *cara*. She also plays the flute, I believe.'

Flame nodded, picturing instruments of gold and silver, violins with exaggerated, sinuous curves . . . 'She has a sense of fun, the Principessa?' she asked anxiously, and Giulietta laughed.

'And of the outrageous. She was the first to wear seethrough blouses when they first came out. Caused quite a stir . . .' Giulietta lapsed into fond remembrances, while Flame nodded, her mind racing.

So the Principessa could be outrageous too. Now that was exciting . . . Flame became lost in a world of gems. Only Reece Dexter could compete with it, and she had to fight to keep his face from swimming up in front of her, ruining her mental designs. Oh, Reece!

Giulietta heard her heave a sigh and frowned. She was so proud, this great-granddaughter of hers. Proud and stubborn. Things had obviously gone wrong between her and that lovely big American. Giulietta could only hope that, whatever it was, they would repair the damage soon. Flame was too young and far too beautiful to be left alone for long . . .

* * *

Owen got a call from Reece later that day, and finally learned of the cave-in. Owen wanted to fly out immediately, but Reece pointed out that there was nothing his father could do that he, Reece, hadn't already thought of. But the news was bad. 'As far as I can tell, the worst of the cave-in began around dawn. Unfortunately, it came during the takeover of shifts. We're not sure yet how many were down there. I've got a head count of the outgoing night shift more or less completed, but it's getting harder to gauge how many of the day shift had gone in. It hasn't helped that reporters have waylaid some of them. Some are in hospital suffering from shock, but nobody thought to count them out. I'm getting conflicting reports from everyone.'

Owen listened grimly. 'Keep me informed, son,' he said, knowing there was nothing more he could do to help. 'And be careful.'

'I will. Oh, and, Dad, we have another problem.' Quickly, Reece outlined what he'd overhead about Justin's plans to shame Flame and Francesca into selling out to him, using the fewest words possible. He was anxious to get back to the shaft, and Owen let him go, promising to look into it. It was the least he could do. The last thing he needed was for Reece to be worrying about what was happening back in England when he went into the mines. A mine was a dangerous place after a cave-in. Secondary tremors were not unheard of.

Owen hung up, his face worried, as he offered up a silent prayer for the safety of the emergency services. He knew Reece knew how to take care of himself, but even so. He wished he was there. But, he sighed deeply, first things first. He straightened his shoulders and went in search of his stepson, knowing he'd either be in the stables or in the study, the only two places Justin seemed at ease. He knocked on the study door, saw Justin and carefully closed the door behind him, unwilling for anyone to overhear what he had to say. Things were probably going to get ugly.

Justin looked up, his face instantly shuttered as he saw his stepfather. Owen walked over to the paper-clogged desk and nodded at him. 'Justin,' he said quietly. 'I've just heard from Reece.'

'Oh?'

'He told me about your recent plans to take Flame to court,' he carried on, still in the same smooth, reasonable tone.

'That's no longer—' Justin began, but Owen, who always wanted the unpleasant things over with as quickly and painlessly as possible, raised his hand for silence.

'I want you to understand, right now, Justin, that I won't let you blackmail, browbeat or brainwash either your sister or your mother into doing anything they don't want to do. Is that clear?'

Justin slowly leaned back in his chair and tossed his pen onto the report he'd been reading. 'I don't see how what I do at Halcyone's is any concern of yours,' he said quietly. 'I'll thank you to keep out of my business.' His voice was dangerously quiet, but Owen was in no mood to heed the warnings.

'Justin, make no mistake. If you take on Flame or Francesca, you take me on as well. You may think, living in this great house, and having people call you "my lord", that you're something special. But you're just a man, Justin. Never forget,' Owen warned him, praying he'd take the advice he was about to give, 'I'm a man of wealth and influence too. Don't force me to use either against you. For your mother's sake, if not for your own,' he added, his voice softening at the mention of his wife.

Justin felt a lance of pain hit him square in the solar plexus. Nobody's voice ever softened over *his* name. What was so wrong with him that his father had hated him? Did his so-called friends only use him? Even Flick . . . No. That was defeatist thinking.

He forced himself to shrug nonchalantly. 'I'm well aware of your power, Papa dearest,' he said softly.

Owen felt a cold shiver run down his spine, but he met Justin's eyes head-on. 'If you could only learn to accept what you have, Justin, you'd be so much happier,' he said, sadness and weariness paramount in his voice. 'Your mother loves you. You have looks, a wonderful home, a business . . . everything any man could ever want. Don't let greed, or a misguided desire for vengeance, make you risk it all.'

As Justin watched his stepfather close the door softly behind him, he was already thinking up ways to combat this latest menace. It didn't take him long to select one that suited him best.

* * *

Two nights later, he crept out of his room at two o'clock in the morning, a pretty-handled file in his hand. Carefully and quietly, he filed a short way through the brake linings on Owen's Mercedes. But only a little way. He wanted it to rupture and widen slowly, as Owen drove the car over the following days. By the time it did finally snap, Flame would be back from Venice.

Carefully, he put the file he'd taken from her manicure set back in place. Something for the police forensic people to find when it came time to investigate the accident, which would rapidly prove to be no accident at all.

If he was *really* lucky, Francesca would be in the car with Owen when it happened . . .

CHAPTER 23

Justin lay naked on the narrow single bed, his chin resting on one bent elbow, his eyes never leaving the girl's hand as she slowly began to undo the large white buttons on her cheap summer frock. She was taller than most girls he'd bedded, with long, slim legs and small, up-tilting breasts, with pert, very dark nipples. Her hair was dark and glossy, and her large, heavy-lidded light brown eyes watched him constantly. Her heart thudded. Erin Lacey had lived in the village of Branston-in-the-Wold, which neighboured Ravenscroft, for all of her nineteen years. She knew the Earl, of course, but only on sight. Who didn't? Especially the girls. How many times, Erin thought in bemused excitement as she continued to strip, had she and her friends from the local comprehensive giggled and mooned over the Earl of Ravenscroft's son, the golden Adonis who could be seen every school holiday, cantering over the fields? But who would ever *imagine* that she, Erin Lacey, would be the one to hit the golden jackpot?

She felt slightly nervous. How could he look so suave and elegant when he was naked? How did he manage to make her small bedroom look so tawdry?

It was the eyes, she thought a moment later. Looking into his lovely blue eyes took her to a world she'd never been before. Erin felt her stomach clench and hoped he hadn't noticed. Just looking at him looking at her was giving her a sexual kick she had never experienced with anyone else. Wordlessly she wriggled out of her panties, revealing a thickly dark, luxuriant triangle.

'You're beautiful,' Justin said matter-of-factly as she walked quickly to the bed then hesitated and stood looking down at him. Justin merely looked up at her, one brow slowly raising, and she flushed, feeling hopelessly outclassed. Justin smiled. 'Don't you want to touch me, Erin?'

'Of course I do. You're lovely . . .' she flustered.

Justin smiled, then took her hand and guided it to his chest. Fascinated, Erin watched her hand being drawn over smooth, warm, strong flesh and, when he pulled his hand away, she carried on the exploration without further bidding. Justin sighed. It had been a while since he'd had a woman. It was nice to be reminded that his power in that department hadn't diminished. 'Mmm. That's nice, Erin.' He leaned back on the bed, offering himself like some kind of pagan sacrifice. Slowly, teasingly, Erin made her way to his nipples, first tweaking them with her fingers and then running her hands flatly over them. She felt his breathing alter, change, deepen, and felt a thrill of power. Her hands stilled momentarily on his smooth, concave stomach as her eyes moved down to where his straining manhood stood at stiff, red attention. He was big, she thought, and glanced up at him. His jaw was tight with desire, his face a little pale, his eyes a glittering, passion-filled blue. She thought she had never seen a man so . . . sexily beautiful before. Slowly he rose to a sitting position, and, with one hand on the back of her head, brought her lips to his and kissed her. Weakly she leaned against him.

'Kiss me . . . here.' Justin touched the spot beneath his jaw and eagerly she obliged. 'Now here.' He touched his collarbone, and her lips immediately followed. 'Here,' he said next, and drew her head to his chest, gritting his teeth as her lips encircled his nipple. Slowly he leaned back on the bed, his eyes wide open and staring at the ceiling. Without being told, Erin moved to his other nipple, then, at a gentle pressure on her head, moved down. Justin stopped her at his navel; obligingly her small pink tongue delved into the indent and Justin felt the reactive jerking of his hips and legs. He closed his eyes, gritting his teeth. He mustn't make a sound. Not one. Gently, not quite sure how experienced the girl was, he pushed her head lower. But she knew what he wanted.

Nervously, she began to feel her way into it, licking the insides of his thighs, then nudging his testicles first with her nose, then with her lips, then with her tongue. She found them wonderfully, almost astonishingly soft, and when his legs thrashed either side of her, she felt a bolt of giddying, addictive power. Her hands on his thighs tightened and, tentatively at first, but with growing confidence and delight, she began to lick his shaft, finding it incredibly hot against her tongue. Justin continued to stare open-eyed at the ceiling, his jaw beginning to ache now as his strong teeth clamped together. Knowing he could stand little more, he dislodged her and, with strong hands under her arms, drew her up his body. Moving his hands to her hips, he positioned her over his straining manhood and looked deeply into her eyes for a moment, reading the excitement, the almost pitiful anticipation in her face. Then, to her utter amazement, he slowly leaned back against the bed.

'Don't you want . . . well . . . you know?' she murmured, wondering why he hadn't turned her around and pushed into her.

'Of course I do. Don't you want me?'

Erin stared at him puzzled, then, when he looked down at their bodies, so close to a full mating, she suddenly realised what he intended her to do. No man had ever offered to let her lead before. Intrigued, delighted, a little nervous, she gingerly lowered herself on to his up-thrusting shaft, as if impaling herself would hurt. It didn't, of course — it felt *wonderful*. As she began to move, up and down, regulating the speed for herself, she found that her pleasure was magnified a hundred times. Now she could do as *she* liked. She massaged his penis head over her clitoris and immediately climaxed, then pushed deeply down on him, hearing him catch his breath. Looking down, she saw that he was gripping the headboard above him with white-knuckled hands and that his eyes were tightly closed. His face was taut with desire and tension, and Erin felt an almost overwhelming sense of compassion. Suddenly she wanted to please this man more than he'd ever been pleasured before. She wanted to make him love her, want her, need her. She wanted to thank him for trusting her like this. There, on her little single bed, in her little single room, she felt as if he'd given her the world. And she wanted to give it back.

Justin kept his eyes tightly shut, his lips even more so, and thought only of the pleasure that was coming, and the girl's father.

Jack Lacey. Who owned and ran the local garage.

* * *

Flame had now returned to Ravenscroft, arriving armed with notebooks full of information on the Principessa di Maggiore. She was sure the Principessa would be intrigued by her use of the more unusual metals, but, of course, they could only be used for the 'fun' section. The 'classical' section would be dominated by gold and silver.

The stones were a different matter. For the classical designs, she'd have to stick with the five superstars of the jewellery world — diamonds, emeralds, rubies, sapphires and pearls. But for the fun and dress pieces, Flame was considering many of the other kinds of stones available to her, which would, she hoped, intrigue the Principessa. She knew the Principessa had a semi-serious fixation on astrology, and knew her birthstone was amethyst, one of Flame's own favourites. Already she had decided on dedicating some pieces to the astrological signs — not necessarily just the Principessa's own, but also those of her husband and daughter, who, luckily, had different signs. She also knew the Principessa had been charmed by the enamel pendant she had made in the workshop, and she was determined to build on that and design quite a few enamelled pieces, and add lapis lazuli to this theme. She'd already made plans to visit the Fabergé collection currently on show at the Victoria and Albert Museum.

She was in the library, trying to pull the different tentacles of her thoughts, ideas and research into some sort of coherent whole when she heard two cars pull up. Looking through the open window, she saw her mother and Owen get out of one and, just behind, Justin emerge from the other. She caught snatches of conversation as she walked out into the hall to meet them. Francesca's voice: 'Why don't we go to Beaulieu tomorrow, darling? You know how fascinated you are by old cars.' Owen, answering: 'OK. But we'd better take your car. The brakes seem a bit mushy on mine.' Justin, unusually joining in: 'The local man, Lacey, over in Branston is good.'

Flame followed them into the blue salon, plopping down into a comfortable chair. Francesca looked at her daughter anxiously. She'd lost weight since Reece had left, and she was definitely more pale and drawn than usual.

'Justin, do you want to see what I've done so far?' Flame asked, causing her brother to glance at her, the picture of surprise. 'I don't mind, you know, if you have any suggestions,' Flame added. 'The enamel pendant for the Principessa was a such good idea.'

'So glad you approve,' Justin said drolly.

'Perhaps we should throw a party to celebrate the commission?' Flame mused. 'We could invite all the Halcyone staff, perhaps even the press. We—'

'What a good idea,' Francesca said, at the same instant that Justin said dampeningly, 'We don't do that sort of thing in England.' Everyone was quiet for a moment, and Flame flushed in both embarrassment and anger.

'Surely, Justin, all that stiff-upper-lip stuff has long gone,' she challenged. 'Promotion, PR, glitz and all that has crossed the Channel, you know. Companies like publicity — they like to blow their own trumpets. It lets the customers know we're out there.'

'If you're selling fizzy drinks, perhaps,' Justin admitted, careful to keep his voice explanatory and not contemptuous. 'But Halcyone's has a certain standard that says we don't *have* to crow. Everyone who counts already knows we have the contract. To rub it in people's faces with a party would smack of . . . arrogance. It simply isn't done. Mother, you lived here once. Try and explain.'

Francesca, caught off guard, looked from her son to her daughter. She could understand both points of view, but this was the first time Justin had ever asked her for anything, and she couldn't *not* do as he asked.

'Justin's right, Flame. Over here . . . well . . . Why don't you organise a big celebratory party for when the commission is complete? The Principessa will expect it, I'm sure, and it will give her the perfect chance to show off and wear the best pieces. That way we can invite all the press we want, and draw up a celebrity guest list as well. We'll hold it in London — at one of the big hotels. What do you say, darling?'

Flame took one look at her mother's pleading eyes and nodded. 'Sure. Why not. That can be my responsibility. Right, Justin?' She looked him in the eye, determined to stand up for herself.

Justin smiled, looked right back and said softly, 'Of course. It'll be your party — all the way.' For a second, Flame went cold. Justin handed Owen a glass of lemonade and the moment passed.

But later, much later, Flame would remember those words.

* * *

The temperature was 110°F in the shade, and Reece was drunk. No miners had been trapped, praise God, and the mine was almost back to normal. He was in the Koolaborra tavern, the main building in the twenty-three-building town of Koolaborra deep in Queensland's outback. Reece sighed into his glass and brushed a hand across his sweating forehead. The bourbon didn't exactly complement the hot weather but he didn't care. Today, he didn't care about anything much. And it was all to do with her, of course. Flame. Why hadn't she called him? And why was she always out when he called her? He wanted her so much. He could feel her pull on him, even now, from the other side of the globe. At night she invaded his dreams; during the day she invaded his concentration. The atmosphere at the mine was still tense and he felt as if he'd been through a meat grinder and back again. He was worried about her, and still felt guilty over leaving her the way he had. Grimly he screwed the top back on the bottle of bourbon. Once he'd worked himself into exhaustion he'd feel better. But he already knew that nothing but her kisses, her warm, loving body and soft voice would make him feel better.

Damn her, why didn't she call?

* * *

Owen slowed down behind a tractor, amused to find himself so patient with the lumbering vehicle. He'd long since lost his habit of aggressive American driving. Now, as the Mercedes purred along behind the swaying tractor, he found himself humming a tune and even grinning at the black and white sheepdog that stared back at him from the tractor's cab.

Eventually the tractor turned off up a dirt road and Owen accelerated, going at a steady forty on the twisting roads. He was out to buy Francesca a birthday present, something exquisite and unusual, something that would please her. He'd left his wife and stepdaughter poring over jewellery designs back home, and he was a well-contented man.

He saw the black and white arrows that warned of a sharp bend, and pressed his foot gently against the brake, anticipating changing down a gear. To his surprise, his foot continued down and the car didn't change speed. A sudden shaft of fear lanced up his spine as he pressed harder, the pedal beneath his foot flapping uselessly. Quickly, with the bend already upon him, he changed down a gear, the engine growling angrily. He reached forward and switched off the engine, and the silence was terrifying. Yet Owen felt curiously calm as he assessed the situation, and realised that he'd never make the bend.

And nor did he. Owen felt the seatbelt constrict painfully across his chest as the car hit the hedge, and then lurched into a ditch before flipping over in a perfect cartwheel to land on its roof. Owen saw the world around him turn upside down. There was a roaring, grating sound of metal as flashes of green, much too close, seemed to ram right into his eyes. Then there was nothing.

In the balmy September air, the four wheels of the Mercedes revolved slowly for several minutes, then became still.

CHAPTER 24

Reece's Learjet landed at the airport of Kidlington, the nearest Flame had been able to find with a long enough runway to accommodate the private Dexter plane. It had been the middle of the night when Bill had knocked, grumbling, on his door to tell him that he had an urgent call on the pub's single telephone downstairs. She'd called at last! But the message that her sweet voice carried soon changed his euphoria to cold dread. Even now, hours later, he could still recall her exact words.

'Reece! Oh, thank God I've got you at last. I've been ringing for ages. Reece, it's Owen.'

'Dad?' Reece had gone cold, shivering in the pub's large, airy room. 'Is it . . . his heart?'

'No. Reece, he . . . he crashed the car.'

'Is he . . . He's still alive, isn't he?'

'Yes, they've rushed him to the John Radcliffe.' After that, time had blurred, but now, through the fog of worry over his father, Reece could feel a warm, comforting tide just beneath his subconscious. He knew she would be here to meet the jet, and she was. It was just getting dark and a light rain was falling. She was wearing a light grey mac, and it swirled around her legs as she moved, her hair rippling free in the breeze. Reece found himself moving towards her like a magnet drawn to iron filings, and when she was at last within his reach, he took her into his arms, holding her close, drinking in the warmth of her body, the smell of her hair, the slight sounds of her breathing.

'Reece. I'm so glad you're home,' she whispered against his shoulder, the trauma and anxiety of the last awful day seeming to slip away from her in his strong, protecting embrace. Then Reece pulled away and she looked up to see that his grey eyes looked dull with fatigue, and his face, usually so tanned and strong, was now pale with worry.

'How is he?'

'He's still holding on. Come on, let's get in the car. The hospital's only twenty minutes away.'

Reece nodded and pulled away, his thoughts on his father. Nevertheless, they walked hand in hand to Flame's car, and when they were forced to let go she felt unaccountably bereft.

* * *

Justin had been working at Halcyone's when he'd heard. Francesca, ringing from the John Radcliffe hospital, kept the call blissfully short. 'Justin, it's Owen.' Her distraught voice made his hand clutch the receiver in a white-knuckled grip. He went deathly pale, and the telephone receiver in his hand creaked and threatened to crack.

'Oh, Justin, his car crashed. I do-don't know any more yet, but it's bad. I'll call you later, all right?' She sounded suddenly very vulnerable, and his heart lurched.

'Yes, Mother,' he said, and hung up. In their joint states of shock, neither realised that it was the first time Justin had ever called her that. For a second he stared at the blank wall, his mind in turmoil. The accident might not have had anything to do with the brakes. And he probably wouldn't die. He had never really meant for Owen to die, after all. At the most he'd been thinking of a broken leg. But Francesca had sounded so . . . terrified. And suddenly Justin felt terrified too. He swallowed bile and his stomach revolted. He rushed through a fire door and across the open yard to the toilets. Plunging into the nearest cubicle, he just managed to fall to his knees before bringing up his breakfast. For long minutes his body was racked with dry, sobbing heaves. His ribs and throat began to ache, but he couldn't stop. He wasn't aware of shaking all over, but his hands jerked wildly against the cold toilet bowl as he hung on. This wasn't fair. It wasn't how he had meant it to be. And what if . . . ? Suddenly, the trembling stopped and he went as still as a statue. What if they found out? A vision of the dark, airless, lifeless cellar at Ravenscroft rose up in his mind. Suddenly he was back there, ten years old, with not even a rat for company. Only rows and rows of dusty wine bottles. And the door banging closed and the key turning. 'No, Dad. Don't. Please!'

The sound of his own voice snapped him out of it. He blinked and groaned. Feeling numb, he flushed the toilet and, bent double and still hugging his stomach, walked at a half-crouch to the basins. He ran the cold water and splashed it on his face, trying to rinse out his mouth as best he could.

Eventually he dried his face and hands, then turned and left. He drove carefully and with intense concentration, and by the time he arrived at Ravenscroft he was feeling better. He headed straight for the library, poured himself a huge brandy, then carried the phone to his favourite chair, sat down and dialled a number. Eventually a voice came on the other end. 'Lacey's.'

'Hello. Is Erin there, please?'

'Just a minute.'

More time passing. Justin glanced up and out of the window. It was raining. Good; the late potatoes needed the rain. He found his fingers were drumming frantically on the edge of the chair, and he looked down at them, almost surprised. He took a deep breath, and then he heard a female voice. He jumped, looked to the door, but there was nothing. Then he pulled himself together with a snap. 'Hello!

Erin.' His voice, he was pleased to notice, came out warm and caressing. 'How are you, poppet?'

'Justin?' The voice, tentative, excited, made him grimace. 'I'm glad you called. I thought you wouldn't.'

'Don't be silly. Actually, I wanted to ask you out again but things here are a bit fraught.'

'Oh, I know,' Erin sighed. 'I was really sorry to hear about your stepfather. You should see his car! Dad's just towed it in.'

'What we can't understand is how it happened,' he continued carefully. 'Owen's such a good driver.'

'I know,' Erin said, eager to add her own information. 'But there were no other cars involved, apparently.'

Justin sighed with relief. 'Well, we want to know what happened. I don't suppose your dad's had a chance to look at the car yet?'

'Are you kidding? He was all over it the moment he got it back here. He says the only thing that could have caused it was the brakes.'

'The brakes?' Justin felt his throat go dry.

'Mm. He said they were worn.'

'That's strange,' Justin said as casually as he could manage. 'The car was fairly new.'

'Dad wondered about that too. He can't figure out why your stepdad didn't bring the car in before. He said the brakes must have been soft.'

'They were. I heard him say just before the accident that he'd have to take it in to a garage. Damn! Look, someone's just come back. It might be Mother with news from the hospital. I'll call you back some time, OK?'

'Sure. And tell your mum I'm rooting for her.'

'I will,' Justin said drolly, and quickly hung up. He leaned back in the chair, his mind working quickly. The situation was perfect. If Owen died, Justin would probably let things ride. Dexter would be out of the way, and who knew, with Reece back, his dear stepbrother might take his bloody sister off his hands. But if Owen recovered . . . then he'd have to feed Flame to the police. Work on Erin's father — get his suspicious roused. Then Justin could tell the cops how he saw his sister go into the garages in the middle of the night. Of course he didn't think anything of it at the time . . . Yes, it could work out well. But he'd have to time it right. She'd have to have completed the Principessa's designs. And he'd have to have the money for the jewellery in the company's bank account before the scandal broke . . .

* * *

Owen looked white and frail against the hospital sheets. With tubes in his nose and arm, a monitor hooked to his chest and head, he looked like a small, valiant piece of humanity lost in a plethora of hard science. Reece looked down at his father, his heart thumping. Flame, by his side, saw the look of agony in his eyes and quickly slipped her hand over his arm, squeezing tightly. 'The doctors say he has four cracked ribs, but it's the head injury that's the worst.'

Reece nodded. 'And he hasn't regained consciousness since they brought him in?'

Francesca shook her head. 'No,' she said helplessly, raising her head to look at him. Reece winced to see how changed she was. She looked old suddenly, her face lined with pain and worry.

'Francesca, Dad will be all right. I know him — he's tough. He'll pull through.' His words, though, sounded hollow, and he could bear to be in the room no longer. He left in search of a doctor and within minutes he was fully briefed on his father's condition. The areas of the brain most likely to be affected, the doctor told him, were those controlling memory and co-ordination.

Reece paced outside for a while, trying to marshal his thoughts. He was standing at a window, looking out over the rain-filled night, when he heard someone cough discreetly behind him. When he turned around, he saw a man of medium height with light brown hair, light blue eyes and a rather carroty-coloured moustache and beard.

'I'm sorry to disturb you,' the man began, his voice as bland and smooth as his appearance. 'But are you Mr Owen Dexter's son? My name is Ivor Oliver.'

Reece held out his hand. 'You have something to tell me?' He got straight to the point, and was rewarded by a look of approval. The man nodded, and Reece indicated the waiting room, which was currently empty.

Mr Oliver opened his briefcase and took out a plain buff folder. 'Six days before your father's accident he came to see me at my office in Summertown.' He handed over a card. It read simply 'Ivor Macklin Oliver — Enquiry Agent' and was followed by a telephone number. 'Before I show you this,' he tapped the folder, 'I must ask you something and I'd appreciate a straight answer.'

Reece nodded. Ivor smiled rather cynically, but asked his question. 'What do you know about Justin Syramore-Forbes?'

Reece found he wasn't at all surprised by the man's opening gambit. 'I think,' Reece said eventually, 'that my stepbrother is probably seriously disturbed.'

Ivor leaned back in his chair, nodding slowly. 'I would go farther. I think he has sociopathic tendencies.'

Reece felt the word hit him, penetrate and seep in. But his face betrayed not a flicker of emotion. 'I think you'd better show me what you found,' Reece said quietly, and without a word Ivor handed over the folder and watched him read. He, of course, already knew the contents. They included the attempted murder of George Campbell-Bean, the rather odd circumstances surrounding the late Earl's death, and nasty rumours about Malcolm's 'discipline' methods for his son. And, although Ivor had no degrees or diplomas in psychology, he was very astute when it came to identifying mental disorders. The manipulation of women was only one of many pathetic straws that Justin Syramore-Forbes clung on to. It must have cost him dear to lose Flick Mainwaring.

Reece turned the last page and shut the folder. His face, as ever, was expressionless. 'I agree with your interpretations. About Campbell-Bean, I mean.'

Ivor nodded and watched Reece Dexter turn to look at the door to his father's hospital room. His eyes began to burn. Ivor tensed. So, he was on to that too. Reece slowly changed the direction of his eyes to the man seated opposite him. 'My father's accident. What do you know about it?'

'I know there was no other car involved. I checked the scene of the accident as well as talking to the police. I know he was not drunk. I know the car is at the local garage, owned by a Mr Jack Lacey. I know that Justin recently took Jack Lacey's daughter, Erin, to bed.'

Reece blinked, digested the information in silence and finally asked, 'You've seen the car?' Ivor shook his head. 'I want you to check it out.' His voice was totally emotionless, but behind his eyes something dark roiled. 'And this Jack Lacey.'

Ivor nodded. He stood up, made no effort to retrieve the folder he'd given him, and left without a further word. Reece watched him go, his face immobile. Only his eyes glittered dangerously.

* * *

It was two days later when Owen first opened his eyes. He stared blankly at the people around him, wondered briefly why the two beautiful women were crying, wondered even more briefly why the big man with the grey eyes called him Dad, and went back to sleep.

The doctors were pleased. Francesca was ecstatic.

He was going to live.

CHAPTER 25

Owen grimaced as the nurse came into the room. 'Here comes the bloodsucker,' he grumbled good-humouredly, his voice slurred and tired. The nurse took the sample of blood from his arm regardless and gave Francesca a broad wink.

'Does he always complain this much?'

'Always,' Francesca grinned back, then glanced at her husband, fighting back a wave of fear. Owen still didn't remember her. It had been two weeks since he'd first opened his eyes, and during those two weeks Francesca had ridden an emotional rollercoaster that had taken her from elation to despair.

At first, as could only be expected, Owen had been totally confused, but for two weeks now Francesca had stayed by his bedside, talking of their life together, and slowly, very slowly, Owen began to get to know his wife all over again. Small things helped. Yesterday, he'd remembered that the sherry trifle she'd brought in for him was one of his favourites. Francesca told him that was why she'd chosen it, and Owen had another tenuous link to cling to. And so it went on. Reece had some of his father's personal possessions flown over from San Francisco and had shown them all to Owen one afternoon. Pictures of his wedding to Clare, photographs of Reece growing up, press clippings, the more recent wedding photos to Francesca. All of them worked ceaselessly to help Owen build up a picture of his life as it had once been.

Yet they were still strangers to him. But beloved strangers. Owen wasn't quite sure what he'd do if he awoke one morning and the beautiful face of Francesca wasn't there. He could feel her love and support like a palpable wave. And that alone, he sometimes thought, was what kept him sane. He had no memories of the empire he was supposed to have built, but he was made of strong stuff. It was there in his nature, letting him call on it day by day. It healed his body and aided him in his fight against the frustration of having no memory to anchor himself with. Even the doctors were amazed by his stamina. Slowly, he came to realise that it was only his memory that was gone — the love he felt for his son and wife and stepdaughter was still there, deep and safe inside him.

Now, as the nurse finished taking the blood sample, the door opened and Flame and Reece walked in. They were a perfect complement for each other. Reece, with his thick dark hair, tanned skin and tall, straight body, was like jet. And Flame, with her glorious hair, light skin, slender body, was like amber. Jet and amber — together they were magnificent.

'Hello, you two,' he said, his voice still slurred but stronger than it was yesterday. 'How are things at . . . ?'

'Halcyone's?' Flame prompted. 'They're going fine.'

'I'll say,' Reece cut in drily. 'She's been drawing like a demented Picasso. Day and night, she's driving me crazy.'

'I've brought them with me,' Flame said. The doctors had told them to make Owen use his brain, think, reason, and exercise his faculties. What better way than to get him to make an aesthetic judgement on some drawings?

Owen sat up further in the bed, wincing at the pain in his ribs. But he was looking better. Gone was the frightening pallor, the shortness of breath and the distressing need to fall asleep every few minutes.

'Let me at 'em.' Owen knew how much it lightened Francesca's load to see him show signs of spark. He determinedly opened the folder and looked at the first page. What he saw made him gasp. Flame had not only drawn in pencil every facet of every stone, including complicated measurements indicated by lines of figures attached to arrows, but she had also painted on the bottom half of the huge sheets of paper a likeness of what the finished articles would actually look like. Flame knew the Principessa would react far better to them if she could have a picture of the finished article in her mind's eye. Owen felt his tiredness slip away as he stared down at a starburst of white diamonds. It was a pendant, to be hung from a heavy gold chain, and something in its beautiful but almost savagely geometric design reminded him of something . . . Damn, what was it?

'It reminds me . . . I've seen something like this before. But I can't remember . . .'

Hearing the frustration in his voice, Francesca quickly looked over his shoulder, and gasped. 'It's a snowflake,' she said, then looked closer. 'How on earth did you manage to get it so . . . perfect? Can it be done?' Quickly Francesca looked at the technical drawing above, but was lost in the waves of mathematical calculations, technical notes and instructions to the stonecutter.

'It can,' Flame said. 'I checked it with Gunther Voss before adding it to the collection. And he should know.'

Owen began to turn the pages with growing satisfaction. The paintings showed things as varied as a pewter brooch depicting a ridiculously pompadoured poodle in the pose of a rampant lion, to a rose-diamond tiara with the palest of rubies. 'They're fantastic.' He glanced at Francesca and reached for her hand. 'Did I tell you the quacks have said I can get out of here soon?' he slurred, his voice losing its clarity as he tired. 'I can't wait to go home.'

Francesca looked at Reece, her eyes pleading. 'I thought, Reece, I would take him to my grandmother's house in Venice.'

'Venice?' Owen said, recognizing the name of the city.

'It's a beautiful place, as you well know.' Francesca was anxious to persuade him. Looking Reece straight in the eye, she added softly, 'We who live there call it La Serenissima. A serene place. It's quiet, and beautiful.'

'It's also damp, as I remember,' Reece pointed out. He'd thought of taking his father home to San Francisco.

It was Flame who came to her mother's defence. 'Grandy lives in the Palazzo d'Oro,' she explained for Owen's benefit. 'As it sounds, it's a palace, and Grandy has had the rooms fully draught-proofed and fitted with central heating.' She looked at Reece, silently willing him to agree.

Reece slowly nodded. 'OK,' he said softly, and then, as Owen tried to stifle a yawn, insisted they leave him to get some sleep.

As they walked out into the chilly October air, Francesca shivered. Reece said quietly, 'There's more to it than wanting a quiet place for Dad to recover, isn't there?'

'No. I don't think so,' Francesca denied. But even as she said it, she wondered. Why did she so dread taking Owen back to Ravenscroft? Malcolm was no longer a threat. It was something else. *Someone* else . . . Abruptly Francesca pulled her thoughts back to more practical matters. She'd have to pack warm clothes for Owen. She let her mind drift away from more dangerous currents, but her heart thudded, as if she'd stepped too close to the edge of a cliff and looked down.

* * *

Reece looked up and watched his stepbrother carefully shut the door behind him. He was dressed for riding, and had a riding crop in one hand. 'Chamberlain said you wanted to see me.'

'Yes,' Reece said, and pointed at a chair. 'Sit down.' Justin stiffened. He gave Reece a long, considering look, then shrugged and took to his favourite wing-backed chair, stretching his long legs out in front of him.

'I have something I want you to read,' Reece said, handing over the folder Ivor Oliver had given him a couple of weeks ago. Since then, Ivor had added the information gleaned from Jack Lacey. Reece was afraid for Flame, and he was determined to nullify the threat against her before he left. Since he'd returned, she'd made no move to come to him. He wished he knew why it was over between them, but . . .

'Can't this wait?' Justin asked in a bored tone of voice. 'I have a mare saddled and—'

'Read it,' Reece cut in, his voice hard. He watched Justin's jaw tighten a fraction, and, as he slowly began to read more and more, his eyes darkened from sky blue to a stormy grey. Apart from that, he showed no reaction at all. When he'd finished, he closed the folder and handed it back to Reece.

'Very interesting.'

'You think that's all it is?'

'What else?' Justin raised an eyebrow. When Reece leaned forward, his gaze level, Justin knew with terrifying unease that this man was not at all afraid of him. Even knowing what he did, he was not afraid of him. Justin found himself floundering, unable to grasp any thread of his emotion or character that could stabilize him.

'I think, Justin, that you are twisted,' Reece began softly. 'I don't blame you for that. I know that children are totally vulnerable to their environment. Nobody taught you what was right and what was wrong, did they? Or was it worse than that? Why don't you tell me about Malcolm?' he asked softly, but with steely determination in his voice.

Justin went cold, then hot. 'Why don't you get to the point?'

Reece nodded. 'That hurt, didn't it, Justin? What else hurts you? Flame? She hurts you, doesn't she? And what about your mother? What about Flick Mainwaring . . . ?' Reece trailed off as Justin flinched visibly. He felt a shaft of compassion shoot through him for this poor, mixed-up bastard, then thought of Owen, and pushed the dangerous pity back to a safer distance.

'What do you want?' Justin said, his voice little more than a whisper. Waves of fear crashed over him, almost paralyzing him. For a second he couldn't think where he was.

Reece saw the panic in his eyes and could almost taste his terrible fear. 'Justin!' he said sharply and watched his stepbrother flinch then sink back against the chair, his contorted muscles collapsing. For a few seconds, Reece had thought the boy was going to go into some sort of fit. 'Justin, let's negotiate a deal,' he began carefully, accurately guessing that this was the only tightrope Justin was capable of walking, with its pitiful semblance of normality. 'You know that the evidence in there is damning. I can go to the police with it.'

'Do that,' Justin said quickly, anxious to play his ace card, almost rabid in his need to get back into some sort of position of authority. 'They'll find it was Flame's nail file that did the damage to your father's car. They'll find that the gardener saw her going into the garage late at night, and will swear to it, under oath. They'll find—'

'I wasn't talking about the accident,' Reece gritted, fighting back his own instinctive rage. It took everything in him to stop himself from taking Justin by the scruff of the neck and strangling him. Only the thought of Flame's pain, and Francesca's, stopped him. Besides, it was Justin who had no sense of morality, not himself. 'I was talking about George Campbell-Bean.'

Quickly Justin thought back to that day. 'You've got no proof,' he said, his instinct for self-preservation belatedly kicking into life. 'Nothing that will stand up in court.'

'It won't have to stand up in court, Justin,' Reece said quietly. 'Only in the press.'

Justin stared at him. 'You think I care what people say about me?' he asked incredulously. 'That was my father's hang-up — never mine.' He half rose out of the chair, his voice rising with him as he lost even more control. 'I don't care a damn what people say about me. All my life—' Suddenly he stopped, realising how close he was to admitting everything, how nearly this man had tricked him. Slowly he sank back in the chair, unaware that he was gulping in air like a beached fish, that his face had turned into a tortured and haunted mask.

'I heard that your father nearly whipped you to death once,' Reece said slowly, recalling a particularly graphic detail in Ivor's report. 'You were fourteen.' The pity refused to stay out of Reece's voice, and Justin quickly looked away.

'Yes, but that wasn't so bad,' Justin said, his voice hardly more than a whisper. Reece shivered, reacting to the evil of Malcolm's malign presence.

'What else?' Reece urged gently. 'Just what did that bastard do to you, Justin?'

'The cellar.'

Reece went even colder. 'What about the cellar?' he probed softly, aware that he was walking on very thin ice. Justin didn't answer, but the images wouldn't go away. He'd always been afraid of the dark. He feared that far more than mere pain. And Malcolm knew it. Justin shuddered, remembering the times he'd been locked in down there, sometimes for days at a time, if he was home from school in the holidays.

'He locked you in the cellar, didn't he?' Reece pressed, relieved that when Justin turned and looked at him his dazed eyes were clearing. With a huge effort, he dragged himself back from the precipice.

'I shouldn't read anything into that, old man,' Justin drawled, a sickly grin once more back on his face. 'Worse things happened at Eton.'

Reece looked at him, his face bleak. 'I'm sure they did,' he said compassionately, and Justin launched himself out of the chair, hating the man for bringing back the memories. One boy, Jake Urquhart, had particularly hurt him. He was a cheerful, outgoing sort of a boy, one who could get on with anybody. Justin was drawn to him — like a cold moth to a warm flame. Then the teasing started, the boys chanting 'queer' whenever he tried to talk to him, and Justin had started to pick fights with his friend. Not only was Jake smaller than he, but it simply wasn't in his placid nature to fight. Within months, Jake had hated the sight of him.

Reece, tensed to defend himself, watched the confusion and pain cross Justin's face and felt a wave of guilt hit him.

Then he remembered why he *had* to do it, and his resolved hardened. 'Sit down, Justin,' he said, and gently placed his hands on the boy's shaking shoulders. 'You and I both know that Halcyone's won't stand a scandal. And we both know you don't want to face Flick again. Don't we?'

'Flick?' Justin repeated numbly, sinking back into his chair. 'I once dreamt of going to sleep in her arms,' he mumbled. 'I've never done that before, you see.' He looked at Reece, wondering who he was. He seemed like a friend.

'So let's make a deal,' Reece said, and the words were like a catapult. Suddenly Justin found himself back in the real world where everything was for sale.

'What kind of deal?'

Reece saw clearly, in that instant, the kaleidoscope that must be Justin's life, and took a deep breath, knowing that the next few minutes would be vital for them all. 'In exchange for not turning you over to the police or the press,' Reece said calmly and clearly, 'I want you to get help. I want you to book yourself voluntarily into one of those clinics.'

Justin took the list Reece held out to him. 'When?'

'Straight away.'

'No,' Justin snapped at once. 'I can't leave now. The Principessa is due to approve the designs in less than two weeks. I've *earned* the right to see the commission through.'

'All right.' Reece was prepared for just this reaction. 'We'll compromise. You'll wait until the commission is finished, then join a clinic. In the meantime, you'll have a doctor stay here with you at the house. You can say he's a friend, or a business associate — anything you want. But he stays here. And you talk to him. I get daily reports on your progress and you stay away from your sister and your mother.'

'You have someone in mind?'

'I do,' Reece admitted. 'A friend of mine from the States. He's a wonderful therapist. He hates pain, you see,' Reece said, watching Justin closely. 'He takes it personally. He'll be good for you, Justin. And he'll be good *to* you, I promise you that.'

Justin stared at him in silence for a couple of minutes, then nodded. 'All right. Deal.'

'And no more scheming,' Reece warned. 'Frank will know, Justin. And if I even suspect you're up to something, I'll have you committed so fast you'll miss it if you blink. Don't think I can't do it. Or won't,' Reece added, meaning it.

Justin smiled with his usual brand of crooked contempt. 'Whatever you say. May I go now? I am still able to come and go as I please?'

'Of course you are,' Reece said wearily, watching as he opened the door. 'And, Justin? I know you'd turn on your own mother and sister, given half the chance. Let me tell you now, if you hurt either of them, I might decide that an asylum is too good for you. Do you understand me?'

Justin smiled coolly, gave him a mocking salute, then closed the door behind him. Once outside, though, he swayed in the hallway, and reached out to lean against a wall.

He heard a furtive, scuttling sound and almost cried out. He spun around just in time to see Roger moving quickly up the stairs. He almost wilted in relief. His simpleton of an uncle. He'd forgotten he even existed.

Perhaps he should join good old Uncle Roger up in the attics, he mused. Become another legendary Syramore-Forbes madman.

Justin began to laugh, and once he'd started, he found he couldn't stop.

CHAPTER 26

Venice

Flame and Reece returned from the Verde, the open-air theatre on the Isola di San Giorgio Maggiore, still full of the spectacle of *Romeo and Juliet*. In the salon, Owen glanced up from a pile of photographs and smiled. The Corraldo women had inundated him with love, care and entertaining ideas, treating him like a long-lost son. And he loved it. Better still, over the past week he'd begun to regain more and more of his memory. Last night, he and Francesca had made love for the first time since the accident. It had been a gentle relearning experience for both of them and now, for the first time, he was beginning to truly believe things would work out.

'Hi, you two. Come over here and have a look at these,' he greeted them cheerfully, and Flame and Reece obligingly sat down either side of him. Giulietta glanced at Flame thoughtfully, then moved her gaze across to Reece. Flame intercepted the look, and nodded slightly. The time had come to tackle Reece about that last day at Ravenscroft — about what he'd overheard and misunderstood. Reece had been so aloof since Owen's accident, and it was driving her crazy. She'd far rather he railed at her than ignored her!

'How are the designs coming, *cara*?' Francesca asked, and Flame gave a heartfelt sigh of relief.

'I've done all the set pieces,' she admitted with satisfaction, 'but I want to do something . . . *flamboyant.* Something the Principessa will only see for the first time at the presentation.'

As the women nodded in perfect understanding, Owen frowned. 'Isn't that dangerous? What if she doesn't like it?'

Flame shrugged. 'I know it's risky. But . . .' She struggled to explain, and it was Giulietta who came to the rescue.

'Every great jewellery exhibition needs something that will bring gasps from the audience as well as the recipient,' she explained. 'And the Principessa is a woman who appreciates grand gestures. I think it's an excellent idea, *cara*,' she encouraged.

Flame smiled. Good advice. But what could she do? What could she think of that she hadn't already incorporated into the collection?

'Those are lovely,' Reece said, knowing the pressure she was under and trying to change the subject. Flame glanced down at the photograph he was holding, her eyes softening at the romance of it. It was sepia with age, and showed a beautiful young woman in a long flowing evening gown.

'Grandy, is that you?' Flame asked, gasping. She was stunning.

Giulietta smiled. 'A ball in 1941,' she admitted. 'Even in war, Venice knew how to hold a masked ball.' Her voice was rich with indulgence and memory.

Flame glanced again at the picture and inspected the mask her Grandy was holding. It was a traditional mask, wispy at the edges with faded feathers, very slanted eyeholes, and gaudy with sequins. Suddenly she drew her breath in sharply, and her eyes became as round as saucers. 'Grandy, do you still have that magazine picture of the Principessa?' They'd had it enlarged, and now Giulietta handed it over, her lips twitching. She recognized that look in Flame's eye. It was her 'brainstorming' look.

Flame stared at the face of the Principessa di Maggiore, noting the high cheekbones and the almost savage line of her jaw. It was a commanding rather than beautiful face. It was a face that demanded to be looked at. Suddenly, and without a word, Flame leaped off the sofa and ran for her room. They could hear her footsteps as she ran up the stairs and, a second later, the slamming of her door.

'Bye, Flame,' Reece said drolly, and everyone burst into laughter.

'I take it she just thought of something outrageous,' Owen said, now feeling at total ease with this tight-knit Italian family. The horror and darkness of the accident and memory loss were rapidly fading. He reached across for Francesca, and her hand was immediately in his, strong, warm, encouraging.

Maria laughed at Owen's comment, and Francesca's smile became crafty as it turned to Reece. 'My daughter is a spontaneous creature, all right,' she murmured, and then frowned as Reece, instead of smiling or making a witty comeback, winced instead. A look of pain crossed his face that made Giulietta sigh. Whatever had happened between the youngsters, she only hoped Flame would make her move to put it right soon.

Flame did.

* * *

After working feverishly all that evening, by the time she was satisfied she'd captured every nuance of her idea, it was after midnight. Flame was far too worked up to sleep, so she took a quick shower and, smiling slightly, selected her sheerest negligee. It was pure white and swung just above her knees. She brushed out her long, glorious hair, letting it lie straight down her back, almost reaching her waist. Then she tiptoed across the corridor and opened Reece's door. A faint breeze stirred the lace curtain at his open window as she crept to his bed and looked down.

He was wonderfully naked. In the moonlight she could see the rise and fall of his well-muscled chest, and her throat went dry. Feeling a little unsure, she reached out with one hand tentatively to touch his nipple. Instantly, his hand shot out and grabbed her wrist, and she gave a small strangled cry of surprise. His grip was like iron.

Reece's eyes shot open, all his senses on alert. But this was no bushman out to rob, or constricting snake out to feed on him, but a beautiful vision in white. He blinked, then laughed softly. 'You shouldn't creep up on a man like that,' he whispered, his hand curling around her neck to pull her down on to the four-poster bed. Their lips met in a gentle kiss that so quickly became urgent that within seconds she was naked too. She gasped as his hands rose to cup her breasts, his calloused thumb rubbing wonderfully against her throbbing nipples. She moaned, deep in her throat, and felt her blood race as he all but threw her on to her back, her body welcoming the heavy weight of his. She felt her thighs being forced apart by his stronger ones, and her body instantly melted.

'Oh, Reece,' she said, which was all she could manage. All thoughts of explaining herself had vanished.

Reece lunged into her, and instantly her inner muscles contracted fiercely around him, dragging a ragged breath from the very bottom of his lungs. Her legs wound around his back, trapping him, a willing prisoner of her body. He gathered his strength to lunge again, his eyes closing on a look of near-agony. 'Damn you,' he gritted. 'What kept you so long?'

* * *

Frank Jensen moved with the stealth of a cat. The magnificent house was in darkness, but he'd long since become acclimatized to Ravenscroft. He'd arrived the same day Reece had left for Venice, and they'd had little time to talk. Not that Frank had needed it. Just one meeting with Justin Syramore-Forbes had convinced him that the boy needed help. Badly.

They'd met in the library, where Justin had played the role of Earl superbly. But Frank knew the disguise for what it was. He'd taken the cool greeting and the undisguised hostility in Justin's eyes with a simple acceptance that had terrified Justin. For the first few days, Justin had managed to pretend that nothing was wrong. He was free of his dreaded family, and prayed they'd stay in Venice forever. Frank Jensen wasn't perpetually asking awkward questions, as he'd expected, and soon Justin found himself talking quite openly with him about the safer topics. Frank was interested in how a great estate was run, and Justin obliged. He didn't know, then, how much of his personality he was revealing to a man who was an expert at listening.

Now Frank paused, peering into the darkness. He glanced up at the stairs leading to the attic. He had met Roger, but knowing how much Justin needed to be the centre of someone's, *anyone's* attention, had deliberately kept himself strictly to the matter at hand. Justin had at first been bewildered by the psychiatrist's attention, then terrified, then . . . reluctantly, gratified. Frank was satisfied with the progress. Now, he carried on down the corridor, his agile and sympathetic mind calculating every eventuality. He knew what a profound effect meeting his mother had had on Justin, and how it had impacted on his already considerable paranoia. They would have to tackle that soon. But first . . . When he got to Justin's door he opened it very carefully, and slipped inside. Justin lay sleeping, looking lost in the huge Queen Anne bed. Noiselessly, Frank pulled up a chair, sat down and waited.

* * *

Reece slipped out of bed and stood at the window, content, sated but restless. He knew why, of course. He simply had to get back to Queensland, but how could he leave her? The miners were happy to go back to work, but Reece needed to oversee the repairs for himself first, and satisfy himself the mine was safe once more.

He turned, his face anxious, to look down at her asleep on the bed. She was gloriously naked, her hair a tangle of flame on the pillow, her breasts gleaming like pale orbs, and his body responded immediately to the sight of her. She was like a drug, and he was an addict.

It was at that moment, as if sensing his scrutiny, that her eyelashes flickered open. She looked up at him, unafraid, still sleepy, but instinctively understanding *that* look in his eyes.

'Reece,' she murmured. Before she took him to bed again, she needed to get the mess sorted out. 'About Scott. I know you overheard everything but it wasn't true. I—'

'Of course it wasn't true,' Reece interrupted. 'I hope you gave him hell. Cheeky son-of-a-bitch.'

Flame blinked at him, totally nonplussed. 'But . . . why did you leave, then?'

Reece scowled. 'The cave-in. Didn't you get my note?'

'Note?' Flame stared at him blankly, then sighed. 'No. No note.' For a moment they said nothing, each of them knowing who must have taken it.

'Oh, damn,' Reece finally said. 'Is that why you never got in touch?'

Flame bit her lip. 'Your father told me about the cave-in when I got back from Venice, but I didn't know when you got the call about it. You left so abruptly, I thought it had to be what you'd heard. Oh, Reece, what's it going to take to get us to trust each other?' she asked, her voice both weary and angry. 'And why didn't you call me?' she challenged. It wasn't all her fault, after all.

'You were always out,' Reece said flatly. Then added, 'According to Chamberlain.' And, again, they both knew who pulled Chamberlain's strings.

'That's it!' Flame said, her voice strong and defiant. 'From now on, if you come back to me smothered in cheap perfume with lipstick on your collar and a silly smirk on your face and you tell me you've been working late at the office, I'll believe you!'

Reece threw back his head and laughed. 'Like hell you will. You'll probably throw something at me.'

'True. The biggest and heaviest something I can find.'

Reece growled, and fell onto the bed to gather her in his arms, his eyes ablaze. He felt her nipples, like tiny pebbles, digging into his chest, and made a small, inarticulate sound that set her blood raging. Quickly, she pulled him down to the centre of the bed, and yelped as she felt him take her ankles in his hands and yank.

She gasped, staring up at the ceiling, as he kissed first the instep of her foot, then the back of her calves, before rising to the tender dip in the back of her knee. Her eyes closed as his lips blazed a trail to her thighs, then gasped as his head dipped to sip at the nectar he found within the triangle of flame-coloured hair. His tongue found her clitoris and stroked mercilessly as she began to thrash her head from side to side, his strong hands keeping a firm grip on her knees, keeping her legs apart. Her mouth fell open in a silent scream of ecstasy as the first orgasm hit and rolled across her in a hot, obliterating wave.

* * *

Justin awoke with a scream. He snapped on the lamp with frantic fingers and sat, heaving for breath. He looked white, his eyes still dark with remembered terror. And then he saw Frank. For a second the terror intensified, then, strangely, began to seep away. 'What are you doing here?' he asked, trying to inject some kind of authority into his voice and failing. He was a man in torment, and for once his acting skills were not going to save him.

'I was waiting for you to wake up,' Frank said, his voice as gentle as a summer rain.

'Why?'

'So we could discuss your nightmares.'

Justin stared at him, amazed. 'But . . . how did you know . . . ?'

Frank sighed. 'Justin, I know you must have been plagued with nightmares all your life. I know the kind of pain you've been in. I want to help. Why don't you let me?'

Justin quickly looked away, but Frank stayed obstinately put. Sighing, he lifted his knees under the bedclothes and rested his chin on them in a classic self-defensive gesture. How young he is, Frank thought, empathy rising up in him. An empathy he kept very professionally controlled.

'They're nothing, really,' Justin finally said. 'Why don't you go back to your own room? Or are you queer?' he sneered.

Frank leaned back in the chair. 'You're not going to frighten me away,' he said, and watched Justin sink back against the pillows, his handsome face gaunt. 'You're so tired, aren't you? You've been struggling for years to keep your head above water and now, almost all your strength is gone.' He saw the boy swallow hard. 'So, Justin, what are you going to do about it?'

Justin turned to him. 'You know,' he said thoughtfully, 'you're the most ruthless man I ever met.'

Frank nodded. 'I'm determined to help you.'

Justin's face contorted with fear, hope and something else. Something . . . desperate. 'No matter what?' he finally said.

Frank met his eyes head-on. 'Yes, Justin. No matter what.'

CHAPTER 27

Flame had never felt so nervous, and her stomach tightened into an ever-increasing knot as the Principessa Sofia Elena di Maggiore turned yet another page of the portfolio in total silence. Flame, strain as she might, could detect not even the faintest sigh or gasp to use as a pointer to the Principessa's true feelings. Her face was perfectly expressionless as she turned yet another page, which made six in all. Six designs, and not a word. Flame felt her throat constrict, and was forced to take a rather ragged breath. She was not sure she could stand much more of this. She had expected the voluble Principessa to coo or carp with every sketch. Not this . . . nerve-racking silence!

They were in the most elegant of Ravenscroft's salons. Outside, the trees in the wood were turning to copper, magenta, pale yellow and burnished brown. A cool wind, whipping raindrops against the window, was the only sound in the room. Flame glanced at Justin, who was sitting in his usual high-backed chair, dressed in an impeccable navy-blue suit yet managing to look the picture of indolence. She noticed the Principessa's eye stray to Justin from time to time, and who could blame her? What woman would not want to look at Justin?

The rustle of another page turning drove Flame's attention back to the Principessa, and by craning her neck she could see the design number: 10. Her heart jumped. If any piece could be called 'risqué' this was it. It was, as she'd labelled it at the top corner, a 'body brooch' of a particularly large and spectacular design. Flame had noticed that stiff velvet gowns were once more in fashion in Venice, and she knew that velvet was a material well able to support the biggest of brooches. Consequently, she'd designed a brooch that was to cover much of the upper body, from a few inches above the waist to just below the shoulder. Naturally she'd used the lightest of materials available, and the brooch had the lowest density ratio of all her work. It was in the design of a perfect spider-web, woven of silver and platinum, with diamond dewdrops and a jet and agate spider in one corner. It looked breathtaking as a sketch and would be eye-popping as a finished piece of jewellery. But did the Principessa feel the same, or did she find it too absurd? Ugly? Perhaps too young or outrageous for a middle-aged woman? It was impossible to tell. But it was not her imagination that the Principessa lingered over it for a much longer period than usual, before continuing her nerve-racking scrutiny and turning yet another page.

Flame twisted in her seat. If only Reece were not in Queensland but sitting next to her, winking at her, reassuring her that this was hardly the end of the world after all. Her mind drifted back to memories of their long nights of love-making and whispered, laughing conversations. She could feel again his strong, hirsute leg nudging hers aside, his lips fastening on to her . . .

'Well, Lady Flame, I must say this is a most . . . interesting, extensive and . . . *original* set of designs.' The Principessa's voice cut across Flame's erotic thoughts like an icy knife, and had her coming to the edge of her seat. Was there a 'but' in that statement? she wondered nervously. But the Principessa closed the folder and for the first time allowed a wide smile to transform her face. 'I love them,' she said simply, and Flame felt the breath explode out of her in a huge wave of relief.

'I'm so glad,' Flame said, then laughed, wondering if she'd ever before uttered such a profound understatement. The two women beamed at each other in mutual understanding and excitement.

Justin slowly rose. 'We were hoping, Principessa, that you would join us for lunch?' His voice was perfectly courteous, totally hiding his simmering rage. Despite the setback it would have meant to Halcyone's, he'd been half-hoping that the Principessa would despise his sister's designs.

But he smiled charmingly as Sofia di Maggiore gladly accepted the invitation to lunch. As he led her to the sumptuously appointed dining room, he let his hand slightly caress her lower back. As he seated her with outrageous gallantry, Flame saw Frank Jensen walk past the open window, one of Justin's dogs trotting happily by his side.

Flame knew why Frank was there, of course. She'd been present when Reece had given him a file on Justin just before they left for Venice. Flame had not asked what was in the file — she wasn't sure she wanted to know. She only hoped that the psychiatrist would be able to do her brother good, and, after meeting Frank, she was convinced that would be the case. There was something so warmly compassionate and yet strong about Frank that she herself responded to. And she'd noticed that Justin talked to him far more readily than Flame had ever expected. She was making an effort to keep out of their way as much as possible. Owen and Francesca had offered to fly back with her for moral support when she met the Principessa, but Reece had told them that Frank wanted a clear field. Francesca had made no objection. She knew as well as anyone that Justin needed all the help Frank could give him.

'So,' the Principessa said to Flame, as the first course was served. 'You will oversee the manufacture of the designs, *si?*' she asked, excited and impatient now to get her hands on the pieces.

'Once the stones are cut, yes,' Flame said. 'But stone-cutting is Gunther's province. And, of course,' she said, catching Justin's eye, 'my brother will have an even bigger part to play, making sure we have all the supplies we need ordered, and work schedules made out, and . . . oh, a hundred and one other things I wouldn't even think of!'

Justin smiled over gritted teeth as the Principessa laid a hand on his arm, her well-manicured nails bright pink against his suit. 'Oh, I know how well-organised Lord Justin is,' she purred, and fingered the enamel pendant she had 'made' on her last visit to Woodstock. She didn't notice how Justin's eyes glittered in fury. He forced himself to smile at her, when all he really wanted to do was scream. He didn't need his twin to sing his praises, damn her condescending hide.

Sophia turned back to Flame, her eyes twinkling. 'So, Lady Flame, you will have some spare time before your lovely designs are made into the real thing. I hope you plan to make the most of it?'

Flame's face lit up like a candle. 'Oh, I will!' she said fervently. 'I'm going to Australia.' She beamed, and Sofia sighed. Ahh, what it was like to be young and in love. For the Principessa was sure that the lovely redhead was not off down under just to see the kangaroos!

* * *

Reece, hundreds of feet beneath the red, baked Australian earth, glanced up nervously as the overhead lighting began to sway. He didn't like it. 'How long's it been doing this exactly?' he asked Mike Faraway, the shaft foreman.

Mike, a grizzled, experienced miner, shook his head. 'Days. But, like I said, we can't find anything wrong.'

Reece nodded. He'd ordered all work stopped when Mike had come to him with his report, and now he looked around, as puzzled as his employee. Everything seemed fine, the engineers had given the mine the go-ahead, all the safety regulations were being strictly adhered to and yet . . . 'What does the seismograph say?' he asked briskly.

Mike shrugged, and removed his safety helmet only long enough to wipe the sweat from his forehead. 'Nothing,' he said, his voice husky with dryness and worry. 'It's been clear since the cave-in.'

Reece nodded. The mine had been working as normal for several days before he'd called this latest halt in production. If Mike Faraway was worried, Reece was worried. 'Do me a favour, Mike, and go and see if anything's registered now.' The lights were no longer swaying, but it still didn't feel right.

Mike nodded and left, and a few minutes later Reece heard the familiar whine of the main-shaft lift as it headed up. He stared up above him for a long while, then moved to the main shoring beams. He pushed hard against one, but it was, as expected, rock-solid.

The whine of the lift returning made him frown. It couldn't be Mike coming back already, and he wondered who'd disobeyed his orders to keep the mine clear until the problem was sorted. He shrugged and moved on to the next beam and heaved, and immediately felt the ice hit his back. Somewhere, high above him, something had moved. He looked up as a fine mist of dust rained down on his face . . .

'Hello, handsome,' Flame said, and Reece almost cried out. For a moment he thought gas must have leaked into the chamber, causing him to hallucinate. Then he turned and saw her, and she launched herself into his arms, knocking him backwards in her exuberance.

'Flame? What the hell . . . ?' Who had let her come down here? But then he knew better than anybody that it was no use trying to say no to Flame when she got an idea into her head.

'I just couldn't stay away a moment longer,' Flame said, and drew his head to hers to kiss him so deeply that Reece thought she was trying to suck his boots off. His arms tightened around her in instant reaction as his heart thumped happily. When he broke away, his eyes glittered in the dim light.

'You shouldn't be down here. It's not safe . . .' No sooner had the last word left his mouth than he felt the vibration in his ear. His face paled. 'Oh, God, no,' he whispered. 'Not now!'

'Reece?' Flame said, then heard it herself. A low, ominous rumble. Beneath her, the ground started to vibrate. It felt as if she was on a bridge, with a high-speed train rocketing through beneath her. She blinked as the shadows began to elongate in an eerie, terrifying way and the lights above her swayed alarmingly. A wave of mind-numbing fear hit her. 'Reece?' Her voice was raised into an alarmed, high-pitched squeal as she reached for him and clung desperately to his solid width. The rumble grew to an all-pervading crash as she screamed what she was sure would be her final words to him. 'Reece, I love you.'

Reece didn't hear her. Desperately he threw her to the ground, then threw himself on top of her as the lights failed and they were suddenly plunged into a darkness so profound it seared the soul. Flame sensed, rather than saw, the collapsing earth and rock coming down around them, and had time for one last thought.

At least they would die together.

* * *

Walt Matthews looked up in surprise as Justin walked into his office. 'Lord Justin. I didn't know you were coming up to London.' He hastily indicated a chair. 'Congratulations on yesterday, my lord,' he allowed his voice to soften and warm. 'I hear the Principessa raved about the collection.'

Justin smiled. His eyes, however, seemed curiously dead, and Walt watched him cautiously. 'Indeed,' Justin agreed, his own voice warming. 'That's why I've come to see your specs.' Walt had by far the most technically detailed of all the specifications of Flame's original designs. She and Reece had had a small cabinet safe brought to Flame's room, with a combination no one was going to give out to him. As if that would stop him, he thought sneeringly. Now he leaned back in the chair and smiled easily at Walt. Scott was due to make the phone call in five minutes. He'd better get on with it. 'I need to calculate supplies and manpower,' he explained, 'and we want the collection finished by the end of the year.'

Walt nodded. It made sense. And yet . . . Walt didn't trust the Earl of Ravenscroft at the best of times. Nevertheless, he knew he couldn't deny him what he wanted. He had no reason to. He walked to his safe, but carefully kept his broad back in front of it as he dialled the combination. Reluctantly he handed the specs to Justin, who pulled out a notebook and began taking diligent notes.

Walt watched him, wondering why he should feel so uneasy. Justin was a superb manager, and no one doubted that his input was invaluable. His thoughts were interrupted by the ringing of the telephone, and when he answered it, Justin saw his face pale. 'Oh no! Is she all right?' There was a pause, then Walt swallowed hard. 'I'll be there right away.' He hung up and rose quickly, then hesitated, glancing at Justin. 'I have to leave, my lord. There's been an accident. My wife . . .'

Justin waved his hand. Good old Scott! 'Goodness, of course you must go, Walt. I do hope she's all right. And don't worry about these,' he tapped the portfolio. 'I'll see they get put back into the safe.'

Walt nodded and hurried out. But on the way past his secretary's desk he stopped. 'Miss Winter, pull the plug on the photocopying machine.' He pointed at the piece of office equipment. 'And put an "Out of Order" sign on it. If the Earl of Ravenscroft tries to use it, you're to say it's broken. All right?'

Miss Winter blinked, but nodded and efficiently carried out her boss's orders. She shook her head over the foibles of the rich and famous as she did so, but the Earl never left Walt's office to ask to use the machine.

Justin had no need to. He had a small but sophisticated camera hidden in his pocket. He very carefully took three pictures of all the specs before putting the folder diligently back into the safe.

He smiled very charmingly at Miss Winter on the way out.

CHAPTER 28

In the darkness, Flame could hear the twin pounding of their hearts — hers quick and panicked, those of Reece, still pressed on top of her, slowing now, becoming regularly and reassuringly strong. He began to stir, lifting himself up on to his elbows as Flame clung to him in the darkness, afraid suddenly that if he left her she would never find him again in this awful blackness.

'It's all right — I have to light the back-up lamps.' His voice was strong, sure, and so blissfully alive. She forced her hands to slide reluctantly away from his warmth, and waited for what seemed like ages. Then a small, wavering beam of light pierced the darkness, and she could see that he was holding the light attached to his helmet. Around her, the floor was a mass of rubble. She knew she would probably be dead if it had not been for Reece's sheltering arms and body.

Knowing he had little time and little light left, Reece searched quickly, while Flame wondered how much air they might have left. She tried to take shallow breaths, but the dust hanging in the air caught in her throat, making her cough wretchedly. She felt infinitely better, however, when first one light, then another came on. Slowly, she turned over on to her hands and knees and gingerly stood up. She felt sore all over.

'You should have lain still.' Reece loomed out of the murky light, looking so wonderfully familiar that she felt tears smart in her eyes. 'You might have broken something.'

'I'm fine,' she said, her voice coming out remarkably strong and sure under the circumstances. She looked around. The passageway through which she had come was no more than a wall of rock and debris. Great beams of wood criss-crossed the cave like a bizarre obstacle course. Reece nevertheless checked her over, and only then went to the rockfall and explored it in minute detail. Knowing she couldn't help, Flame found a large rock in what looked like a clear and safe area and sat down, her legs shaking helplessly. Slowly, the consequences of their situation began to sink in. And it was the stuff of nightmares. To be buried alive, perhaps never to be found. To slowly suffocate, to feel your life slipping away. She found a sob rising in her throat and quickly swallowed it back. She would not give way to panic or hysteria. Besides, Reece was with her, and immediately as she thought it, she felt the worst of the despair drain away. She watched him moving about in the dimness, content now in the strong, sure presence of the man she loved. Reece came back within a few minutes, and knelt down in front of her to take her cold hands in his warm ones. There was not a trace of fear on his face.

'It's not as bad as it looks. From the measured marks on the wall, I don't think the fall is very dense. They'll certainly have heard it upstairs and must already be on their way.'

Flame nodded. If that was the way he wanted it, she would go along. Pretend everything would be all right.

'The first thing they'll do is find a way to send a wire to us.'

'Wire?' she echoed, puzzled.

'A hose. For air, and to talk to us.'

'How much air do you think we have?' She forced the question out. Reece's eyes narrowed as he stared down at her bent head and lifted her chin. Only when her frightened brown eyes were looking into his did he smile gently.

'Air is no problem, Flame. This is one of the central shafts. Look over there.' He swung the lamp in the direction that led further into the mine and she could see a long tunnel, only semi-blocked, leading further away.

'Can't we get out down that way?' Hope rose up, only to be dashed as he shook his head.

'No, sweetheart, we can't. But the point is, those tunnels are littered with ventilation shafts — we'll have air for as long as we need it.' He did not add that he had found only one spare water bottle, and that that had been broken, leaving barely a few swallows in the bottom for each of them. 'Do me a favour.' He drew her smoothly to her feet. 'Come here and watch this wall for me . . .' Carefully he led her over the debris of the mineshaft to where the rockfall loomed above her. 'I want you to stay here and listen. The moment you hear anything, anything at all, I want you to call me. OK?'

Flame nodded, then, as he turned away from her, tugged on his hands. 'Where will you be?'

Reece turned, cursing himself for his thoughtlessness. 'Now, where would I go?' he asked. Never before had her soft chuckle sounded so wonderful. 'I want to look around — make sure there are no more weak spots, test the walls for any possible subsidiary slide.'

'OK.' Her small voice sounded determinedly brave and bright, and Reece found his heart swelling in pride. Gently he bent down and drew her to him, her warm body clinging to his like a kitten's. Slowly he stroked her hair, reassuring her silently, then he lowered his lips to hers. They tasted dusty and sweet, and Reece felt his body quicken. Firmly but tenderly, he pushed her away. There was no time for that now. 'Don't worry. They'll be here soon, and we always have special equipment on hand. We'll be out in time for cocktails.'

Flame laughed, even though she knew he was only saying it to cheer her up. But, when he left her, she didn't feel so afraid. Turning back to the wall of rock in front of her, she sighed deeply, and pressed her ear to the rock and listened intently. Behind her, Reece searched in vain for water.

* * *

Hatton Garden it isn't, Justin thought with a wry smile as he parked his car near the river, far from London's new, much-touted Docklands. The streets here were grim and grey, but in front of him was a warehouse owned by Felix Barstowe, and that was all that mattered. Justin walked up to the high tin doors and knocked, the sound echoing eerily beyond. Recalling what Scott Tate had said about Barstowe, he wondered idly how the criminal underworld fared these days.

The thought made him smile, and the coldness of it was enough to intrigue the man who was watching him from inside the warehouse on the monitor attached to a hidden camera. Felix Barstowe was forty, extremely lean, extremely intelligent, and extremely crooked. His right-hand man, known only as Sandy, shifted beside him.

'Let the Earl in, Sandy,' Barstowe said, his voice so soft it was almost a whisper. When Justin entered the office, he was clutching his small leather briefcase in a white-knuckled grip, and had to fight to remember all of Scott's instructions. Felix Barstowe was a professional crook, Scott had briefed him, with the emphasis on 'professional'. Make the deal straight, simple and sure, and there would be no problem. It had all sounded so easy and *safe* in the sanctuary of Ravenscroft's library. Now, it felt anything but. Justin nodded at Barstowe.

'Lord Justin. Please come in.'

Justin blinked at the softness of the voice but took the chair and, without preamble, opened his briefcase. Barstowe steepled his fingers and watched Justin closely as he extracted a sheaf of papers. 'I believe my associate, Mr Tate, has informed you that I wish to do some business with you?' Justin began cautiously.

Barstowe nodded. 'What exactly is it that you have in mind?'

Wordlessly, Justin handed over the photographs. Felix looked through them in silence. When he'd finished, he looked at Justin curiously. 'These wouldn't be the designs for that Italian princess's jewellery, would they?'

Justin was not surprised that Barstowe was well up on the news. 'Some of them, yes,' he admitted crisply. 'I want you to have paste jewels made in the exact proportions as those stones marked on the photos. On the night before the pieces are to be presented, I want your people to replace the real stones with the counterfeit.'

'That's dangerous and skilled work,' Barstowe pointed out.

'I own the workshop where the finished items will be stored,' Justin informed him. 'You'll find the alarms will be turned off. I also have the combination to the vault.'

Barstowe looked through the photos again. He had people who could make the paste, all right, but it would take a skilled artisan to remove the real gems and replace them with the paste. 'I take it you want the replacements done so that no one but a skilled jeweller will know the difference?'

'That's right,' Justin said. He wanted it good enough so that the Principessa wouldn't be able to tell the junk from the good. Only when she had it independently appraised would the pieces be exposed as tainted.

'It will be the end of Halcyone's,' Barstowe said, his voice curious.

Justin smiled coldly. 'I know,' he acknowledged, but made no further comment. Instead he opened his briefcase again, lifted back a secret flap of leather, and began to place wads of cash on the desk. 'Ten thousand pounds up front. Another fifty when the substitutions are made.'

Felix Barstowe nodded, rose slowly to his feet, and held out a long, well-manicured hand. 'Done.'

* * *

'Hello in there . . . Can you hear me, Mr Dexter?' The voice was muffled and came through a long white plastic tube that had suddenly appeared between a crack in the rocks like a subterranean worm.

Flame stood up with a little squeal. 'Reece! Come quickly. Look!'

Reece scrambled up the rock and carefully pulled the pipe further into the cavity. Putting his mouth to it, he shouted loudly. 'Yes, I can hear you. I'm not alone down here — Lady Flame Syramore-Forbes is with me. Do you have that?'

There was a second or two of startled silence, then the voice came back. 'I understand. There are two of you down there. Is anyone injured?'

'No. No injuries. The shaft is clear at the back, so air's no problem.' He hoped Flame hadn't understood the meaning of his emphasis on 'air', at the same time hoping that Mike Faraway, whose voice he'd recognized, had.

'I understand. *Air* is not the problem,' Mike's voice came back, letting him know that he'd understood perfectly. 'Do you have a receptacle?'

'My helmet,' Reece yelled, and glanced down at Flame to see her looking at him, her brows pulled into a puzzled frown.

'Stand by,' Mike yelled back. Flame watched, more puzzled than ever when Reece took off his metal helmet and held it beneath the hose. Only when she saw water pour from the hose did she understand. Never for a single moment had she given water, and what they might drink, a passing thought. When the helmet was full, Reece gave the hose a firm tug, and a few seconds later the flow of water ceased. Wordlessly, Reece held the brimming helmet down to her, and Flame took it from him. She walked very carefully with the precious cargo and found two rocks close together. There she carefully positioned the helmet between them, not spilling a drop.

'How does it look, Mike?' Reece yelled into the hose, and Flame quickly moved back to the rockfall, wanting to hear what was going on.

'Not too bad, boss. We'll have you out of there within ten to sixteen hours, I reckon.'

Reece nodded, then yelled back into the hose, 'OK. What machinery are you going to use?' Flame listened to the highly technical talk that followed, slowly realising that it was going to be all right after all. They were going to live! Both of them!

Outside, Mike Faraway walked away from the rockfall, Reece Dexter having told him all he needed to know. The roof was hardly secure. They would have to be careful. Very damned careful indeed. The men were clustered around the lift as he rose into the light. Briefly he gave them a rundown on the position, and there was obvious tension in the air when he informed them that a woman had gone down into the shaft. Heads would roll for that, but right now there were more important things to think about.

Mike moved quickly to the office, taking three of his best men with him. There he outlined the plan. But Mike knew that he had one more task to perform before the rescue operation got under way. Wearily he lifted the phone, looked out Reece Dexter's personal phone book, and began to dial.

* * *

The butler took the call and immediately went in search of Giulietta, who was in the main salon, overseeing a game of bridge that Owen and Francesca were currently winning. She left the card game with a murmured apology and took the call in near silence, listening to Mike Faraway's words with a grim expression on her face. Only when she was told that Flame was also trapped in the landfall did she speak.

'We shall be there as soon as possible. In the meantime, continue the rescue operation as you see fit.'

Mike Faraway, thousands of miles away, couldn't help but smile gamely at the tone of voice. He had thought it best not to speak to Reece's father, Owen, concerned for his well-being after his recent accident. Mike knew he'd be informed about his son if it was considered the best course of action. He assured Giulietta they would do all they could, then hung up. He glanced at his waiting men. 'Let's get on with it,' he said grimly. He didn't need to add anything more. They all knew the risks. If the roof gave in while they were levering the rockfall away . . .

* * *

Frank Jensen watched closely as Justin put down the phone. They had been having dinner when Chamberlain had brought in the telephone, citing an urgent call as an excuse for the interruption. From the moment Justin had snapped, 'Yes,' he'd felt his shoulder blades tense in foreboding. Watching his patient's face closely, he saw a strange gamut of emotion cross his blue eyes — surprise, delight, anger, anxiety, and, finally, an almost ironic humour. When he hung up, he was smiling that cold, almost desperate smile that still confused Frank. Justin was a challenging case — both victim and potential threat, a patient and yet a dangerous adversary.

Justin's mind was whirling. Reece and Flame buried in a mining accident. It was too good to be true. His two greatest enemies might die, without him even having to lift a finger.

'That was Mother,' he said quietly. 'Apparently there's been a cave-in at one of Reece's mines.' He returned to his dinner, but Frank was not fooled.

'Is anyone hurt?'

Justin shrugged. 'Reece and Flame are trapped. They're going to try and dig them out.' Justin speared a new potato and ate it with apparent enjoyment.

Frank watched him. 'You expect me to call you heartless? To rant and rave about how cold you are?' Frank too lifted his knife and fork and began to eat. He could do nothing for his friend, except worry and pray. Right now, the man sat opposite him was the only one he could possibly help. 'Sorry,' Frank said, reaching for his wine goblet. 'I don't think you're either. Your face made very interesting viewing just then, Justin,' he continued, noticing how the younger man tensed violently. 'Very interesting indeed. Why don't you tell me why this accident is so ironic?'

Justin stared at him, fighting off the honeyed panic that only Frank Jensen could arouse. Justin wanted to pour his heart out to him so much that it was almost a physical ache. But it was not possible that he knew about Felix Barstowe and the paste gems, and if Flame and Reece did die, no one else would know either. Justin could keep a secret better than anyone. He'd simply pay Barstowe off, abort the plan, and take all the credit for the commission. His life would be perfect again.

Then he felt his eyes being dragged back to Frank Jensen again, who was still watching him with his usual relentless patience and compassion, and he wondered with a painful pang just who he thought he was kidding.

CHAPTER 29

Flame felt the rocks begin to slide under her feet, and her arms shot out wildly in a desperate bid to steady herself. Ahead of her she heard Reece call out a warning, and a moment later strong hands grasped hers, making her feel infinitely safe again. Flame looked behind her, but in the ever-dimming light she could make out little. Which was just as well. She gauged they must have climbed at least six feet over the pile of rock that separated them from the tunnel that led deeper into the mine. 'Why . . . exactly . . . are . . . we . . . doing this?' she puffed around her laboured breathing. Fit as she was, the climb over shifting rock in near-darkness while breathing dust-laden stuffy air was taking its toll on her and she could feel the sweat trickle between her shoulder blades and run down her back. Reece reached the top and peered down, arching the lamp overhead, his eyes narrowed as he tried to pick out the best descent for them. 'Reece?'

He turned at the half-angry, half-amused voice and saw her lift herself up to stand beside him. 'When they start digging us out over there,' he pointed back to the chamber they had just left, 'it's more than likely that it'll dislodge some more rocks and debris from the roof.'

Flame bit her lip. 'So we'll be safer in here?'

'I think so.'

Flame looked at him. He looked dirty, angry, entirely male, and Flame felt an utterly feminine longing stir deep in her womb. Seeing that the ceiling was only an inch or two above Reece's dark head, a sudden thought made her shiver. 'Reece. What if, when they're digging us out, another fall comes on top of here and seals us in? Won't they have to dig us out all over again?'

Reece nodded. 'It's possible. But if it does happen, they *can* dig us out. If we stay in there and the rockfall buries us . . .' He peered carefully over the edge of the rockfall and put one foot down, listening to the ominous slither of stone and dust as he tested his weight. 'Come on, the more we stand here dithering the worse it will seem. Try and step exactly where I step as we descend, and remember one thing.' He turned to her, his voice sombre, his eyes glowing softly as he looked at her pale, worried face. She tilted her head, alerted to the seriousness of his tone, and raised questioning eyes to his.

'Yes, Reece? Remember that you love me?' she said softly. 'I know. I love you too.'

Reece leaned towards her and gently placing both hands on either side of her cheeks, rubbed his thumb lovingly across her nose. 'Well, that as well,' he whispered softly. 'Actually, I was going to say, if you fall, remember I'm in front so try not to fling the last of our water out of my hands.'

Flame blinked, saw his lips begin to curl into laughter, and growled. 'Oh, you . . . you . . . wretched man!' Then she began to laugh as well, and for several moments the dark cave around them echoed with his deep, rich baritone and her light, tinkling laughter.

'Come on.' Reece took her hand, his fingers closing softly and reassuringly around hers, and together they began the climb down to safety. Sometimes Reece would slip, and he'd let go of her hand immediately, in case he dragged her with him. Then Flame would slip and cannon into his back, rock-steady and always preventing her from injury. When they finally reached the rock floor, Flame was panting hard.

Reece immediately set about finding a good place for them to wait. He chose a turn in the tunnel, where, in the event of more rockfall, they would be best protected. He gauged they had at least twelve hours of light left on the lamp. Already six hours had passed.

Flame sank down next to him like an exhausted child. 'How long do you think it will be?' she asked softly, wiping a hand across her sweating forehead. She supposed she must look a sight, with her matted dusty hair, dirty face and drooping dungarees.

'It could be a while,' Reece warned her gently. 'It's been six hours so far, so by Mike's estimation we'll be waiting anywhere between another four to ten hours. However, we need to be prepared for twenty-four hours.'

'A day?' Flame squeaked, trying to keep her voice from sounding as appalled as she felt. She crawled across to him and rested her head against his chest. Reece drew in a sharp breath. Her nearness was driving him slowly out of his mind. Even the touch of her fingers on his cheek made the blood pound through his veins. He hoped that in the dim light she couldn't see the swelling that began to burgeon under his tight jeans.

'Gosh, it's hot,' Flame murmured, and, rising agilely to her feet, she undid the braces on her dungarees and let them fall.

'What are you doing?' Reece gulped, watching in fascinated desire as the baggy canvas material fell to her feet. She was wearing a tight white T-shirt and cut-off denim shorts.

'It's too hot to wear that thing.' Flame kicked the inoffensive dungarees, then spread her legs, resting her hands on her hips and looking down at him. 'And speaking of uncomfortable,' she said softly, 'aren't those jeans getting awfully . . . tight? If you're not careful they'll cut off your . . . circulation. Or something even more important,' she added, her eyes twinkling in irrepressible humour.

Reece grunted. 'Minx. I might have known your greedy little eyes wouldn't have missed that.' He unbuttoned the top of his jeans and unzipped his flies on a sigh of relief, unable to prevent a self-mocking grin as Flame laughed softly at his obvious predicament.

'You know,' Flame said thoughtfully, looking around her, 'it's too hot for this as well.' She plucked at her T-shirt disgustedly, then, with a swift, single movement, crossed her arms, grasped its hem and lifted it over her head. Reece stared up at her, unable to move. Flame looked down at him, then at her bare, pale skin, glowing in the dim light. Slowly, one exquisite eyebrow began to arch. 'And you say I have greedy eyes.' She shook her head at him in mock disappointment. Reece swallowed hard, then reached for the broken water bottle, taking a small sip.

'I'm still too hot,' Flame sighed, standing akimbo above him. 'Reece, what should I do?'

Reece licked his lips. 'You could take off the shorts,' he suggested hoarsely, and Flame looked down in exaggerated surprise, enjoying the game. At least he'd lost that awful sense of wariness. Was he at last beginning to accept that they belonged together? 'Why, Reece, you're quite right. All that heavy denim.' Her eyes burned like dark coals as she watched him watching her. Slowly she found her zip and listened at the angry sound it made as she undid it. A moment later, she stepped out of them, adding them to the pile.

Reece felt the stillness around them shimmer, waiting for the next moment. It came quickly. 'Isn't it amazing how even a piece of cotton like this,' Flame gently plucked the elasticated waist of her white cotton briefs with a careless finger, 'can feel as cloying as a blanket on a hot day? I think they'll have to go too.' Reece watched as her last item of clothing was shucked off, and heard his harsh rasping breath echo loudly in the tunnel. Wordlessly, he held out his arms and Flame came into them, kneeling either side of his thighs, her arms looping around his neck as her lips found his. Reece could feel the hardened points of her nipples pressing against his chest, and quickly ripped open his shirt, uncaring that the buttons scattered into the darkness with tiny 'pings' against the rock.

Quickly her hands slid between them, falling to his hardening manhood. Reece groaned, his legs jerking in instant reaction. Smiling in feline satisfaction, Flame gently lifted her lips from his then licked his mouth, tasting his maleness on her tongue. Then she ducked her head and neatly sucked one of his nipples into her mouth, almost losing her balance on his lap as Reece bucked beneath her, his eyes closing in helpless delight. 'Flame,' he murmured, obediently lying back at the urging of her hands, lifting his hips as she pulled down his jeans. Dimly, in the back of his mind, he understood her urgency, her passion. The nearness of death was a spur that ate at them. Psychologists believed that the act of love was an act of defiance against death, the very act of procreation a way of denying death its final victory.

And as Flame's tongue dipped into his navel, making his whole torso shudder in ecstasy, he realised that it was true — he had never felt more alive in his life than he did at this moment, with the spectre of death closing in all around them.

Gently, almost reverently, Flame's hand encircled his shaft, her small gasp mute testimony to the heat and velvet strength she could feel beneath her fingertips. Then the world turned and she found herself on her back, the coldness of the stone against her spine and shoulders, the hot searing heat of his skin on her stomach, breasts, and legs as he moved on top of her. She felt his hands, urgent and strong on her legs, moving them apart, and she closed her eyes, ready — oh so ready — for the hot intrusion of his maleness into the very heart of her femininity. When he entered her with one smooth, deeply penetrating movement, Flame screamed, a pure, simple, unashamed sound of deepest pleasure. She felt the delicate inner walls of her womanhood expand to accommodate its beloved invader, and when her eyes opened a moment later she found herself looking into the hot, stormy gaze of the man she would love with all her heart, body and soul, for the rest of her life. However short, or long, that might be. 'Reece,' she said, tears of joy making

281

her eyes shimmer like jet. 'Make love to me as we've never made love before. Please.'

Reece kissed her deeply, trying to convey with a caress of his lips what his voice couldn't communicate. And in that moment, Flame thought that no woman had ever been loved so much and so well — not Juliet, not Helen of Troy, not Catherine Earnshaw, not Cleopatra. When he lifted his head she was crying softly, but her legs locked around his lower back, her spine arched strongly, and Reece became lost in their passion. Eagerly, willingly, he lost himself in the savage, beautiful, greedy dance of love, loving her until the last of his titanic strength was gone, spilling his seed of life into her in a hot gushing torrent, the echo of her own screams of fulfilment and ecstasy still ringing in his ears.

* * *

Justin pushed open the door to the workshop in the Woodstock emporium, and looked around. Gunther Voss sweated in one corner, currently working on a pendeloque cut for a top-quality £350,000 diamond that would be the main stone of the entire collection. Elsewhere, the pace was frantic. Quietly, so as not to disturb or distract a single craftsman, Justin moved to Gunther Voss's corner. Somewhere, right at this very moment, an exact replica of this stone was being made. Justin smiled grimly as he thought about the furore in the Principessa's camp when her experts declared this diamond, along with other major stones, to be fakes, an insult to the Principessa and the jewellery world in general. Briefly Justin's heart ached for Halcyone's, but it was all Flame's fault. He glanced at his watch. It was almost fifteen hours since he'd heard. Surely they were dead by now?

* * *

Mike glanced at the entrance to the elevator, and then at the men waiting beside it. Grimly he raised the radio to his mouth and gave the order. Deep below, the charge was detonated. A large slab of rock, too large to shift even by haulage machinery, had been blocking the shaft. Only dynamite could shift it. A second later, they heard the low rumble deep below ground and from the mine's entrance a great cloud of dust was spat from the earth.

Inside, Flame screamed. She couldn't help it, for there had been no warning. They'd dressed after making love, and had been lying on the floor in each other's arms when the explosion had rocked them, roaring in their ears and bringing down fresh cascades of dust on to their faces.

'Damn. I never thought of that,' she heard Reece's gravelly voice, somewhere above her, as he fumbled to turn the lamp back on. 'They must have hit a rock they couldn't shift except with dynamite.'

Shakily, Flame got to her feet. 'Did it work?'

But there was only one way to find out, and in grim silence they started back up the rockface, not knowing what they'd find on the other side — freedom, or a tomb.

* * *

At last, the elevator came into view and one of the group of waiting men quickly pulled back the metal door. For a second there was total silence as the men who had slaved non-stop for the last eighteen hours waited to see whether the lives they had sweated for had been saved. Then a figure stepped into the sunlight, a figure that had hair the same colour as the setting sun, a figure that was slender as a reed with a face as beautiful as a goddess. A massive cheer split the air. Grinning, Mike Faraway stepped from the elevator and turned as Reece Dexter followed him. Reece felt the slaps on his back from all sides, grinning at the feeling of comradeship all around him as he shook hands and shouted thanks into scores of dirty, sweaty, grinning faces.

Flame looked in awe at the beauty of the sunset all around her. She breathed deeply of the air that seemed as fresh, cool and dew-laden as any air on a frosty English winter's morning. 'It's so *good* to be alive!' she yelled.

CHAPTER 30

Flame still didn't know where the last three months had gone; they had passed in such a whirl of hectic, almost panic-stricken activity. Reece had had to stay on in Australia, promising to come to England the moment the mine was safe and fully operational again. Flame, firmly putting the nightmare of the accident behind her, was determined to get back to normal, which meant overseeing the commission. She'd been surprised to find, on entering Halcyone's Woodstock workshop, that work was already in progress. Moreover, after a few discreet questions, it didn't take long to realise that none of her staff had heard about the mining accident. Her brother hadn't bothered to inform them. Justin must really hate her, she'd thought sadly, to be so offhand.

On her second day back at Ravenscroft, however, Frank Jensen had cornered her in the library and given her a run-down on his progress with her brother so far. And, listening to Frank explain the reasons behind Justin's mental state, understanding fully, at last, the loneliness, the pressure, the sheer pain that had been her brother's childhood, she could have forgiven him anything. And over the next few weeks, while she had waited impatiently for Reece, and watched her drawings become the real, sparkling, three-dimensional things, Flame had seen for herself that Frank was getting closer to Justin, inch by hard-fought inch. And Francesca and Owen were both delighted by his progress.

But something was wrong. She could feel it. Her brother no longer looked at her with such cold, calculating hatred, and, perversely, that worried her. There had been moments, fleeting but growing in number, when she felt certain that Justin was simply waiting for something.

But then Reece had returned, and she'd felt instantly better. In his arms, she didn't awaken sweating and shaking, imagining the roof was caving in on her or that her twin brother was stalking through the house with a hatchet. Now, three months, two weeks and five days since the accident, Flame walked down the grand staircase and into the dining room. Giulietta and Maria had arrived yesterday, and she went to them first, kissing each of them on the cheek. 'I'm so glad you're here,' she whispered to her Grandy, giving the old woman, dressed in an impeccable sapphire-coloured satin blouse and long beige suede skirt, a warm hug.

'I wouldn't miss this evening for all the world,' Giulietta assured her.

Flame sat down beside Reece, who wordlessly took her hand in his and gave it a squeeze.

Flame knew, even as she helped herself to toast, that she wouldn't be able to eat it. If she had thought herself nervous before, when the Principessa had been looking at her designs, it was nothing to how she felt now. In just twelve hours, the Principessa would be looking at the real thing. Plus her surprise gift. Who knew how she'd react to it?

'Well, at least we can have breakfast in peace for once,' she sighed, the absence of carpenters, painters, decorators, restorers, art renovators and professional carpet-cleaners making the atmosphere feel almost idyllic. The party was not to be held in London as originally planned, but at Ravenscroft itself. She'd chosen the ballroom as the main arena — it was huge, had a high, cavernous ceiling, a black and white tiled floor and a large row of French windows. The four surrounding rooms, mainly salons, would be used as dining rooms. She'd checked everything only yesterday, and even she was impressed anew by Ravenscroft's elegant charm and beauty. She could only imagine the photographers' delight at seeing the old house themselves, for all the quality magazines and newspapers had been invited.

Chamberlain came in, long-faced, and announced that the caterers had arrived. Flame groaned, reached for a paper, ducked behind it, and got an acute case of deafness. Giulietta chuckled softly, and Francesca and Maria exchanged telling glances. 'I'll see to them, Chamberlain,' Francesca said, and on leaving the table gave her daughter's flame-coloured head an affectionate tousle. Owen looked at Reece.

'I think I feel an attack of fishing coming on.'

'Me too,' Reece said, and winced as Flame gave him a swift kick under the table.

From the corner of her mouth she hissed from behind the paper, 'Traitor. Coward.'

Grinning, the two men left. The doorbell went again, and Chamberlain came back, his face longer still. 'The musicians, my lady. They say they need to set up *amplifiers*.' Flame groaned, but was saved from answering by the summons of yet another ring. Chamberlain came back, the picture of long-sufferance. 'The electricians, my lady. You ordered special lighting for the ballroom?' She had. On the table where the jewels were to be displayed.

'What have I done?' she muttered behind her paper and, with a sigh, folded it angrily.

Frank Jensen chose that moment to step jauntily into the room. 'There's a gaggle of villainous-looking men out in the hall.'

'Don't worry, *cara*,' Giulietta said to Flame, her eyes twinkling. 'There's only the security team and the florists yet to come.'

Flame shot her a look and let rip with a mild scream and a very Italian wave of her hands. She stormed out, enjoying herself enormously. When she'd got everyone sorted and returned to the table, Justin came in. Frank looked up but said nothing as his patient helped himself to coffee and sat down.

Justin checked his watch. Ten-thirty. If Felix Barstowe's men had been caught in the workshop, he would have heard by now. So it was all on. His eyes met those of his sister. Would she go to prison? Probably. He only knew that he was safe — it was common knowledge that he had had little if anything to do with the actual hands-on work. But by then, he thought with a sudden smile, he'd be off in some nuthouse with Frank Jensen.

Flame felt a familiar sense of rising panic. Justin was up to something, she just knew it. But what could he have done? Everything was perfect — she herself had seen the pieces yesterday evening, and they were all magnificent. But still shivers of foreboding clung to her.

She was not alone. Frank was also alert to something being amiss. Justin was talking to him too unguardedly. It was as if Justin had . . . given up. As if he was at last prepared to let go of his hatred. But Frank knew him too well. He would not be so malleable now unless he was confident that he had won. To Justin, winning was everything.

Frank didn't like it. Even as he left the room with his patient, who had agreed to take him upstairs to visit Roger, he made a mental note to have a word with Reece the moment he put in an appearance. And to warn him to watch Justin like a hawk.

* * *

The first guests began to arrive at six. Rolls-Royces, Bentleys, Daimlers, Jaguars, and the more sporty Ferraris, Lamborghinis and Porsches began to fill the drive. Flame, along with the family, stood in the hallway, greeting everyone as if they were royalty themselves. The guests were a mixed bunch: English and Italian aristocracy, newspaper people, friends old and new, the Halcyone craftsmen of course, and key executives.

Flame winked at Walt Matthews, and gave Gunther Voss, who had done such a magnificent job cutting the stones, a kiss on the cheek. Owen, Reece and Justin all wore dinner jackets — Reece and Owen black ones, Justin white. How handsome they looked, Flame thought, her eyes resting on Reece. Giulietta, too, made a startling impact on the guests. With her silver hair piled high on her head and her slender figure encased from head to toe in deep red silk, she was still, in her eighties, a figure that somehow radiated beauty. Francesca, in emerald velvet, and Maria, in blue tulle, were impeccably groomed and gracious, but it was Flame who drew the most gasps, the most male smiles, the most envious female stares. Not wanting to outshine the Principessa, she had decided on a midnight-black dress of velvet, cut so simply it was little more than a modestly V-necked, V-backed swathe of material that left her arms and shoulders bare. A slit from ankle to mid-thigh had been necessary to enable her to walk in her high silver heels. A beaten-silver bracelet watch on one arm and silver and diamond-drop earrings were the only pieces of jewellery she wore. One of her own designs, of course. Aware that they were here to celebrate jewellery, every female guest had worn her best, determined not to be overshadowed. But with her hair loose in cascades of flame-coloured waves, a stark and impressive contrast against her black and silver ensemble, it was Flame who drew the eye, not the sea of sparkling gems worn by other women.

At seven o'clock precisely, the guest of honour arrived. The Principessa swept into the hall, drawing instant gasps of admiration. Flame was delighted to see that she was wearing a simple white velvet dress that left her arms and neck bare. She was wearing not a single piece of jewellery.

Flame gave a genuine smile of welcome as she reached for the Principessa, and to the delight of their audience they embraced happily to the flashbulb hysteria of the photographers. '*Cara*, I'd like you to meet the paragon I've been telling you about,' the Principessa said, drawing the squat, handsome man at her side towards Flame. 'This is my husband,

Guido Luciano. Guido, Lady Halcyone Syramore-Forbes. Known to all her friends as Flame.'

Guido stepped forward, his black eyes twinkling in appreciative good humour. 'I can understand why,' he murmured gallantly, and kissed her hand. Again, camera bulbs flashed. Slowly, the royal couple began to tour the rooms, meeting guests, chatting to old friends, admiring the beautiful paintings and their surrounding grandeur. Flame gave the orchestra the nod and they began to play a Strauss waltz, the royal couple taking the floor and leading off the dancing. Flame crossed her fingers and glanced at her watch. The security van that was bringing the collection was due to leave in an hour. She jumped as a warm hand slipped around her waist, then melted into Reece's embrace.

'Dance with me, pretty lady.'

'I thought you'd never ask,' she whispered back, and together they moved around the floor, oblivious to the photographs being taken of them that would, the following morning, adorn the papers in the society columns under the outrageous heading: 'The Jewellery Queen and the Gold-Digger!'

For the delicate move from the ballroom to the main dining salon and the three others, Flame relied on Giulietta. It was done, at eight o'clock prompt, with gracious ease. At a nod from Flame the music stopped, and in the ensuing silence the Ravenscroft gong, a present from a prince regent, echoed musically from the hall. 'Ladies and gentlemen,' Giulietta said, her imperious voice ringing out and demanding and receiving an immediate, respectful silence. 'Dinner is served. Principessa,' Giulietta turned to her and her husband, 'may Lord Justin take you in to dinner?'

Justin stepped forward, impossibly handsome, while Guido Luciano gallantly looked to Giulietta. 'Charmed, Contessa.'

Slowly, the throng followed them into the salons, the more important guests led to the main salon, where the Principessa was being seated, the lesser guests being shown into the other salons by impeccably liveried footmen. As she took her own place, Flame glanced nervously at her watch, which was cunningly set into her beaten-silver bracelet.

'Relax.' At her side, Reece whispered into her ear. 'The van's guarded better than Fort Knox. It'll get here.'

'I know. I know!' she groaned back, and came to attention as the food was served. Apart from the finest of champagnes and wines, caviars and pâtés, there was duck, grouse, pheasant, beef, lamb, venison, trout, salmon and lobster. For the vegetarians there were dishes with origins in Greece, India, Polynesia and China. Desserts came and went that resembled works of art — towering gateaux of every fruit imaginable, flambés that were lit to the accompaniment of blue flame and gasps of pleasure and ripples of applause. And a platter of cheeses that boasted no less than fifty-four varieties. Real Venetian coffee was served, but for Philistines there were also choices of Colombian, Kenyan and Costa Rican. With the guests mellow from good food and wine, and gossiping happily among themselves, the excitement rose as the big unveiling came closer and closer.

Flame was able to excuse herself and go back to the empty ballroom. The security team waited, and on the long black-velvet-lined table rested the boxes of jewels. Flame quickly set about arranging them on the tiers, pedestals and stands. She had gone over this arrangement a hundred times, using stand-in pieces of jewellery, and she finished it in remarkably short time. The ropes that would keep the guests at bay until after the Principessa and her husband had toured the table for themselves were already in place, and as she placed the finishing touches of silver and crystal bowls of creamy gardenias at strategic points on the table, she took a deep, steadying breath. Displayed to artistic advantage on the black velvet under blazing lights that picked up and displayed every faceted colour, the jewels seemed alive. And Flame's surprise for the Principessa was hidden in a mysterious black box at the centre of the table.

Flame smiled her approval, nodded to the guards, checked that her own staff were standing in strategic places just in case, and then left. She walked to the main salon on legs that felt wooden and approached the head of the table. The Principessa caught her eye, saw the tight, pale face and smiled gently. 'It is time, *si*?'

Flame nodded. The room fell silent as the Principessa rose, the culmination of the evening leaving everyone poised in silent anticipation. With Flame walking on her left, and her husband on her right, they moved from the salon to the ballroom, the guests not far behind. No one needed to be told to stay behind the ropes as Flame and her royal guests moved on to the black tables that held their glittering exhibits.

Walt watched Justin, who seemed unconcerned at being out of the limelight. Walt hadn't forgotten the hoax phone call he'd received during Justin's last visit. However, his secretary had been adamant the Earl hadn't stayed long, hadn't made any phone calls, and hadn't used the photocopier or fax machine. Still, Walt wondered. And worried.

Standing a little to one side, Flame tried not to stare at the Principessa as she looked at the first item. It was a brooch in the Belle Époque style, depicting a ruby-winged hummingbird and a sapphire and emerald flower with tiny seed pearls depicting the sprays of nectar the bird was sipping. Gingerly, the Principessa lifted it from its velvet bed, raised it to her eyes and studied it closely. Sofia thought she had never seen anything so exquisite, so perfectly made. She glanced at Flame and smiled. 'Perfect, *cara*,' she said softly, but in the silence her voice carried to the people waiting their own turn to view the gems, and a tiny sigh of relief and congratulation ran around the room. After that, Flame felt herself relaxing. She'd been wrong to be so nervous. Everything had gone well and was still going well. If the Principessa was aware of the crowd behind her, impatiently awaiting their own turn to view the treasures on display, she didn't show it, taking her time, fingering the odd piece here or there, asking Flame to explain where the inspiration came from for this or how the original idea was born for that. And nobody really minded.

After all, she had paid for this bonanza, and rumour had it that it was worth almost ten million. Trays of earrings, rows of rings, trees of bracelets that hung from the finest ebony frames were all examined, and met with a smile of approval. Calm though she was, the Principessa's cheeks glowed with excited colour and her eyes were semi-dazed, as if she could hardly believe these sparkling treasures were all hers. Finally, her tour of the long table complete, the Principessa came to a stop by the spider's-web body brooch. With her back to the crowd, she raised a questioning brow at Flame, who instantly caught on. Lifting it from its bed, careful to stand in front of the Principessa and so prevent the crowd from seeing, Flame fixed it to the front of the plain white dress, hooking the pins at the web's end into the fabric. The jet spider was a sensation against the white silk and the silver and diamond web glittered in perfect harmony across the material.

'Now,' the Principessa turned, aware of the stunned gasp from behind her as even from a distance of several yards the guests could see the startling spectacle of a brooch that almost covered the Principessa's entire top half, 'let us invite our guests to join us. *Si?*' Guido led her down to the agog crowd. The brooch was arched in the centre, which explained why it fit so snugly over the bosom, and the pagan beauty and horror of the jet spider made many a female spine tremble in fear and covetous envy.

As the security team moved the ropes to just a foot around the table, giving all the people who instantly rushed there the chance to see, but not to touch, Flame found herself gasping for air. It was over, and everyone knew it was a roaring success. Reece was at her side a moment later, and together they stood watching in amusement as the elegant crowd jostled for position around the tables. Photographers had a field day, and not one piece, not even the humblest black-pearl drop earring, escaped the cameras' lenses. It was nearing midnight, and the crowd around the table were still reluctant to move away, when Flame gathered up her last piece of courage and walked to the small dais slightly to the right of the table. 'Ladies and gentlemen,' she called, having to say it twice before the gabbling voices quietened. 'Your Royal Highness.' Flame nodded to the Principessa, who was watching her with a quizzically raised eyebrow. 'You have now seen all but one piece of the Halcyone Collection.'

There was an instant buzz. Slowly, the Principessa began to smile. 'You have a surprise for me, Lady Flame, *si*?'

Flame smiled. 'Indeed I have, Your Highness. This is a piece you have not yet seen. It is a gift, from Halcyone's to our patroness. I only hope that you approve.'

Curious, the Principessa and her husband followed Flame behind the ropes, and only when she lifted the black box from under a mound of gardenias did they realise it had been there all the time. Wordlessly, Flame turned and held out a large box to the Principessa. Slowly, teasingly, the Principessa lifted the lid and looked inside — and audibly gasped. Suddenly the atmosphere was ice-brittle. What could be more spectacular than the body brooch? Than the main necklace, earring and tiara set that comprised huge, glittering diamonds? The Principessa muttered a word in Italian that made those who spoke the language grin knowingly. Then she slowly lifted her eyes to Flame.

'My dear Lady Flame. You have excelled yourself.' And, so saying, she reached into the box and drew out the jewelled tiara that lay inside. But it was not just any tiara. It wouldn't just sit on her head in a row of precious stones. No. This tiara was also partly a mask. Holding it in her hands, it felt as light as a feather, yet the Principessa recognized diamonds, onyx, the darkest of sapphires, jet, amber and the deepest of smoky topazes. It shone in her hands like a deep, dark secret.

Wordlessly, her eyes showing her amazed disbelief, the Principessa put it on. And it was only then that it truly came into its own. For, sweeping down over one eye and into a gentle arch on her cheek, the piece fit as snugly as any mask made of material. Through the single eyehole, perfectly positioned, the Principessa's eye shone in exultant excitement, making her look delightfully feline.

The crowd, after an initial, stunned silence, broke out into rapturous applause. The Principessa waited impatiently as the photographers went wild, then turned to the full-length mirror standing to one side of the table and stared at herself in amazement. With the body brooch sparkling on her breast, and the tiara/mask covering her face, she looked the epitome of a seductress, a woman of limitless mystery. A photographer took a picture that would travel the globe, sending shockwaves through the jewellery world that would never be repeated. It was a picture of a woman smothered in jewels and yet not swamped by them, staring at her imperious reflection, her left eye bare, the right glittering from behind a mask. With clever and careful work, the effect looked feathery, almost surreal. The picture was destined to be a classic. It was then, at the heart of her triumph, with all eyes turned to the Principessa, that Flame happened to look down at the table, the main diamond of the entire collection catching her eye. And Flame froze. For she could see that the tapered collet was not the same. It was dented, very, very slightly at the ends. No craftsman would have been satisfied to leave it like that! Luckily no guest would have the knowledge to spot the error. She dragged her eyes from it, looking around desperately. It was Gunther Voss who saw the panic in her eyes, and quickly joined her.

'Gunther. The collet — on the premier diamond. It's bent,' she whispered frantically, keeping her eyes fixed on the photographers who, thankfully, were interested only in the Principessa. Taking a quick glance around, making sure no one saw him, Gunther bent over the diamond, drew his breath in quickly and straightened. 'It is not the collet we need to worry about, your ladyship,' the stonecutter whispered into her ear, his German accent thick with panic. 'It is the diamond. It's paste!'

CHAPTER 31

Flame stared at him, not sure that she had heard correctly. But the stricken look in his eyes was unmistakable. 'Paste?' she echoed faintly, then snapped to attention as a light bulb flashed in her face. Instantly she produced what she hoped was a dazzling, confident smile, as the young reporter thrust a mini recorder under her nose. 'Lady Halcyone, how does it feel to have a sensational hit on your hands?'

Flame fought back the hysterical desire to laugh out loud. Hit? She had a catastrophe. *Think!* her brain screamed at her. 'Well, of course, we at Halcyone's are very glad that the Principessa di Maggiore is satisfied with the collection.' She smiled sweetly, her mind in turmoil. She had to keep the jewels under her control until the mess could be sorted out. Obviously, every piece of the collection had to be gone over with a microscope. But how? The Principessa was expecting the collection to go straight to her private plane, which was waiting at Kidlington airport.

'I'm sure everyone, including our readers, will want to know exactly where you came up with such an idea for the tiara. Or is it a mask?'

Flame smiled again, although her face felt as if it were cracking. What could she do? She couldn't let the collection go as it was. The paste diamond would be discovered and Halcyone's would be ruined. 'If you've ever attended a masked ball in Venice, you'd know where the inspiration came from.' She heard her voice, light and teasing and happy, and felt distinctly unreal. 'Would you excuse me please for just a moment? This is Gunther Voss, the craftsman responsible for cutting the stones. I'm sure he can give your readers a fascinating insight into the jewellery business's most glamorous job.' She looked at Gunther, her eyes apologizing and pleading for help. Gunther, dear gentleman that he was, didn't let her down. Leading the reporter away from the collection, she could hear him flannelling the eager young reporter with tales of woe, hardship and glory in pre-Hitler Germany. Frantically, Flame looked around. The guests and reporters were still clustered around the Principessa, gaping in amazement at the body brooch and tiara-mask.

It was then that she saw Justin. He, too, was watching the scene, but his lips were twisted into an ironic rather than admiring smile, and suddenly Flame knew. The paste diamond was Justin's doing. No wonder he had been so relaxed lately. He thought he had won. And — her blood turned to ice — he might still have won unless she could think of an excuse to keep the collection until the diamond could be replaced.

Flame's blood turned even colder. What if the diamond was not the only paste gem? There were several stones — large emeralds, rubies and sapphires — that were also cornerstone pieces in the collection. Flame closed her eyes briefly and took a deep, shaking breath. She couldn't stand here doing nothing while her whole career was about to go down the tubes. But what to do? Flame looked at the Principessa herself, who was still admiring her reflection in the mirror, and her backbone stiffened. The Principessa obviously respected and admired her designer. Flame straightened her shoulders. Yes, she had to face this head-on. But what to tell her? She could hardly say . . .

'What's wrong?'

Flame jumped. She'd been so intent on thinking the problem through that she'd forgotten Frank Jensen and his radar for people in distress. In a whisper, she told Frank what Gunther Voss had spotted. Frank's face was grim as he looked at Justin, but all he could do was offer sympathy and agree to back her up on whatever she decided to do. She nodded her thanks, asked him to tell Reece what was going on, and then, with her back ramrod-straight, her head high, her heart pounding in sick fear, she left the podium, gave instructions to the guards to move the ropes back another foot, just in case some eagle-eyed matron who knew a thing about good jewels spotted that there was something wrong, and then slowly made her way through the crowd to the Principessa.

There, Sofia di Maggiore turned from her reflection at last and sighed happily at the young woman who had designed the gems that would be the talk of the town for months to come. '*Cara*. It is magnificent. You are magnificent. What can I say?' She lapsed into voluble Italian, and Flame, seizing the opportunity to add a touch of intimacy and patriotism to her request, replied to her in the same language.

'I'm glad you approve, Principessa. Of course, to make absolutely sure that everything is perfect, we should give you a fitting of all the main items. Just to make sure they fall right. After all, a necklace that rests against a collarbone may have its symmetry altered. And earrings that scrape the shoulders need to be shortened slightly.' Flame knew she was talking rubbish — the Principessa's neck, ear-to-shoulder length and every other measurement needed had already been taken and meticulously adhered to. But she was gambling that the Principessa, with her delight in her new collection at its height, would want it to be absolutely perfect. If she could just play on that . . . 'As you know, the tiara was made very much in secret, and it may not fit just right on the head. Or . . . do you mind?' Flame very gently cupped the Principessa's chin and turned her head to the right, flashlights popping at the unexpected photo opportunity. 'Hmm, I thought so. The mask doesn't fit quite right on the cheek — after a while it may chafe, and that would be terrible. It's nothing drastic,' she continued to reassure her in confident Italian, 'just a matter of soldering an extra piece of metal here or there. But I know you'll want the collection to be as great as it can be.'

The Principessa nodded slowly, but Flame could see she wasn't happy. The thought of having her lovely new sparkling toys taken away from her was not a pleasant one. 'Of course, it would only take a week,' Flame said, wondering if they could possibly find new stones, cut and replace them in that time. 'You'll still be able to wear whatever you like during the season.' It was the right thing to say. Instantly the Principessa's reluctance faded.

'You are right, *cara*,' she agreed. 'This collection deserves to be perfect.'

Flame nearly wilted in relief.

The Principessa, spotting her husband over Flame's shoulder, excused herself and swept away. Flame nodded to the orchestra, who struck up a charming little 1920s waltz. Quickly Flame found the chief of security and told him of the change of plan, and that the collection was to be taken back to Halcyone's immediately. When she turned, Reece was there. He nodded to the Principessa. 'You've convinced her to leave the jewels with us?'

Flame nodded and licked her paper-dry lips. 'Oh, Reece, I was so scared. I told the Principessa she could have the collection back within a week. But can we do it in time?'

Reece's eyes narrowed suddenly and when she turned, she saw that he was watching Justin. 'It depends,' he said softly. 'If we can find the originals, Gunther can have them reset within a day. If not . . .'

'If not?' Flame echoed fearfully.

Reece smiled. 'Darling, I mine jewels, remember? I'll find replacements in my stockpiles.'

Flame nodded. But could it be done in time? 'I'd better find Gunther and tell him what's happening,' she murmured. Her adrenalin had ebbed away, leaving her feeling sick and ill and so very, very tired.

Reece nodded, his eyes back on Justin. 'Yes, darling, you do that.' Gently he pushed her away and she disappeared into the dancing crowd, as Reece made his way across the floor to his stepbrother.

Justin watched him approach, his face outwardly calm. But Reece's first words floored him. 'We've discovered the paste, Justin,' Reece said quietly. 'The guards are going to take the jewels back to Woodstock, not the Principessa's plane. We're going to replace the stone, or stones, and return them within a week. Now, are you going to make it easy and tell us where the real jewels are? Or do you fancy a long spell being detained at Her Majesty's pleasure?'

If Justin had been thinking straight, he would have realised at once that Reece wouldn't inform the police. And if he'd been thinking like a normal man, confident of his mother's love, he'd have known that Francesca herself would never allow it. He was her son, and she loved him fiercely. She'd never allow him to go to prison. But Justin wasn't thinking straight. In fact, he was hardly thinking at all.

The emotional powder keg inside him suddenly exploded, his mind screaming. He felt himself rock, both physically and mentally, and Reece watched him take a staggering step back, his face draining totally of all colour. Reece felt a familiar rush of reluctant pity wash over him. It was the sympathy he felt for any animal in pain.

'I don't know what you're talking about,' Justin heard himself say, but it was automatic, as if some lifeless robot had pushed a button and the words had emerged, a collection of meaningless sounds. Inside, deep inside his head, the anger, fear, rage, despair, frustration, hatred, self-hatred, self-pity and self-destructive masochism were like pieces of shrapnel, shredding his grip on reality like knives. He could feel himself slipping off some unreal cliff and falling through ugly space. The music around him receded into a dull clanging. He had to get away from the people who were crowding around him, threatening to squash him into the walls. Wordlessly, blindly, he pushed past Reece. Reece saw Frank

Jensen rush out of the room, quick on his patient's heels, and shook his head.

He looked around and saw Flame talking to a white-faced Walt Matthews. What a woman she was. When most people would have panicked, she had stayed calm, taking control of the situation and giving them a working chance when all the odds seemed against them. Quickly Reece left the ballroom and found a phone in a quiet study. Getting International Directory Enquiries, he began to make some important phone calls. They'd need gems. And quick!

Justin had fled to the games room. Dimly he'd realised Frank Jensen was following him, and he used his intimate knowledge of the house to lose him. Now, in the darkness, he could see the stuffed animal heads looking down on him, victims of his father. Foxes, badgers, otters . . . Justin sank to the floor, unable to meet their accusing eyes. 'It's not my fault,' he told them, his voice angry and indignant. 'I didn't shoot you.' He curled into a tight ball, hugging his knees against his chest, his eyes tightly closed. It had gone wrong, again. His sister had won, again. He was the one who was being punished, again. Suddenly it was too dark and he ran around the room like a madman, snapping on every light he could find. He needed to do something normal.

Quickly, Justin unlocked the cabinet that housed his gun, went to the drawer and pulled out the gun oil and cleaning rags, and began to clean the Purdey gun. It felt good in his hands — heavy and reassuring, the actions of his hands smooth and sure, and blessedly familiar. Yes, it felt good, holding the gun. Suddenly, Justin's stroking fingers stopped, and he stared down at the gun in his hands. He stared at it for a long, long time.

* * *

Outside, the guests were beginning to leave. The Principessa had already left for her Oxford hotel, and, better yet, the press had all left.

'Don't worry, my lady,' Gunther Voss assured Flame about the craftsmen and their ability to keep a secret. 'They all know that their own livelihoods rely on keeping their mouths shut.'

When the last guest was gone, Flame gave in to the strain and sank down on to the nearest chair. Wearily, she told the rest of her family what had happened. In the appalled silence, Reece reached down and dragged Flame back to her feet. 'Don't worry. I'm having all our biggest stones flown over to Woodstock. Gunther won't let us down.'

Owen glanced at his wife, opened his mouth, then shut it again. Francesca felt the tears start in her eyes and determinedly bit them back. 'Where is Justin?' she asked at last, her quiet voice breaking the tense silence in the hall.

'I don't know. The last I saw of him he was rushing from the ballroom, Frank close behind,' Reece admitted. Then, walking over to his stepmother, he gently put his arms around her, meeting his father's eyes over her bent head. 'Don't worry, Francesca. Frank will be able to help him. He knows the perfect place.'

Francesca shuddered in his arms. 'It's all my fault. I shouldn't have left him. I should have paid some men to kidnap him from this place when he was still a baby. I knew what Malcolm was like. I *knew*!'

'Don't be silly, Mamma,' Flame said sharply. 'It's nobody's fault, not even Justin's.'

Giulietta took the opportunity to say that she was exhausted and was going to bed, and Maria instantly went to accompany her. Owen nodded towards the two departing women. 'Come on, angel face,' he said softly to his wife. 'I think your mother and grandmother have the right idea.'

Francesca hesitated. 'What about Justin?'

Reece smiled gently. 'We'll handle Justin.'

'You won't . . . hurt him, will you?'

Reece gently shook his head. 'No, Mother, we won't hurt him. He's been hurt enough.'

Francesca's eyes filled with tears. 'Thank you, Reece . . . son . . .' she added and, with her husband, mounted the stairs and walked silently away. Flame watched them go, tears of her own threatening to spill. She took a deep shaking breath. 'I should be getting to Halcyone's. Gunther will have had a chance to check the pieces by now.'

Reece nodded. 'Right. Let's go,' he said briskly.

Flame looked up at him, so sure and strong, with love and determination shining in his eyes. She laughed softly. Together, they could do anything, even the impossible!

* * *

It was cold out on the roof. Justin looked up at the sky, unaware that he was shivering uncontrollably. The gun rested in the crook of his arm. Beneath his feet, the roof was frosted and slippery. He moved closer to the edge. He wasn't sure what had made him leave the gun room and come out onto the roof. Perhaps he had wanted to come, for the first time ever, to the place where his father had fallen to his death. But when he looked down, and in the bright light of the full moon saw his sister and her lover walking out over the gravel towards her car, he knew he had been guided to this spot, at this time, by a fate that had at last decided to be good to him. He felt his arm move and saw the gun rise into his field of vision. It felt like an extension of his hand. He had the girl directly in his sights, but his finger stayed still on the trigger. He'd wait a second longer.

The silence of the night was deafening. And in that silence, as his finger still refused to pull the trigger, Justin heard a sound. Just as, over a year ago, his father had heard a sound. And, just like his father, Justin spun around in surprise.

The man behind him was standing in the shadow of the great chimney pots. Then, awkwardly, he moved forward, the silver moonlight striking clearly on his face. It was a handsome face, round and innocent. And yet it was frightening. 'Uncle Roger,' Justin said, blinking in surprise.

302

On the landing below, Frank heard the door to the roof click shut and within moments was racing up into the attic.

Justin stared at his uncle, desperately trying to clear his mind. Behind and below him, he heard a car door open. Quickly he swung back and saw Reece opening the door for his sister. They were getting away. Quickly he raised the shotgun again. He was young and fast, and could have killed them both, but again he waited. Just another moment. He could do it if he waited another moment.

'No.' The word was simple, quiet, commonplace, but it lanced through Justin like a knife. He turned once more to face his uncle. He didn't hear the roof door open or see Frank Jensen step out into the shadows.

'Uncle Roger, go back to your room,' Justin said angrily, not sure where his fear came from. This was his dotty uncle, the phantom painter of Ravenscroft. He began to laugh, unable to help it. 'Go back to the attic, Uncle Roger. It's better than the cellar.'

Roger walked stubbornly forward, his baby face tight with determination. 'No,' he said again. 'You hurt Flame.' The mention of her name made Justin look around again. And in that second, Roger did something so unexpected, Justin couldn't believe it. He moved — quickly, precisely, silently. Suddenly his clumsy, shuffling Uncle Roger was gone, and in his place was a man who clamped on to Justin with the strength of a limpet. He felt himself stagger back, and panic screamed in his head as he thought he was going to fall. But Roger held on to the gun, his surprising strength whiplashing Justin around and forward, bringing them both away from the roof's edge.

'Let go of the gun, damn you,' Justin snarled, hearing the car start up behind him. 'They're getting away.'

Frank Jensen moved closer, his heart pounding. He too had heard Reece and Flame's voices, and knew what Justin had intended. He hesitated, unsure what to do for the best. Two men were fighting over a loaded gun at the edge of a treacherous drop. He felt helpless, useless. He moved closer, still not sure what he could do.

'Not let go gun,' Roger said. 'You hurt Flame. You bad man, like Malcolm. I not let Malcolm hurt Francesca.'

'What are you talking about, you imbecile?' Justin snarled, tugging on the gun, unable to believe for one second that Roger, barmy Uncle Roger, could be this strong. Then, as his eyes met that vacant blue stare only inches from his face, Justin's grip on the gun suddenly went limp. His eyes widened a fraction as he stared at his uncle, an awful understanding creeping into his consciousness. 'It was you,' he said, his voice small and disbelieving. 'You pushed him.'

Roger nodded. 'Bad man,' he said again, and pulled abruptly on the gun. Justin clung on by reflex, and then, as he realised his uncle meant to kill him too, panic lent him strength. He felt his finger tighten on the trigger as he made a last, desperate effort to pull the gun free, and suddenly the shotgun went off. He felt its vibration race through his hands and shoot up his arm, his ears tingling at the proximity of the loud sound.

Roger's eyes changed. Suddenly they were no longer vacant but filled with puzzlement. He let go of the gun and moved back and it was only then that Justin saw the blood. It stained Roger's chest like a wet, clinging blanket, and he felt sick, a sickness that travelled from his stomach and seemed to seep into his very soul. He stared down at the gun in his hands, an alien thing of silver and black, and felt it drop from his nerveless fingers. Below, the car engine shut off.

'What the hell was that?' Reece said, looking behind him, seeing nothing but the looming bulk of the house. 'It sounded like a gunshot.'

'From the roof. Or somewhere high up,' Flame agreed, and they looked at one another, both having the same thought at the same time. 'Justin!' Flame screamed, and the next moment they were both out of the car and running.

On the roof, Frank Jensen moved at last. He had been stunned by the blast, and the first Justin knew of his presence was when he leaped out of the shadows just in time to catch Roger Syramore-Forbes as he began to fall to the ground.

'Justin, call an ambulance — NOW!' Frank ordered.

But Justin stood there dumbfounded. 'Uncle Roger,' he said, dimly beginning to realise what he had done. 'Uncle Roger, I didn't mean . . .'

Roger blinked, his eyes still puzzled. He recognized the nice man immediately. Flame and Francesca brought him to the attics often to see him. 'Hello,' he said.

Frank Jensen smiled. 'Hello, Roger.'

Roger looked at Justin. 'Bad man,' he said.

'No, Roger. Not bad. Hurt. Malcolm hurt him.'

Roger frowned, and began to cough, spitting blood over Frank's arm. 'I . . . kill Malcolm. Was that bad?'

Frank looked down at the gaping hole in Roger's chest, saw the whiteness of his face and the blood foaming in his mouth, and knew he was dying. 'No, Roger. It wasn't bad. You're not a bad man.'

Roger felt cold. Cold meant dying. Francesca had talked to him once about dying. She said it was when God took you away to another place. 'God will look after me now, won't he?' Roger said, looking at the nice man, who nodded, tears falling down his face. Roger didn't like tears. He wished he would stop. Nice men shouldn't cry.

'Yes, Roger,' Frank said, his voice thick. 'God will look after you now.'

Roger nodded and closed his eyes for the final time.

A moment later, everyone spilled out on to the roof, for everyone had heard the shot. Flame and Reece were first. They saw Frank Jensen holding a sobbing Justin in his arms. On the ground next to him lay Roger Syramore-Forbes and a smoking shotgun. Flame looked at her uncle's beautiful, peaceful face and gave a low moan. Quickly Reece turned her away from the sight and buried her face in his chest, his arms holding her with a comforting, protecting strength. Over her shaking shoulders, his eyes met those of Frank. Owen, Francesca, Maria and Giulietta stepped back, unable to take in the tragedy. Frank, still rocking the hysterically sobbing Justin in his arms, nodded at Roger. 'He was the one who pushed Malcolm off the roof. He came up here to stop Justin using that . . .' he nodded at the shotgun '. . . on you and Flame.'

'Justin killed Roger?' Owen asked, appalled.

'No!' Frank said sharply. 'It was an accident. I saw it all.' He looked at Reece, holding his friend's eye in a steady gaze. 'Roger was trying to get the gun from Justin. It was between them when it went off. It could have been either of them that got hit . . .' He broke off as Justin begin to moan through his tears. 'It's all right. Shushhhh.'

'I didn't mean it,' Justin sobbed, over and over. 'I didn't mean it. I loved my un-uncle.'

The men gently ushered the women down onto the landing. Francesca looked at Reece with wide, frightened eyes. They were all silent for a long while, but it was Giulietta, suddenly looking her age, who spoke first. 'We must call the police,' she said matter-of-factly. 'There has been a shooting and a death.' She looked from Owen to Reece, her eyes thoughtful and full of strength. 'The question is,' she added meaningfully, *'what* do we tell them?'

EPILOGUE

Flame stood in front of the full-length mirror in the master bedroom and looked solemnly at her reflection. Her wedding dress had been designed for her by the Principessa di Maggiore's personal couturier, a lavish white creation with a long train and seeded pearls sewn into the lacy panniers at her waist. Through the veil, her sunset hair gleamed vibrantly. Francesca surreptitiously wiped away a tear.

'Well, Mamma, how do I look?'

'You look the way a girl should look on her wedding day,' Francesca said, her voice choked with emotion. Through the open window, the sound of church bells rang joyously in the still, hot May air. Through the trees in the distance they could see the solid square tower of the Ravenscroft village church. If all had gone according to plan, her guests and husband-to-be waited for her inside.

Flame took a deep, nervous breath. 'What if I trip in the aisle?' she asked on a fluttery laugh.

'Owen will pick you up again, Reece will call you a clumsy so-and-so, the vicar will have a quiet snicker and everything will proceed as normal,' Francesca said helpfully.

Flame stuck her tongue out. 'That's what I like about you, Mamma. You're always so reassuring.'

The two women were still laughing when there came a timid knock on the door. 'Come in,' Francesca called, and a moment later Walt Matthews, smart in grey morning dress, entered gingerly, clutching his top hat nervously and looking as if he'd rather be anywhere else than where he was. 'Sorry to interrupt, Lady Halcyone. But I have one last duty to perform. For your great-grandmother, Jessica.'

'What is it, Walt?' Flame asked easily, her glance dropping to the aged blue velvet box he was carrying. Walt quickly thrust it at her, as if glad to get rid of it.

'Well, before she died, your great-grandmother gave me this. She said I was to give it to you on the day you got married. So, here it is.' He backed out, mumbling something about getting to the church on time, and high-tailed it out of the room like a frightened rabbit. Francesca and Flame burst into laughter the moment the door closed behind him.

Flame looked down at the box. 'Well, the wedding dress is new, I'm wearing a blue garter, and I'm wearing your borrowed pearl earrings. And this box looks old.'

'Well, open it!' Francesca exclaimed, leaning over her daughter as Flame flicked the lid. And gasped.

'It's the pearls,' she said reverently, looking down at the finest strand she'd ever seen. 'The ones Jessica was wearing in the portrait down the hall.' Carefully Flame put them on. Resting against her bare neck, they looked as if they'd been made to go with her dress and her colouring. 'Mamma,' Flame breathed. 'They're perfect.'

'And old,' Francesca smiled. She had known nothing could spoil this perfect day. Then she thought of her son, and her smile dimmed. But Justin was safe with Frank Jensen, who assured them he was improving every day.

They'd told the police that the shooting of Roger Syramore-Forbes had been an accident, as it had been, but the true story they had kept to themselves. Roger, they'd said, had become excited and wanted to fire off the gun in celebration. Justin, worried about him, had tried to take the gun away and it had gone off. With an independent, reputable witness in Frank Jensen to confirm it as an accident, plus the fact the Syramore-Forbes family were well known and respected, the story had been accepted and quietly played down. It had been a sad day when Francesca had seen Roger buried, but this time the visit to the church was going to be one of celebration, one of love, hope and life. Impulsively Francesca hugged her daughter fiercely, and Flame, after a startled moment, hugged her back every inch as tightly.

'Oh, Mamma, I'm so happy. I love Reece so much.'

'I know. And he loves you. I'm glad you've decided to make Ravenscroft your home. This house deserves a loving family. Just wait until you have children. They'll love it — the lawns, the horses, the river just over the field . . .'

Flame nodded. 'I wish Justin could be here,' she said softly, but knew that it was impossible. The shock of killing his uncle had affected him deeply, but it had also opened the floodgates that had kept him a prisoner of his own pain. In time, she was sure, he would be able to leave the clinic and live a much kinder life. Everyone would be there to help and support him. Owen, Flame was sure, would be a great help, when the time came. Owen, who could be the father that Malcolm had never been. Flame glanced at her mother, gave one final look at her reflection in the mirror, and took a deep breath. 'Well, I suppose we'd better go, before Reece gets impatient and sends out a search party!'

Francesca laughed and hurried to open the door for her, helping her with her train as they walked down the narrow corridor and on to the stairs. They had elected to ride to the church together, breaking tradition but not caring.

As they walked down the stairs, Flame paused by the portrait of Jessica Syramore-Forbes. Looking up into a smiling, beautiful face, framed by red hair, the painted pearls that now rested around Flame's neck glowing dimly in the filtered sunlight, Flame felt a lump rise in her throat. 'I wonder if she knew,' Flame whispered. 'I wonder if she knew all along how it would be?'

Francesca too looked at the portrait, remembering an old woman, full of determination and strength. 'Perhaps she did, *cara,*' Francesca murmured, squeezing her daughter's arm. 'Perhaps she did.'

Then they left the painful past behind them and walked ahead to a glorious future. A future where the men they loved waited for them.

THE END

ALSO BY FAITH MARTIN

DI HILLARY GREENE SERIES

JENNY STARLING MYSTERIES

MONICA NOBLE MYSTERIES

GREAT READS
THE LYING GAME
AN OXFORD REVENGE
AN OXFORD SCANDAL
AN OXFORD ENEMY
AN OXFORD SECRET
More coming soon!

Join our mailing list to be the first to hear about NEW FAITH MARTIN releases!
www.joffebooks.com

FREE KINDLE BOOKS AND OFFERS

Do you love mysteries, historical fiction and romance? Join 1000s of readers enjoying great books through our mailing list. You'll get new releases and great deals every week from one of the UK's leading independent publishers.

Join today, and you'll get your first bargain book this month!

Follow us on Facebook, Twitter and Instagram

@joffebooks

DO YOU LOVE **FREE AND BARGAIN** BOOKS?

We hate typos too but sometimes they slip through. Please send any errors you find to corrections@joffebooks. com. We'll get them fixed ASAP. We're very grateful to eagle-eyed readers who take the time to contact us.

Made in the USA
Las Vegas, NV
25 January 2021

16512222R00184